W9-BYZ-744

ADMISSIONS

ADMISSIONS

NANCY LIEBERMAN

NEW YORK BOSTON

This book is a work of fiction. Names, characters, places, and incidents are the product of the author's imagination or are used fictitiously. Any resemblance to actual events, locales, or persons, living or dead, is coincidental.

Warner Books

Time Warner Book Group
1271 Avenue of the Americas, New York, NY 10020
Visit our Web site at www.twbookmark.com

Printed in the United States of America

First Printing: September 2004
10 9 8 7 6 5 4 3 2 1

Library of Congress Cataloging-in-Publication Data

Lieberman, Nancy.
Admissions / Nancy Lieberman.
p. cm.
ISBN 0-446-53303-3
1. Television producers and directors—Family relationships—Fiction. 2. Manhattan (New York, N.Y.)—Fiction. 3. Women school principals—Fiction. 4. Mothers and daughters—Fiction. 5. Children of the rich—Fiction. 6. Female friendship—Fiction. 7. Private schools—Fiction. 8. Girls—Fiction. I. Title.
PS3612.I335A66 2004
813'.6—dc22

2004005779

To David

For helping me see the humor in all this.

ADMISSIONS

SEPTEMBER

The Tuesday after Labor Day marked the official start of admissions season, the Manhattan parents' version of a blood sport. The ferocity with which Wall Street traders worked the floor, mergers-and-acquisitions lawyers closed their deals, magazine editors staked their claims on a hot new trend, and ladies who lunched jockeyed for position at the fall shows couldn't hold a candle to the intense competition between families to secure that most coveted of accessories: a space for their child in the school of their choice.

Anticipating the onslaught, Sara Nash arrived at The School early and found her new assistant, Brandi, already at her desk, speaking rapidly into the receiver while casting a wary eye at her phone's four other blinking red lights. Every blip signaled an incoming call from an anxious New York parent, each more desperate than the last to obtain an application for one of the few available spots in The School's renowned Kindergarten.

"Your name and address, please. Yes, we do require The Kindergarten Admissions Test. How nice; I'm impressed, and I'm sure Ms. Nash will be, too. Yes, she is our director of admissions, and all correspondence should be addressed to her. No, there is no 'G' in 'Nash'—just like it sounds. Yes, that would be perfect. Thank you.

Goodbye." Brandi hung up, gulped down a swig of her double skim latte, and resolutely moved on to the next call.

"Child's last name, please, if different from yours. Hmmm, that is different. It's spelled 'X-I-E'?" She quickly scribbled the information before taking the next call.

As Sara plugged in the kettle to make a pot of chamomile tea, she nodded with approval at the tele-patter emanating from the outer office.

"Yes. Once we receive the application, we'll call you to schedule the tour and interview. Yes. Both parents should try to come. There are four of you? Then, yes, by all means, all of you come."

Sara exhaled a sigh of relief; Brandi's tone conveyed just the right blend of solicitous and officious, helpful but hardly encouraging. She hoped she would turn out to be a good hire.

"Yes, we do require the child to be potty-trained. *How* old is your son?"

Just keeping the applicants' names straight was a challenge, even for a well-seasoned professional like Sara. Last year's applicants included five-year-old Thiruvikraman Hathiramani, the son of Chandrakanta Subramanian and Ramesh Hathiramani, the famous Bollywood filmmakers who had recently relocated from Bombay to Tribeca. Throughout the admissions process, Sara struggled to keep them straight, and just barely managed to address them properly at the interview—no small feat from a girl from Omaha. When she discovered that the boy not only could spell all these names but was trilingual, ambidextrous, and an accomplished T-ball player, she marked an emphatic "accept" on his application forms on the spot.

Then there was the family with the adopted child and same-sex parents—the Chuan Lee Tsao-Silverbergs. The daughter, Lili-Xin, was bright, talented, and well behaved, but Sara decided that the parents, Drs. Jaehoon Chuan Lee Tsao and Steven Silverberg, were just too high-maintenance. Not only was their interview one of the longest on record, she then spent hours on the phone with them discussing The School's position on multiculturalism and alternative lifestyles.

"Miss Nash, I was curious about your use of the word 'seminal' when you were describing The School's policies on tolerance to us last week," Dr. Silverberg probed in the course of their fourth phone conversation.

"Yes," Dr. Tsao chimed in. "It's important to us that The School not just talk the talk—you must walk the walk, as I tell all my patients."

Sara wondered how his patients kept their patience. Losing her own, she placed their application in the Life's Too Short pile.

Philosophically she supported their family structure, just not when both parents were shrinks.

Perhaps the most difficult admissions call of the prior year had been the Bangston fiasco. While considering an application for the spoiled rotten, high-strung, and mean-spirited daughter of Stuart Bangston, a hostile, hostile takeover specialist, Sara inadvertently learned that the father's firm had made an unprecedentedly grandiose contribution to The School. The one-million-dollar gift was the largest individual donation in the history of The School and, to Sara's ethical nose, reeked of corrupt intent. After an in-school battle that pitted the office of admissions (or, when it came down to it, Sara) against the powers that be, the board of trustees stepped in and pronounced that the five-year-old tantrumer was "unquestionably a highly qualified applicant," and instructed Sara, under no uncertain terms, to accept her forthwith.

Thus admissions decisions were made at The School.

Seven blocks north, on another tree-lined street in upper Manhattan, Helen Drager sat in her office / dining alcove, determinedly pushing the redial button on her phone. Helen had begun her morning under the cheerful misconception that phoning a few schools to request high school applications for her daughter, Zoe, would be a fairly straightforward project. She delighted in plunging into simple tasks that could be ticked off on her daily mental to-do list without much fuss and bother. This seemingly minor chore, however, was beginning to remind her of the time she had spent days calling all over town in search of the Tickle Me Elmo doll Zoe desperately wanted for her fifth birthday, only to be told there was a three-month wait. Unused to denying her daughter her heart's desire, Helen had pulled every string she could think of to hasten the toy's arrival and managed to cut the wait down to three weeks. Unfortunately, by the time it finally arrived, Zoe had lost interest in Elmo and was on to the next big thing: a repellent purple and green television dinosaur.

Dolls and dinosaurs were minor speed bumps—applications to high schools were another issue entirely. The day before the admissions process began, she and her husband, Michael, had vowed to keep their sense of humor intact. *Well, it's always good to set goals,* Helen thought wryly while adjusting the hands-free-to-multitask headset, which allowed her to pay bills, send e-mail, and wipe the breakfast crumbs off the table while patiently standing by for her call to be answered by the first available admissions assistant.

Press "one" if you are requesting an application for a child who aspires to attend Harvard, Princeton, or Yale only, she joked to herself. See, the whole thing really could be funny. It would just take some extra effort on her part. Still waiting, Helen looked critically around to determine the next task to fill the on-hold-Muzak void.

The Dragers' 1920 Deco-style apartment, although smaller than the "classic seven" Helen had ideally wished for, was elegant in its simplicity. A disciple of the modernist aesthetic, she appreciated good design at its cleanest and sparest; despite its rampant overuse by marketers and branding consultants, "keep it simple" was her mantra for both her home and her appearance. As a result, she had been able to spend money sparingly on good pieces, to pleasing overall effect. Most of the Dragers' furniture bore the imprimatur of an important twentieth-century designer, and Zoe had learned at an early age to refer to "the Eames chairs" or the "Mackintosh table" when speaking of the things in their household. Even Michael, who was avowedly more interested in Le Cordon Bleu than Le Corbusier, appreciated her good taste. She, in turn, indulged his appetite by agreeing to splurge on a professional kitchen, albeit a small one, which, with its industrial appliances and stainless steel counters, conformed to her style as well.

Still in a tele-holding pattern, Helen glanced approvingly across their modestly proportioned living room, admiring the successful compromise between design and comfort she felt she had achieved. The two downy ecru sofas and a plush, geometrically patterned area rug provided a soft contrast to the austerity of the other furnishings. Disdainful of clutter, she remembered what a relief it had been to replace the Playskool kitchen with the Barcelona lounger and reinstate the Aalto vase in its rightful place on the Nakashima table when Zoe finally outgrew the baby-proofing stage.

A house full of toys was a small price to pay for the joy we got from Zoe when she was a toddler, she thought wistfully as her gaze rested on a small photograph, the only object atop the smooth sea-green credenza that separated the foyer from the living room. The frame held a picture of Zoe as a small child, chasing a balloon on a windy beach, the glee on her face unmistakably that of a carefree spirit.

Helen thought back to the time that photo had been taken: Zoe had been five, and the Dragers had just finished applying to Kindergarten. The only requirement was that her child look presentable, know her ABC's, and not pick her nose during the interview, although even that would probably have been acceptable at some of the more progressive schools. It certainly had been a carefree time—although the private schools cultivated an air of selectivity, the population had been so different in New York back then that schools had to hide the fact that they accepted a large percentage of the applicants.

Damn. Why didn't we apply to one of the K–12 schools back then? If we had chosen one of those instead of The School, we wouldn't be going through this now, she chastised herself while sealing and stamping an envelope.

Nine years ago, both she and Michael had agreed that the intimate and nurturing ambiance of a K–8 school was appealing and that delaying interaction with high schoolers for as long as possible was a good idea.

"It isn't a life-or-death decision; it's just kindergarten," they repeatedly told each other back then, never imagining they would ever have to worry about admissions again. The School staked its reputation on being a "feeder to the feeders," meaning that its graduating eighth-grade students were assured entrance into New York's top high schools, which ultimately fed into the Ivy League.

But in recent years the rules of the game had changed: the players had become increasingly more cutthroat, and the playing field had turned treacherous. With a slew of children born to ambitious baby-boomers with six-figure incomes, gaining entrée into one of the top private schools had become not only an enormous financial challenge but a torturously uncertain odds-against-you gamble as well.

To further complicate matters, Helen's confidence in her advisor, Pamela Rothschild, the head of The School, had started to wane. Once the pinnacle of professionalism, over the past several months Pamela had often failed to return phone calls and e-mails and, in general, seemed peculiar and remote. Her personal counsel—and more important, her wide-ranging influence—were what Helen had counted on to make this process bearable. But recently, Pamela's erratic behavior was troublesome. Confronting that problem could mean losing her as an ally, so Helen was reduced to feeling like the wallflower who needed to befriend the popular cheerleader in order to be invited to the fun parties. In this case, though, the outcome of not being invited to the right parties meant more than just staying home on a Saturday night; it could mean never getting into college, holding down a job . . . Before Zoe knew it, she'd be destitute, looking for a handout . . .

"May I help you?" the voice broke in, mercifully putting an end to Helen's nightmarish vision. Helen quickly dropped her pen, straightened her spine, and cleared her throat.

"Oh, yes, hello. Yes, please. I would like to receive an application for my daughter, Zoe Drager, for grade nine. A wait list? Just for the application? Well, yes, I suppose I would like to be added to the list. Thank you. And a letter stating our interest? Hand-delivered? Okay. Right away. Sure, yes, thank you so much for your help. Goodbye." Three down, three to go. Helen groaned.

Groveling with admissions people was especially difficult for Helen, who, as president of the Parents' Association for the past three years, had earned VIP status and insider access at The School. Even The School's receptionist, Miss Lulu, recognized her voice whenever she called, and always managed to come up with a timely comment like, "Zoe looks so adorable without her front teeth," or "I bet you made Zoe's scarecrow costume, didn'chya?"

She was glad Michael and Zoe were not home to witness her frustration, preferring her family not see her in the abject role of underdog. She had ceremoniously announced "Today's the day!" as Michael was leaving for work this morning, and he'd responded casually with some remark like "I'd wish you luck but I can't imagine you'll need it."

Ignorance is bliss, she thought, on hold for school number four.

Unlike Michael, Zoe was visibly nervous and had started biting her nails again, even though she had kicked the habit four years ago. The anxiety was contagious and had likely been caught from her classmates, many of whom had spent a good part of the summer talking about applying to high school and speculating on who would be accepted at which schools.

Two hours later Helen finished up the last of her calls, having made contact with all six schools, to varying degrees of success. Convinced that her morning's work represented a victory of sorts, she filled in the scorecard she had created for herself during the course of the morning:

SCHOOL	PHONE #	DIRECTOR OF ADMISSIONS	STATUS
The Fancy Girls' School	674–9876	Justine Frampton	YES! Sending application Sept. 4
The Progressive School	563–9827	Soledad Gibson	YES! Sending application Sept. 4
The Bucolic Campus School	475–8392	Vincent Gargano	YES! Sending application Sept. 4
The Safety School	498–5937	Shirley Livingston	YES! Sending application Sept. 4
The Very Brainy Girls' School	938–8475	Eva Hopkins	Sept. 4 wait listed for application- Send letter
The Downtown School	483–8473	Taisha Anguilla	Sept. 4 wait listed for application- Nothing to do but wait . . .

That done, she forced herself to dash off a lighthearted e-mail to the head of The School.

Pamela-

Got all my requests done this a.m. the first day after Labor Day! Isn't that great! We're getting applications from all the schools you suggested except for two. We're wait listed at those. You didn't warn me about wait lists, or were they invented just to torture poor parents like me? :) See you tonight.

Helen

She also sent an e-mail to her close friend Sara Nash.

Hey Sara,

Made my calls today. A few schools have wait-listed us already—for applications, not admissions! Can you believe it! I guess we're awaiting security clearance, or more likely, Social Register clearance.
You must be having a crazy day. See you tonight at the Topplers'. Watcha wearing?

xoxo Helen

It was some hours later before Sara responded:

Helen

Congrats on the apps. Don't worry, you WILL clear wait lists.
It IS nuts here today. Anxious to see if Brandi survives.
Looking forward to seeing you at the Over-the Topplers.
My usual bland ensemble.

Sara

Helen and Sara had met ten years ago on a 5K bike-athon that The School's student council had organized to raise money to help retired New York City carriage horses find homes in greener pastures. As the children slowly looped around Central Park, the older ones on two-wheelers, the younger on three, Helen and Sara brought up the rear, making sure there were no pokey bikers left in the dust. Sara was a newcomer to the group, having just been hired as Pamela Rothschild's assistant, and Helen, as the mother of a Kindergartner, was new to The School, too. Knowing none of the other chaperones, the two women were glad for each other's company, and the bike-athon turned into a talk-athon as they spent the entire 5K in nonstop conversation.

The first two kilometers were spent exchanging general biographical details. Sara was the first person Helen had ever met who grew up in Nebraska, and she found the description of small-town life fascinating in contrast to her own Philadelphia childhood. While Sara attended a small, highly touted Midwestern college, Helen was studying in New York and Paris (junior year abroad), and when Sara moved to New York to get a degree in social work, Helen was in Berlin doing research for her dissertation. After completing social work school, Sara ran a city-financed early education program and, in order to make ends meet, taught a few after-school music classes at The School.

"Eventually I just burned out on working two jobs and took the easy way out. I couldn't resist the higher salary and better benefits that The School offered," Sara confessed.

"Don't apologize. That's a totally legitimate decision. I did the same thing when I decided to quit academia. I realized I could work less and spend more time with Zoe if I wrote and curated instead of taught. I'm really glad I made that choice."

By the end of the third kilometer they had covered parents, siblings—Sara's three, Helen's zero—and significant others.

"I guess I'm what people call 'very single,'" Sara confided with a sad smile.

"Then I guess I'm what people called 'very married,'" Helen responded, going through her mental Rolodex to see who she knew that might be available.

"Michael sounds pretty great, and you're so lucky to have Zoe. She is too cute. Just look at her," Sara said, pointing to the pigtailed biker madly pedaling to keep up with a small blond child on a pink trike.

"Go, Zoe, you can do it!" Helen shouted ahead.

"She's one determined little girl. Look at her trying to overtake Julia."

"It's Julian," Helen corrected. "A boy."

"Oops."

"And now watch. If I know my daughter, she'll pedal really fast to catch up to him and then slow down and follow behind. She's always been reluctant to take the lead," Helen laughed, both proud of and annoyed by her daughter's noncompetitive nature.

"That could be developmental. She might surprise you one day with a killer instinct you never thought she had," Sara volunteered.

"She'd better. Or she'll never survive in this town!"

By the fifth kilometer they were giddy, laughing at the absurdity of the bike-athon itself (couldn't The School have found a worthier cause than old horses?), at several of their fellow chaperones, who at this point were slavishly carrying both their children *and* their children's bikes, and at the taunts of one jeering onlooker: "Hey, what about me? I don't have a retirement fund!"

When the bike-athon was finally completed, Zoe was in need of a nap, and Helen, feeling buoyant at the prospect of cultivating a new friendship, invited Sara back to her apartment for lunch. They spent the better part of the afternoon delving deeper into their life stories, struck more by the differences than the similarities, and by the time Zoe woke up, they were on their way to becoming fast friends, entranced by what each perceived to be the other's exotic background.

In the years Sara had lived in New York, she had acquired a modicum of sophistication while somehow managing to retain her deeply ingrained Midwestern sensibility. Her outward persona was straight-shooting American Gothic, but those who knew her well were privy to her sharp wit and droll style. These traits would serve her well in admissions, where a poker face was mandatory but a funny bone was the key to survival. Helen, on the other hand, was urbane to the core, with a cynicism that allowed her to see the humor in most of life's travails—that is, most of those she had encountered so far.

Over the years, their friendship blossomed. They saw each other regularly in The School's admissions office, where, after five years as Rothschild's assistant, Sara became the director of admissions, and Helen volunteered as a tour guide for prospective Kindergarten applicants. And they both participated in the many activities that were scattered throughout the school calendar, particularly once Helen was elected president of the Parents' Association and her presence at these events was required. Beyond that, they made an effort to see each other socially, as frequently as their divergent and demanding New York schedules permitted, which admittedly was not as much as either would have liked.

In addition to all her other responsibilities, Sara was the director of The School's extracurricular choral group, of which Zoe was an enthusiastic and talented participant. After years of in-school interaction, Sara had come to know Zoe not only as Helen's daughter but as a highly valued member of the School community, a gifted musician, and a solid though not stellar student. In turn, Zoe looked up to Sara and, unbeknownst to Helen, had also recently sought her advice on the subject of high school admissions. Sara recognized the risk involved in separately counseling two members of the same family but told herself that as long as she exercised the utmost discretion, her objectivity might be helpful. And since the Dragers were the closest thing she had to family in New York, she was willing to run the risk of ruffling a few feathers to make sure Zoe ended up in the school that was right for her.

Pamela Rothschild did not arrive at The School until noon. It was unusual, on the first day of school, for the head not to be poised at the front gate, a smile ready for the shy first-time students, a compliment on a new haircut for a returning fifth-grader. In past years, Pamela could always be counted on to be there, the figurehead at the bow of the ship. But this year she was feeling complacent. The School was running well, enrollment was robust, and money was pouring in from several recently enrolled families who viewed their hefty contributions as the least they could do to express their relief at having been granted admission into her exclusive enclave. But even more to the point, proffering enormous donations helped these new parents sleep at night, assuming that their little ones would receive preferential treatment the minute they were enrolled in their new school.

Pamela unlocked her office, admiring the shiny brass plaque she had had engraved over the summer and affixed to her door.

Headmasters have powers at their disposal
with which prime ministers have never yet been invested.

"Brilliant, isn't it?" she crowed to her assistant, Margaret, who still wasn't sure what message the new plaque was intended to convey: "Keep out"? "The doctor is in"? Or simply "Beware"?

As Pamela stood in front of her office mirror rearranging her hair, she remembered the one thing she *had* to do before the evening party: check to see if Julian Toppler was appropriately dressed for the first day of school.

During the course of the past summer, Pamela had spent many hours counseling John and Lauren Toppler about their eighth-grade son, who seemed to be in the midst of a rather disturbing adolescent identity crisis.

"I strongly suggest that when Julian is away at camp, you purge his room of all cosmetics and feminine accessories. And when he returns, you must forbid him to enter his mother's dressing room or touch her jewelry," she declared with utmost authority. A believer in tough love, Pamela told the Topplers that they could only hope to set Julian straight on his gender confusion by setting limits *and* enforcing them through strict disciplinary measures.

"That means no more eyeliner—even if he tells you all the kids are using it," she commanded sternly.

Mr. Toppler agreed with Pamela, but his wife did not.

"I'm more inclined to explore a kinder, gentler, therapeutic approach. Maybe we need to consult a professional," Lauren ventured tentatively.

"Are you suggesting that I'm not a professional?" Pamela replied haughtily, and looked to John for support. He nodded in agreement. "In my years of experience I can't tell you how many parents think their children need touchy-feely intervention when, in fact, their children are crying out for discipline! They're looking for limits! And it's up to you to set them!" she addressed her speech to Lauren, whom she had pegged as the pushover. It was two against one, and for the time being, John Toppler and Pamela prevailed.

Stepping back from the mirror, she experimented with a side part and a new rhinestone-studded barrette, her beloved charm bracelet jangling each time she flipped her wrist.

An innocent bystander's glance in the general direction of her hand was Pamela's cue to recite the unabridged story behind each of the fifteen charms. The first year she was the head of The School, the graduating class presented her with the bracelet, simply adorned with a single gold apple in celebration of her recent relocation to the Big Apple. The annual gift of a charm became a tradition at The School, and each eighth-grade class presented her with one on the day of their graduation. The class representatives spent weeks trying to find the perfect charm, wanting theirs to be more precious and personally significant than the last. Over the years she had been given a lucky horseshoe, a ruler, a little teapot, a riding crop, and her favorite of all, a perfect little replica of The School, complete with a tiny red door and a minuscule schoolmistress standing in front. While fondling the most recent addition, a tiny gold ladle commemorating the days she spent with last year's graduating class at the local soup kitchen, she remembered her offer, made in an uncharacteristically magnanimous moment, to bring an appetizer to the Topplers' party. But over the weekend she had been too busy to shop for the ingredients and, quite frankly, regretted ever having made the offer.

"Margaret!" she shouted. "Where can I procure decent pissaladiere? I need enough for a crowd. For tonight," she barked.

"I'll get right back to you on that," Margaret replied, pretending to know what Pamela wanted. It sounded like some sort of French undergarment for accident-prone children, but why would such a thing be needed for a cocktail party? She scrambled to her desk and grabbed the dictionary.

"Jeez, was I off base—a Provençal finger food! I'd better phone Bruce. If anyone can help me, he can," she thought, quickly dialing an old college friend who, she had read on Page Six, was now an up-and-coming caterer.

Margaret had been working for Pamela for five years. The pace of the school day appealed to her, the kids were endlessly amusing, and she enjoyed her colleagues immensely. But it was the opportunity to work directly with the legendary Pamela Rothschild that had initially sold Margaret on the job. She was respected for overseeing what was considered to be one of the most rigorous, traditional elementary schools in the city.

In addition, Margaret equated "British" with "learned" and had convinced herself that there were many things she could learn from Pamela. And it was true, there were. But recently some of Pamela's requests had been falling into the not-in-my-job-description category—like today's, for example. Or into the I'm-not-so-sure-this-is-ethical category, like the time last year when Pamela asked her to wrap a Murano glass vase that had been donated for The School auction and re-gift it to Pamela's recently married cousin. The most annoying aspect of her job, however, was the frequency with which she was required to invent excuses to conceal her boss's habitual absenteeism. But at least she could always rely on the stimulation of new challenges.

So here she was, hustling a caterer while Pamela was sequestered in her office, "catching up on some pressing correspondence," as she regularly announced with an air of self-importance. After hearing the same phrase for months, Margaret had figured out that it meant a few minutes of legitimate e-mail followed by hours on the Internet, which, as far as she could tell, involved nothing remotely school-related. Once she caught her searching eBay for bargains on Staffordshire porcelains. Other times she nabbed her yacking up a storm in a chat room with fellow Windsor watchers. And then there were the frequent games of solitaire, which, if Margaret happened to walk in on, would magically vanish from the screen in a nanosecond.

Meanwhile, ensconced in her graciously appointed office, Pamela cast a wary eye at her computer. As it was day one of the admissions season, it was not surprising that her in-box contained over a dozen messages from eighth-grade parents, all reporting on their application progress. "What a bloody bore," she murmured to herself as she reluctantly clicked on the first message in her box.

Pamela-

Should I inform the schools that Nathan is on Ritalin when I request the applications, in the applications, or wait until the interviews?

J. MacGuire

What sheer stupidity! Have you been sampling the meds yourself? Pamela wondered, and responded:

Jean-

I won't tell if you don't tell. Ever. End of story.

Pamela

Next was an e-mail from Neal Moore, the most nebbishy parent in The School and the bane of her existence.

Pamela,

Marianne has suddenly done an about face and doesn't want to apply to any of the schools you suggested. When we met with you in June, you strongly recommended a single-sex school for Nicholas and we both agreed with you. At least I thought we did. Now she suddenly thinks a boys' school is the wrong way to go. What should I do?

Neal Moore

What a weenie! This is exactly why poor Nicholas needs a boys' school—he has no masculine role model, Pamela sneered, and wrote:

Neal,

Who wears the pants in your family? If Marianne is unwilling to call for the applications, then you do it! But deal with this right away! The schools must not sense her ambivalence! You both must appear single-minded and confident in your choice. If she is not, then she should not go on the interviews. But we will talk about that later. Now just get the applications!

Pamela

These people need more hand-holding than a kindergarten class on a field trip, Pamela moaned.

Pamela,

I wanted to inform you that Marissa will be taking the qualifying exam for the selective public schools. Richard and I have agreed that we do not wish to apply to any of the private schools you have suggested. We have a deep commitment to public education and have decided to pursue that route. We look forward to, and have all confidence, that our pursuit will have a successful outcome. Thank you for your continued interest in Marissa's education.

Denise Doyle-Gillis

A successful outcome indeed, Pamela sniffed. *If they want to scrimp on their own daughter's education, that's their business. I always thought Dick was a bargain hunter. Anyway, it's one less student I have to worry about. Young Marissa's loss will be my gain.*

She didn't dignify the e-mail with a response.

And then there was Helen Drager's, which required no more than a two-word response like "good job" or, if she were feeling friendly, which she was not today, "go, girl." Since Zoe was a relatively competent and presentable adolescent and her parents had been appropriately generous to The School with both their time and checkbooks, she was currently holding a space on Pamela's "eminently placeable" list. But that could change any time, particularly since Pamela had learned that Helen had committed a major breach of Rothschild's Admissions Etiquette.

During the summer Pamela had heard a rumor via the eighth-grade grapevine that the Dragers were considering coed schools for Zoe, after Pamela had specifically instructed them, when they met last spring, to apply only to the girls' schools. Her fury was fueled as much by their audacity as by her anger at having her authority called into question. And to make matters worse, she learned that the Dragers' decision was made on the basis of advice received from, of all people, her former assistant Sara Nash. Pamela knew that Helen and Sara were close, and, resentful of their friendship on multiple levels, she took this as a personal and professional affront and sent Helen a strongly worded e-mail in which she commanded her not to discuss admissions with anyone other than herself. She had since realized that Sara's advice was well founded, given the limited number of spots in the girls' schools, but she wasn't about to admit that.

Pamela frequently congratulated herself on her omnipotence within The School, always finding the concept of her limitless influence headily intoxicating. She relished her role as ruling puppeteer, pulling the strings that controlled the actions of the people she referred to as her "marionettes." Every year there were many moments in the admissions drama when she was tempted to assert her power. She was well aware of her range of options, from simply not returning phone calls to out-and-out sabotage, and she would exercise them as she saw fit.

But that would come later. Now she had to hustle down to the auditorium, where she was expected to make an appearance at the afternoon welcoming ceremony, where while the elementary chorus was singing "My country 'tis of thee," she quietly sang "God Save the Queen."

* * *

Brandi appeared to be slightly frazzled by the relentless ringing of the phone. No sooner had she finalized a breathy conversation with a soft-talker from the West Village than the screamer from Chelsea called back with a zip code correction. But despite her inexperience with the codified hierarchy of New York society, Brandi caught on faster than Sara could ever have predicted.

Sara was so relieved at last to have an assistant that she was willing to overlook the fact that Brandi was a twenty-two-year-old recent graduate of a southern party school with no real experience to recommend her. In the past Sara had manned The School's admissions office entirely unassisted, but the volume had increased to the point that it became unmanageable for one, and after much back-and-forth, Pamela finally agreed to hire an additional employee. Sara posted the job on the Internet and received a pile of resumes but never actually had an opportunity to interview anyone. No sooner had Pamela approved the position than she informed Sara that she had taken the liberty of hiring Brandi, who just happened to be the niece of one of The School's trustees. Sara was less than enthusiastic when she saw her resume, a sparse one-pager describing three summers playing Minnie Mouse at Disney World and an internship at the House of Blues. However, on meeting her she was pleasantly surprised. What she lacked in experience, Brandi definitely made up for with enthusiasm and, Sara had to admit, there was something refreshing about a perky sorority girl with a cheerful disposition. *And by the time January rolls around,* she mused, *the admissions department will definitely benefit from an infusion of pep squad rah-rah and sunshine.*

The hiring of Brandi was the last positive professional contact Sara had with Pamela. In fact, she hadn't spoken to Pamela since June, before they both went off on vacation—Sara to a New Age spa in Taos to do tai chi, sun salutations, and meditation, Pamela to a cooking school in the south of France owned by Justine Frampton, the director of admissions at The Fancy Girls' School. Pamela had spent her vacation at Justine's cooking school every summer for the past five years. Not coincidentally, for the past five years, The Fancy Girls' School had admitted a disproportionately large number of Pamela's graduating female students.

Before leaving for the day, Sara asked Brandi for an up-to-the-minute tally of application requests.

"One hundred and seventeen calls. Is this a record or what?" Brandi announced proudly.

"One for the *Guinness Book*. Tomorrow may bring even more. Think about all the people who never got through today," she sighed, sweeping her keys into the utilitarian green canvas backpack she carried every day. "I've got to get home quickly to change and then get myself over to the party. See you tomorrow. And by the way, good first day," she smiled, awkwardly patting Brandi on the shoulder before turning to dash out.

Sara's third-floor walk-up apartment was filled from floor to ceiling with self-help books and CDs. Her taste was eclectic, running the gamut from *The Origin of Chinese Deities* to *Who Moved My Cheese?* and from Neil Young (post–Buffalo Springfield) to Norah Jones.

Not particularly tuned in to the nuances of decorating, Sara had in her apartment much of the same furniture she had in her college dorm room, including the steamer trunk she had used to ship all her worldly goods to and from campus twenty years ago. Only now it functioned as a coffee table, stacked high with educational newsletters, New Age publications, and assorted magazines, the piles topped with the two books that were currently in use: *The Joys of Yiddish*—a gift from Helen on her last birthday—and *Thinner Thighs in Thirty Days,* an old standby she revisited every few years. Her sofa was covered with a muslin one-size-fits-all slipcover she had ordered from a catalogue—a misnomer since it never seemed to fit her particular sofa properly.

Hanging on her "exposed brick wall" (a phrase her realtor had chirped over and over when selling her on the virtues of the apartment) was the patchwork quilt made by the children of room D from dozens of their daddies' discarded Italian silk ties—one of the many items she had bought over the years at the annual school auction. On the table sat the room C ceramic vase, decorated with all the children's names in Chinese calligraphy, although how they translated names like Courtney and Ashley into Mandarin was anyone's guess. On the floor lay the hooked wool rug that the fifth grade had roughly patterned with a map of the Lewis and Clark expedition, complete with a tiny figure of Sacagawea in the lower right-hand corner. Having grown up with Ethan Allen, Sara thought of the colorful, whimsical student creations as adventurous home décor, while at the same time they qualified as contributions (and tax deductible, too!) to The School—the only monetary contributions she could make on her paltry salary.

Sara's last big purchase, outside of the auction items, was the stationary bike she had bought with the intention of pedaling for thirty minutes a day while watching Jim Lehrer. She was embarrassed when Helen was last over and pointed out that the bike, draped with piles of clothing, looked more like a coatrack than a piece of exercise equipment.

Sara's wardrobe also lacked pizazz. She would have been happy wearing jeans and a sweatshirt every day, but unfortunately, the dress code for her job was more Talbot's than tattered, confronting her with the daily challenge of assembling a presentable outfit. When Pamela promoted her to the position of director of admissions, she admonished Sara that she would be "the first contact the public has with The School, and you must dress with that in mind." She remembered thinking what a chore that would be, and she had been right; particularly since she had gained a pound a year since she started at The School, and half her clothes didn't fit. She blamed that on the frequent school bake sales, which inundated the admissions office with a constant flow of minimuffins, cupcakes, Rice Krispy treats, and other so-called child-friendly confections.

After searching despairingly through the chaos of her closet, Sara threw on her standard school event uniform: straight gray skirt, pink sweater set, and practical flats. She struggled with a new pair of panty hose, annoyed that size D, which, according to the pseudoscientific height/weight chart on the back of the package, should fit, barely did. Glancing in the mirror, she dabbed some petroleum jelly on her lips, ran a comb through her thick, unruly hair, then caught a cab to the Topplers'.

The elevator door opened directly into the Topplers' luxurious Fifth Avenue duplex apartment; Sara had been in enough of these buildings to know that one apartment per floor was always a sign that grandeur lay ahead. Stepping into the foyer, she remembered Helen describing it as "a treatise on artifice." With every surface painted to look like something it wasn't—ceiling as sky with clouds, vertical beams as Doric columns, walls as Aegean vistas—it was truly a triumph of trompe l'oeil. The vast living room beyond contained three discrete seating areas, each of which was upholstered with heavy brocades, jacquards, and velvets, with silky tassels dangling off every corner of every pillow, every knob of every drawer, and every edge of every lampshade. Extending outward from the living room were several long hallways, each one softly lit by a complex network of recessed fixtures and costly dimmers. One hallway led to the master suite, one to the children's wing: a series of four bedrooms occupied by Julian, his two stepsisters, who lived most of the time with John's first wife in Los Angeles, and his stepbrother, who lived most of the time with John's second wife in Honolulu. A third hallway led to the library, music room, and a variety of other underused, overdecorated spaces. Throughout the apartment, the walls were covered with fabrics, veneers, mirrors, marbles, and tiles but were otherwise strikingly bare. The absolute absence of art seemed incongruous amid this level of splendor. But, as Helen had explained to Sara at the last Toppler-hosted school function, "the Topplers' apartment is about texture, not culture."

"Miss Nash. How good of you to come," Sara was greeted by a deep curtsy and great aplomb. "Pink. What a lovely color on you," Julian added, waving a white feather duster in the air. Apparently his parents had neglected to inform him, upon his return from camp, that the maid's closet was off limits, too.

"Hello, Julian. How was your summer?" Sara asked warmly.

"FAB-ulous. Camp itself was nothing to get excited about, but I got the leading role in the summer play, *Auntie Mame*! The other kids were totally freaked by that, but the director was really, really supportive and went way out on a limb to give me the part."

"Did your parents get to see the show?" she asked.

"Regrettably not," he replied pouting.

Knowing how much time Pamela had spent counseling the Topplers over the summer, Sara was surprised to see Julian flaunting the feather duster. She couldn't help but wonder what Pamela's response would be.

John Toppler was a wildly successful class action attorney, well known from his advertisements in subway cars and bus shelters. He was also one of The School's wealthiest parents and had made no bones about the size of the donation he planned to make upon Julian's admission to the right high school, although in this case "right" did not necessarily mean the school that was right for Julian as much as right for him. Originally from the Bronx, he aspired to more for his son than DeWitt Clinton High School. He had made the blanket assumption that between his money and Pamela's alleged clout, his son would be handed an automatic acceptance by the same New England prep school his neighbor's son attended. What Toppler chose not to acknowledge was that these days there were no guarantees, particularly in a school that had more interest in filling its freshman class with lacrosse players than with cross-dressers.

Pamela frequently complained about this type of father—the man who made unrealistic demands, relinquished all responsibility, and then became apoplectic when the outcome did not meet his expectations. She often proclaimed to have "zero tolerance for these self-important bastards," except in the case of John Toppler. With him she had no choice—she had already scheduled a dedication ceremony for The School's new auditorium, Toppler Hall.

Looking around the room, Sara was happy to see Helen gliding towards her, looking lovely in a sleeveless, black crepe de chine cocktail dress, strappy black sandals, and a triple strand of water pearls. Sara marveled at her friend's ability to look her best no matter how stressful a day she had had, and to do this on half the clothing budget of most of the women in this room. Helen knew exactly how to make the most of her lithe, willowy frame by wearing well-cut, tailored clothing. She always managed to look fashionable but never trendy. Even her hair, which had been shoulder-length for years, was always straight and bluntly cut, framing her high-cheekboned face perfectly. Sara cringed when she once heard one of the mothers cattily whisper what a pity it was that Helen's nose was too large for her to be considered truly beautiful. To Sara's eye, Helen's excellent posture, spectacular figure, and elegant style more than made up for an aquiline nose. She knew she would benefit from implementing even a few of Helen's fashion suggestions and, picking at a pill on her sweater sleeve, vowed to follow her advice the next time it was offered.

"You look gorgeous. I always feel so shlebby next to you," Sara greeted her warmly.

"Do you mean shlubby or schleppy?" Helen teased.

"Both," Sara laughed as she grabbed two wineglasses from a passing waiter and handed one to Helen.

"To the new school year"—Helen clicked her glass against Sara's—"and all that comes with it," she whispered, rolling her eyes.

"You're such a headmistress's pet," Sara teased, knowing Helen had been one of the eager beavers who started making her calls at eight a.m. the day after Labor Day, according to Pamela's instructions.

"Well, I'm glad to get the calls out of the way, and I'm looking forward to the school visits and interviews. I've got to remember to make sure Zoe gets involved and doesn't feel bulldozed. I know I have a tendency to get wrapped up in a project and get really bossy. I don't want to be like some of these other people"—she lowered her voice and gestured towards the other guests—"and lose sight of what's best for my child. You know what I mean?"

"I can't imagine who you might be referring to," Sara deadpanned as she and Helen observed Julian across the room, rose between his teeth, leading his flustered mother in a mock tango.

"I haven't seen Pamela. Is she coming tonight?" Helen asked innocently.

"I assume so. It *is* the kickoff event of the school year. One would at least expect her to make an appearance." And she added in a whisper, "Especially given the hosts' net worth."

Pamela's comings and goings had always been unpredictable, and occasionally raised eyebrows, even among the members of her devoted fan club, the head-of-School-can-do-no-wrongers. Helen remembered the time she was working at The School's book fair with Cally Reynolds, and Cally whispered to her conspiratorially, "Last Saturday, at two a.m., Jake saw Pamela at Gruffy's—you know, that leather bar in the village. What do you make of that?"

Helen looked at her incredulously and said, "I have no idea. How weird," while actually thinking, *And you're not wondering what your husband was doing there?*

Seeing that Michael had arrived, Helen went over to rescue him before Peter Newman, one of The School's biggest windbags, had a chance to corner him. Peter was a Civil War buff, and Michael had once made the mistake of mentioning a business trip he had made to Fredericksburg, Virginia, leading Peter, who missed the word "business," to assume that Michael shared his interest in the battle site. As a result, whenever he saw Michael at school functions, he subjected him to an 1864-based monologue. Helen grabbed Michael's arm just as Peter was beginning a discourse on a new theory about Lincoln's assassination, and whisked him off to get some food.

"Thanks. Dodged a bullet that time," he said, appreciatively kissing his wife on the cheek.

"Two bullets. John Wilkes Booth and Newman," she replied, warmly returning his greeting.

"How was your day?" he asked.

"I've developed a case of carpal tunnel finger. I must have pushed the redial button three thousand times today. When I finally got through, it was to be put on hold. But I did finally manage to speak to a few admissions office flunkies and, by noon, had succeeded in wangling applications out of four of them. The other two schools put us on wait lists, and we now actually have to write one of them a letter telling them *why* we're willing to wait. Can you believe it? And the groveling is just beginning!"

"They'll come through, don't worry. It's just a little test. They want us to prove that we know how to play by their rules," he said reassuringly. After her morning of petty indignities, she found Michael's mechanical optimism slightly irritating.

As they stood around nibbling on goat cheese tartlets and chicken saté, Margaret rushed in, balancing a large tray of hors d'oeuvres on one arm while adjusting her tote bag, purse, and gym bag on the other.

"Ms. Rothschild's contribution." She grimaced and plunked the tray down on the table. "Pissaladiere, in case you're not familiar with it."

"Yummy," purred Dana Winter, mother of eighth-grader April and member of The School's board of trustees. "I love everything Pamela cooks. This must be her rendition of the famous Justine Frampton recipe, right, Margaret?"

Margaret was about to blurt out that that was only possible if Bruce McCall was channeling Justine while he worked, but then remembered Pamela's instructions: "Make sure the pissaladiere appears to be my own creation."

"I'm really not sure where the recipe came from," she replied vaguely. Meanwhile, Toppler refused a piece of pissaladiere faster than he would a no-fault insurance claim, and cross-examined Sara about Pamela's whereabouts. Sara, now convinced Pamela was AWOL, tried to concoct a plausible explanation, all the while resentful that this burden had fallen on her. In classic Pamela fashion, her arrogance had left her insensitive to the Topplers' true agenda in offering to host the party—their desire to have the head of School in their home for an evening. Every year, Sara watched the eighth-grade parents compete with one another to get in Pamela's good graces. They kissed up to her in every way imaginable, thinking that would guarantee them admission to the school of their choice. The sad reality was, it generally worked. Pamela pulled strings for a short list of families—only the few she deemed worthy, regardless of the child's qualifications. And "worthy" could mean anything from the virtuous (donating generously to the Capital Campaign or sewing costumes for the School play) to the smarmy (loaning the country house to Pamela for her personal use during spring break or sending the family masseuse to Pamela's apartment on a weekly basis).

Dana Winter had moved on to the crabmeat dip, scooping and shoveling with an endive leaf. A stocky redhead with ruddy skin, coarse hair, and nicotine-stained teeth, Dana widened her squinty eyes when she spied Helen sipping wine by the bar.

"Hey, there! How was your summer? Any interesting travel?" Not waiting for an answer, Dana continued, "We had the BEST summer. Patrick has always wanted to go to cooking school, so I surprised him with two weeks at Justine Frampton's École de la Cuisine de Provence."

"Fun, fun," Helen replied distractedly. She was never fond of the Winters, and had grown to dislike them intensely over the past year, when their daughter, April, tried to steal Zoe's best friend Julian by bribing him with designer hand-me-downs.

"Did you call for your applications today?" Dana asked.

"Of course," Helen answered lightly. The last thing she wanted to do was swap admissions stories with Dana.

"Do you know what your first choice is?"

"How could we possibly know that so soon? We haven't even seen the schools. Do you?"

"Well, after spending a few weeks with Justine Frampton, we're pretty sold on The Fancy Girls' School. It was so nice for her to get to spend some quality time with April and get to know her in a nonacademic context. Could be helpful, too," Dana winked.

Helen raised her brow and murmured, "Good for you," as she glanced over Dana's shoulder in search of a friendlier face. "Oh, I need a refill. Please excuse me."

Denise Doyle-Gillis waved, and Helen went over and gave her a warm hello. Denise had volunteered to chair The School auction this year, a Parents' Association function that Helen was glad to hand off to somebody as well qualified as Denise. Over the years Denise had held many positions of responsibility in The School, from lieutenant of the playground patrol squad to dance chaperone coordinator. In each case she took her role as seriously as could be expected, and then some.

Helen had known most of the people at this party for many years and had spent numerous memorable occasions with them. Together they had attended holiday galas, school plays, art fairs, field days, and fund-raisers and watched each other's children grow from adorable toddlers to gawky adolescents. She and Michael had become quite close to several of the couples, which added yet another grueling dimension to the admissions process; their friends had suddenly become rivals as they battled one another for the limited spots in the city's most desirable schools. Each acceptance meant someone else's rejection, and Helen couldn't stop herself from looking around the room and sizing up the competition.

April Winter is bright, Helen grudgingly admitted to herself, *but I hear her anorexia has really gotten in the way of her academic performance. Poor thing. I can't imagine that most schools wouldn't consider April a mental health liability and reject her on that basis alone. But who knows? Maybe their summer sojourn clinched them a spot in The Fancy Girls' School. God knows, that place must be crawling with girls with eating disorders . . . There are the O'Neals. I seem to recall their mentioning that Katie's test scores weren't very good last year. I wonder if they had her tutored over the summer. Hmmm . . . I'll have to ask Zoe. Oh, and I think I remember Neal Moore saying that Pamela told them Nicholas should only apply to the boys' schools. That will free up one more spot in the coed schools.*

She despised herself for thinking this way. No matter how hard she tried to stay above it, being thrown together with the other eighth-grade parents seemed to bring out the worst in her these days. Looking around for a diversion, she saw Sara, no longer being interrogated by Toppler but, worse, trapped in a conversation with a mother who, Helen knew, had a second child she was desperate to enroll at The School. She sidled over and joined their conversation.

"Sara, I'm not totally clear on The School's sibling policy. Can I assume Ari's acceptance is a fait accompli?" Norit Ben-Adler inquired.

"We have no articulated policy as such. Each application is considered on an individual basis. There are no guarantees. I must encourage you to apply to other schools as well," Sara said, sounding more aloof than she intended.

Norit looked infuriated. This wasn't the answer she had hoped to hear.

"Relax, Norit. These things always have a way of working out for the best," Helen added supportively, mindful that as president of the Parents' Association it was her duty to exercise diplomacy. Sara nodded affirmatively; she just hoped that when it came to Helen's own situation, she would have the insight to practice what she preached.

Pamela still hadn't shown up, and by eight o'clock John Toppler was seething.

"I'm sick and tired of watching your son play coochie-coo with the guests," he hissed at his wife. "Jesus Christ! Look at him!" He glared furiously at the sight of Julian tickling Peter Newman's behind with his feather duster. "Enough, dammit! I'm starting without her!" he growled. He yanked a silk handkerchief out of the pocket of his pinstriped double-breasted jacket to wipe his sweaty palms, grabbed a knife, and clanged it loudly against the rim of a glass. Several people shushed the crowd.

"Welcome, eighth-grade parents. Tonight, as we say in the legal profession, I'll be brief, heh, heh. This is a significant milestone for all of us. We have certainly been together for a long time and have enjoyed celebrating many occasions in our children's lives. I wish everyone here great success in their trials, heh heh, and hope that the jury deliberations fall in everyone's favor. As we all say at the law firm of Toppler and Whitney, may we all get our just rewards, heh heh. Let's hope for the best." He raised his glass to the crowd, and everyone did the same.

Let's hope for the best . . . for the children, Sara thought, knowing that what was best for his child was the furthest thing from John Toppler's mind.

The next morning Pamela sent carnations to the Topplers, intending for the flowers to be accompanied by a handwritten apology explaining why she had been unable to attend last night's soiree. However, the florist erred and sent the Topplers the note that was intended to accompany Pamela's other order—the dozen roses sent to Brooklyn Heights.

Roses are Red
Violets are Blue
I had a super evening
Et tu?

When Lauren Toppler read the note and realized it had been intended for someone else, she immediately called her friend Jean MacGuire.

"I give up. Who's the lucky man?" Jean giggled.

"I have no clue. I thought you might," Lauren responded, fully aware that gossip spread like wildfire in The School and that Jean could always be counted on to fan the flames.

"It couldn't possibly be anyone at school. She'd never be that indiscreet," Jean said with conviction. She had always been one of the true believers who accepted everything Pamela said as gospel, even her order to keep Nathan's use of Ritalin a secret.

"I wouldn't put it past her," Lauren said flatly. The truth was that Lauren was actually relieved that Pamela hadn't attended the party, since Julian's behavior would inevitably have provoked another unwelcome discourse on discipline. But she sought revenge nonetheless and thought the best way to do that was by providing grist for the rumor mill.

When John got home that night and saw first the cheesy flowers and then the provocative note, he exploded.

"That fickle bitch! She was probably out nailing some two-bit polo player. And then she has the nerve to send us this six-dollar piece-of-shit flower arrangement! Who the hell does she think she's dealing with here? Our donation is history if she doesn't watch her ass!" he shouted, and stormed out of the room.

By the end of the second week, Brandi announced that she had fulfilled 556 requests for applications.

"How many children do you anticipate admitting?" she asked Sara with a worried wrinkle in her normally smooth brow.

"No more than fifty."

"Wow. Pretty tough odds for a gambler." Brandi shook her head in disbelief.

"Killer odds for a paranoid parent," Sara answered.

Sara was amazed by how quickly so many of the parents had returned their completed applications, some even within a few days. Did these people think that admissions decisions were made on a first come, first served basis or that they would receive brownie points for punctuality?

Her first year as director of admissions, she had received a whole batch of essays that gave elaborate responses to a question that was not even on the application. Puzzled, she brought them to Pamela, who laughed and said that these parents had gotten last year's application to prepare for the process over the summer and never bothered to check whether the questions had been altered. Sara had made it a point to change her questions every year since.

The application essay functioned as a way for the parents to introduce themselves and their child to The School. Sara often wondered whether the essay had any basis in reality, since it often just seemed to reflect a parent's calculated guess of what The School was looking for. After all, intelligent applicants knew they had nothing to gain by hanging their dirty laundry out to dry—they learned that in

Offspring Marketing for Dummies. But by reading between the lines and exercising astute analytical skills, Sara managed to learn quite a bit about both the parents and their children.

Occasionally an application was straightforward, no-nonsense, and heartfelt, and in these cases Sara looked forward to meeting the families. Unfortunately, they were the exception rather than the rule, and more often the essays were superficial, transparent, and occasionally flat-out hilarious.

Every year there was a group of parents who weren't shy about proclaiming their child a budding Einstein. This year's winners in that category were the Belzers. After explaining that their son Sam was a "genius" and extolling his many brilliant traits, they added:

> But we are happy to report that there are still ways in which he's still a normal kid and even goes so far as to exhibit a few teeny tiny signs of his youth—he delights in catching fireflies in a jar at our country house, but while other boys his age tire of the game quickly and set their lightning bugs free, Sam keeps them in the jar for days, using the exercise as a method of studying the habits of insects up close. We're so proud of our budding entomologist!

Sara was put off by the boy who delighted in holding bugs captive as long as possible whereas other children's normal compassion compelled them to set theirs free. She continued to read:

> Like many boys Sam's age, he loves trains, planes and automobiles. But where most young boys possess superficial knowledge of these things, Sam knows the New York subway system inside out. He can recite every stop (express and local) on every line, and the same goes for buses! Last week his grandmother even called him for directions to get from Far Rockaway to Arthur Avenue. We're so proud of his navigational skills! And I haven't mentioned his reading ability . . .

Sara made a note to herself to ask Brandi if this was the parent who asked whether toilet training was a requirement for Kindergarten entry. She had learned that young children who were victims of extreme performance pressure often manifested their anxiety through regressive behavior in the scatological department.

Another of her favorites was the parent who tossed in a small negative about the child in an effort to make the application seem more sincere. The negative was cleverly calibrated to convey an attribute that any educator knew was a positive, but the parent slyly pretended not to know. This year's master of this subtle art was Mrs. Mansfield.

> Wyatt is everything a mother could want her child to be—bright, industrious and most importantly to me, honest and humble. A prime example of his lack of airs occurs when Wyatt reads. Sometimes when he is reading to me out loud he comes across a word he doesn't know. He will struggle for a long time to sound it out. He repeats the word over and over, every which way, until he finally gets it right. It may take a while but the satisfaction he gets from succeeding, without my help, is thrilling. As you can tell, I have gotten immense pleasure from participating in Wyatt's early learning and I look forward to a day-to-day partnership with The School as we tackle new challenges together.

Obviously this parent was counting on the admissions director's response being something along the lines of "It's so extraordinary that your child demonstrates such great perseverance! And you. What good judgment and parenting you exhibit!"

But Sara was far too savvy for that, and in her notes she scribbled, *Manipulative and meddling.*

Sara remembered how, years ago, she and Pamela used to spend collegial afternoons together reading the applications, often laughing heartily. It was one of the few occasions when Pamela would let down her regal airs and behave almost girlishly. Sharing these confidential documents with an outsider would have been completely unethical; sharing them with Pamela had been wicked fun. Regrettably, that pastime was now history, and given the current state of their relationship, it was hard for Sara even to imagine spending a few minutes alone in the same room, let alone giggling together.

Their last real contact had been a dinner in early June at The Bistro, a restaurant that was around the corner from The School. It was one of the many places in Manhattan that served passable, traditional French fare, annually advertised the arrival of Beaujolais nouveau, and staged elaborate Bastille Day celebrations. The special of the day was the bouillabaisse, and they both ordered it. Pamela was critical of the dinner, insisting that bouillabaisse should never be made without native Mediterranean fish, and why anyone would try to do so was incomprehensible. Sara knew her well enough to know not to ask why she ordered it. She just prayed that Pamela would not summon the waiter and demand its removal from the table and the bill.

It was at that dinner that Pamela had expressed her growing ambivalence about The School.

"I'm positively sick and tired of the parents and their constant complaining. You'd think they had better ways to spend their time than in endless meetings with me. Do you know, last week I spent over two hours with the Blanchards because they were upset that Anthony's classmates called him 'tubby.' I wanted to tell them that it's their own fault for allowing their son to become such a fatty. But of course I held my tongue. And then there are the excuse makers. If I get one more call from a parent blaming a lost piece of homework on a new housekeeper, I think I'm going to lose it! Don't they realize what kind of message that gives their kids? And you won't believe this! Just yesterday I got a call from that ridiculous Wachtel woman, asking if I thought it would be okay for Telulah to miss midterms so the family could go to the Galapagos Islands before the hurricane season kicked up. I said, 'Sure, if you don't mind if she fails seventh grade.' What did she think I would say?"

Sara listened quietly. She had to admit, those were legitimate gripes.

"What I'm about to tell you should go no further. Do I have your word?" Pamela lowered her voice.

"Of course. You know that."

"I'm considering a career change. I'm seriously thinking about making this next school year my last," Pamela whispered while dipping a heel of baguette in the last of her bouillabaisse broth, clearly having decided to overlook its inauthenticity.

"Really? But what would you do then?" Sara asked, maintaining neutrality. She had sensed Pamela's dissatisfaction but had never imagined she would ever actually leave.

Pamela didn't answer her question. Instead she droned about how The School was like her child and that leaving it in someone else's hands was unimaginable, and she moaned about how difficult it would be to find a successor. Sara marveled both at Pamela's over-inflated sense of indispensability and at her arrogance in thinking that The School would perish without her.

"I really understand how you feel," Sara sympathized. "I've been restless, too, and sometimes think I could use a new professional challenge. Maybe I should apply for your job. You might feel more open to the idea of leaving if you knew you would be passing the torch to me rather than to someone from outside The School."

Sara knew she had committed an egregious error before she even finished the sentence. Looking as if she had swallowed a rotten *moule,* Pamela pressed her napkin to her mouth, coughed a few times, and said, "I'm going to the ladies'. Summon the idiotic waiter and get us the check."

Minutes passed, the check arrived, and Pamela still hadn't returned, so Sara used her own overextended credit card to pay for a dinner that should have been charged to Pamela's expense account. When Pamela finally waltzed back to the table and saw Sara signing for the check, she said haughtily, "It's the least you could do to make up for your ludicrous suggestion."

However awkward Pamela's cold-shoulder treatment had been to endure, Sara's aspirations had not been derailed by that conversation. Quite the contrary: it gave her hope that The School might be seeking a new head sooner than she had ever anticipated. But after such a disastrous interchange, she knew she'd be fooling herself to think that Pamela could be counted on to support her candidacy, and she doubted that she would have any chance without her endorsement. She pushed the whole idea to the back of her mind; it was one of those "we'll have to wait and see" situations—a phrase she repeatedly used with anxious applicants.

Getting back to work, she read the next application.

> As a mid-career painter with gallery representation, with the added luxury of financial security provided by my investment banker husband, you can imagine how gratifying it was when I discovered that my daughter Miranda was passionate about "the dance." Miranda is what's known in the field as a pre-professional classical ballerina, having received a certificate of recognition from New York Toddlers on Toe. I have taken the liberty of sending you a tape of her most recent performance of "The Prince and the Pauper" at the Prime-A-Donna Children's Theater. I hope you enjoy watching it as much as we do. You should also know that, if accepted at The School, Miranda would be more than happy to perform in any and all school performances.

Oh great, one more nascent diva, Sara groaned, promising herself she would read just one more before going home for the night.

> As a single father I have learned so much about myself from my son Shane. It's odd to think that my five-year-old son could possess so much wisdom and have so much to teach me. When I look at him I see an old soul. I think he may have been here before . . .

I think he may have, too, Sara thought, *in at least forty-six previous applications.* It was definitely time to quit, before total cynicism threatened to short-circuit her brain. Tomorrow would bring another deluge, and she needed to be well rested. Her agenda for the next day included a tutorial with Brandi on the ins and outs of scheduling tours and interviews. That could take a while.

Having received four applications, the Dragers had a family meeting to divvy up their assignments. Each application required both an essay from Zoe and a statement from the parents, which precipitated a squabble between Michael and Helen.

"Why would you assume that I should be solely responsible for all of the applications?" Helen demanded.

"Because you're the writer in this couple?" he shot back.

"I'm an art critic. I critique art, not our child. You're as capable of waxing poetic about Zoe as I am," she replied angrily. "You minored in poetry, for God's sake!"

"Well, you've got more time than I do right now. We're about to start production on the new show, and the two chefs aren't speaking," Michael was feeling pressure on multiple fronts and did not respond well to that. As a producer for the Cooking Network, he frequently seemed to be in the midst of a calamity. Helen was accustomed to his crisis mentality and had learned not to get nearly as alarmed about each so-called catastrophe as he did.

"I'm on a deadline, too, you know. I have three articles due in the next month and I haven't started any of them!"

"Stop! You sound like the Bickersons," Zoe yelled. "I can't believe you're arguing about who's going to do this. I thought you both wanted to help as much as possible."

She's right, Helen thought wryly, *but she sure is Phi Beta Kappa when it comes to guilt tripping.* Catching sight of Zoe's tear-filled eyes, Helen offered her daughter a hug.

Zoe's face was straight out of a Florentine fresco: olive skin, heavy-lidded dark eyes, pouty lips, and lustrous brown hair. When she assumed the mournful look of a distressed Madonna, as she did now, Helen invariably melted.

"Oh, sweetie, we're so sorry. Of course we both want to do whatever we can," Helen soothed. "We're all just feeling a lot of pressure right now. Michael, I'll write the essays. You can write the checks."

"Out of the joint account, right?" he asked, looking at her with some concern. Even after they were married, Helen and Michael held on to their separate checking accounts, using them to pay for the occasional expenditure they didn't necessarily want to justify to each other, such as self-indulgent beauty treatments or extraneous pieces of sporting equipment. They maintained a joint checking account for all household expenses and most things that pertained to Zoe.

"I think it would be fairer if it came out of your account since I'm doing all the work. Don't you?" she suggested. At fifty dollars each, she calculated that the application fees would be around three hundred. "That way, you can contribute, too." It was the perfect solution, Helen realized; not only would Michael foot the bill, but by not having to dicker with him over the contents of every application, she would save herself hours of work.

"Whatever," he acquiesced, deciding it wasn't worth arguing about.

"Zoe, are you happy with the school choices?" Helen asked, remembering her promise to keep her daughter involved.

"I guess so."

"You guess or you are okay?" Helen asked impatiently, and then reminded herself to soften her tone. Oh, dear, she sounded shrill, even to herself. If she didn't watch it, she would be one of those shrieking harridans she made fun of at school events, nagging both husband and child at every opportunity. She took a deep breath and tried to refocus her energy towards supporting Zoe. "If there are any other schools you want me to call, just let me know, okay, cutie?"

"Okay."

"Have you thought of any that aren't on our list?"

"No."

"So I take that to mean you're fine with the choices?" Helen asked, struggling to disguise her frustration.

"Yeah," Zoe replied glumly. Throughout most of her childhood, Zoe had been a communicative child. Never shy in the presence of adults, she was always comfortable participating in grown-up conversations, readily offering answers to questions and being generally sociable and charming. Thankfully, she had retained those qualities as she entered adolescence, and her parents often expressed appreciation that their teenager seemed to be more civilized than most. So it was particularly alarming to Helen that this monosyllabic style seemed recently to have crept into her daughter's repertoire.

When Zoe behaved in an objectionable way, Helen often looked to Michael for help and was disappointed if she didn't get it. Her approach was to push Zoe to express her feelings, even when she didn't appear to want to, whereas Michael took a more passive approach, believing it was important to give Zoe space to withdraw and even to sulk, if that was what she was inclined to do. Sometimes Helen found their family dynamic troublesome; when it came to discipline, she often ended up playing bad parent, which by default made Michael good dad. When Helen felt that her family was ganging up on her, she often retreated to the bedroom, leaving the two of them alone to whisper about Mom's bad temper.

Helen thought of the master bedroom as her sanctuary, and it was in this room only that she loosened her insistence that form follow function and indulged in a little whimsy. The centerpiece of the room was the large picture window, which she had draped with a pale, gauzy swag that shimmered at night with the distant twinkle of the lights across Central Park. She was so pleased with its softening effect that on a trip to Delhi she bought yards and yards of richly embroidered silk, with which she upholstered a chaise longue for the corner and made piles of throw pillows to scatter about their dark cherry-wood sleigh bed. But the Dragers' most prized possession was the huge silk Fortuny lamp shade they had bought in Venice on their honeymoon, and which hung from the ceiling like a huge upside-down parasol. The light seemed to float on the ceiling above the bed, softly emitting an exquisite glow while evoking memories of faraway places. The bedroom exuded exoticism, and Michael frequently called it his harem.

"Does that mean I have to call you 'pasha'?" Helen teased.

"Only in bed," he responded flirtatiously.

As Helen settled in with a stack of school catalogues, she glanced wistfully at the framed photographs that hung above their bureaus, part of the small but significant collection of 1920s avant-garde photography she had begun collecting while doing graduate work in Berlin twenty years ago. However, since Zoe began school, whatever disposable income they had was used to pay for tuition, resulting in a substantial reduction in their art acquisition and decorating activity. It was the natural progression to stop buying for oneself and save for your child, but still, Helen longed to go on a mini decorating spree again, just to remind herself that she counted, too. When Zoe got into a good school, she promised herself she would splurge on one more photograph to celebrate. She returned to the catalogues with renewed interest.

A little while later, Michael joined her and plopped down with the current issue of *Gourmet.* Reclining against the plump stack of pillows, Michael had a relaxed and blissful air; he got as much pleasure from a four-page spread on Memphis pulled pork as other men got from a *Playboy* centerfold. Helen glanced at the spare tire that had gradually begun to create a gap between Michael's T-shirt and boxers, and found herself hoping it was just particularly pronounced in this position. But, appreciative of the fact that he was generally nonjudgmental on the subject of her looks, she kept her thoughts to herself. He still had his boyish face, a disarming, dimpled smile, and some hair on his head, which was more than she could say for a lot of his peers. Eighteen years ago, when Helen first introduced Michael to her family, her mother called him a mensch. He was still that same mensch, just a slightly chubbier one.

"These schools *all* look excellent. Listen to this: classics, ecology, biogenetics, printmaking, architectural history, Iranian literature. I wish I could be in high school again," she mused. "Without the raging hormones this time."

"I wish I had known you when your hormones were raging. That would have been exciting."

"If you think I'm moody now, I was truly impossible back then."

"You mean like Zoe is now?"

"Worse."

"That's hard to imagine."

"Trust me. But really, Michael, all these schools look great. I hope Zoe is able to figure out which is best for her."

"Of course she will."

"But then she has to get in." Helen sounded doubtful.

"Helen, why are you being skeptical? Zoe has always landed on her feet. Have a little confidence in her. It will be helpful to both of you."

"Mea culpa," Helen admitted reluctantly, and returned to perusing the catalogues.

"Are the tuitions at these new schools much higher than we're paying now?"

"Uh-huh," she muttered.

"Do you think we would ever qualify for financial aid?" he asked.

"I doubt it."

"Do you think I should talk to my parents about their maybe contributing a bit?"

"That would be nice."

"Do you think we should be looking at public schools as well?"

That got her attention. She put down the catalogue and yanked off her reading glasses, suddenly bringing him into sharper focus.

"Michael. We've had this conversation umpteen times already. We agreed that we would have just one child so we could afford to stay in New York and send her to private school. I'm working my ass off, juggling articles and multiple exhibitions so that we can do that. I don't want to discuss this again!" She flipped off the light and turned away from him, glad that they had finally invested in a king-sized bed. But even the new bed did not help her to get the sleep she so desperately needed.

Helen had always been a sound sleeper, rarely suffering from the sleep deprivation many of her friends complained about. That is, until recently. Since the beginning of August she had experienced the horrors of insomnia, awakening at three a.m., unable to fall back to sleep until five or six, when it was time to wake up again. During these hours she found herself obsessing about admissions. Which schools had vacancies? What were considered acceptable test scores? Would Zoe's make the cut? How many kids were applying from The School? Would Pamela give them the help they needed? Would they be able to afford the tuition for the next four years and then pay for college on top of that? Would Zoe interview well? Would Michael interview well? Were their professions interesting enough? Would her presidency of the Parents' Association be helpful? Would Zoe's musical talent help? Did she prefer girls' schools or coed? Which was best for Zoe? Around and around she went, never finding answers to any of these questions, tossing and turning for hours while Michael was snoring away beside her. At one point she sneezed, reached across him for a tissue, and then accidentally grazed him with her elbow. He groggily asked her what was wrong.

"Nocturnal admissions," she moaned.

* * *

Sara spent the morning briefing Brandi on the tricky art of scheduling tours and interviews. As soon as the applications arrived and the checks were deposited and cleared, Brandi was instructed to phone the family to set up their appointment. Sara had learned from experience that it was best to get a jump on this before the applicants' agendas filled up. With every imaginable lesson, enrichment class, therapy session, play date, prescribed uptime, downtime, quiet time, nap time, vacation time, and time-outs, not to mention visits to other schools, the four-year-old applicants were scheduled within an inch of their lives. Add to that the difficulty of synchronizing the schedules of all three family members, and Brandi could count on taking up to ten minutes to pin down a single appointment—and those were the easy ones.

With a whole pile of applicants ready to be scheduled, Sara pulled up a chair and coached Brandi through the first call.

BRANDI: Hello, Ms. Riley? This is Brandi McHenry in the admissions office at The School. We've received your application for Butterscotch and would like to set up a visit for you. The visit will include a tour and an interview, and you will need to be with us for about two hours. May I suggest a date? How about October fourteenth at eleven a.m.?

MS. RILEY: Let me get my Palm Pilot . . . (forty-five seconds pass) . . . Hmmm. The fourteenth is difficult. Butterscotch has Merry Music Makers that morning, and I have an appointment with my Reiki practitioner.

BRANDI: Are afternoons better for you?

MS. RILEY: It depends on the day. What do you have available?

BRANDI: October twenty-third at two p.m.?

MS. RILEY: Hmmm. I'll have to check with my husband's secretary. I have penciled in "away," and I don't now remember what that means. It could mean out of town . . . but then again . . . it could mean . . .

Brandi (interrupting, which earned a thumbs-up from Sara): How about the afternoon of October sixteenth? Two p.m.?

Ms. Riley: No. Harold and I are at Canyon Ranch that week. We simply have to get away—these applications have been so stressful! Josette, our caregiver, could bring her. Would that work?

Brandi: Afraid not. We would like to meet you and your husband and assume you both would like to meet us and see The School. What about October twenty-seventh at ten a.m.?

Ms. Riley: Let's see. Butterscotch has her Mandarin lesson, but I could switch that to Wednesday. I have fencing, but I'll leave a few minutes early and have Josette bring Butterscotch and I'll meet them there. Harold should be in town that day. I think that works. Touché.

Brandi: Okay. I'm slotting you in. Please come a few minutes early so we can get started punctually.

Ms. Riley: Oh, dear, I might not have had time to shower first. But I'll bring clothes with me and change quickly and I can do my makeup in the cab and—

Brandi (she interrupted again, scoring a beaming nod of approval from Sara): We'll look forward to meeting you on October twenty-seventh.

Ms. Riley (unaware Brandi had hung up): . . . my hair may be a bit of a mess but I can get . . .

"Touché to you, too. Now you understand what I meant when I said these people act like they're doing us a favor," Sara sighed. "One down, hundreds more to go."

Brandi took a deep breath and picked up the phone to call Mr. and Ms. Jackson, who were divorced and had phone numbers with different area codes. "Does this mean they live in different states?" Brandi asked nervously. Sara bent over to take a look.

"Different boroughs. He's in Manhattan; she's stuck out on Staten Island. Typical."

Sara had a free moment and, disgusted by her own participation in the ridiculous standoff, decided it was time to go and try to speak to Pamela. What kind of adult shut down like a petulant fifth-grade queen bee just because she was told something that she didn't want to hear? Sara became riled up every time she thought about it, and decided that her anger was beginning to have a deleterious effect on her mental health. She took a moment to visualize a positive encounter, then climbed the stairs to Pamela's office.

"Do you have an appointment?" Margaret asked curtly, guarding Pamela's office like the palace sentry.

"No. I thought I would just pop up for a quick chat," Sara replied casually, as though she were still on pop-in terms with Pamela.

"I don't think that's going to work today. She's in with Mrs. Winter now and then has to leave immediately for an appointment."

Sara shook her head conspiratorially and stood with her ear cocked towards Pamela's door as a distraught Dana Winter carped about her daughter, April.

"I really thought the visit to Justine's cooking school would solve *all* our problems. I had hopes that April would enjoy the food and eat enough to put on a few pounds. April did eat, but then she developed a new trick. She chewed her food, then spit it into her napkin and hid it. I spent the whole vacation worrying that Justine would discover a wad of premasticated foie gras in an armoire. You were there with us. Do you think Justine saw what was going on? I would just die if she knew. What do you think she thinks of April?" Dana whined plaintively.

"It doesn't matter what Justine thinks of April. If The Fancy Girls' School is your first choice, then that is where April shall go. Justine and I have an understanding—a, shall we say, quid pro quo," Pamela declared imperiously.

"Oh Pamela, you *are* the best. I'm so relieved," Dana sobbed. "Patrick will be, too. He thought the summer trip was a big waste of money. Now he will see it was worth it. And now I'm sure I can get him to contribute our home in Telluride *and* his corporate jet for the spring auction."

Margaret shook her head and said softly to Sara, "*Now* you understand why they all go to that cooking school."

"Kid pro quo." Sara shook her head in disgust and headed back down to the admissions office.

With a pounding headache that threatened to develop into a full-blown migraine, Sara decided she needed to get some air. It was a beautiful Indian summer day, and she counted on a short walk to help clear her thoughts and relax her throbbing temples. As she strode down the avenue, she recounted all she knew about the megalomaniacal woman who was her boss.

Pamela Rothschild was inscrutable to the point of unknowable, a master at cultivating an air of mystery by mixing and swirling the details of her past. She had an upper-class English accent and High Church manners, but her swarthy complexion, propensity to *parlez français*, and penchant for spicy foods and sunny climes befuddled anyone who tried to decipher her actual ethnic identity. If her father were one of *the* Rothschilds, as Pamela often implied, then that would make her Jewish. But she often spoke about going to church, made a big fuss over Christmas, and was compulsive about eating fish on Fridays, which suggested something else entirely. Then there was the question of her age—she could be thirty or fifty; it was impossible to tell.

Sara seemed to recall that Pamela had been enrolled at some point in an English school, but something made her think it might have been in India. But then again, Pamela often spoke about a Swiss boarding school, which would explain her annoying use of French, unless it was the German side of Switzerland . . . It was impossible to know. The questions went unanswered, the stories remained muddled, and Sara was never any closer to knowing who the real Pamela Rothschild really was.

Then there was the ultimate head-scratcher: the embarrassing incident last May when, together at a private school expo, they ran into a British gent who claimed to recognize Pamela from their days together in Manchester.

"Oh, my, Pamela Wickham?" the man ventured as he approached them out of the blue.

"It's Rothschild. And you are . . . ?" she replied icily as she dramatically swept her hair off her face, charm bracelet clanging noisily.

"Benjamin Whyte?" he answered in the self-effacing form of a question, clearly unsure whether she recognized him.

"Oh, yes, hello."

"After all these years, it's good to see you. Let me introduce my wife. Clarissa Whyte, this is Pamela Wickham—I mean Rothschild—um, ah, from The Manchester School. Luvvy, do you remember Pamela? She and I taught together for several years. And what brings you to New York?" he asked.

"I live in New York and am head of The School," she announced grandly.

"That's a jolly bit of good luck. We've just moved across the pond with our five-year-old munchkin, Oscar, and are thinking about applying to The School for next year. It's been touted as one of the best. And just imagine, Clarissa, we now have an in," he said, using his pasty fingers to emphasize his quote-unquote use of the word "in."

"By all means. I'll look forward to personally reviewing your application," Pamela responded flatly. Sara, irritated by both Pamela's breach of school protocol and by her manners—she'd been standing there unintroduced the entire time—insinuated herself into their tight little Anglo-Saxon circle.

"Hello. I'm Sara Nash. I work with Pamela. I'm the admissions director of The School," she asserted brightly.

Clarissa and Benjamin lit up. With big smiles they both reached out, grabbed her hand, and pumped it up and down as if they were churning butter in a Devonshire creamery.

"Brilliant," beamed Clarissa, an apple-cheeked milkmaid type. "We've been warned about the difficulties of New York school admissions and have not been looking forward to beetling about, trying to find a spot for our little kipper. Now that we have a friendly face—or two—to attach to The School"—she giggled nervously—"maybe the bits and bobs will fall into place."

"I will look forward to meeting Oscar," Sara said pointedly, making it clear that she was more interested in their child than she was in getting chummy with them.

"Super. Lovely. Thank you," Ben chimed.

"Yes. Super," Clarissa repeated. "Pamela, so, so good to meet you.

I know Benjamin has talked about you in the past. Um, I'm just not sure in what context."

"I can't imagine. *Au revoir.*" Pamela was obviously anxious to leave.

Sara remembered the awkwardness between them as they walked uptown after the unanticipated meeting with the Whytes.

"I'm confused," Sara had said.

"About what?" Pamela feigned oblivion.

"Who is Benjamin Whyte?"

"Some milquetoast I once taught school with. I can't remember a thing about him and would never have known him if he hadn't so rudely accosted me."

"Manchester? That's new. I had a vague recollection you trained at an international school in Switzerland and then taught in London. Where does Manchester fit in?"

Pamela tittered, "You are confused, dear. I taught in Manchester, ever so briefly, before coming to the States. Before that I had been at a boarding school in Lucerne and then was headmistress of an exclusive day school in London. NOW do you get it?"

"He called you Wickham. That's a name I don't know. Why would he call you that?" Sara asked, trying to make light of this.

"How should I know?" she replied impatiently.

"He seemed quite certain about it," Sara pressed.

"What is this? The Spanish Inquisition? I must go. I have an early meeting tomorrow with the Ethics Committee."

That was the first and last time they ever talked about her past.

The walk helped Sara achieve a modicum of serenity and enabled her to return to the office in an improved state of mind. She asked Brandi if an application had come in for a child named Oscar Whyte, and in no time flat, Brandi had it on Sara's desk.

> We are ever so grateful to Ms. Rothschild for taking little Oscar under her wing. Inviting him to the zoo last weekend was the kindest thing anyone could have done. It did wonders for Oscar's self-confidence and has made a difficult transition so much easier for us as well as him. The outing with her was

so special, so generous, that he feels he is already part of The School community, and he hasn't even begun! We cannot begin to express our gratitude for this generosity and look forward to enrolling Oscar in The School next year.

Sara stared in shock at the words before her. Pamela had offered carte-blanche admission to the five-year-old son of a former colleague whom, four months earlier, she had disdainfully referred to as a nobody. And she had done so without consulting the director of admissions! And taking the child on a solo trip to the zoo! What was this all about?

Watching a clan of hairy primates expose their pink bums to a crowd of shrieking children is hardly Pamela's cup of tea, Sara thought, remembering back to the time Pamela nixed a biography of Jane Goodall from the fourth-grade reading list, asking the teacher, "What possible reason can you give me for wasting time reading a book about apes?" When the teacher timidly replied, "Evolution?" Pamela scoffed.

Pamela's unilateral decision to accept Oscar Whyte did not bode well for the future of the admissions office, and Sara worried about the implications this could have to her job. If this was how admissions were going to be handled in The School, her position had suddenly become untenable. She turned to her computer to vent her frustration.

Helen-

P. is playing games. I feel like I'm about to be led off to the Tower of London. I really need to have it out with the Be-Head of School, but she's not giving me a chance. I am just spoiling for a fight here, and the longer she puts off speaking with me, the worse it gets!! I am ready to SCREAM!

S.N.

Helen replied almost instantaneously.

Sara-

Please hold off on a confrontation until after Zoe gets an acceptance letter. If P. wants your head on a platter she will want mine too. Knowing her, she'll find some way to get both of us via Zoe's admissions. PLEASE PLEASE don't do anything rash.

H.

Sara was surprised by the tone of panic in Helen's response, and hurt by her friend's disregard for her own plight. However, over the past years she had learned never to underestimate Pamela's ability to wreak havoc on other people's lives, and realized she couldn't fault Helen for being concerned. Pamela, in true Machiavellian style, was perfectly capable of intentionally undermining Zoe as a way to simultaneously punish Sara for her insubordination and Helen for her friendship with Sara. Though it seemed far-fetched, Sara knew that Pamela's arsenal contained just this type of mental torture device.

Deciding she absolutely *had* to clear the air, Sara called Margaret to see if Pamela was by some remote chance free to meet with her now, and was dismayed to learn that she had left the office and wouldn't be back for the rest of the day.

"Oh, right . . . the head-of-School meeting at The Safety School?" Sara suggested, covertly attempting to get Margaret to reveal her whereabouts.

"No, that's next Tuesday. She has a . . . personal appointment this afternoon," Margaret replied with a tightness in her voice.

"Medical?" Sara proposed.

Poor Margaret had lately been suffering from feelings of guilt and betrayal. The truth was, she liked Sara much more than she liked Pamela, and wished she worked for her instead. She was tired of having to be evasive with Sara and was tempted to blurt out, "She's out at a tack shop in New Jersey, shopping for a new saddle," but bit her tongue and remained vague.

* * *

Leaving nothing to chance in her high-stakes endeavor, Helen had reluctantly requested a meeting with Pamela to review all the steps of the admissions process. Arriving at her office the following morning, she did a double take when she saw the new brass plaque on the door, "Where did that come from?"

"Sir Winston Churchill," Margaret answered without missing a beat. It wasn't the first time she had been asked this week.

"Is she free?" Helen asked.

"Why don't you stick your head in? She's expecting you," Margaret answered.

Pamela was seated at her desk, a repository of veddy British novelty items that included an official Fortnum and Mason quilted tea cozy, a Simpson's on the Strand ashtray (pilfered), a polo mallet autographed by Prince Charles, and the purple Princess Diana Commemorative Beanie Baby Bear. If her desk were seen as an homage to the Union Jack, the walls represented an homage to Pamela Rothschild, with framed photographs of the intrepid head of The School, always front and center, at groundbreakings, ribbon cuttings, awards ceremonies, and horse shows, each a visual testament to her lifelong commitment to self-aggrandizement.

"I don't have much time. What do you need from me?" Pamela demanded.

"The applications all say to submit the results of the SAPS test no later than January first. Sounds like a test for a sexually transmitted disease," Helen tried to start off lightly.

Tapping a riding crop against her palm, Pamela shot Helen her dreaded schoolmarm stare. "It's something far more deadly, my dear. The Standard Assessment for Private Schools is no laughing matter, particularly with a testing record like Zoe's. You had better get her a tutor, *tout de suite*."

What a bitch, Helen bristled inwardly. *How dare she imply that Zoe's test skills are substandard?*

"Isn't that something The School should provide?" she shot back. "I would think that test preparation would be included in the twenty-six thousand we pay for tuition. After all, it seems to be such an integral part of education these days."

"Absolutely not. It's certainly not The School's fault that Zoe doesn't test well. We have many students who don't require tutoring. It wouldn't be fair to use school resources for the unfortunate misérables who need help."

Thank you, Victor Hugo, Helen thought. Remembering that she could not afford to alienate this woman at this stage of the game, she conceded. "I suppose you're right. Do you have a particular tutor to recommend?"

"Bertha Kauffmann. Anyone else is a waste of time. Get her number from Margaret and call her immediately. Zoe needs to see her at least twice a week for the next three months."

"What will this cost?" Helen asked.

"You have no choice."

"That doesn't answer my question."

"The cost is irrelevant. You can't afford not to. But don't wait. She books up very quickly. And don't forget to schedule the SAPS. Book the latest available date."

"Yes ma'am." Helen smiled grimly and lowered her knees in a mock curtsy.

That evening, Michael arrived home to find his wife and daughter huddled at the dining room table.

"Tuesdays at four and Thursdays at five forty-five in October, but not during the week of the twenty-third. And then in November, Mondays at five fifteen and Thursdays at four thirty. Yes. We've scheduled the SAPS for December tenth. So you'll let us know if you think she needs to see you up until the last week, right?" Zoe nodded and scribbled in her agenda as Helen repeated the dates she'd been given by Ms. Kauffmann.

"Oh, and by the way, what do you charge? . . . Per month? . . . Per session!" Helen gasped.

Michael leaned over to kiss Zoe and peered into her agenda to see the word "tutor" scrawled here and there.

"What's this about?" he asked innocently.

"This is about thousands of dollars transferring out of our account into that of some woman called Bertha Kauffmann who claims she will increase Zoe's SAPS scores by thirty percent."

"Is there a money-back guarantee?"

"Not funny, Michael. Rothschild said in no uncertain terms that if Zoe's test scores don't improve, we're sunk."

"That's just great. First I'm getting all this pressure at home, and now it's coming from Rothschild, too?" Zoe lamented bitterly.

Michael shot Helen a warning look.

"Oh, sweetie. I didn't mean it. The only pressure you're under is to try your hardest and do your best. You're a great kid, and if a school doesn't recognize that, it's their loss. The test scores are just one part of the package. Besides, we wouldn't want you to go to a school that only cares about test scores anyway," Helen said comfortingly, with an arm around Zoe.

"Yeah, but Mrs. Rothschild does," Zoe replied in a defeated tone.

"Screw Rothschild," Michael said angrily.

"If she doesn't screw us first," Helen answered wryly.

Zoe slammed down her notebook in exasperation and announced, "I'm going to Julian's. We're practicing a scene together for drama class."

"That's wonderful, dear. What's the play?"

"Romeo and Juliet."

Helen wondered who was playing Juliet.

"Dad and I thought we would go out for sushi. Shall we bring back something for you?" Helen offered.

"No, thanks. I'll eat at the Topplers'. Their chef makes us whatever we want," Zoe answered.

"Maybe we should all go to the Topplers'," Michael teased.

"You're not invited," Zoe said, and as she yanked on her denim jacket, she freed her long hair from under the collar with the same flip of the wrist Helen used. In fact, she looked and moved so much like her mother that, from behind, it was becoming hard to tell the two apart. She threw her backpack over her shoulders and walked out.

"Why don't we have a chef?" Helen asked. "You're a producer on the Cooking Network. Can't you trick one into coming home with you? You could say you're holding auditions in your home to see how well the chef works in a tiny New York apartment. Call it 'Pullman Kitchen Confidential.'"

"Hmmm. That's a good idea. I'll pitch it at the next development meeting."

"And credit your wife. I could use some credit around here these days," she said, allowing a note of weariness to creep into her voice.

"And I could use some dinner."

Whenever Zoe hung out in Julian's bedroom, she was struck by how tiny hers seemed in comparison. But she actually never felt jealous, because even though his room was enormous, it didn't feel like it really belonged to him the way that her room did. Even when she was young, she realized there were big differences in the way their families did things. When she audaciously covered her bureau with decals and bumper stickers and tie-dyed her bedspread orange and pink, her dad said it looked cool. When she made the windowsill a permanent home for her snow globe collection, her mother congratulated her on her ingenuity. When she sloppily painted clouds on the blue wall behind her bed, her parents were charmed. So when Julian told her about the time his father, on a rare visit to his room, freaked out when he saw the Judy Garland, Elizabeth Taylor, and Joan Crawford posters, she felt sorry for him. Soon after that discovery, the Topplers commissioned their decorator to masculinize their son's bedroom as quickly as possible, which was how, almost overnight, it was transformed into something akin to an upscale electronics showroom.

Now in place of the posters were an oversized flat-screen television and a multicomponent music system. On the surface of a very large matte steel table was an unfathomably slender brushed-titanium laptop computer, lit by a high-tech system of halogen lamps. In one corner of the room sat an electric shoe polisher; in another corner, an electronically powered massage chair; and in the closet, an electronic rotating tie rack, which, Julian was pleased to discover, provided a good storage system for his secret collection of feather boas.

"New paint color, too?" Zoe inquired as she looked around the room.

"Wall treatment," he replied, mimicking the decorator.

"Wow, it's soft." She ran her hand over the pale gray surface. "What is it?"

"Cashmere," he confessed, and then, seeing her confusion, added, "Don't ask."

"Oh," Zoe gulped, quickly calculating what it must have cost based on the exorbitant price of the pink cashmere sweater she had been begging her mother to buy her for months.

As they were reciting the lines from the play, Zoe's eye caught a stack of school applications on Julian's desk.

Not recognizing any of the names, she ventured, "I wonder if we're applying to any of the same schools." The last thing she wanted was to be in direct competition with Julian. She was one of the few kids in her class who were never comfortable comparing grades, and often invented an excuse to rush away whenever she sensed that one of her classmates was approaching to ask her what she got on a test.

"Doubt it, unless your parents have decided to send you to a boarding school, too," Julian answered sadly.

"Wow, boarding school. That's cool. Believe me, I'd go in a heartbeat, but my parents would never let me. They get weird when I go to camp for a month. I think I'll have to live at home for the rest of my life," she declared theatrically. Zoe wanted to make Julian feel like the lucky one, even though she knew she would never want to go away to school.

"I look at these and feel like I don't belong at these places. The kids all look so straight," Julian commented as he disdainfully flipped through a few of the catalogues, pointing to photographs of ultra buff athletes romping on manicured fields, and well-groomed prepsters huddled around reference-book-laden library tables.

"The catalogues for the city schools look basically the same," Zoe responded.

"But we know they're not. You get all kinds of kids at the New York City schools. But these schools cater to another breed entirely."

"You're so adaptable. You'll manage to fit in somehow," Zoe said encouragingly.

"No, you don't understand, sweetheart. I'm deathly allergic to WASPs," he deadpanned.

She laughed. "So is boarding school an option or a final decision?"

"As Dad says, the verdict is in and it's nonnegotiable," he answered glumly.

"My mom's being really bossy about the whole school application thing, too. She keeps pretending like she's concerned about my feelings but then goes ahead and does whatever she wants. She's acting like a real Miss Buttinsky."

"Your mom's usually so cool. Can't you tell her to butt outsky?"

"I wish." Feeling vaguely disloyal, Zoe suggested they get back to the play, and the two eagerly lost themselves in another couple's troubles.

When they arrived at their neighborhood Japanese restaurant, Michael and Helen were greeted with smiles and bows by two knife-bearing kimono-clad chefs, who motioned for them to take a seat at the sleekly varnished sushi bar. Against a backdrop of tatami mats and Japanese porcelain, the Dragers nibbled at yellowtail hand-rolls while sipping warm sake.

"I haven't filled you in lately on the Pamela and Sara tiff, have I?" Helen inquired between mouthfuls of raw fish.

"Uh-uh," Michael garbled.

"They seem to be having a bit of a standoff and haven't spoken in a few months."

"That sounds like more than a tiff to me."

"You never know with Pamela. Remember when she didn't speak to Dana Winter for six months after Dana sent that memo to the board?"

"The one pointing out that Pamela's salary was higher than that of any other head of school in New York? Whatever happened with that?" Michael asked.

"Nothing. You know how reluctant the board is to ever cross Pamela. The incident passed, and Pamela and Dana seem to be buddy-buddy again."

"How did that happen?"

"Cavorting together last summer at Justine Frampton's cooking school in the South of France."

"She's the one who's also the director of admissions at The Fancy Girls' School, right?"

"Yup."

"Are we applying to her school?"

"It's on our list. It's supposed to be an excellent school, and Pamela highly recommends it for Zoe. Plus, I've recently read a lot about the advantages of a single-sex education and, despite Sara's opinion, still think it makes a lot of sense. How do you feel about all-girls' versus coed?"

"As far as I'm concerned, the longer we can delay her dating, the better. You know me. I'd be happy if Zoe were a virgin on her wedding day," he joked.

"Come on, admit it. You'd probably be happy if she *never* married," she laughed.

"Or became a nun," he said teasingly.

"That would solve the school problem. We could send her to a convent."

"It would be a lot less expensive than private school."

"Seriously, Michael. I'm really concerned about Pamela and Sara. If there's trouble between them, I'm afraid we'll be on Pamela's shit list."

"Just because you're an F.O.S.?"

"What's that?"

"Friend of Sara," he answered.

"Yeah. Because I'm an F.O.S., I'll end up an E.O.P."

"It sounds like schoolyard talk," he said, laughing.

"Hello. It *is* the schoolyard. But in this movie, the parts of the children are being played by the adults," she answered darkly.

"You don't really think she would be that vindictive, do you?"

"I hope I'm overreacting. But nothing would surprise me when it comes to Pamela."

"Let's not worry about it," Michael said dismissively, and returned to his dinner. But after a few moments he put down his chopsticks and asked, "Do you really think she might try to make trouble? I mean, in your worst nightmares, what could she actually do?"

"A lot . . . or nothing. Either could be damaging," Helen answered.

"Have some sea urchin. It'll put hair on your chest," he suggested lightly.

"The last thing I need is *another* depilatory challenge." She picked it up and swallowed it whole.

* * *

Sara was reading applications in her office, half-listening to Brandi, who was scheduling a tour and interview with a three-parent family with twins.

BRANDI: Mrs. Barton, I'm going to have to leave it to you to coordinate with your ex and his wife. I've already accommodated you and the twins.

MRS. BARTON: My ex has to be there. He pays the tuition.

BRANDI: I completely understand. But when I spoke to his wife, she said she wasn't able to commit to a date, and he hasn't returned my calls.

MRS. BARTON: That lousy bastard. He never returns my calls, either. In fact, he didn't even return my calls when we were married, which is how I figured out he was having an affair with our nanny, who, by the way, is now his wife.

BRANDI: I'm terribly sorry, but for the moment I think we should just focus on the issue at hand. I will leave you in on the twenty-first and assume we will see at least you and the twins. I'll leave your ex's participation up to you. As far as his wife goes, from our perspective, she's ancillary.

MRS. BARTON: That's a nice word for what she is.

BRANDI: Let's not get into *that*. We'll look forward to meeting you on the twenty-first.

When Brandi related the conversation, Sara responded enthusiastically. "Good work. You handled that perfectly. Want to make a bet on who shows up for the interview?" Brandi laughed, and she added, "Five dollars, only Mrs. Barton."

"I'll make it ten that it's her, her ex-husband, and wife number two," said Brandi, accepting the challenge. They shook on it, and then Brandi got busy trying to find an interpreter to help conduct next week's interview with a non–English-speaking Korean family.

* * *

After an hour-long workout at the gym, Helen got dressed in black slacks, black boots, and a white tailored shirt, her standard uniform for gallery prowling. With her hair down, a pale pink pashmina shawl around her shoulders, and large silver hooped earrings, she was instantly transformed from at-home admissions drone to art critic—unquestionably her preferred role. With a deadline looming, she was looking forward to finally getting started on her article, "Images of the Cockfight in Contemporary American Painting."

On the subway ride downtown, she double-checked the list of paintings she needed to see, and hoped she had enough time to fit them all in. She arrived at the first gallery—Marco Puttanesco—and, using all her strength, she pushed the industrial-weight cast-iron door that opened into the cavernous, garagelike space. Marco Puttanesco was an art world wunderkind who, at thirty-three, was one of New York's most successful dealers of the school of painting known as "arte ricca," a movement that emerged in response to the now passé "arte povera."

Of course, Puttanesco wouldn't be caught dead in his gallery this early in the morning, so instead, Helen was greeted by the gallery director, Gabriel, who sported the requisite soul patch, hair gel, and heavy, black-rimmed glasses. He escorted her to the back room to view a black velvet painting by the Latino artist Carlos Gallomuerto. She was surprised to see how closely the work resembled the kitsch she saw at the Albuquerque flea market when she was in New Mexico last year doing research for an article on kachina dolls.

"The referential quality of the work is quintessentially postmodern," Gabriel explained. "The velvet imbues the paint with an eroticism that one would not generally associate with the cockfight." He looked to her for a nod of agreement but didn't stop when he didn't get it. "Of course, the irony isn't lost in the translation from the vernacular subject to the more metaphorical. Do you agree?" He stopped, demanding a response from Helen.

"Exactly, that's why I'm here. Could I sit down and spend a few minutes alone with the piece?" she asked, hoping to compose her own thoughts independently of this verbose twenty-two-year-old who, even though she hated to admit it, was actually quite astute. She wondered where he went to college, and then remembered that she made herself a promise not even to *think* about schools today.

By the late afternoon she was ready to tackle the last gallery on her list. There a svelte young woman with spiky red hair that bore a striking resemblance to the chickens she had been viewing all day dragged out an enormous canvas. Her first impression was that it looked like a study of eviscerated poultry. On close inspection she discovered she was right: there were feathers embedded in actual chicken gizzards, necks, and livers, with a few razor blades scattered here and there. As she stepped a few feet back to take in the entire work, the gallery assistant piped in, "Are you aware of the name of the painting? It's called *Cocktales*."

"I see. Thank you." Helen smothered a giggle and jotted it down in her notebook, thinking that might make a good title for her article.

Finishing up the last of her notes, she heard her name and turned to see an approaching woman pushing a baby in a stroller, with a café latte in an attached cup holder.

"Helen Drager! I haven't seen you in years! Not since Mommy & Me!" the woman shrieked in a grating outer-borough accent. "How is Zoe?"

After a brief lapse of memory, Helen recognized Diane Spilcher, a fellow toddler group attendee of twelve years ago. Although Diane kissed her enthusiastically, Helen was more interested in the cup holder and wished that brilliant innovation had been around when Zoe was stroller age.

"Zoe is great. How about MacKenzie?" she asked, proud of herself for dredging that one up. "I seem to remember she's a year or so older than Zoe, so that makes her what? Fifteen? Sixteen?"

"Good memory. She just started high school. And this is Ryan. He's just two."

Helen wondered about the huge age difference but decided it would be rude to ask and probably involved more than she really wanted to know. "He's darling. And you—what are you up to these days?"

"Well, we moved to Jersey, so essentially, I've spent the last year mall-crawling on Route 17."

"Wow, that's a shift. I think of you as such an, uh, urban person,"

Helen said, careful not to sound condescending. The urban-suburban debate was one that Helen had gotten into one time too many and had finally learned to avoid altogether.

"Believe me, it's the last thing I wanted to do. But between us, we made the move last year when MacKenzie was dinged by every private school in the city. We could have papered her walls with rejection letters," Diane whispered, as though there were anyone in this gallery who was remotely interested in her humiliating setback.

Oh, God. So that could actually happen? Helen shivered. She really hadn't entertained *that* possibility. "We're just starting the ordeal and finding it rather stressful, too. Any words of wisdom?"

"Two. Backup plan."

"Yeah, a backup plan. Good advice," Helen responded, having no idea what theirs would be, since the suburbs, in her mind, were not an option. She was starting to feel sick to her stomach.

"You just never know. These schools are brutal. They get hundreds of applications for such a small number of spots. God only knows how they make their selections. If you figure it out, let me know, okay?" Diane sneered.

Helen changed the topic, "What are you doing here? I don't think of you as the, uh, gallery type."

"You know, I sometimes think that I culturally short-shifted MacKenzie and maybe that's what she was lacking. So I'm trying to make up for it with Ryan."

Helen thought she had better drag Zoe along the next time she went out to look at art. They hadn't been to a museum together in ages.

With no hint about the agenda, Pamela had called a faculty and administration meeting for that afternoon. At the appointed time, Sara and her colleagues filed into the auditorium. As Pamela ceremoniously entered, there was a perceptible downgrade in the noise level.

"All sit," Pamela ordered, as if addressing a room full of first-graders.

Sara wondered where Pamela had come up with the hideous mustard-yellow double-knit suit, recalling a similar garment she saw on Camilla Parker-Bowles in a recent PBS special on the demise of the royal family.

"The purpose of this meeting is to announce a new appointment in The School," Pamela began grandly. "Effective immediately, Felicity Cozette, the head of our French department, will be taking over the newly established position of associate head of School. All administrative departments will report directly to Mademoiselle Cozette, including admissions," she announced, looking peevishly at Sara. "Mademoiselle Cozette will be responsible for the day-to-day activity in these areas and will keep me informed on a need-to-know basis. I will continue to retain full responsibility for our grade eight outplacement, faculty, the board of trustees, and, of course, finance. That is all. *Merci beaucoup.*"

"Class dismissed," someone in the back of the room whispered.

"Long live the queen," Brandi whispered to Sara.

Sara looked at her and smiled, pleased to know that her take on Pamela was in sync with her own these days.

When Helen returned that evening, Michael was already at home—often a sign that things at work were not going well. He was glued to the computer, surfing NBA.com, while simultaneously watching the Cooking Network on television. Helen often wondered how she ended up married to a man who subscribed to both *Food & Wine* and *Sports Illustrated.* The food part she understood and even appreciated, particularly since he could be counted on a few times a week to cook dinners that far outshined her own efforts. But she had a much harder time accepting what she considered to be the inordinate amount of time he wasted on basketball. Whenever she got riled up about it, she had to remind herself that in the panoply of husbandly vices, this one was fairly benign. And in a cruel twist of fate, Zoe loved basketball, too.

"How was your day?" she inquired brightly.

"Shitty."

"Oh. Sorry," she said, secretly wishing the conversation could end here.

"The chefs are still not speaking, and each is refusing to do the show if the other is still part of it. Now the Italian Mushroom Growers' Association has canceled their sponsorship. They're saying that they contracted to sponsor a show called 'Two FunGuys,' and don't think that 'One FunGuy' will work. It's a disaster."

"Sweetheart, in the big scheme of things, this can hardly be called a disaster. You have several other shows in production and a few in development. Why don't you put the mushrooms aside and spend your time on new material? Like, what about the series about legumes you presented to Xavier last month? He was totally behind it, wasn't he?"

"Yeah, Xavier approved it. But now our legal department is embroiled in what seems like an endless negotiation with *Mr. Bean*'s agent."

"But at least it's still alive. I love *Mr. Bean*! I always thought that would make a great show," she continued coddling.

"How was your day? You seem up," he said in a tone of voice modulated to make sure she didn't forget that he wasn't.

"My day was mostly good. I spent it looking at cocks," she joked, expecting to get a rise from him. When she didn't, she continued, "I was really enjoying myself until I ran into a woman I knew from Mommy & Me, twelve years ago. Remember Diane Spilcher?"

"No."

"There's no reason you should. We were never close. She moved to New Jersey last year after her daughter, MacKenzie, was rejected by every private high school they applied to in the city."

"And that upset you? That's ridiculous. For all you know, her daughter is an illiterate juvenile delinquent with pierced eyebrows."

"You're right. I hadn't stopped to wonder why. I just panicked. But before hearing her story I hadn't really considered the possibility of that happening to us."

"Don't. It won't."

"That sounds definitive. And may I ask what exactly this staunch belief in fairness and justice is based on?" she inquired.

"Zoe. My faith in Zoe. She's a great kid. We have nothing to worry about. And we have Rothschild. She gets all of the kids into good schools," he said.

Helen wished it were that simple.

A little while later Zoe came home and reported that her French teacher, Mademoiselle Cozette, had been promoted to become the new associate head of School. Helen was a bit surprised, having heard nothing about this from Sara, but didn't dwell on it until later that evening, when she checked her e-mail.

Helen-

P. has done something very weird. She's promoted that dippy French teacher Cozette to be her second in command. Can you sniff around for me and find out what this is about? Like did The Board approve the position? Did they approve her choice? Anything you can dig up would be appreciated.
Thanks,

Sara

She sent off a quick reply.

Sara-

I'll learn what I can. There's a parents' coffee on Friday. I wasn't planning on going (you know how both Michael and I feel about coffee mornings) but I'll go just for you. You owe me one.

Helen

On Friday morning, Helen dutifully attended the parents' coffee klatsch, held this month at the Winters'. When Zoe was younger, Helen used to look forward to these get-togethers, grateful to have a chance to exchange ideas with other mothers who were tackling some of the same child-rearing issues she was. It was always reassuring to discover that she wasn't the only one who felt guilty about letting her daughter watch two hours of cartoons on Saturday morning so she and Michael could sleep past six a.m. Or to learn that other six-year-olds ate pasta with butter and cheese every night for dinner.

But having reached the stage, both in Zoe's life and in her own career as a mother, when comparing notes resulted more often in feelings of insecurity than in any sense of solace, she made a decision to boycott these get-togethers. Having a strong hunch that much of today's conversation would be centered on high school admissions, and knowing that the last thing she needed was for her shaky confidence to be undermined, she promised herself she would only stay a short time.

"Casual Friday?" Dana laughed as she opened the door and critically eyeballed Helen's jeans and black turtleneck.

"I make it a rule to never overdress," she replied coolly as she critically surveyed Dana's shiny red leather pants. *God, she looks like a side of beef in those. How fitting. This foyer looks like a meat locker,* Helen thought, looking disapprovingly at the glossy, gray walls.

Dana's decorator, Clyde Mason, was commonly known in Manhattan decorating circles as "Slide," and for good reason: he had a penchant for Plexiglas, polished chrome, and casters, and a patent for the custom-made mobile units that his clients used for seating, storage, room dividing, and whatnot. Everything in the Winters' home was on wheels and constructed out of putrid shades of Formica, Corian, Lucite, or whatever other slick materials Clyde found remaindered and got away with marking up to the hilt. And the garbage the Winters called art! Helen was stunned to see the three-foot-tall glass seal in the living room, recognizing the piece from a recent Sotheby's auction catalogue, estimated at around forty thousand dollars. At the time she thought it looked more like a carved-ice wedding table centerpiece than a piece of sculpture, and viewing it up close, she concluded that her first impression had been correct.

Ducking into the kitchen for a cup of coffee, Helen was immediately struck by its dinginess; the last time she saw harvest-gold and avocado-green was when she visited Michael's great-aunt Gertie in Canarsie. And the filth! A dark sheen of thirty-year-old grease coated every cabinet door, countertop, and appliance.

She was startled by a large cockroach scurrying across the floor, and then by the piercing sound of Dana's voice. "You're probably wondering how the kitchen could possibly look so dreadful when the rest of the apartment is so done. We've been desperate for Clyde to finalize the plans and begin a gut renovation, but he's just impossible to pin down. It's been three years since we moved in. I can't tell you how frustrating it's been."

"I can't imagine," Helen said in mock sympathy, wondering how Dana, a woman who didn't work and had limitless funds, could tolerate this disgusting kitchen. No wonder April refused to eat—it was nauseating!

She returned to the living room to the sight of a dozen or so women and two men seated rigidly, feet firmly planted on the floor in a valiant effort to prevent their chairs from rolling around the slickly varnished floors. *The stay-at-home dads always look so uncomfortable at these gatherings,* Helen thought, remembering back to the first and only time she had gotten Michael to attend. He had been the only male present that morning and eventually left in a huff when several irate women began a husband-bashing session, the subject of which was the pathological inability of men to detect a dirty diaper.

She gingerly lowered herself onto a moving hassock and slithered over to Lisa Fontaine, the chair of the board of trustees of The School. Helen relied on Lisa to keep her up to date on board matters and considered her one of the few trustees who were capable of impartiality and levelheadedness. Not inconsequentially, Lisa's children were substantially younger than Zoe, making it possible for Helen to have a conversation with her about something other than admissions. After the usual pleasantries, Helen broached the subject of Felicity Cozette.

"Outrageous," Lisa whispered. "The board learned about it the evening *after* it was announced to the faculty. There are some members who would like to see the decision reversed. I think that wouldn't be healthy for The School, but I do think Pamela deserves a slap on the wrist. At the summer meeting we discussed the need for a succession plan—you know, in the event something happened to the head. I suppose Pamela assumed that gave her license to make the appointment. But Felicity Cozette?"

"I wonder why Pamela chose her. Any idea?" Helen probed.

"None whatsoever. The only thing I can imagine is the French connection. You know Pamela—our resident Francophile. Let's ask

Dana. They were all together at some cooking school last summer. Dana, you were in France with Pamela over the summer, weren't you?"

"We were," she trilled, thrilled to be asked about her vacation. "At the École de la Cuisine de Provence. It was divine. I can't recommend it highly enough."

"I thought I heard Felicity Cozette was there, too."

"She was. In fact, she and Pamela roomed together."

"How coz-ette," Helen said, louder than intended. Eager to shift attention away from her snarky remark, she turned to her hostess and asked, "Did April enjoy herself?" fully aware that this was a loaded question.

"Oh, you know, as much as one would expect a teenager to. April's not much of a foodie," Dana answered.

That's an understatement, thought Helen.

Fortunately for Dana, someone directed a question to Denise Doyle-Gillis about The School auction.

"Do you think we will achieve our fund-raising goal for the year, Denise?"

"If certain targeted individuals step up to the plate, we will. Present company included," Denise replied, looking directly at Dana.

Dana seemed initially taken aback by Denise's directness, but recovered her composure and answered, "I'm sure *we* will do our part. We're just waiting for a few . . . issues to be resolved."

"And what issues are those?" Denise, the quintessential fundraiser, never let her prospect off the hook easily.

"Admissions. What else is there?" Dana said slyly. "Right, Helen?" She winked.

Helen pretended not to hear the last question as she tried to plan her escape. Just as she was moving toward the front door, Neal Moore called her name and followed her out. Damn! Trapped in the elevator with the shlub. Neal, a man who wore the same sweatpants and college fraternity T-shirt every day and, as a result, smelled a little moldy, was the couch potato father of one of Zoe's classmates, Nicholas, and husband of Marianne, a dynamic ob-gyn who delivered at least twenty babies a month. Helen braced for the inevitable.

"How are you doing with your applications?" he inquired, exactly on cue.

"Just fine. They're almost complete. In fact, I'm in a hurry to get home now and finish up the last of them. And you?" she felt obligated to ask.

"Well . . . Marianne is on call this month, so she put me in charge of the whole mess, and I'm finding it rather overwhelming. Plus, you know, we're also trying to get Nina into The School, for Kindergarten. I hoped I would be getting a bit more guidance from Pamela, but she failed to show up for three appointments and hasn't returned my phone calls."

"Have you tried e-mail?" she suggested.

"I did a few weeks ago, but our Internet provider just went belly-up and I haven't hooked up with a new one yet," he whined nasally.

What a wuss, she thought, turning away to hail a cab.

"Are you getting helpful input from Pamela?" he continued, thwarting her efforts to ditch him and end the conversation.

"Input, yes; helpful, I'm not sure. The jury's still out on that." *Thank God, a taxi.* "Bye. Good luck." She waved and hopped in the cab, feeling just a tad guilty abandoning this sad sack.

She got home and, humming the theme song to *Mission Impossible,* immediately headed to her computer.

Sara-

Ad-Mission accomplished. The Board is not happy with the appointment and with the fact that they were not consulted. Board doesn't understand choice of Felicity. I learned that P. and F. were at Frampton cooking school together last summer AND were "roommates"!! Hmmmmmmmmm.

Helen

Sara responded immediately:

H.

Thanks a lot. You rock. Are you implying an incestuous relationship within our royal family? Who's your source?

S.

Helen wrote back:

Deep Throat.

No big whoop. Half the heads of New York's private schools are homosexuals, and Helen and I have always suspected that about Pamela, Sara thought. *And as Helen always says, that would make her the world's first lipstick lesbian with no fashion sense. So, Felicity Cozette is sleeping her way to the middle. Hmmm . . . that's interesting.* But she was certainly relieved to learn that the board did not sanction Pamela's new appointment, and looked forward to hearing what the repercussions of that would be.

Under the circumstances, I think a little schadenfreude is permissible . . . or is it bad karma? she wondered, searching her memory for what it was that the Dalai Lama had said about other people's misfortunes.

She returned to reading applications. They were still pouring in by the dozens on a daily basis.

> Our daughter, Silvia, has a few allergies. She is allergic to peanuts, milk, wheat, eggs, citrus, strawberries, and all members of the nightshade family. We are interested in finding a school that can provide us with assurance that Silvia will never consume any of these foods while she is on school premises. Because Silvia has had to lead such a cautious life, she is an exceptionally sensitive child. She approaches everything she does with the care and concern she has been trained to exercise towards her diet. Consequently, she is a perfectionist in life and in everything she does. For example, Silvia will not even touch a book until she sprays the front and

back cover with antibacterial liquid and dries it thoroughly. She will never sit on a chair, bench or toilet seat without first running an electromagnetically charged particle dust cloth over the surface. With this kind of attention to detail, you can imagine what an asset she would be to any classroom. Mrs. Rothschild has told us that The School is peanut free and, from this, we have extrapolated that The School has heightened awareness and sensitivity towards the problems faced by the allergic child. For this reason I am sure you will agree we are the kind of family The School endeavors to serve.

"Uh-oh. I forgot. Brandi, don't tell anyone I brought a peanut butter sandwich for lunch today, okay?"

"Okay," Brandi answered with a puzzled look on her face.

Sara stuck this application in a file labeled "Children with Special Needs," a pile that seemed to be growing disproportionately larger than any other.

The next applicant in her stack was for the son of a major television celebrity—Sara had the eerie feeling she was suddenly in a supporting role on *Lifestyles of the Rich and Desperate*. Tally Easton was one of the most recognizable faces in America. Her daytime talk show was number one in the ratings. her prime-time specials served as an inspiration both for the working mother and for the downtrodden, stay-at-home mother of eight. She was the role model for millions of women everywhere who quoted her magazine, *Tally Ho,* like the gospel, wore her line of clothing like a badge, and drank her dietary weight-loss supplement by the gallon. Both an activist and a philanthropist, Tally had recently franchised her support group, MOTBOB—Mothers of Turkey Baster Originated Babies—whose members included many of her celebrity single-mother friends.

Attached to the application was a personal note from Lydia Waxman, principal of the firm, Ivy Bound Ltd. Lydia was the archetypal New York entrepreneur, who, after educating five difficult children (three biological, two steps) in at least a dozen different private schools, used her personal experience to build a business advising overextended and insecure parents in their quest to enroll their little darlings in prestigious kindergartens. She specialized in challenging cases, particularly postgraduates, those children who were spending an extra year in nursery school after failing to secure a spot in kindergarten on their first go-round. But she was more than happy to work with anyone who was willing to pay her exorbitant fee, which, much to the chagrin of several disgruntled former clients, was nonrefundable even in the event of across-the-board rejection.

Sara,

As you know, Tally Easton is one of the most well known daytime television personalities in the world. It goes without saying that her son, Montana, has lived a life of privilege and luxury that probably exceeds that of any other child in The School. Tally is remarkably down-to-earth and would like nothing better than for Montana to be educated in a school environment where he will be treated like any other child. There is one little caveat I would be remiss if I didn't alert you to up front—a bodyguard will drive Montana to and from school and must accompany him throughout the day. We assume that The School will find a way to accept these terms and offer Montana enrollment. As compensation for this inconvenience, his mother has agreed to donate one percent of the net profits of one of her mutually agreed upon publications, on an annual basis. I hope this meets with your approval.

See you at the Emmys,
Lydia

Over the years, The School had accepted its share of celebrities' children, and they generally created a bigger brouhaha than they were worth. The parents usually had such extreme attitudes of entitlement that The School ended up having to bend over backwards to accommodate them, at great cost and inconvenience. In most cases, Sara believed it was in The School's best interest to reject these applicants; however, protocol mandated that when a celebrity application was submitted, she bring it to Pamela's attention.

She had a choice: she could either try to schedule a meeting with Pamela or discuss this application with the newly appointed associate head. Viewing this as a prime opportunity to acquaint herself with Felicity, she popped upstairs and found the petite femme behind her desk, busily filing her French-manicured nails. Seeing Sara, she quickly slipped the emery board into her desk drawer and, parting her lustrous lips, flashed a juicy smile. Her laser-whitened teeth, peroxide-blond hair, and preternaturally pert breasts made speculation on the authenticity (or lack thereof) of Felicity's physiognomy a favorite topic in the faculty lunchroom.

Graciously, Sara congratulated Felicity on her new post and told her how pleased she was at the prospect of working together. *As if* . . . As she delivered an overview on the state of the admissions department, bandying about terms such as KAT percentile rankings, financial-aid-to-revenue ratios, and minority outreach initiatives, she watched Felicity fidget, confirming what she already assumed was the case: that Felicity was in way over her head. That established, Sara placed the star-studded application on Felicity's desk and, in the most deferential tone she could muster, said, "I would really like your opinion on this application. I'm not sure what to do with it."

Felicity read the name and said in her girlish Gallic accent, "Isn't zis a—how you say—shoo-in?"

" 'Shoo-in' is not a term I would recommend tossing around in admissions circles," Sara suggested diplomatically. "And, by the way, our policy states that we use multiple criteria when evaluating every application," she said, struggling to maintain her professionalism.

"Oh? Do we have such a policy?" Felicity asked, pronouncing it "police-y."

"Of course we do!"

"Then I will have to ask Madame Rothschild about zis," Felicity responded shakily.

"Good idea. I'm sure she'll want to spend some time acquainting you with our admissions 'police-y,' " Sara said brusquely, and left the office.

Ha! Now she had a pretty clear picture of how things were going to work. She would be reporting to Felicity, who would make no decisions without consulting Pamela, thus permitting Pamela to retain her power over the admissions office, while severing all communication with Sara. If Pamela was in fact still planning to depart, then promoting Felicity was undoubtedly her first step in trying to control the selection of her successor, and it was clearly not going to be Sara.

Screw it, Sara thought as she returned to her desk. *By the time Pamela leaves, The School will be scorched earth. It will take years to resurrect it. I don't even want the job!* She slammed her door closed and dug around in her desk drawer, looking for some valerian root extract to calm her nerves. She lit a scented candle, recalling something an aromatherapist recently told her about lavender and anger suppression.

She had just begun to regain her composure when Brandi buzzed to tell her that there was a call on line one from Simone Savage. As the head of one of Manhattan's poshest nursery schools, or, as the cognoscenti called them, "developmentally oriented readiness programs," Simone was universally understood to be *the* grande dame of the kindergarten admissions world. The coveted spots in her pre-K program went to Manhattan's A-list families, who thereby guaranteed their three-year-old entrée to the city's most sought-after elementary schools. Each September, Simone presented several "choice" candidates for admission to The School's Kindergarten class. And each February, The School accepted one or two of the "choicest," based almost entirely on Simone's recommendations.

"Sara, dahling, have you had a chance to review the Von Hansdorff application?" she demanded, and then lowered her voice to a barely perceptible whisper. "You know, dahling, they are the real thing."

"The real what?" Sara snapped. The name didn't register.

"The Hapsburgian Von Hansdorffs, of course. You remember. They chaired last year's Viennese waltz at the Wiener Werkstätte Society. They were all over the press."

"Oh, *those* Von Hansdorffs. Silly me," Sara replied, racking her brain to remember whether the Wiener Werkstätte Society provided social services to dachshunds or had something to do with bratwurst. "We've been absolutely inundated with applications this year, and I haven't had a moment to breathe. I'll look at theirs as soon as possible."

"And one more, Sara, dahling. The Dondi-Marghelletti family. They are a couple of young, gorgeous Italians in the hotel business.

Think Villa d'Este meets Cipriani, you know, Old World—new money, or old money—new economy. Oh, you know what I mean. And their little Aurora is precious beyond words. A true *principessa*," Simone gushed.

Sounds more like a Euro-trash version of Eloise, Sara thought. "Lovely, Simone. I can't wait to meet them."

"I'll check in to hear how much you adored them after your meetings."

"I'm sure you will, Simone. Take care, now."

"Brandi, would you please pull out the applications for Von Hansdorff and Dondi-Marghelletti," Sara called as she replaced the receiver.

In an instant, Brandi had them on Sara's desk. "This is weird. The handwriting on both applications is the same," Brandi said, and then, sniffing the folders, said, "and they both reek of expensive perfume. Chanel Number Five?"

Sara laughed. "Good nose you've got there, Watson." She launched into an explanation of Simone Savage and her ethically questionable habit of personally writing the applications for all her students.

"And when will we have the honor of meeting these two imperial families?"

Brandi consulted the appointment chart. "I'm waiting for a return call from the Von Hansdorffs' secretary. She said she would consult with the *Frau* and get back to me with their available dates. And Signora Dondi-Marghelletti faxed from Milano and said she would call once they knew when they were returning from Europe."

"I so look forward to making their acquaintance, Brandi, dahling, don't you?"

It was the last day of September, the deadline Helen had set for completing the applications. She sat at the Mackintosh table in the corner of her foyer/dining alcove, which, when she was working, she called her desk; when they were eating, she called the dining room table; and which at all other times functioned as a receptacle for all the junk mail, press clippings, journals, catalogues, recipes, bills, and school notices that cluttered the Dragers' lives. In a separate pile of high-priority items was her folder labeled "admissions."

As she reviewed the applications, she was tempted to call Sara, wanting her final approval on the essays. She wondered what Sara's reaction would be to the style of her writing, her descriptions of Michael, her use of hyperbole when writing about Zoe. But she decided against it, thinking it would be an imposition to ask Sara to spend the time right now, and could even put her in an awkward position if she disapproved of any of Helen's tactics.

The most difficult essay to write was the one for The Bucolic Campus School because that one asked for a description of the parents. Helen spent days weighing the desirability of various parental profiles. Should she go for creative Helen/successful Michael, or intellectual Helen/athletic Michael, or nurturing Helen/comedic Michael, or some other combination? She settled on a carefully worded blend of professionally oriented Michael and emotionally available Helen, implying that Zoe's home life was perfectly balanced and that all her physical, emotional, and material needs were met.

Another application asked the question "What are you looking for in a school for your child?" and Helen was glad that she was able to modify an essay she had written for another school, which asked her to "describe your ideal school." With a little creative editing she was able to keep her essay writing to a minimum.

The essay she most enjoyed writing was the one for The Progressive School, which asked the parents to write a letter to their child, expressing what they liked most about him or her.

". . . The close relationships you have formed with teachers and many other adults are inspiring. You are truly a social creature. The enthusiasm and care with which you approach your work is commendable . . ." she proofread. *Icchhh, I'm so embarrassed to think that someone out there is actually going to be reading this drivel.* Helen cringed and then directed her attention to completing the section of the applications that asked:

"Number of siblings?" "0"

"Relatives who have attended the school in the past?" "0"

"Languages other than English spoken at home?" "0"

She feared that all these zeros looked very undistinguished and added up to a big nothing. At least in the section where the applications asked, "With whom does the child live?" she wrote, "mother and father," but she doubted whether that answer would score them any points—conventional families were a dime a dozen. She could not believe she was thinking this way, and was anxious to get the damn things in the mail. All she needed were the checks (from Michael) and Zoe's essays.

In a recent conversation, Zoe had been very clear: she insisted that she wanted to write the essays alone and that parental input was unwelcome. But she did agree to share them when she was finished, as long as Helen and Michael agreed not to make any changes.

Before Zoe went to bed that night, Helen asked her to leave the essays on her desk so that she could put all the elements together and sign, seal, and mail them. As she assembled the packets, she anxiously picked up the first essay and read:

> My parents have been the most important influence in my life so far. They provide me with excellent role models for leading a moral and ethical life, and I am ever grateful that I have them as a constant and consistent beacon of light and strength.
>
> My Dad is smart, successful, athletic and funny. He has taught me how to tell a joke, dribble a basketball, make profiteroles and balance a checkbook. He is always available for a laugh, a tickle, a game of one on one and a bedtime story.
>
> My Mom is wise, stylish, creative and kind. She has taught me how to write a book report, embroider, look at art and stand up straight. She is always available for homework help, girl talk, hair braiding and moral support.
>
> But the most important lesson I have learned from both of my parents is to be a loving family member and a caring citizen. They both exemplify these characteristics on a daily basis and teach me, in the smallest ways, how to live a life I can feel good about. I love them both for this more than anything. Through these daily lessons they have given me the tools to achieve whatever it is I choose to do with my life. I

don't yet know what that will be but I am confident that I can
be successful on any path I follow.

Hearing Helen sniffling, Michael approached and put a hand on her shoulder.

"What's up?"

"Take a look at this." She handed him Zoe's essay.

As Michael read, Helen watched his face for a reaction.

"It's beautiful," he blubbered. Helen had always loved the fact that Michael teared up almost as easily as she did.

"I'm incredibly touched by it. Is it possible this is genuine? Or has she been as calculating as I have?" Helen wondered aloud.

"She couldn't possibly be that cynical. Not at her age. Besides, it's all true, isn't it?"

"When was the last time you made profiteroles?" she teased.

"I think it was the same year you did embroidery," he replied.

OCTOBER

Sara always loved when the lush greens of September turned into the burnt oranges and golds of October. It meant that the lunacy of the admissions season was one month closer to being over. Her thirteen-block walk to work constituted the only exercise she would get that day, but she figured it was better than nothing, and at least it provided a tranquil start to what would inevitably be a hectic day. She was transferring her high-protein, low-carb lunch from her backpack into the office's small refrigerator when Brandi buzzed to tell her Simone Savage was on line three.

"Sara, dahling. After all the years we've known each other I think of you as more of a friend than a colleague, and even more than a friend I think of you as . . . a confidante."

There was a long pause on the line before Sara replied, "I feel the same way, Simone."

"And sometimes friends—confidantes—have got to keep secrets from each other . . . Do you trust me, Sara? Really trust me?"

"Of course I trust you," Sara lied.

"Then it is of utmost necessity that you do not repeat a word of what I'm about to tell you."

"My lips are sealed," Sara replied, quoting the title of her favorite old Go-Go's song.

"Then just between you, me, and the lamppost, this is about the most outstanding student I have ever had. He makes every other child in the room pale in comparison. He is an extraordinary talent, yet utterly down to earth. He is truly the ideal student. His parents have asked me to use whatever *little* influence I might have to get him into The School . . ."

"So who is this boy wonder?" Sara asked impatiently. The preamble was becoming tedious.

"Due to a confidentiality agreement I am not at liberty to reveal his identity."

"Excuse me?"

"I cannot reveal the child's name at this time."

"And when will you?"

"After the child has been accepted to The School, of course."

"Simone, you know I can't do that."

"Sara! Don't you know who this family is?"

"How would I? You haven't told me!"

"Let me give you a hint, then: connections—big connections."

"The Con Ed man?"

"Not funny. Think, power . . . access . . . wealth . . . touch football on the White House lawn . . . Easter egg hunts with the pope."

"What is this, twenty questions? Simone, this is getting absurd. Are you going to tell me the name or not?"

"Not until I have your word that you will unconditionally accept him," Simone said, knowing she was asking for the impossible but trying her luck anyway.

"That's out of the question! You know I can't do that. The way you've described him, he sounds like Monica Lewinsky's love child."

"You're getting warm."

"Simone, I don't have time to play this game." Sara was ready to hang up when Simone interjected, "Pamela will be very disappointed if I tell her you wouldn't even consider him."

Sara quickly weighed her options and then replied, "I no longer report to Pamela. Our new associate head is overseeing the admissions department."

"And who is that, may I ask?" Simone asked indignantly.

"Felicity Cozette."

"WHO?" Simone gasped.

"Exactly," Sara answered.

The Dragers were preparing for their first interview. From what little they knew about it, The Safety School was in no way their first choice, but, unsure of what their real options would be, Helen insisted that they approach it as though it were. So when Zoe emerged from her bedroom wearing a faded pair of hip-hugger jeans and a tight ribbed shirt that exposed about three inches of midriff depending on how she positioned her arms, Helen voiced her disapproval.

"I don't approve of your outfit, either, Mom," Zoe bit her back.

"What's wrong with what I'm wearing?" Helen had carefully chosen a navy pencil skirt, blue-and-white-striped blouse, and pale yellow cardigan—the ultimate uptown-mom look.

"That skirt is so not cool. It makes you look really chunky." Zoe knew exactly which button to push.

"I'll change my skirt if you change your shirt. Deal?" Helen proposed, suddenly aware that her skirt did feel a little tight.

"Okay. Deal."

"No exposed belly buttons, right?"

"Okay, okay," Zoe replied resignedly.

"Helen, do I need to wear a tie?" Michael asked as he emerged from the bedroom.

"You can dress yourself. I'm not your mother." She realized she was overreacting, but she was on edge about their interview. "By the way, the answer is yes."

"Sorry, just asking," Michael replied.

Their morning visit to The Safety School began with a tour led by an eleventh-grade student named Katrina Stroheimer. As soon as they were introduced, Helen and Zoe, simultaneously noticed Katrina's pierced belly button and then, as she turned around, the artfully rendered yin-yang symbol tattooed at the base of her spine, both made visible by the insufficiency of her shirt—a size 4 on a size-12 girl. Zoe stuck out her tongue at her mother while, at the same time,

Michael, who had noted that the other three fathers in their tour group were tieless, glowered at Helen.

When did I become the official Drager family wardrobe watch-dog? she wondered.

There were three other families in their group: two with boys, and the third with a girl. Helen noted that the girl was minus a mother and that the father was quite attractive—a "yummy daddy," as her gay friends called attractive men with children. She wondered where the mother was. Away on a modeling shoot? A Doctor Without Borders? It was unusual for a mother to miss such an important event in her daughter's school career. The motherless girl was a lovely, frail Pre-Raphaelite type with a slightly melancholic air about her. The father also had a sort of dreaminess about him, or was he merely tired? She couldn't decide whether he was a hapless romantic or a sleep-deprived somnambulist.

The bespectacled boy in their group had dressed the part of Encyclopedia Brown, with horn-rimmed glasses, schoolboy blazer, and voluminous book in hand. Helen tilted her head to read the title: *The Complete Works of Homer.* She tried to remember the last book Zoe read, and seemed to recall its having gnomes on the cover. The boy's tweedily dressed father was also toting a weighty tome—the third volume of the Durants' *History of Civilization.*

God, how obnoxious, Helen thought. *Who do they think they're kidding with these props?* She checked out the mother, who had also dressed the part in a Mitford-sisters-on-a-garden-tour–type suit, a leather-bound book in hand, in which she was busily scrawling notes. Helen craned her neck to read: "Latin required—*only* four periods per week. Sanskrit not offered—mediocre language department."

The fourth family in their little group provided a study in contrast. The parents looked like characters out of a 1950s sitcom, strikingly ordinary throwbacks to a simpler decade. But their son, with his Nirvana sweatshirt, sebaceous skin, slacker posture, and expression of abject boredom, was the quintessential disaffected adolescent. The parents and their child, through their mirrored body language, expressed one common sentiment: estrangement.

Hmmm. If faced with a choice between these two boys for Zoe, which would get my vote? The namby-pamby son of the intellectually insecure overcompensators, or Kurt Cobain, the despondent son of the vanilla people? Helen wondered, weighing the lesser of the two evils.

With her group in tow, Katrina raced around the school at a breakneck pace. Breathlessly struggling to keep up with her long-legged strides, not wanting to ask her to slow down, because that would suggest they were out of shape, the Dragers scrambled to keep up.

The Safety School was in the midst of a major construction project, so that everywhere they turned, they were confronted with scaffolding, masonry, and stacks of Sheetrock. But even more disruptive was the intermittent pounding of jackhammers that made it nearly impossible to hear Katrina as she explained the expansion plan. Helen thought she heard the words "ten million dollars" and "new gym," but missed everything else in between. She was sure she heard Katrina swear up and down that the project would be completed before the start of the next school year, but then caught the eye of one of the construction workers as he snickered, shook his head, and, with his right hand curled as though holding a large salami, performed a familiar obscene gesture that Helen took to mean "in your dreams, lady."

Katrina opened a classroom door, gestured for them to enter, and then silently instructed them to stand in the back to observe a tenth-grade English class in action. The teacher, who looked to be just a few years older than Zoe, was doing what Helen thought was a credible job of comparing the rogue in nineteenth-century picaresque literature to dot-com executives in Silicon Valley. Helen marveled at his ability to conduct such a heady discussion amidst the chaos of the construction project and thought that if Zoe were a student here, she would be inclined to register a complaint about the ear-splitting noise. She smiled when she caught the teacher's eye, and he flashed her one back; he took her smile to mean that she approved of his teaching, while his contained a hint of sympathy because he knew her daughter's chances of becoming his student were slim.

In an adjacent classroom, a group of Latin students were conjugating the verb "*sum*" aloud over the roar of a buzz saw. "*Sum, es, est, sumus, estis, sunt . . .*" She thought she heard a practical joker sneak in the forbidden "C" word, but with such a racket, she couldn't be sure.

As Katrina led them out, Helen thought she caught Mr. Cobain staring at Katrina's ass. She checked to see if Michael was doing the same but, worse, caught him speaking convivially with Mr. Encyclopedia Brown.

"This is the first school we've toured," she overheard Michael say.

"Where else are you applying?" Mr. Brown asked.

Helen yanked on Michael's arm.

"What?" he whispered, looking bewildered.

"Don't divulge any strategic information," she ordered under her breath.

"You're kidding, right?"

A few minutes later, Katrina deposited them back at the office, and the associate director of admissions came out to greet them.

"I hope you enjoyed your tour with Katrina and got to know a bit about who we are. Now, please make yourselves comfortable. You will be called momentarily for your interviews. While you're waiting, are there any questions?" he offered collegially.

"Is literature taught in the original language, i.e.: Günter Grass in German?" who else but Mrs. Brown asked.

I hate when people say "i.e.": it's one thing to write it, but to say it, icchh, Helen thought.

"Um, that's a question for the head of the English, or, uh, is that for the language department? I'll have to get back to you on that," the associate fumbled.

"This school has the reputation of being pretty druggy. Do you think there's much drug use among the students?" Mr. Cobain asked.

The associate looked at the family and paused before replying. Helen bet he was wondering not whether their son was into drugs, but which ones. He then answered defensively, "I have very little patience for this kind of question. I don't know how these rumors get started, but there is absolutely no truth to them, and in fact, we have a highly effective antidrug policy. But, we also feel that ultimately it is the responsibility of each family to monitor and discipline their children as regards drug use." He stared accusatorially at the

Cobains, and Helen could almost hear him make a mental note to pull their file and mark it with a red flag.

"Their chances just went up in a puff of marijuana smoke," Helen whispered to Michael.

After this admonition, Helen shied away from asking about the construction completion date, afraid the associate might perceive her to be a troublemaker. In response to the Cobains' query, the yummy daddy recommended an article on teenage drug use that recently appeared in a highbrow psychoanalytical journal, with which Helen was familiar but which she doubted the Cobains would have ever encountered. She liked the sound of his voice and the generosity he exhibited by offering the suggestion. He also had a gentle, considerate manner with his daughter—warmly protective but not overbearing. She appeared to adore him and stayed by his side at all times. And finally, Helen noted the absence of a wedding ring, which, for reasons she couldn't explain, intrigued her.

After an annoyingly long wait, all three Dragers were called for their interview with The Safety School admissions director, Shirley Livingston. After introducing herself, she threw them all off guard with her first question. "Zoe, how would you describe your relationship with your mother?" Helen thought this a highly provocative way to begin an interview and waited breathlessly for Zoe's response.

"We're very close, most of the time. Sometimes we—" Livingston cut her off.

"My daughter and I were also very close. Particularly when she was living at home. Now she's in college . . . thankfully in the Northeast . . . in Boston . . . well, more precisely, Cambridge . . . Harvard, to be exact, and we're still very close."

Helen smiled, glad to know that Shirley's daughter made it to the Ivy League, but couldn't help but wonder where this was leading, and about its relevance to Zoe.

"And Michael. What do you like to do best with Zoe?"

"Oh, you know, go to the park and play a little ball or—"

Shirley interrupted again. "Oh! You play football?"

"Well no, actually, we play basket—"

Shirley interrupted yet again. "My son is a great football player. He made the varsity in his sophomore year and is ever so sweet about inviting us to all the games. Do you know, they still do tailgate parties at Princeton?"

"Boola-boola," muttered Helen.

"It sounds like The Safety School has a pretty strong record of getting their graduates into the Ivy League. Your kids did go to school here, didn't they?" Michael asked.

"Well, er, no, actually. Well, I mean they did both start here in kindergarten but then transferred out to The Very Brainy Girls' School and The Very Brainy Boys' School, in fourth and fifth grades respectively. But they were unusual cases," Shirley hedged awkwardly.

Michael smiled at Shirley and then glanced at Helen, who was also grinning falsely. Zoe kicked Michael under the table.

"Helen. You're an art critic? How fascinating! We have a wonderful art program here. Would you be interested in doing some lecturing? Many parents often volunteer to do that and enjoy it tremendously. We are very open to that kind of parental involvement. My husband, Chauncy, is a horticulturalist, and he gives a lecture every semester on the . . ." She talked nonstop for the next five minutes about her husband and his breakthrough research in the field of orchid hybridization. She stopped to take a breath, and just as the Dragers thought she was about to give them a chance to tell her *something* about themselves, she looked at her watch, stood up, shook hands, thanked them for a wonderful interview, and said goodbye.

As the door closed behind them, they looked at one another and covered their mouths to stifle their laughter. Helen shushed them until they were outside.

"Okay, I know I haven't had much experience with this kind of thing, but was that the most ridiculous interview either of you have ever had?" Zoe asked her parents.

"I wouldn't even call that an interview. It was a monologue performed by a compulsive egomaniac," Helen responded with a combination of disgust and amusement.

"I want to see her write-up on us. What could she possibly say?" Michael asked.

"That we're good listeners?" Zoe said with a straight face, eliciting more laughter from her parents.

"I told you, Mom, bare midriffs are totally in. All the girls dress that way. You saw Katrina," Zoe, who was more interested in assessing The Safety School's dress code than its academic attributes, complained as they walked uptown.

"You couldn't miss her. Michael, what did you think?"

"About Katrina's tattoo?" he asked.

"Glad you noticed. So did Mr. Cobain. What I meant was, what did you think about The Safety School?"

"Let's compare notes tonight. I've got to get to the office. I'm late for a meeting," Michael said. Quickly kissing his wife and daughter, he rushed off.

When Helen dropped Zoe off in front of The School, she felt a distinct sense of relief; its familiarity was comforting after the morning's journey into alien territory. She then wended her way to the Nouveau Russe Gallery on Madison Avenue to review an exhibition of contemporary glass sculpture for one of the monthly art magazines.

The exquisite little gallery occupied a ground-floor storefront on Manhattan's Upper East Side gold coast, with a rent so astronomically high that the proprietors were under constant pressure to sell just to break even. The space was designed to emphasize the delicacy and exclusivity of their goods, with several locked glass cases built into the walls displaying a selection of delicate breakables and a long velvet-covered surface on which the objects could be examined. Two satin settees were strategically placed in the center of the room, inviting the clientele to linger while, in the best of circumstances, contemplating a purchase.

Helen was surprised and delighted by the stunning complexity of the works on display. As she examined the pieces, she jotted in her notebook, "Egglike shapes. Colors—deep, iridescent, translucent. Inspired by Faberge."

"Fab-u, aren't they?" Her concentration was disrupted.

"Donald, hello!" She walked over to him, and they air-kissed on both cheeks—the prescribed way of greeting in this sort of shop, where touching was not allowed.

"What a spectacular show! When I was assigned this review I had no idea what to expect! The pieces are absolutely phenomenal. I see you've sold quite a few." She smiled, pointing to the red dots on the exhibition price list that indicated that a piece had been sold. She noted the lofty prices and thought that Donald and his partner, Josh, must be doing rather well.

He giggled and said, "And eight more pieces are on hold. We're in the money," he sang à la Ethel Merman. "Joshie," he called out, "Look who's here. It's Helen Drager!"

Once the same kiss-kiss routine was out of the way, Josh asked, "How's that adorable little girl of yours?"

"Zoe? She's not so little anymore," she laughed. "And your children?" Several years ago Donald and Josh announced they were acquiring twins—by what means she wasn't certain—and now the twins were almost five years old.

"They're precious as can be," Donald swooned.

"And if I remember correctly, Zoe goes to The School, right?" Josh asked.

"She's graduating this year," Helen answered, and reluctantly gave them a brief, sanitized version of her admissions plight. "And what are you doing about school for the twins?" she asked politely.

"We're in the process of applying to kindergartens all over town. You can imagine, it's doubly complicated with two." Donald dramatically pressed the back of his hand to his forehead.

"Coinky-dinky, The School is our first choice. When we go for our interview in a few weeks, can we say we are friends of yours?" Josh asked.

"It won't do you much good, but by all means mention it. Sara Nash is a friend, and I'll put in a word for you." Helen offered this tidbit, but no more. She saw a look of disappointment creep across Josh's face; he was hoping for more from her. But she hardly knew them well enough to offer a full-blown recommendation, particularly since she had never even set eyes on the children. She pointedly returned her attention to her note taking.

When at last she had finished and was saying goodbye, Josh blurted, "One last thing. Would you say The School is gay-friendly?"

"The School's colors are pink and gray," Helen answered with a laugh, and opened the door.

"Just like Vassar's. Say no more," Josh hooted, and waved her out.

* * *

Walking home from the gallery, Helen stopped along the way to look in shop windows, particularly those containing footwear. She hated to admit it, but she had a thing for shoes, and she marveled at how particularly sexy this year's designs were. A pair of pumpkin suede slingbacks caught her eye and drew her in to try them on. As she was studying her feet in a mirror, a salesperson sidled over.

"And of course you know that pumpkin is the new black. You can wear it with absolutely everything."

"Really?" She pretended to seriously consider this inane statement.

She wondered whether Michael would like them and then reminded herself that he rarely noticed what she was wearing these days. She was sure Zoe would say they were "phat" and would probably want to borrow them. As she contemplated the purchase, she recalled her calendar for the upcoming months, and all she could envision were school tours, interviews, and tutor appointments; therefore, she decided she couldn't justify the purchase, and left the store empty-handed, reminding herself to polish her navy pumps before the interview next week at The Fancy Girls' School.

The Belzer-cum-Einstein family was the first of the back-to-back interviews Sara had scheduled for the day. After briefly meeting the son, Sam, Sara sent him down the hall to be vetted by a Kindergarten teacher while his parents, Marsha and Alvin, slowly plodded into her office. Huddled tightly in the middle of her sofa, they formed one lump sum, an amorphous blob of characterless hair, skin, polyester, and rayon, frayed at the edges, faded and dull.

Interpreting their cleaving as a sign of nervousness, Sara attempted to help them relax with a standard icebreaker.

"It's been a beautiful fall, hasn't it?" she asked.

"It's been nice," Marsha replied flatly.

"Have you gotten out of the city to see the foliage at all?" she tried again.

"No. But I took the crosstown bus through the Park yesterday," Marsha answered.

"Oh, the Park is lovely this time of year, isn't it?" Sara persevered.

"It's nice," Marsha answered.

"Sam looks like a very big boy," she changed tack.

"He *is* tall for his age. He's in the ninety-sixth percentile for weight and the ninety-eight for height. And his head is enormous. Apparently, according to the neurologists we've consulted, that's quite common in children of Sam's superior intelligence," Alvin explained.

"You said in your application that you think Sam is, quote, "a genius." I'm wondering if you meant to say that you think he's literally a genius, that is, of extraordinary IQ, and if so, what has led you to this belief?"

"Of course there are many intelligent children around, but you must understand, Sam is exceptional," Alvin began. "He reads newspapers, medical journals, car manuals, court transcripts, whatever he can get his hands on."

"It's not that unusual for a five-year-old to read that voraciously, but there's the question of comprehension. Have you explored that with Sam? Does he understand what he's reading?" Sara probed gently.

"Why would he continue to read these things if he weren't getting something out of them?" Marsha questioned defensively.

"Maybe he receives a lot of praise and positive reinforcement from you both," she said. *And constantly hears you bragging to anyone who will listen,* she thought.

"That's not the case," Alvin responded defensively while Marsha cringed with embarrassment. "He's also solving complex mathematical problems and doing intricate scientific analysis," Alvin emphasized, speaking loudly and slowly, as if Sara couldn't possibly understand the magnitude of Sam's accomplishments.

"That's wonderful." Sara backed off. "You mentioned in the application that you feel Sam is immature in certain areas. Could you elaborate on that?"

Alvin hissed to Marsha. "You wrote *what*?"

Sara saw Alvin pinch Marsha's thigh and hated to imagine the bruise that would result. Poor Marsha was going to hear from him about this when they got home.

"What I meant was, despite his brilliance, Sam acts like a normal five-year-old . . . most of the time. That's really what I meant," Marsha finessed.

"There is a wide range of behavior that is considered normal for this age group. I wonder if what you call 'normal' falls within the range of what The School calls normal. Take, for example, toilet training. There are differing opinions as to what qualifies as normalcy in this area, but The School has a strict requirement that all children must be toilet trained before admittance to Kindergarten. Will this be a problem for Sam?" Sara watched Alvin jab Marsha's thigh again. Aha, that *was* the stickler.

"It shouldn't be. We'll give him a copy of Dr. Spock. He'll toilet train himself immediately," Marsha insisted.

Alvin strategically changed the subject. "What kind of gifted program does The School offer?"

"None. We feel our program is sufficiently challenging for all of our students. And every teacher is trained to offer enrichment projects for students who are asking for more stimulation. I can assure you, Sam would not be bored," Sara explained.

"Humph," Alvin grunted.

"If you're partial to gifted programs, you might want to explore other options," Sara replied tersely. *I defy you to find one that doesn't require toilet training,* she thought.

She wrapped up the interview, escorted them to the door, and pointed them down the hall to where Sam was waiting.

Before her next interview she pulled aside the Kindergarten teacher who had met with Sam, and asked, "What was your take on Einstein?"

"He seems like a pretty angry kid of average intelligence. Who decided he's Mini Mensa?"

"Who do you think? Mr. and Mrs. Mensa."

"That's typical. He was actually quite uncooperative and fidgeted the whole time we were together. I kept asking him if he needed to use the toilet, and he told me to 'mind my own beeswax.' I'm pretty sure he soiled himself," she reported in the objective manner she had been trained to use when evaluating children for admissions.

"Eeeww," moaned Sara. "I'm sorry about that."

"It wasn't the first time that's happened in my classroom," the teacher replied.

Fifteen minutes early and not accustomed to being kept waiting were the Von Hansdorffs, the "Hapsburgian" family from Simone Savage's "developmentally oriented readiness program." In contrast to the decidedly off-the-rack Belzers, these people were straight off a page of *Schloss Rhinelander,* the Bavarian equivalent of *Town and Country.* Sporting multiple layers of expensive plaid woolens, pastel cardigans around shoulders, blond hair, and icy blue eyes, the Von Hansdorffs personified "Teutonic." The *Herr* held one of those boxy little leather purses that only European men can get away with; the *Frau,* a custom-made handbag that cost more than Sara's monthly take-home pay. Their daughter was outfitted in the standard upper-class-child-on-school-interview uniform: navy blue quilted jacket with plaid lining, pleated gray skirt, and velvet hair band. While feasting her eyes on their Aryan perfection, Sara overheard the mother's strict orders.

"Greta, dear, be sure to tell Miss Nash how much you like de drawing of de bunny you saw in der front lobby. And remember vat Ursula taught you—sit up straight and look directly at der lady ven you speak to her. And don't forget, just like at home, speak only ven spoken to."

Sara invited the parents into her office and closed the door while Miss Stubinsky, the room C Kindergarten teacher, invited Greta to "play"—the term used to describe the process of interviewing a four-and-a-half-year-old who had no understanding of why she was there, what she was expected to do, or why her parents seemed so apprehensive.

Greta's "playtime" with Miss Stubinsky was not a whole lot of fun for either teacher or child. Greta did everything she was told, was careful and tidy, said please and thank you, but initiated no activity or dialogue and never once cracked a smile, even when Miss Stubinsky showed her the sloppy finger painting on the bathroom door and said, "Look at the silly tushy that Jason painted." In fact, Greta blanched when she saw it, and Miss Stubinsky had a moment of worry over the possibility that she could be accused of behaving unprofessionally if Greta were to report to her parents that "the teacher said a naughty word."

She had Greta put together a puzzle, stack some blocks, sew a giant button onto a piece of felt, and perform other equally challenging and compelling tasks, all of which Greta completed willingly and silently. Miss Stubinsky decided she needed to probe if she hoped to learn anything about Greta.

MISS STUBINSKY: Greta, what is your favorite thing to do at home?

GRETA: Watch Ursula make strudel.

MISS STUBINSKY: What fun! Does she let you help?

GRETA: No. Mother says it's messy.

MISS STUBINSKY: Oh, that's too bad. Do you and Mommy do things together?

GRETA: Only on Sunday.

MISS STUBINSKY: Why only Sunday?

GRETA: Ursula go away on Sunday.

MISS STUBINSKY: And what do you and Mommy do on Sunday?

GRETA: Go to church.

MISS STUBINSKY: Is that fun?

GRETA: No.

Miss Stubinsky could have simply described Greta Von Hansdorff as "not a happy camper" and Sara would have known exactly what she meant. But because she was obligated to write her two-hundred-word report in Educanto, the universal language of the admissions world, she described Greta as "a noncommunicative perfectionist with a negative affect who would greatly benefit from a stronger attachment to her mother." Miss Stubinsky's report essentially downgraded Greta from a possible to a probably not.

On her way home that evening Helen realized that her family hadn't eaten together all week. The other day she had been stuck waiting in her dentist's office and, driven by boredom, opened a parenting magazine. She'd been utterly captivated by an article about how kids who ate dinner with their families scored higher on standardized tests, and had resolved to make this more of a priority. Now, making good on her vow, she stopped into the local gourmet shop to pick up pasta and salad greens so they could enjoy what the article called "a healthy, conversation-stimulating meal as a family unit."

Once her family was assembled and the meal was underway, Helen began brightly, "Why don't we take turns bringing each other up to date on each of our lives!" exactly as the article suggested. After shooting each other worried looks, Zoe and Michael complied, and soon all three were happily chattering away about work, school, friends, colleagues, and, naturally, admissions. They laughed again about the absurdly one-sided so-called interview at The Safety School and about the other families in their group, particularly the Encyclopedia Browns. At first, Helen didn't react when Zoe mentioned the "clingy girl with the handsome father," but when she added, "I guess I would be insecure, too, if my mother had recently died." Helen failed to disguise her curiosity.

"Oh, how terrible. How do you know that?"

"I heard her father telling the admissions dude."

"Poor girl," Helen *tsk*ed sympathetically, and then casually added, "Did you happen to catch her name?"

"Catherine something. Why do you ask?"

"It's just good to know who we're up against. The devil you know is better than the enemy you don't." Helen was prone to the unintentional malapropism.

"You mean the devil you know is better than the devil you don't know?" Michael corrected, chuckling.

"Whatever."

In bed that night Michael suggested they make love. Helen responded with a huge yawn and a promise to do it the following night.

"Do I need to confirm my reservation with you tomorrow morning?" he asked facetiously.

"Before noon," she joked, and rolled over.

Even though she was tired, she had trouble falling asleep. She couldn't erase the image of the motherless girl and her dishy widowed father. The thought of the two of them navigating their way through the perplexing admissions maze without the support of a mother seemed tragic. She couldn't imagine how Michael and Zoe could possibly manage to get the laundry done if she weren't in the picture, let alone get Zoe into high school.

Instead of counting sheep, she counted all the motherless girls in literature she could think of, starting with Emma Woodhouse, Eliza Dolittle, Scout Finch, Cordelia, Lady Chatterley, Nancy Drew . . . and finally fell asleep.

Sara walked into her office the next morning just in time to field a call from the irrepressible Simone Savage, who insisted on knowing how the interview went with the Von Hansdorffs. Searching for something positive to say about a family she found to be as frigid and impenetrable as a polar ice cap (before global warming), Sara finessed with "Greta's posture is flawless."

"Greta has had only the best and is proof of how effective a good governess can be," Simone replied with the confidence of one who had extensive experience assessing domestic help.

"I wasn't aware that anyone still refers to child care providers as governesses."

"*Anyone* doesn't. The Von Hansdorffs do. Impressive, isn't it?"

"I am more impressed when I see a strong parent-child attachment counterbalanced with an appropriate level of independence. In their case, I saw neither," she answered, and hurried on to give Simone no opportunity for rebuttal. "We can discuss Greta further once her file is complete and the KAT scores are in."

Reviewing her list of appointments for the day, she was puzzled when she saw that Oscar Whyte, who had been on her list, had been crossed out. She called Brandi to ask her whether the Whytes had rescheduled or had canceled the appointment entirely.

"Felicity called yesterday to say that the Whytes will be interviewed by Pamela today," Brandi told her.

"Get me Felicity's extension right away . . . please," she demanded angrily.

Sara took three deep breaths and then called Felicity and, as calmly as possible, asked why Pamela was going to be conducting the Whyte family interview. Felicity repeated what Pamela had told her—that the Whytes had requested that Pamela interview Oscar because of the difficulty he was having understanding the American language.

"How will he manage with the KAT test? It's an oral examination, in case you didn't know," Sara countered huffily.

"As I understand eet, Pamela told zee Whytes zat she would waive zee KAT," Felicity said cautiously, as if aware that Sara was not going to be pleased when she heard her response.

She was correct. "Are you kidding me?" Sara shouted. So much for centering oneself through breathing.

"She said something like, because zee KAT has no equivalent in zee British educational system it was useless for Oscar to take eet," Felicity tried to explain, but lacked the vocabulary even to fake it.

"He's only five! He knows no education system, British or otherwise!" Sara was shouting now. "I need to discuss this with Pamela before they arrive."

"She's not in today," Felicity calmly informed her.

"But their interview is today. Aren't they coming?"

"No, zey are not. Pamela is going to zem. She said a home visit is appropriate under zee circumstances."

"What circumstances?"

"Zair recent arrival in America and zee child's fears," Felicity explained feebly.

"They're from England, for Christ's sake, not New Guinea! I have applicants right off the boat from third world countries that manage to get it together to come in for an interview. What's wrong with these people?" She didn't wait for an answer and slammed down the phone.

It dawned on Sara that the Whytes were the first people she had ever met—or, for that matter, had ever heard of—who had some connection to Pamela's past life. And she had a sneaky feeling that the Whytes were aware of some skeletons that Pamela would prefer remained closeted, which would explain why she was going out of her way to make sure that Sara had absolutely no contact with them.

But she had no time to dwell on this now. She had an appointment for an interview with a disabled mother who was having trouble maneuvering her wheelchair through the door of the admissions office. She could hear the woman threatening Brandi in a menacing voice, “This school isn't handicapped-accessible? Do you know you're in violation of the Disability Act? I could get this placed closed down like that”—she snapped her fingers.

How the hell could Pamela have overlooked this detail? Sara shook her head in disbelief, then rushed out to do damage control.

A flotilla of Town Cars and Range Rovers jammed the street in front of The Fancy Girls' School, making it difficult for the Dragers' taxi to deliver them to their destination. When they finally reached the entrance to the school, they were introduced to their tour guide, Morgan Striker, an immaculately groomed and coltish twelfth-grader who had the most evenly tanned and muscular calves Helen had ever seen, and, miraculously, thighs of the same circumference.

I never looked like that, even at seventeen, Helen thought.

Morgan was articulate and knowledgeable and, while conducting the tour, managed to offhandedly let them know she was the captain of the field hockey team, editor of the yearbook, and had applied early decision to Princeton. As they clambered through the halls behind her, they passed several other little tour groups led by girls who looked a lot like Morgan, all in The Fancy Girls' School uniform of short, short blue skirts and white, white collared blouses. By some fluke of nature, they all had the same long, straight, shiny blondish hair, light eyes, and full lips suggesting either that homogeneity reigned supreme at The Fancy Girls' School or that they were all related. They waved to one another and called out as they passed in the halls, “Hey, Taylor,” “Howzit goin', Jordan?”

“Don't you hate these surnames for girls?” Helen whispered to Michael, making a mental note to discuss the sociological implications of this trend with Sara.

“Yeah. What happened to Ashley, Brooke, and Tiffany? I liked those names,” he whispered back.

As they shuffled through the well-scrubbed halls, Morgan drew their attention to the bulletin boards lining the walls, each of which served as an information center for the school's many clubs. They looked closely at the ski club's hub and saw a sign-up sheet for a December ski trip to Cortina d'Ampezzo that generously invited nonskiing Italian-club members to tag along. The sheet was surrounded by notices posted by students selling ski paraphernalia, including a sign advertising a twenty-five-hundred-dollar fur-lined ski jacket, on which the seller had scribbled, "just the thing for a weekend in Gstaad!!!" Proceeding down the hallway, they came to the film society's board, which featured an invitation to preview this year's Academy Award–nominated films in a student's private screening room. The final board on the hallway was that of the gourmet club. Instead of the expected posters for the high school version of the Pillsbury Bake-Off, there were six different sheets to sign up for two-hundred-dollar prix fixe dinners at four-star restaurants, a petition protesting the serving of the endangered Chilean sea bass in the school cafeteria, and, tucked discreetly into the corner, a promotional brochure for a summer cooking program in Provence, on which someone had scribbled, "Frampton Sucks."

Next Morgan took the Dragers to the school's gargantuan library, with wall-to-wall carpeting, mahogany bookshelves, and plushly upholstered easy chairs that beckoned even the least bookish student to enter. The three gymnasiums accommodated a huge variety of sports and athletic activities and were decked out with banners celebrating victories over the many rival schools. The science and computer labs contained all the latest equipment. But it was the music department, with its faculty of accomplished musicians and singers and a full twenty-four-track recording studio, that most impressed the Dragers. If Zoe should be inclined to continue her musical education, this was certainly a place to support her efforts.

At the appointed time, Morgan deposited the Dragers in the auditorium, where they would witness a well-choreographed presentation by The Fancy Girls' School's top brass. Two ample women were seated on the stage, waiting impatiently as dozens of hopeful applicants scurried about, trying to snag the most advantageous seats in the house.

"It's the big skirts," Michael said, pointing discreetly to the women on the stage.

"Teletubbies," Zoe giggled.

"Interesting how little they resemble their nubile students' bodies," Michael whispered to Helen, who, in mock exasperation, swatted him with the school catalogue.

When the audience was finally seated, the program began with the standard welcoming spiel delivered by the head of The Fancy Girls' School, the éminence grise of New York City's girls' schools. Reputed to be a superb educator and respected theorist on feminist adolescent psychology, she exuded an air of gravitas, an attribute that served her well in a school with such a high-powered parent body and a star-studded board of trustees. Her speech began with some statistics about her students' superb performance on the SATs and their high percentage of Ivy League acceptances, with a quiet mention of the few girls who had gone on to slightly less prestigious colleges but, of course, for justifiable reasons like athletic scholarships. Having gotten the critical facts and figures out of the way, she eased into some psychobabble about emotional intelligence, self-esteem, body image, teen cruelty, sexual responsibility—all the universally agreed-upon justifications for single-sex education. The audience was SOLD. With a few cleverly worded phrases, she had convinced them that they would unequivocally get their money's worth if their daughters were lucky enough to be accepted. After an enthusiastic round of applause, the head introduced Justine Frampton, director of admissions of The Fancy Girls' School.

Justine was tall, buxom, and bottom-heavy, with the longest hair Helen had ever seen on a professional woman over the age of forty. Her sallow complexion was exacerbated by excessive pigmentation, and as a result, her dark eyes receded deeply beneath her simian brow. When she perspired, droplets of moisture beaded on the dark growth of hair that fringed her upper lip, and she was often seen fanning herself with a school catalogue while muttering, "Pardon me, it's my private summer." Helen was surprised that no one had told her that her slip hung about two inches below the hemline of her skirt.

"I'm so pleased to see so many enthusiastic faces. If after tonight's presentation you're still interested in The Fancy Girls' School, please submit your applications as soon as possible and then call my office to schedule interviews for yourselves and your daughters. That will give us a chance to get to know you while you're getting to know us."

As Justine rattled on, Helen looked around the room to see who else was there from The School. She saw the Winters seated front and center and was struck by how wan and ashen April appeared, as if a slight gust of wind (or the hot air blowing off the stage) could knock her over. Dana appeared captivated, eagerly trying to make eye contact with Justine while hanging on her every word. Patrick Winter, on the other hand, was using his new Internet-access cell phone to track his stocks while getting an up-to-the-minute forecast on the weather at Pebble Beach. Helen continued to scan the crowd, noting a few other familiar faces and then a face she recognized from their visit to The Safety School. It was the yummy daddy, looking even yummier than she remembered. Was it the light? His clothes? New haircut? Propped lightly against him was Catherine, also looking even more ethereal than she remembered.

Justine wrapped up her superficial remarks and asked if there were any questions. The first person she called on was an elegantly dressed African-American woman whom Helen recognized as a former principal dancer with the Alvin Ailey dance ensemble.

"I haven't seen much evidence that this school supports diversity. In fact, I haven't seen a single person of color in the entire place. I'm curious, what *is* your position on racial integration?" the woman asked confrontationally. A hush filled the room.

Deftly sidestepping this minefield, Justine invited her boss to answer the question. Always ready to tackle this one, the head delivered a long-winded treatise on their commitment to diversity and then apologized for the fact that none of their MANY African-American students were present today. She explained that they were all attending a conference entitled: "The Race Race: Manhattan Schools Compete to Diversify." She graciously invited the woman to attend "our magnificent all-school Kwanza celebration in December." The woman nudged her daughter and rolled her eyes.

"They're in," Helen whispered to Michael.

Next, some brave soul asked the one question to which everyone wanted to hear the answer—"Exactly how many applicants will be accepted for grade nine?"

Justine was prepared for this one. She tittered and proceeded, "That's the sixty-four-thousand-dollar question, and even *I* don't know the answer."

Bullshit, Helen thought.

Justine continued in this insincere vein, "It will depend on so many factors. I only wish I could tell you there is a place for each and every one of you. But I can assure you, in the end it will all work out for the best."

"What a politician," Michael murmured.

"Bush league," Helen answered.

As the Dragers walked out of The Fancy Girls' School, Helen hooked her arm through Zoe's.

"So what do you think sweetie?"

"It's a pretty incredible place. And the music department looks amazing," Zoe answered.

"What was your impression of the girls?" Helen asked.

"Hot," Michael said with a leer.

"Maybe you should apply," Helen laughed. "But I meant Zoe's."

"I don't know. They all sort of looked the same. You know, that Upper East Side, summer-in-the-Hamptons kind of look. That was kind of scary," Zoe said tentatively.

"Yeah. I know what you mean. But I'm sure they're not all like that. And the fact is, you'd have no trouble fitting into that kind of crowd. You've pretty much got the look down," Helen replied brightly, hoping to spark Zoe's enthusiasm.

"Yeah, if I dyed my hair blond and went to a tanning salon," Zoe said sarcastically.

"And she'd have to change her name to Spencer or Blake," Michael added.

"But anyway, I'm still not convinced I even *want* to go to an all-girls school," Zoe added.

"We haven't even had our interview here yet. Let's wait until we see all the schools before we get into that debate. We don't have to make any decisions, now," Michael answered, raising an eyebrow towards Helen to say, "right?"

"Good idea," she added.

They all kissed goodbye on the corner, and as Michael and Zoe went off to see the Knicks play at Madison Square Garden, Helen went to meet Sara for dinner in Chinatown.

All week Helen had been looking forward to seeing Sara; except at the Toppler party, she hadn't seen her friend for almost a month.

They had made plans to meet at the Shanghai-style seafood restaurant on Mott Street with the enormous fish tank in the front window that allegedly contained the creatures that ended up on the customer's plates.

"I'm so happy to see you. We haven't had a good smooze in ages," Sara said, giving Helen a warm hug.

"Or a good shmooze, either," Helen laughed.

Sipping cosmopolitans, they caught up on events of the past few weeks and then rolled up their sleeves and dug into a heaping pile of crabs. Up to their elbows in shells, scallions, and ginger sauce, they cracked and picked and licked their fingers while having a side-splitting, no-holds-barred hen session in which none of their mutual acquaintances were spared.

They each ordered a second cosmopolitan, and Helen changed the conversation to a more serious topic: "Not to be a downer, but I'm a little worried about Zoe. She's been withdrawn lately. I'm not sure if she's stressed out by the admissions stuff or if it's just typical adolescent moodiness. I'm wondering if she's been this way at school. Have you noticed anything?"

Just yesterday Zoe had asked Sara if they could talk and ended up crying in her office. She confessed that she was feeling completely overwhelmed by the pressure she was getting from her mother, who, as Zoe put it, "is acting nutso about admissions," and she wanted some advice from Sara on how to cope. Sara consoled her and advised her to let Helen know how she was feeling. If she didn't think she could do that, Sara suggested she speak to her father.

Careful not to betray Zoe's confidence, she replied, "I think she *is* stressed about admissions. There's good reason to be. I see this with all the eighth-graders and their parents. My advice is, if at all possible, lighten up. She's under enough external pressure. She shouldn't be getting it at home, too."

"I wasn't aware that she was," Helen said defensively.

"Trust me. She is. Even I can sense your tension every time the subject comes up."

"I just want to do everything I can to make sure she ends up at a good school."

"Helen, the bottom line is, all of the private schools in New York are good schools. Why don't you let Zoe decide what's best for her? She's the one who'll be going every day, not you."

"Okay, okay. I get the message," Helen said abruptly, sorry to have brought up the subject in the first place. It was just that it seemed to be on her mind almost all the time, even in Chinatown, with two cosmos and a half-dozen ginger-scallion crabs under her belt.

They ordered a third drink, and as Sara talked about how impressed she was with Zoe's role in the choral group and her extraordinary musical talent, Helen lapped it up. She certainly hadn't gotten positive feedback like this from Pamela in years.

"I interviewed your friends today," Sara said, slowly stirring her drink with a chopstick.

"Really? I didn't know I had any friends applying to The School. Who's that?"

"Donald Roman, Josh Kirov, and their two children."

"Professional acquaintances, not friends. Pleeease. They own a gallery that I frequently visit. That's the extent of our friendship." Helen insisted on setting the record straight.

"Really? They acted like you're buddies. So what's their story?"

"By now you probably know more than I do. I've never even met their children. I've always been curious—where *did* their kids come from?"

"It seems that Josh is the biological father of one child, and Donald the other. Together the children have four different mothers—two surrogates hired solely to carry and deliver, and two egg donors, chosen for their high IQs and good looks."

"Are you kidding? But that means the children aren't really twins!"

"Technically, they're not even related by blood. But, by some divine miracle, they were born within hours of one another, so they're being raised like twins even though they're not."

"I don't get it. Couldn't they have used two women instead of four? Wouldn't that have been a hell of a lot easier?"

"They chose to use every trick in the fertility book to maximize their level of control. They shopped for the best eggs, the best ovens, as they refer to the surrogates—which must have cost God knows how many thousands of dollars—and now act like their creations are, without question, perfect. Boy, are they in for a surprise."

"Very Dolly the sheep meets Frankenstein," Helen proclaimed, pronouncing it "frong-ken-shtein." "What are the children like?"

"The girl is all right, but the boy is a bit delayed and not quite ready for school yet. Actually, he's quite immature. I was a little surprised when they arrived in a stroller."

"That's not so unusual for four-year-olds."

"No, you're right. But they were also both sucking on pacifiers the entire time they were at The School. It made talking to them rather difficult."

"Oh. That *is* weird. What are their names?"

"Are you ready for this? Anastasia and Alexi."

"And their last name is what? Roman or Kirov?" Helen asked.

"That's the kicker—it's Romanov."

"No way!" Helen cracked up. "You can call them the tsar and the tsarina."

"Good idea. I have another applicant who is a *principessa.* If we accept all of them, we'll have an entire royal family."

"You've already got your queen. She would like nothing better than to expand her empire," Helen cracked.

"That's reason alone to not accept any of them."

"So what's up with you two? Have you finally gotten a chance to ask Pamela what's up her bugaboo?"

"No chance whatsoever. I'm just doing my job and staying out of her way. The biggest hitch is reporting to Felicity. God is that woman stupid." Again Sara reminded herself that it would be a big mistake to tell Helen what she really thought was at the root of her Pamela rift. She was also dying to tell her the Whyte story but instead opened her fortune cookie and read aloud, "A wise man will keep his suspicions muzzled, but he will keep them awake."

"Hmmmm . . . what do you think that means?"

"Dunno," Sara answered as she tore it in half and dropped it into her teacup. "What's yours?"

"The chains of marriage are so heavy that it takes two to bear them, and sometimes three."

"Hmmmm . . . what do you think *that* means?"

* * *

Helen woke up the next morning feeling groggy and achy, regretful about last night's third (or was it fourth?) cosmopolitan, particularly in light of the busy day ahead. Cup of coffee in hand, she struggled to finish her review of the glass exhibition, faxed it to the editor, and then quickly updated her spreadsheet before heading out for the day.

SCHOOL	PHONE #	DIRECTOR OF ADMISSIONS	STATUS
The Fancy Girls' School	674–9876	Justine Frampton	Open House Oct. 6 Interview scheduled Oct. 14
The Progressive School	563–9827	Soledad Gibson	Interview scheduled Oct. 20
The Bucolic Campus School	475–8392	Vincent Gargano	Interview scheduled Nov. 5
The Safety School	498–5937	Shirley Livingston	Tour & Interview Oct. 4 Sent thank you note.
The Very Brainy Girls' School	938–8475	Eva Hopkins	Still wait listed-called Oct. 5
The Downtown School	483–8473	Taisha Anguilla	Still wait listed-called Oct. 5

Gathering a scarf and gloves, Helen glanced at her computer screen and saw that an e-mail from Sara had just arrived.

Helen-

Thanks for the great evening. I must confess I'm getting too old to drink like that. Ugh! Hope you're okay. See you later for your tour—I have an extra special family lined up for you. The child is a graduate of "Isadora for Children." Need I say more?

Sara

Arriving at The School, Helen went directly to the admissions office, where Brandi was waiting to introduce her to the attractive and trendy Swansons and their daughter Miranda. Helen's eye was immediately drawn to the wife's pumpkin-colored shoes. Having reviewed Miranda's curriculum vitae (voluntarily submitted with the application) prior to meeting the Swansons, Helen knew that Miranda was not only a highly accomplished dancer but had also completed two semesters of Mallets and Strings and three semesters of Spatter, Smear and Stipple, the highly selective toddler art program at the Painters' Alliance. When Zoe was preschool age, Helen had investigated the possibility of enrolling her in this program and called for an application. When the enticing brochure arrived, she was shocked to learn the cost—twelve hundred dollars for ten sessions—but out of curiosity went ahead and set up an appointment to visit a class. She was wowed by the classroom, and the teachers seemed appropriately bohemian; but she just couldn't see the logic behind paying a fortune for Zoe to learn finger painting by numbers and to sculpt with recyclable papier-mâché, and opted instead to invest forty dollars in an easel, a pad of newsprint, and a set of water-based paints, enabling Zoe to create masterpieces in the privacy of her room.

"I understand Miranda is quite a little culture vulture. The School's artistic offerings will probably interest you. Where would you like to begin?" she patronizingly asked the Swansons.

"Why don't we start with art, move on to music, and save the most important for last? Miranda is very excited about your dance program, aren't you, cuddly bear?" Miranda hid behind her mother's leg, clinging to her well-cut pants. "She's an extraordinarily talented dancer," whispered Mrs. Swanson.

The first stop was a Kindergarten art class, where they found the children painting wooden spools and then stringing them on colored yarn.

Bad choice, Helen thought. *This is about as interesting as watching paint dry. Oh, dear, we are watching paint dry.* She wished she had chosen a class that was engaged in a more ambitious project, like the one she dropped in on last week in Miss Atari's room, where the children had painted a map of the world, highlighting the countries of origin of each student's caregiver. When Helen was in kindergarten, she had never heard of Trinidad or Tobago, but thanks to their multinational caregivers, these kids knew not only the names of numerous countries in the Southern Hemisphere but their capitals, language spoken, and, most important, best resorts, since their parents often planned vacations expressly "to see where Yolanda grew up."

Next Helen steered the Swansons to the music room, where a Kindergarten class was banging on tom-toms and singing the "Indian War Song" from *Peter Pan.* She prayed that the Native American number was not in some way offensive to them, and was relieved when Miranda, obviously having seen the Disney version, was able to sing along, pleasing her mother no end.

"Lovely singing, pussycat," Mrs. Swanson purred.

When they arrived at the dance studio, Helen was relieved to find the room awhirl with a bevy of children draped with colored scarves, leaping and spinning to *Swan Lake.* At last Miranda emerged from behind her mother's leg and whispered, "Miranda wants to dance."

Her mother bent and whispered, "No dancing today, ladybug. Next time."

Not accustomed to hearing the words "no" and "dancing" uttered in the same sentence, Miranda ran into the middle of the room, pulled her dress up over her head, exposing her underpants to the entire class, and shrieked, "I HATE THIS SCHOOL!" The mother looked mortified as she ran to comfort Miranda. The father stayed with Helen and made light of the situation with an emotional detachment she found chilling. As quickly as possible, Helen rounded them up and herded them back to the admissions office, hardly able to contain her impulse to run in and share the story with Sara.

Her tour guide duty out of the way, she went to the lobby to wait for Zoe and ran into Lisa Fontaine, who had just heard about the Swansons.

"The School will be abuzz with this one for days, right, honeybee?" Helen chuckled.

"You can bet this one will travel fast," Lisa concurred with a grin.

"So, Lisa, what's the board up to these days?" Helen asked.

Lisa took Helen by the arm and led her to a hidden corner of the lobby and, sotto voce, began, "The board has hired an independent accounting firm to conduct an emergency audit. There seems to be an inexplicable shortage of cash, and the operating budget is showing a deficit. Pamela has stonewalled everyone who has tried to discuss it with her, forcing us to solicit outside counsel. This is, of course, highly confidential. You must give me your word you'll keep it under your hat," she begged.

"Mum's the word," Helen whispered, and zipped her lips closed.

Helen had never understood the board's unwillingness to challenge Pamela's authority, or the wisdom of allowing Pamela unrestricted access to The School's funds. So today's news, though not surprising, was certainly alarming. As she was pondering the potentially dire implications, she saw Zoe come cheerfully bounding down the stairs, and immediately her mood improved. A ten-minute cab ride got them across town, just in time for their four o'clock appointment with Bertha Kauffmann.

They rang the bell, and a loud gravelly voice commanded, "Let yourselves in."

As they shyly squeezed into the three-foot-wide foyer, Helen, a typically real-estate-obsessed New Yorker, quickly appraised the apartment: a two-bedroom, two-bath prewar in a doorman building between Madison and Park. In other words, like many of Bertha's students, it had potential. But talk about fixer-upper!

Cardboard cartons were stacked on every available surface, making the apartment appear smaller and darker than it actually was. Some of the boxes, logically, contained textbooks, workbooks, notebooks, files, and binders, but even more contained candy: every variety of neon-colored, newfangled, braces-busting confection on the market, leading Helen to suspect that Bertha was in cahoots with the orthodontist around the corner.

Through years of experience, Bertha had developed a brilliant strategy: by plying her students with limitless quantities of candy, she gave them a heightened state of euphoria that they associated with their tutoring sessions. Her students eagerly looked forward to seeing her when, in fact, what they really craved was their regular sugar fix. Conveniently, by the time the inevitable postglycemic crash occurred, the child was under someone else's supervision.

The living room was lined with overloaded bookshelves and wooden file cabinets, spilling over with the tools of her trade. In the center of the room sat an enormous desk covered with piles of creased and torn paper, an assortment of stationery and office doodads, the remains of Bertha's past three meals, and, of course, buckets of candy. As Helen spotted Bertha herself amidst the hodgepodge, she was reminded of one of Zoe's favorite childhood books, *Where's Waldo?*

Pushing aside a stack of books and several boxes, Bertha ordered Helen and Zoe to sit down at the table for a discussion of the game plan. With the ultimate insider's view of private school mania, and an opportunistic outlook, Bertha had built a successful business, catering to the needs of neurotic New York parents as well as to those of their progeny. One of her patented techniques was to begin the first session with a standard proclamation.

"Your child is unquestionably bright, obviously capable, and will undoubtedly increase her test scores and be accepted at the school of her choice if . . ." (pause for impact) ". . . you are committed to seeing me twice a week." She had yet to come across a parent who didn't buy into her program.

Helen was instructed to leave and then return to pick up Zoe in one hour. So, doing what any remotely self-indulgent New York mother with an hour to kill would do, she went for a manicure and pedicure at the neighborhood Korean nail salon. With eyes fixed on the bobbing head of the esthetician polishing her toenails, her mind wandered to the events of the afternoon. Lisa Fontaine's confidential story about the "independent emergency audit," sounded fairly ominous. If the audit were to uncover a serious malfeasance, the implications for The School could be devastating. If Pamela's reputation in the private school network were tarnished, where would that leave them on the admissions front? Helen had no doubt that Pamela was capable of shady dealings, but she desperately hoped that none of them would be uncovered before February 12.

An hour later she returned to Bertha's and was delighted to hear that her daughter was one of "*the* brightest young ladies" Bertha had ever met and that working with her was "*pure pleasure.*" She loaded Zoe down with workbooks, invited her "take some candy for the road," and said she would look forward to seeing her in three days.

Just as they were getting ready to depart, there was a shrill buzz, and Bertha shouted, "The door's open." Helen and Zoe pressed against the wall to let the next client enter and simultaneously registered recognition—it was Catherine, the girl from The Safety School tour, and her handsome widowed father. They all shuffled about and awkwardly switched places in the cramped space, averting their eyes while muttering hellos and goodbyes. Helen grabbed Zoe's arm after they left, and held her close, grateful for the mundane luxury of being there for her daughter on an ordinary weekday afternoon.

The School had been on celebrity alert all morning—Tally and Montana Easton were due any minute for their interview. Margaret was looking spiffy in Tally's signature line of clothing, Brandi was chatting up a sixth-grade English teacher about Tally's latest literary recommendation, and three Kindergarten teachers were lingering in the admissions office with disposable cameras.

"Remember, no pictures," Sara scolded as the door swung open.

First in was an impeccably tailored six-foot-five African-American man, resplendent in a tapered jumpsuit, black beret, and leather jacket, revealing just the slightest outline of the Tech-9 that was cradled in a shoulder holster. After giving the room a well-practiced once-over and confiscating the Kindergarten teachers' disposable cameras, he nodded over his shoulder as if to say, "Coast is clear, no paparazzi here."

Then in strode the World's Best-Known Daytime Television Personality, Magazine Publisher, and Marketer's Dream and her sparkling five-year-old son, Montana.

The secret of Tally's success was her genuine warmth and familiarity, her everywomanness that made females in America as comfortable speaking with her as they would be with their best friend. Even Sara was seduced.

"Sara. You have the most . . . full-bodied hair," Tally gushed.

"Really, I think it's too big," Sara responded, patting her wild mane, then feeling silly for continuing a conversation about something as trivial as her hair.

"I would give anything for so much hair. A little trim is all you need. How about if I send my Rafael over to give you a snip-snip?" Tally offered graciously.

"Thanks. Maybe you can just give me his number. But, Tally, let's talk about Montana."

"It's so sweet of you to ask about my boy. My life was meaningless until I had him. Do you have children?"

"Er, no," she answered. "But as you can imagine, I adore working with kids."

"Of course you do. You're so compassionate and understanding. I could tell that about you the minute we met."

"Well, thank you." Sara felt herself blushing. *One of the most powerful women in America is showering me with compliments!* she gloated inwardly.

By the end of the interview, Sara was convinced that Tally was the kindest, most empathetic person she had ever met in her life. Whether she thought her son should attend The School was another matter altogether.

"I have one last question for you . . ." Sara hesitated. "It has to do with Montana's bodyguard."

"Quentin?" Tally asked with surprise. "The man's been with me for years. He's as gentle as a pussycat."

"Still, I have to tell you, we can't possibly allow a gun anywhere near The School."

"Not to worry. Quentin is a fifth-degree black belt in both tae kwon do and hapkido. He can take care of Montana and his little schoolmates with his bare hands and a pair of nunchakus, if you're more comfortable with that. The fact is, Quentin played linebacker at the University of Southern Mississippi and trained with the World Wrestling Federation, so he could probably help out with your phys. ed. program. Word on the street is, your athletic department could use a kick in the ass."

"I would have to clear that with the head of School," Sara answered politely.

"Ms. Nash, you have my word. Quentin is like a ninja. The School won't even know he's here."

"Well, we'll certainly have to factor Quentin into the equation when we consider your application, won't we? Do you have any questions?"

"Just one . . ." Tally demurred. "May I ask what The School's position is on Mother's Day and Father's Day?"

Sara had been waiting for this question. She was aware that

MOTBOB had initiated a national campaign to abolish Mother's Day and Father's Day on the grounds that they discriminated against children who might not have a mother or a father.

"As you have seen, The School truly embraces the spirit and values of the nontraditional family," Sara conveyed in her best National Public Radio voice. "We go out of our way to make sure our children feel free to celebrate these holidays by making cards for whomever they choose. We are also proud to have taken a leadership role in converting our Grandparents' Day into 'A Day with a Special Person,' sensitive to the fact that many children don't have living grandparents."

Tally seemed satisfied with Sara's answer. "So can I assume that The School would be open to supporting MOTBOB's initiative to celebrate Turkey Baster Baby Day on Thanksgiving?"

Sara was saved by the bell. Literally. Class was dismissed, and Brandi and Quentin were returning with Montana.

"Did my little butterball like The School?" Tally asked as she smothered her prodigal son between her prodigious breasts. Montana nodded eagerly, and Tally beamed at Sara, shaking her hand warmly as she headed off with her son. "Oh, don't forget about Rafael!"

"Rafael?" Sara repeated, horrified. Surely she hadn't been calling Tally's son by the wrong name this whole time!

"I'll have my assistant call to set up an appointment for shaping. The man works absolute wonders! Bye, now!"

Nervous about the traffic, the Dragers had arrived early for their interview at The Fancy Girls' School. One of Justine's associates greeted them and then whisked Zoe to another room to have a "chat" and do "a little work"—a euphemism for the in-house test they administered, which, in addition to the SAPS, was yet another method of separating the wheat from the chaff.

After an inexcusably long interval, Helen and Michael were ushered into Justine's chintz-filled inner sanctum and offered a seat on a pouffy sofa, where they were kept waiting another five minutes. Michael thumbed through the yearbooks and student newspapers (the standard admissions-office fare) while Helen, who was more interested in what was on the walls, inspected a small grouping of botanical prints, each of which was embellished with a flowery Latin inscription identifying the plant's genus and species.

"*Nymphaea virginalis.*" Helen laughed as she noted the name of one of the flowers. "It's probably the official school flower."

Justine finally rushed in, all blustery and out of breath, and then, taking a few more moments to tuck a few stray hairs into her ridiculously long braid, at last set herself down before them. The whole performance had been carefully orchestrated to impress the Dragers with the fact that, having received an unprecedented number of applications, she was unimaginably busy and was selflessly working day and night in order to give them the fair chance they so deserved.

"Well, at last. Here we are. Welcome to The Fancy Girls' School. I can't tell you how thrilled I am that you are applying for . . . Zoe . . ." She looked down again. ". . . for grade nine."

"So now . . . I see . . . Zoe likes to cook. She wrote in her essay that her father taught her how to make profiteroles. Ah, a girl after my own heart. Michael, are you in the food service industry?"

Come on, Michael, take the bait, Helen prayed silently.

"Yes, I guess you might say I have an interest in the culinary arts. I'm a producer for the Cooking Network."

As if the Pavlovian dinner bell had just rung, Justine's posture suddenly shifted from an indifferent slump to an upright state of alert as she flung her braid over her shoulder.

"I watch the Cooking Network every chance I get!" she squealed, then added, catching herself, "which of course is not often." A woman in her position could not possibly appear to have enough time to, of all things, watch television.

"I just love it, especially when the show features exotic locales. You're probably not aware of this, but I own a cooking school in Provence. I spend every summer there. Oh I forgot, you may have heard about it from Pamela. She has come to stay with us several times!" Justine enthused.

The Dragers pretended that this was the first they had heard about Justine's school, and then oohed and aahed over how wonderful it must be to spend every summer in such an enchanting part of the world. Hating herself for the sycophantic tone, Helen even went so far as to tell her they would love to look into attending one summer.

Operator that she was, Justine was three moves ahead.

"Come in June! I would love for you to see our place. It's just beautiful. Come to think of it, my home in France would be the perfect place to produce a program on Provençal cooking! I don't think such a show exists. Do you know of one?" She turned frenziedly to Michael, and becoming red-faced and rather damp, began to fan herself with their application.

Helen looked at Michael and thought, *Don't blow it, buddy; she's offering us a deal,* and then, not taking any risk, preempted him.

"Michael, what a great idea! You've been on the lookout for a new French show ever since Julia retired. This sounds like an excellent prospect."

Michael was slow on the uptake and stammered, "Was I? Uh, yeah, I guess I was. Hmmm. Provence, could be good."

"Let's continue this conversation soon over a pot-au-feu. Once I'm through with interviews, I would like nothing better than to sit down and talk puff pastry with you."

"Yes, that would be lovely," Michael responded politely.

They finished the interview and headed towards the lobby to meet Zoe, whom they found bubbling with enthusiasm.

"How'd it go, sweetie?" Helen asked, pleased to see her daughter's smile.

"Miss Bradford was really nice. She sings in a gospel chorus in Harlem every Sunday and invited me to come hear them. Can we go sometime?"

"That would be really fun," Helen answered cheerily. "What else did you talk about?"

"She asked me how I felt about going to an all-girls school after having been in a coed school for so many years."

"And you said . . . ?"

"Of course I was totally positive."

"Are you?"

"I don't know. I kind of got into the idea while I was with her. She's a graduate of The Fancy Girls' School and she seemed very cool."

"What else?"

"She asked me a lot of questions about my school. Do you think The School has a good reputation?"

"Absolutely," Helen answered automatically. *At least, it used to,* she thought. "What was the test like?"

"A little bit of math, which was pretty easy. And then I had to write a short essay describing a person who has influenced me in some important way."

"And you wrote about . . . ?" Michael and Helen both asked eagerly.

"Sara," she answered, disappointing them both. "I wrote about how she's taught me how to meditate and find inner peace."

Icchh, that's not gonna score big points at this school, thought Helen as they walked out in silence.

Once they were a safe distance from The Fancy Girls' School, Helen took Michael by the arm and whispered, "Do you get what happened in there?"

"No, what happened?" he asked. Zoe looked confused.

"The cooking school, location, shoot. What part don't you get?" she probed.

"You mean Frampton volunteering her cooking school as a location for a show I have no interest in?"

"Well, you've just got to get interested, or at least figure out how to fake it. Don't you see? It's so obvious. She'll accept Zoe as long as she thinks there's a possibility that you might produce a show at her school."

"Was I in the same meeting? Did I miss something?" Michael asked. He honestly had no idea how Helen had come up with such lunacy.

"Do I have to read you the subtitles?" she demanded impatiently.

Zoe looked perturbed. "Can someone fill me in on what's going on here?"

"Sweetie, it's just some adult nonsense. Believe me, the less you know about it, the better."

"Mom, how can you say that? How can it be better for me not to know what happened in YOUR interview when presumably it was about me and will determine where I'll be going to school next year?

If you don't tell me what happened in there, I won't tell you what happens in my interviews. Ever again." Zoe was inconsolably angry and refused to speak to her mother, while silently holding Michael's hand the entire way home.

As she walked two steps ahead of them, Helen wondered how much of the behind-the-scenes scheming they should be sharing with their daughter. After all, as Sara kept succinctly reminding her, "This is about Zoe." *Choosing* a school was about her, but getting her in was another matter. From the beginning, Helen had followed her maternal instincts and tried to shield Zoe from the underbelly of the admissions process, but today she had been blindsided by Justine Frampton's proposal, and now chastised herself for being so callous as to mention it in front of Zoe. She remembered the way she and Michael used to use spelling when they didn't want Zoe to know what they were talking about—a practice they foolishly continued long after she learned how to read. Like asking each other whether it was N-A-P-T-I-M-E at times when Zoe was cranky. Today she might as well have just spelled out B-L-A-C-K-M-A-I-L for all the sensitivity she'd exercised. Sara was right—she was being way too intense about this whole thing.

At breakfast the next morning, Helen informed Zoe that she would be picking her up after school to take her to Bertha's.

"Mom, that's ridiculous. I can go alone. She won't let you stay anyway, so what's the point of your coming?"

"Okay, okay. But I need to pay her, so I will meet you there at the end of your session," she invented an excuse.

Once her family had left and the beds were made, Helen sat down and sent an e-mail to Pamela.

Pamela,

We had our interview yesterday at The Fancy Girls' School and all came away feeling very positive. Zoe is much more open to all-girls than I expected and even thinks the uniform is cute! You may be right after all! Interview went well.

Justine was very enthusiastic. Please let me know what feedback you get.

Thanks,

Helen

That out of the way, Helen spent the day at home working on an exhibition proposal. As the afternoon approached and it was time to pick up Zoe, she changed clothes, spending more time selecting an outfit than she normally would for a pickup. After careful consideration, she chose a pair of olive-green wool slacks, the side zipper accentuating the flat stomach she'd honed at her thrice-weekly Pilates workouts, and a lemony V-neck sweater that revealed her well-defined collarbones and long neck. A pale-green quartz necklace tied the outfit together, she was pleased to note, both stylistically and coloristically.

Next she wrestled with her hair, pulling it into a loose French twist and then spritzing it with three of Zoe's hair products: one for hold, one for shine, and one for volume. What ever happened to the old-fashioned hair spray that held the answer to all three problems in one can? This seemed like either regressive technology or an ingenious marketing ploy. Bored with her own cosmetics, she rummaged through Zoe's makeup drawer and, finding a few flesh-toned creams and powders, applied several, hoping they would go undetected in daylight. Looking for a mascara, she came up with six choices; some were called lash builders, others called lash lengtheners—what was the difference? Selecting a lipstick was even more complicated; there were thirteen options that ranged from gloss to glistener, matte to shiny, neutral to vermilion. How did Zoe afford all this crap? She needed to have a talk with her about curbing her consumption, maybe establish some sort of cosmetic nonproliferation treaty.

A final glance in the mirror and she was ready to go.

There. Maternal chic, she thought as she grabbed Zoe's denim jacket and green plaid scarf. *Or is that is an oxymoron?*

* * *

Helen arrived at Bertha's a few minutes before the end of the session and let herself in. Zoe was hard at work on a math exercise, with Bertha right beside her, suggesting strategies for increasing speed and accuracy. When they finished the problem, Bertha delivered another rave review, music to the ears of a mother who had spent two hundred dollars for the session.

"I bet your services are in great demand, Bertha. You must have dozens of clients at this time of the year," Helen said to make conversation, delaying their departure.

"Hundreds," Bertha corrected her.

"We must know some of your other students. The other day when we left, your next appointment was arriving . . . a girl named Catherine?"

"Catherine Cashin?" Bertha asked.

"I guess so. We recognized her from a few school visits."

"Oh, yes. She's a lovely girl, very bright and creative. Nice, too. Poor thing. Her mother died last June, and now she has to go through this. I predict she'll receive preferential treatment, not to mention the sympathy vote, from our friends in admissions. Her mother's death will end up working in her favor."

How crass can you get? Helen thought, but suspected that Bertha was probably right.

"How's her father handling all this?" Helen ventured.

"Couldn't be better. Dad is divine. Not hard to look at, either," Bertha winked at Zoe, who was becoming impatient and embarrassed by her mother's probing. "Too bad. No eye candy today. They have an interview."

"Really, where?" Helen tried to conceal her disappointment.

"Mom, can we go now?"

When they returned home, Helen checked her e-mail. There was one from Pamela.

Helen-

Justine was comme ci comme ca about your interview. She said Zoe is a "reasonable" candidate and will remain on her "under consideration" list. She also said something about a television show that Michael wants to shoot in Provence. Come see me to talk about it. Tomorrow morning is good. Ten-ish.

Pamela

Scheduled to lead an admissions tour at The School at ten thirty, Helen arrived a little early, figuring that would give her time to speak to Pamela first.

"She's not in yet. I don't know what her schedule will be once she arrives. There are two other appointments on her calendar for this morning, and if she's late coming in, I'm not sure how her day will fall," Margaret explained politely.

Helen was annoyed. It was ten o'clock; school started at eight, and the head was missing in action.

"I would assume she's somewhere where she can be reached," Helen stated tersely.

"Uh, no, not really," Margaret answered haltingly.

"What would happen if there were an emergency? What if the kosher boy in the fourth grade accidentally mixed meat and milk at lunch and had a psycho-Semitic reaction that required emergency treatment? It wouldn't look good if Pamela were nowhere to be found, would it?"

Margaret was shocked. She had never known Mrs. Drager to be the confrontational type and wondered what was bothering her. There were plenty of other parents who behaved this way, especially parents of eighth-grade students who were caving under the pressure of the admissions process or whose psychopharmaceuticals needed tweaking. But Mrs. Drager had usually understood when meetings were postponed and was generally flexible about rescheduling.

Why the change in attitude? Margaret wondered. *I never pegged her as the Zoloft type, but this admission thing seems to make everyone crazy. Maybe a small dose of St. Mom's wort would help.*

Margaret knew exactly where Ms. Rothschild was this morning. She had left a voice mail message saying that she would be going to a dressage clinic at ten o'clock and might be in by eleven. She instructed Margaret to cancel her morning appointments and, by all means, tell no one where she was. Margaret was resentful; placating irate parents was not the way she had hoped to spend her day. She was tempted to confide in Mrs. Drager but restrained herself, knowing Ms. Rothschild well enough to know that could result in her losing her job. So instead she said, "She will be calling in. Is there a message I can give her?"

"Just that I was here, at ten-ish, as *she* suggested, and was surprised to not find her in," Helen said softening her tone.

After all, it wasn't Margaret's fault.

Dust mites, molds, pollen, airborne viruses, pollutants, and their deleterious effect on their daughter's immune system were the tedious subject of Sara's interview with the parents of the highly allergic girl, Silvia. By the end, she decided to "file them under 'never,' " but then wondered whether that decision could be construed as being discriminatory.

When Helen arrived to give them their tour and the couple was out of hearing range, Sara grabbed her arm and whispered, "Is allergic considered a disability?"

"Better check with legal on that," Helen replied. "These days you never know."

Sara introduced Helen to the Clarins and, as the three of them meandered down the hall, she returned to her office.

Leafing through the applications on her desk, Sara came across Oscar Whyte's. On a whim, she decided to call Benjamin Whyte to see what she could learn about the Manchester School, where he and Pamela had taught together many years ago.

"Hello, Mr. Whyte? This is Sara Nash from the admissions office at The School."

"How lover-ly to hear from you," he replied hyperamiably.

"I gather you have had your interview with Ms. Rothschild?"

"Oh, yes. She insisted that we do it at home so as not to discommode the wee one. So very considerate of her, don't you think?"

"Absolutely. She always knows what's best for the child," Sara replied, going to great lengths to veil her sarcasm.

"But it is a bit odd that we haven't yet seen The School," he said.

"I'm sure Ms. Rothschild will arrange for that soon," she assured him. "But I'm calling about another matter. I thought you might be able to give me some advice to pass on to one of our teachers who is moving to Manchester. She's interested in finding a position there and knows very little about the schools."

Fifteen minutes later she had heard more than she ever wanted to know about the Manchester school system, and Whyte still hadn't mentioned Pamela. She segued clumsily, "So the last school you mentioned, The Manchester School, is the one where you and Ms. Rothschild met, isn't it?"

"Yes, that was where we met. But she was Ms. Wickham then. It was before she married Mr. Rothschild."

For a moment Sara was silent. Pamela's marriage was news to her. Careful not to reveal her surprise, she continued, "Oh, right. Mr. Rothschild is . . ."

"*Was* the headmaster there, that is, until they were both asked to resign. That's an extremely shorthand version of a very complicated story. I certainly don't want to bore you with the details."

"Not at all," she said, thinking she would like nothing better than to be "bored" with the details. "Were you and Pamela friendly when you were both in Manchester?"

"Not really. She's at least ten years older than I, so we didn't run in the same circles. And her little, uh, escapade with the headmaster would have made socializing a bit tricky. I did my best to steer clear of the whole kit and caboodle. Running into Pamela last spring was a stroke of luck. Otherwise, I'm not sure how we would have coped with finding a school for Oscar. New York is trying under the best of circumstances. And now, as a forty-year-old father, I find it exhausting."

Bingo! That made Pamela at least fifty! If Sara could have kept this bloke talking, she might have learned Pamela's entire life story. But unfortunately, they were interrupted by a loud bang and a splatter.

"So sorry, got to ring off. The little kipper's gone and knocked over a crock of clotted cream."

Meanwhile, Helen was in the middle of the tour from hell—crawling through the bowels of The School with Silvia's obsessive-compulsive father, inspecting internal ductwork to determine whether the dust particle level exceeded DEP standards. Somehow he had convinced her that certain dust could have a negative impact on the growth hormones and brain cells of *all* children, not only his own allergic-to-practically-everything daughter. Helen was sufficiently spooked to get down on all fours and collect scrapings from the ventilation system for him to send out for testing, while his slightly saner wife waited upstairs. As they finished the ductwork, he pulled out a pocketknife and pried a few chips of paint from the stairwell walls in order to conduct a lead count. At this point, she realized this guy was a paranoid maniac and that, by crawling around with him, she was voluntarily acting as his enabler. Disgusted and disheveled, she called upstairs and got Brandi to come down and relieve her.

"Tell Sara I caught Legionnaires' disease and I'm suing The School," she said between coughs. She brushed the dust and debris off her clothes and marched upstairs to see if Pamela had returned. She had, and quite unexpectedly, Helen was granted an audience.

"I don't have much time. Bring me up to date on your progress," Pamela ordered as she distractedly shuffled papers around her desk, charm bracelet jangling with every movement.

"We had a tour and interview at The Safety School," Helen began slowly, and was immediately interrupted.

"She will probably not be accepted there because she is overqualified. Next."

Careful to conceal her dismay over Pamela's snappish verdict, Helen continued, "We have our tour and interview at The Progressive School next week."

"You will hate it. It's not for Zoe," Pamela said definitely.

"We go to The Bucolic Campus School the first week in November. I hear very good things about it. What do you think?"

"It is an excellent school. Zoe's test scores will have to improve enormously for her to be even considered. It's a stretch. Next."

"We're wait-listed for applications at both The Very Brainy Girls' School and The Downtown School."

"It is unlikely that you will clear either of those wait lists," Pamela asserted, still seeming to be more interested in something she was looking for on her desk than what Helen had to say.

According to Pamela, they had, for all intents and purposes, rejected or been rejected by five of their six schools, and it was only October.

Am I going to end up like Diane Spilcher? Brain-dead at Starbucks in the Paramus Mall? Helen panicked. She felt ill and wondered whether she actually might have contracted Legionnaires' disease.

"And what did you think of The Fancy Girls' School? *That* is, by the way, the only place Zoe belongs," Pamela declared with absolute authority.

"I told you we liked it very much. But will she get in?" Helen asked with trepidation, praying for a yes.

"It all depends."

"On what?" Helen asked cautiously.

"Justine's École de la Cuisine de Provence. Did you ask her about her cooking school or did she bring it up?"

"Michael was talking about his work and, out of the blue, she suggested that he use the school as a location for a show about Provençal cuisine. Don't you think that was a little presumptuous on her part?" Helen suggested.

"No," Pamela said bluntly. "Not at all. That is, if you are serious about Zoe going to The Fancy Girls' School."

"I thought that was the implication. I just needed a reality check," Helen said, struggling to stay composed.

"I'm not sure you *fully* understand what she has in mind. She is not only interested in Michael producing a show at her school; she also expects to star in the show. She is highly telegenic. You may not remember this, but when she was young, Justine had a recurring role on *Romper Room.* That led to her academic career. But her true love is *la cuisine.* You will be amazed by what she can do with a lamb shank."

Helen was taken aback. "This is crazy! You can't imagine the torture Michael goes through when he's casting a new show. Everyone and their mother gets involved in the decision: the network executives, the sponsors, the directors, producers, casting agents—and then they do focus groups to gauge the viewers' reactions. Justine Frampton isn't going to waltz in and get a starring role on the Cooking Network just because Michael recommends her. That would be an impossible promise to keep. Besides, we don't even know if the network will be interested in the show in the first place!"

"Then clearly, getting them interested should be Michael's first priority."

Helen couldn't believe she was having this conversation, and she knew that Michael would go ballistic when he heard about it.

"So let me get this straight. Justine told you, point-blank, that if Michael produces a show on Provençal cooking starring Justine Frampton, then Zoe will be accepted at The Fancy Girls' School?" She was incredulous.

"*Mon ami.* She is a bit subtler than that. She has informed me that she can only accept one student from The School this year. April Winter was to be that one. Since meeting you and Michael, her position has changed. Now she is saying that, under the right, shall I say, circumstances, the spot could go to Zoe."

"Do you think we would stoop that low?"

"The Fancy Girls' School is the best choice for Zoe, bar none. How low you will stoop is up to you. But keep in mind, admissions-wise, it may be your best shot," Pamela concluded, and stood up to dismiss her.

Helen was speechless and left Pamela's office without a goodbye. As she passed Margaret's desk, she grabbed her cell phone out of her bag and called Michael at his office.

"We have to talk. Now!" she shouted, while Margaret sat looking alarmed. *Is Mrs. Drager old enough to be menopausal?* she wondered.

"Shhhhh," Michael whispered as he gave Helen a light peck on the cheek. "This is the most delicate part of the procedure; the artichoke heart transplant."

Michael was on the sound stage at the Cooking Network shooting a segment for the season premiere of *The Epicurean MD.* They watched silently as the surgeon/chef performed an operation on the thorny-leafed vegetable and then stitched up the outer layer of the turducken. The process complete, Michael led Helen into his office.

"So what's so important that it couldn't wait until tonight?" he asked impatiently.

Barely able to breathe, Helen recounted her entire conversation with Pamela, as close to verbatim as she possibly could.

"Helen, this is extortion. People go to jail for things like this. I can't believe she really means it."

"I know it's crazy. But it's not like it was MY idea!"

"Of course it wasn't. I'm just having a hard time imagining Justine Frampton being *that* unethical, not to mention ludicrous. I can't believe a woman in her position would do this."

Helen was exasperated. "You are *so* naïve. Over the years I have learned to never underestimate Pamela in the sleaze department. And as far as I'm concerned, Justine is sleaze by association."

"Then there's only one thing to do: withdraw our application. Right?" Michael said uncertainly.

Helen hesitated. "I'm not so sure. Why can't we play their game? You could call Justine next week and tell her the network is interested in a new show about Provence. You set up an audition for Justine in late November and have a few meetings with her to look at location photographs, discuss recipes, and drool over her cassoulet. A few weeks later, you tell her that the film test was superb and everyone is gung ho. Throughout December and January you say you're working to tie up a few loose ends and are expecting the final go-ahead any day. The most important part is to drag out the final decision until after the admissions notification date, February twelfth. By then Zoe will have been accepted, and the show gets the guillotine."

"It sounds like an episode of *I Love Lucy*," Michael laughed.

"I guess there's a reason I always liked that show."

"You *are* kidding, aren't you?" He stopped short and stared at Helen.

"Michael, it's a wild idea, but just think—it would give us a sense of empowerment. I'm sick of feeling so helpless with this admissions thing. I'd like to be proactive for a change."

Michael shook his head in disbelief. "Is this my rational, competent wife talking? Helen, first of all, I would have to get approval from Xavier to even do the audition," he began.

"Xavier always gets excited about your ideas. This one should be no different."

She was right about that. "Okay. So we do the audition. There's no way it will be anything but ridiculous. Even she will see that."

"I doubt that she's that self-aware. She'll think she's brilliant whatever happens in the audition."

Michael had to admit she was probably right again.

"Please tell me you're not really serious about this, are you?" he begged one last time.

"Dead serious. That is, if you're willing to do everything in your power to get your daughter into The Fancy Girls' School. I know I am."

"And you accuse Zoe of being a guilt-tripper?" he countered.

Sara's Saturday began with a meditation class and would end with a shiatsu massage, so having to put in a few hours at the office didn't seem too onerous. She knew that she would have been better off doing some rigorous exercise and scheduling a haircut (not with Rafael), but had opted for the path of less resistance. Helen's repeated suggestions that she try Pilates was her way of hinting to Sara that her posture could use some work, and just the other day, Tally Easton had sent her a note offering her trainer for a few private sessions. Still, self-improvement would have to wait until after the admissions season.

The sheer enormousness of this year's applicant pool presented a particularly burdensome set of problems. Between the internal forces within The School, the external influence peddlers, and the applicants themselves, Sara was already suffering from the stress of being pushed, pulled, harangued, and cajoled. This was nothing new; she went through it every year and had more or less learned how to cope. But this year was going to be particularly grueling. The number of applicants was greater, the stakes higher, and the parental frenzy more frantic than ever. And the absence of a legitimate supervisor did not help matters, either. She worried about what would happen in January when selection time arrived. Felicity clearly lacked the sensitivity and sound judgment that was required to get the job done fairly and effectively. She certainly couldn't be counted on to be of any help. Should Sara assume that Pamela planned to play the wizard of Oz and mastermind the admissions process from behind the curtain?

That was too demoralizing even to contemplate. For the time being, she was better off focusing on more tangible problems, like what to do about the application for Alexander Trousdale, the LD, ADHD, HIV-positive son of the type A, hepatitis B, vitamin D–deficient trustee married to the CPA with TMJ and chronic PMS. With no solution in sight, she turned her attention to writing the last of the brief synopses of the applicants she had interviewed that week:

"Marina Rodriguez: Mother Puerto Rican, Father Nicaraguan. Physically aggressive (biter), verbally aggressive (screamer). Academically aggressive? (check KAT report). Overweight. English is second language. Parents self-employed. Own a taquitos truck. Cater school parties?"

Closing the file, she was startled to hear footsteps, but then hearing a familiar jingle-jangle, knew immediately who had arrived.

Pamela stuck her head in Sara's office. "What are *you* doing in today?" implying that it was unusual for Sara to work on the weekend, when in fact it was a Saturday appearance by Pamela that was a rarity. Always amused by the sight of Pamela in head-to-toe equestrian gear, Sara wondered if she was coming from or going to the stable—or wherever it was she went in that getup.

She responded politely, "Catching up on admissions business. And you?"

"Ditto. This year's eighth-grade students are going to be a nightmare to place. There are very few spots, and they're a bunch of losers and duds. Much to do. Ta ta." She waved and sashayed out, her breeches adhering to her buttocks in a most unflattering manner.

Sara shut down her computer, gathered her belongings, and locked her door. As she was leaving the building, she spotted a family of three, furtively approaching The School from the opposite direction. It was the milquetoasty Benjamin, his wife, Clarissa the milkmaid, and their peaches-and-cream-complected, probably lactose-intolerant son, Oscar.

So, the Whytes finally get their tour, conducted in their native language no less, she mused, glad to have somewhere to be that afternoon other than The School.

Politely squeezing past one another as they competed for the bathroom sink and mirror, all three members of the Drager household were bustling about. It was one of the rare mornings when, with all of them due somewhere at the same early hour, their living space felt especially cramped. But they chalked it up to one of the many sacrifices they made to live in New York City. Just as they were about to walk out the door, the phone rang.

"Is this Mom?" Bertha Kauffmann demanded brusquely. For some inexplicable reason Bertha always addressed Helen as Mom, even though she was nearly old enough to be Helen's mother.

"Yes, Bertha." Helen immediately knew it was she, since the only other person who called her Mom was beside her, tying her bootlaces.

"I have to be out of town next week for a conference, so I won't be able to see Zoe. Since the test dates are looming, I wanted to propose that for this time only, I double up the students and see two at a time for two hours. I thought I could work with Zoe and Catherine Cashin today from four to six, if that's okay with you. I spoke to Dad and he said it would be fine. The girls need help in the same areas, so it should work well."

Helen said yes and hung up.

As Zoe was leaving, she told her about the plan, got her approval, and then added, "And I'll pick you up at school to take you over there."

"Mom, please. I'm fourteen years old! I'm perfectly capable of going to my tutor without an escort!"

"I need to pay Bertha, and I don't want you carrying that much cash around. Besides, I have a few errands to do in her neighborhood."

"You mean Birdie. She wants us to call her Birdie," Zoe corrected her.

"All right, then. I will pick you up after school and take you to Birdie's," she said, emphasizing the "B."

"Oh, all right," Zoe muttered, "see you later," and rushed out without kissing her mother goodbye.

Before she walked out the door, Helen paused in front of the hall mirror to assess her ensemble. With the enticing possibility of seeing Phillip Cashin later in the day, she double-checked to make sure that her outfit was right. Deciding she could use a little more color, she tied an orange silk shawl around the shoulders of her black suit jacket, threw some extra lipstick and a few hair ornaments into her bag, and headed out. Her plans for the day included several hours of museum research, a very important lunch with a curator, and, time permitting, a few gallery visits before fetching Zoe.

It was a splendid autumn day, the kind that reminded Helen why she loved New York. The temperature was a perfect sixty-five degrees, the air was clear, the mood in the streets was gracious, and everyone she encountered throughout the day seemed to share her optimism—even the normally cantankerous museum librarian, with whom she managed to exchange a few pleasantries.

At noon she punctually arrived for her lunch meeting with Sir Basil Balfour III at his establishment of choice, The Pretensa Club. Sir Basil's grandfather was one of the founding members of the club, which, until recently, barred women from setting foot on the premises and, even more recently, amended its regulations to permit women to dine in trousers.

The club could not have been fustier. The wood-paneled rooms were gloomy, every window heavily shrouded with drab damask drapes that dated from the 1940s and had never been aired, let alone cleaned. The upholstered furniture smelled musty and was stained in so many spots that last year the club had to spend its entire refurbishment budget on antimacassars, just to conceal the damage inflicted by decades of accumulated hair oils. Helen noticed that the only paintings in the entire club were portraits of Balfours and other crusty former Pretensa members that, from their high perches above stair landings and fireplaces, stared down disapprovingly.

The lunch date had been scheduled months ago, Sir Basil being one of the busiest curators in town, at least to hear him tell, which he did ad nauseam. It was hard to believe that this was the first available date he had in four months, but she was grateful that he had agreed to see her. After all, as Helen had said when his assistant was searching for an opening, "He has to eat, doesn't he?"

Over the summer, while Zoe was away at camp, Helen had labored over an exhibition proposal, design, and budget that entailed numerous meetings with Sir Basil's staff. She was told he had approved her proposal, but since he had attended none of the meetings, she wasn't really sure he was fully briefed on the scope of her concept. Today's lunch was scheduled to bring him up to date and, more important, to finalize her consultancy contract. Unfortunately, Sir Basil had his own ideas about the lunch, specifically, a two-hour recitation on the subject of who's who in the international cultural elite, and how they each spent their summer vacations.

Over the blandest food imaginable, Helen was subjected to a detailed description of Lady Millicent Freestone of the Victoria and Albert and her gracious hostessing on Majorca; the archaeological tour of the Cyclades with Nikos Katzaganis of the Athens National Archaeological Archive that was to die for; the early neoclassical statue of Hercules Basil discovered in a shop on Naxos that looked exactly like Baron Beringer of the Munich Kunsthalle Pinakotek-der Architectonia; and the soiree on Sardinia at the home of the Fontinettis that included all the senior curators from the Accademia del Arte della Commune della Citta di Solingnaria.

Thanks to the rubbery chicken and her incessant nodding and smiling, Helen had developed a throbbing pain in her jaw. Would the man ever stop?

"But I must say, the most sublime part of my summer was the two-week cruise down the Nile with George Bartholemew," he prattled on. At last he had finally dropped a name she knew.

She caught it in midair. "I haven't seen George for years. Is he still at the museum?" she asked, eager for a chance to speak and release the cramp in her mandibular muscles.

"No, he retired last year. But I see him every month at The Bucolic Campus School board meetings. We're both trustees there," he told her matter-of-factly.

"Really," she responded casually, going out of her way to disguise her excitement. Continuing coolly, she told him about her daughter's school situation, careful to create the impression that The Bucolic Campus School was far and away their first choice, not letting on that she had not yet actually set eyes on the place. Having no doubt that a social climber of Sir Basil's caliber was well versed in the art of mutual back-scratching, she asked tentatively, "Would you consider writing a letter of recommendation for us? I mean, if you feel comfortable doing that. A letter from you would be so meaningful."

It worked; he was flattered. "Of course, my dear, it would be an honor. Let me get all the details," he said, and taking a tiny Florentine-leather book and expensive fountain pen out of his breast pocket, he wrote down the pertinent data while seeming to be genuinely pleased to extend her this kindness. After all, since Sir Basil was a card-carrying member of the old-boy network, she saw no reason why the old boy shouldn't network on her behalf.

That out of the way, they both ordered coffee and, for him, a soggy trifle. Helen was aware that they still had not discussed the exhibition, but having already asked him for a favor, she was reluctant to bring it up but then kicked herself for allowing one thing to get in the way of the other. Business was business; social lubrication was social lubrication.

As he signaled the waiter for the check, she reached into her bag and boldly plunked the contract down in front of him.

"Oh, yes, the exhibition. Let's just sign this and get you started," he said, and, fountain pen still in hand, signed on the designated line.

Breathing a sigh of relief, she thought, *And the best news is, my consulting fee will cover school tuition for at least a year.*

It was shaping up to be a productive and lucrative day. Helen spent the next few hours making the rounds of the uptown galleries, consciously avoiding Josh and Donald's, and selected a few shows to review for the monthly art journals. With about an hour to kill before picking up Zoe, she decided to walk. Along the way she passed the shoe store where she had seen the pumpkin-colored suede pumps last month, and having no trouble convincing herself that she deserved a reward, she went in and bought them. The shoes complemented the orange shawl she grabbed that morning, so she decided to wear them out of the store.

"Cool shoes, Mom. Can I borrow them?" Zoe said as soon as she saw Helen.

"Sure, sweetie," Helen replied, gratified to be at the receiving end of her daughter's approval for a change.

Having arrived at Birdie's before Catherine, Helen dawdled, searching her bag for her reading glasses, using Bertha's bathroom, and asking Bertha questions to which she already knew the answers.

"Is the SAPS a timed test?"

"Duh," Zoe said, "If we had unlimited time it wouldn't be so hard."

"Do you recommend Zoe take practice tests beforehand?"

"Get with the program, Mom. What do you think I've been doing with Birdie for the last two weeks?"

The bell rang, announcing the arrival of Catherine and her dad. Bertha brusquely performed the necessary introductions and then sat down to work with the girls, summarily dismissing the lingering parents.

In the elevator, they shyly smiled, and then, as Phillip formally introduced himself, Helen extended her hand, gave his a light squeeze, and then quickly retracted. For some strange reason, she felt herself blush, and was glad that the elevator light was dim.

"I was going to kill a few hours over coffee and a book. Can I buy you a latte or something?" he offered.

Her plans for the next two hours were up in the air and, if she were being completely honest with herself, did include this fantasy. "Sure, that sounds lovely."

They found the closest cafe, ordered their coffees, and sat down at a small table in the corner. As she removed her coat (his assistance gave her the first clue that he was one of the dying breed formerly known as gentlemen) and crossed her legs, he remarked, "Nice shoes. Great color."

She looked down at her recent purchase. "Thank you. I'm told that pumpkin is the new black, but I'm not so sure." Helen felt extremely self-conscious; she was not accustomed to a heterosexual man noticing, much less admiring, a woman's shoes.

"When I first met you at Bertha's, you looked familiar. I think we've seen you at a few of the schools we've visited. The Safety School and maybe The Fancy Girls' School?" she inquired, making conversation about the one subject she knew they had in common.

"I guess we're operating in parallel universes these days," he laughed. "Now that you mention it, I do remember you from The Safety School. We were in a tour group together with two other families. A few oddballs in that group, weren't there?"

They laughed about the Homer-bearing boy and his pompous parents, and both agreed they were glad that their daughters showed no interest in the other boy, the poster child for disaffected youth. Then came the inevitable: comparing notes about where they were each applying, and commiserating about the trials and tribulations of the admissions process. It turned out that their daughters were applying to several of the same schools.

"You've received an application from The Very Brainy Girls' School? That's odd. We're still on the wait list." She was concerned.

"I'm sure you'll get yours any day," he said nonchalantly, and quickly changed the subject. "I must say, going through this alone has been really difficult. This is a time when single-parenting feels really lonely," Phillip confided.

Helen was not sure if she should acknowledge that she knew his wife had died, so she merely murmured sympathetically.

"Since Margot died, Catherine and I have managed pretty well. I made some changes in my work so I can be around more, and she has been incredibly strong. But this admissions thing is not easy. It's exactly the sort of thing Margot was great at. She would have taken complete control of it."

Just like I have, Helen thought, and again wondered how Michael would possibly cope if she were to die.

"The single parents that I know often say that it's manageable as long as everything is going smoothly, but as soon as there's a bump in the road, they find themselves wishing they had a partner," she offered.

"That describes my situation pretty well. I find I actually enjoy being alone with Catherine much of the time. There are many days when I feel like Margot's death has changed my life in surprisingly positive ways, especially in my relationship with Catherine. We never spent this much time together when Margot was alive. But I sometimes worry that we're too close and emotionally dependent on each other. It might make it difficult for either of us to ever get involved with anyone else. You know, classic Electra kind of stuff. Do you think I should be concerned?" he asked her frankly.

Oh, my God, talk about a loaded question, Helen thought, weighing the possible answers.

Helen thought that Phillip sounded as if he was highly therapized, a trait she found extremely attractive in a man. Unless, of course, he went more than twice a week—that usually connoted *deep* neurosis. So few of the men she knew were able to talk about feelings, especially feelings about such emotionally complex subjects as father-daughter relationships or a wife's death. As he continued to reveal his concerns about single-parenting, she found her eyes going back and forth between his hands and his mouth, noting their grace and sensuality.

"Enough about me. Tell me about Zoe. Birdie always raves about her. She says she's one of her favorite students."

"She says the same about Catherine. I attribute her compliments to the fact that Zoe is always on time and I pay promptly, with cash," Helen laughed.

She talked for a few minutes about her daughter, being careful not to say anything that might smack of smugness. The last thing she wanted to do was to make it sound as if Zoe was having an easier time than Catherine because she had a mother. After a rather lengthy description of her daughter, she felt a pang of guilt when she realized she had neglected to mention Michael. Phillip must have sensed the omission, too, and asked about Zoe's father.

"My husband, Michael, and Zoe are quite close. He's involved with her to the extent that his career allows, and he makes an effort to spend a good amount of time alone with her," she explained awkwardly.

What's wrong with me? she asked herself. *I'm making Michael sound like an absentee husband. What can I say to make it clear he isn't? Or am I trying to make it sound like he is?*

To her relief, Phillip didn't seem to be particularly interested in Michael but seemed to be keen on knowing more about her work. They talked about the state of the art world, artists they liked and disliked, and the business of buying and selling art, about all of which he was current and knowledgeable. She asked him how it was that he knew so much about her field, and he explained that the financial firm that he ran was frequently called upon to advise its clients on art acquisitions. She had read quite a bit about the high-rolling world of art investment, and asked him the name of his firm. He mumbled the name: the Cashin Group.

Of course. That's the firm that pioneered the concept of collateralizing fine art, she thought, and then asked, "Is Joseph Cashin your father?"

"He was," he answered modestly. "He died three years ago."

So it's Phillip's firm now, she thought. *BIG bucks.*

Surprised to see that two hours had almost passed, they finished the last of their lattes and reluctantly wandered back to Bertha's.

Having collected their daughters, the four of them crammed into the elevator. On the ride down, Catherine suggested that the following week, when Bertha was out of town, they get together to drill each other on vocabulary. Both parents agreed, and Helen wondered how she might engineer the date to include another rendezvous with Phillip. As the four walked down the street, the girls, pitched forward under their thirty-plus-pound backpacks, chatting amicably, the preoccupied adults were silent. Phillip and Helen seemed to have arrived at a tacit understanding that their whereabouts during the past two hours must remain a secret.

Since Helen never made it to the grocery store, the Dragers resorted to doing what a disproportionately large number of New Yorkers do on any given night: ordered takeout Chinese food. Before the food arrived, they opened a bottle of wine and drank to Helen's success on finalizing her exhibition contract, and toasted Zoe on her can-do attitude and perseverance with the admissions process.

"And to me," Michael said, raising his glass. "I successfully pitched a show to the network execs today."

"Congratulations. Which one?" Helen responded enthusiastically.

"La Cuisine de Provence," he said, exaggerating the French pronunciation.

"Are you serious?"

"They all loved my presentation, especially Xavier." He smiled knowingly at Helen. "If I may say so, I was pretty great. I pulled out all the stops and, voilà, green light. Next step is to audition a certain chef," he explained, pleased with the unexpected success.

"Does that mean we get to go to France next year?" asked Zoe excitedly.

"It's a remote possibility," Helen replied, and then smiled at Michael. "Emphasis on the word 'remote.'"

While daintily nibbling watercress sandwiches and sipping Earl Grey's finest, Pamela and Felicity reminisced about their summer vacation in Provence. Tea at the Palm Court of the Plaza Hotel was one of Pamela's favorite weekend pastimes, and she was tickled to be in the company of such an enthusiastic guest. As the harpsichordist softly plucked "Lara's Theme" from *Dr. Zhivago,* Felicity hungrily devoured every pastry, scone, sweet, and savory that graced their three-tiered silver caddy.

"Don't you miss zee scent of lavender in zee morning?" Felicity feigned a nostalgic tone purely for Pamela's benefit. The fact was, a vacation in France had almost no appeal for Felicity, who had spent her entire youth dreaming of ways to escape her oppressive life in Marseilles.

"Frankly I'm beyond Provence. I'm thinking ahead. Warm sun, blue water, white sand. That's where I intend to spend my winter holiday. You will be joining me?" Pamela asked in a way that sounded more like an order than an invitation.

"I would love to," Felicity cooed coquettishly. "But on my salary I could never afford such a—how you say—extravagance."

"Didn't I tell you about your Christmas bonus? As associate head you are entitled to a substantial sum. That should cover a deluxe vacation and leave you with enough to buy gifts. So shall I make the reservations on St. Barts for two, *moi et toi*?" Pamela asked, fingering the tiny gold palm tree on her charm bracelet.

"Oui, oui." A bonus? She had been in her new job for less than two months.

"By December twentieth your admissions obligations will be out of the way and you can go on holiday with a clear head," Pamela told her.

"Er, about admissions . . . Sara Nash has not been so very—how-you-say—coop-er-atiff. She give me so little time and never tell me what is going on. I have to figure it all out for myself," Felicity lamented.

"Don't worry your petite *tête.* I guarantee, as soon as admissions are complete . . ." she drew a flat hand across her throat in a slicing motion.

"Does that mean you will fire her?"

"More likely, she will quit. I am in the process of making her job unbearable. Having her report to you must be *très* humiliating. That was a stroke of genius, if I may say so," she said callously. "How cheeky of Sara to even entertain the possibility of becoming head of School. Well, she has a surprise coming."

Felicity smiled and purred, "Whatever you say. You're zee boss."

"There's no question about that," Pamela said, nibbling a stem of watercress.

In faded jeans and a skimpy powder-blue shirt with "Brooklyn '54" emblazoned across her chest, and bare flesh exposed across her middle, Zoe emerged from her room on the morning they were scheduled to visit The Progressive School. Not in the mood to play the heavy, Helen swallowed her words, knowing full well that the kids at The Progressive School would be dressed the same way.

Upon their entering the school lobby, a powerful aroma immediately engulfed the Dragers—the herd of teenagers stampeding into the school was redolent of a pungent mix of body odor and cigarette smoke. Anxious to escape, they veered off towards the office, where they were greeted by the director of admissions, Soledad Gibson.

Soledad was a recycled hippie who grew up in a commune in Haight-Ashbury and, when Helen asked her about her curious name, explained that she was named after the eponymous California prison. She informed them that she would show Helen and Michael around the school while Zoe went on her own tour with a girl she introduced as Violet Parsonet. Zoe looked to her parents to see if they approved of her going off alone with Violet, who, with her extensive inventory of pierced body parts, alabaster skin, and waist-length, shoe-polish-black hair, was a dead ringer for Morticia Addams. In black platform-heeled boots, Violet towered over six-foot-two Michael and made Zoe look like the incredible shrinking freshman. Helen nodded and gave Zoe a pat on the back as she followed Violet into the dark recesses of The Progressive School.

"Have you ever thrown a pot?" Soledad cheerfully began their tour.

"Uh, no," Helen hesitated, not sure what she meant.

"Well, you have a treat in store for you! Let's go to the clay room." She led them up a flight of smoke-filled stairs.

"Is smoking allowed in the building?" Michael asked Soledad.

"The student council voted to permit smoking last year. Self-rule is an important component of our philosophy. We find it empowers the students," Soledad explained.

"It's illegal," Helen quietly said to Michael, but Soledad overheard and responded, "Technically not. As an independent institution we're entitled to set our own policy on such matters."

Helen coughed all the way to the third floor and, remembering the tour she recently conducted of The School's ventilation system, shuddered to imagine the objections that Germophobic Father would raise here.

They arrived at their destination, and Soledad ushered them into a dank chamber that smelled and looked like the inside of a cement mixer. The walls, floor, and ceiling were speckled with grayish-colored clay, requiring them all to walk on tiptoes to avoid the slime. Helen was very sorry that she had worn her new suede shoes.

"This is where the high school program begins—the core of our curriculum, if you will," Soledad began. "At the start of their first semester, each student is taught how to throw a pot on the ceramic wheel." She pointed to one of the filthy round devices in the middle of the room. "When the student is able to successfully center a pot, she is ready to graduate, if you will, to the second phase of the curriculum."

"I'm not sure I understand. Where do academics fit into this, ah, curriculum?" Helen asked innocently.

"Usually by the start of the second year, what is traditionally referred to as the sophomore year, the student begins the transition from the studio to the learning center. By spending the first year with the wheel, we insure that all of our students are *centered,* if you will, like a pot. We believe that students are not ready to tackle abstract concepts until they get in touch with their *cores.* The year in the clay room is the time and place where this happens. Let's go to the learning center now."

"She's kidding, right?" Helen whispered to Michael.

They traipsed back down the fetid staircase.

I'll have to have my suit dry-cleaned after this, Helen thought to herself.

They arrived on the second floor of the building, where the "learning center" was situated. The floor was divided into what Soledad described as "virtual classrooms," where small groups of students were assembled around large tables, conversing with teachers they called by first name only. Soledad explained that the academic program was "seminar-based" and that the students decided each week what the subject of the seminar would be. This way, she told them, the curriculum remained "vital and relevant at all times."

Gathered in one of the "virtual classrooms," they listened as a ponytailed teacher asked a group of students for their thoughts on the threat of global warming.

"I was really worried about it but, like, now that I know there's nothing I can do to stop it, I'm not letting it, like, ruin my life or anything," was the first response offered.

"That's one approach," the teacher said resignedly.

The Dragers quietly slipped out and declined Soledad's invitation to listen in on another "seminar."

"Are there papers, tests, homework, grades—any of that old-fashioned stuff we associate with high school?" Helen asked sarcastically.

"If the students decide they want to write papers or have tests, then, yes. Grades, no."

"So college admissions are done . . . how?" Michael asked.

"Oh, very successfully. All the progressive colleges know and love our students. It's not a problem at all."

"Oh, great. Zoe can choose between Antioch and Hampshire," Michael said under his breath.

Or The Rocky Mountain College of Underwater Basket Weaving, Helen thought.

They finished their tour and met Zoe, and as they were leaving the building, a male student in a Stone Temple Pilots sleeveless T-shirt and with a safety pin in his nose sidled up to Michael and whispered, "Want to score some bud, dude?"

Michael looked to Helen for guidance, not wanting to do anything that might humiliate Zoe.

"Keep walking," Helen said through gritted teeth.

Once they were out of earshot of the loitering students, Helen announced to both Michael and Zoe, "If The Progressive School turns out to be our only option, I swear to God, we'll be home-schooling."

A few days later, while painting posters for an upcoming choral performance, Zoe reported to Julian about her visit to The Progressive School and about her tour guide, Violet.

"Do you think most high school kids are, you know, having sex?" she asked. "Violet talked like they all do stuff."

"What kind of stuff?" Julian asked curiously.

"I'm not sure. It was hard to tell from the way she was talking whether she meant, you know, all the way or just oral sex," Zoe asked uncomfortably.

"I've heard everybody gives blow jobs in high school. It's not such a big deal," he explained.

"Do you think girls have to do that to be, you know, popular?"

"You're not gonna be popular if you don't do it, that's for sure," he told her. "I'm not sure about going all the way, though. I think maybe you can just do blow jobs and get by," he explained patiently. He knew that Zoe wasn't what would be called "fast" or a "slut," and he knew that was probably one of the reasons they were such good friends. While many of the other eighth-grade girls at The School were usually in some stage of either looking for a boyfriend, maintaining a boyfriend, or breaking up with a boyfriend, Julian was grateful that Zoe was content to spend most of her free time with him, particularly since there weren't many boys in his class that he considered friends.

With all this swirling around in her head, Zoe was developing a growing sense of dread about high school, magnified today by her visit to The Progressive School, which really turned her off. She was afraid that she was a total nerd compared to the kids there, especially Violet, and wondered if she was incredibly immature for not jumping for joy over all the "righteous" stuff Violet showed her, like the condom machine in the bathrooms and the make-out couch in the utility closet. She knew she didn't fit in there; she would never be happy in such a dirty, weird place surrounded by such freaky kids. Then there was The Fancy Girls' School. Did she fit in there? She was afraid she would always feel like the poor stepsister of all those superrich debutantes. And The Safety School was nothing to get excited about. It felt like the consolation prize. The Bucolic Campus School might be a possibility. She hoped she would like it when they visited next week. From everything she had heard, it might just be the best place for her.

"Why so blue?" Julian was concerned that their little sex talk had upset her.

"The whole school thing. It really sucks," she answered, and they both started to giggle at her choice of words.

NOVEMBER

A palpable frisson radiated from The School's auditorium as several hundred eager parents poured in for the annual open house. Every parent who was applying was advised to attend, as much to learn about The School as to further demonstrate their ardent interest.

As was the tradition, the evening program featured Pamela Rothschild in her award-winning dramatic role as Best Head of School. This was where Pamela truly shined, as she captivated her audience with a bravura, Power Point–aided show-and-tell that left even the formerly skeptical applicant praying for admittance. A long-term veteran of the open-house, Pamela knew that her audience was riddled with fear and doubt, a remarkable fact in light of their high professional status. She scanned the room, taking a quick inventory of CEOs, notable authors, tenured academics, and scions of society. As was her intent, her presentation managed to simultaneously assuage and fuel their collective insecurity.

Sara was relieved to play merely a supporting role at the open house; her only obligation was to stand up, smile, and tilt her head when introduced by Pamela at the conclusion of her performance. She was never one to enjoy the limelight and, in fact, had a pathological fear of public speaking. She knew she would need to get some coaching if she were ever to become head of School, a job for which a commanding presence was a prerequisite. In exchange for the exorbitant tuition, parents wanted assurance that there was an able commander in chief leading their little soldiers into battle.

Sara looked around to see if Tally Easton was present, not really expecting her to be, and instead spotted the Von Hansdorffs, sprechenzing with the Konigsbergs, the bony German lit professor married to the roly-poly Weimar scholar. Scanning the crowd, she caught Judith Ehrlich, a principal partner at Dickenson and Trollope, furtively sneaking a glance over her shoulder to the back of the room, where Abigail Groomer stared stonily ahead. Sara had recently learned that, as two of only a handful of women to hold senior positions in leading merchant banks, Abigail and Judith were often competing for the same deals. Just last week she had caught a segment on *Money Market* about the two women and how, for the first time in their careers, they had cobrokered the hotly contested $5.6 billion megamerger between Totco Ltd. and Kidzbiz Inc. But when it came to admissions, they again found themselves in enemy camps and resumed a contentious stance by sitting at opposite ends of the auditorium.

Felicity Cozette was also making a command appearance; Pamela had instructed her to attend with the promise of a "special something" afterwards that Felicity was hoping meant dinner at a very good restaurant. Pamela had taken to listing these dinners as "faculty development" on her monthly expense report, but oddly, Felicity was the only faculty member to be the beneficiary of these expenditures.

As President of the Parents' Association, Helen was required to make a cameo appearance in the role of most ebullient parent, a stretch given her current frame of mind. Year after year she had religiously attended these open houses, and she was tired of the formulaic palaver and the almost standardized question-and-answer segment. The play never changed, but the audience was becoming noticeably more demanding, like theatergoers who used to affably trot their young to The Paper Bag Players but now were satisfied with nothing short of the phantasmagoria of Cirque du Soleil.

As Pamela approached the podium, she adjusted her black and white faux ermine capelet, the one she wore when trying to look regal, though Helen thought it looked more like something out of Cruella De Vil's closet. She spent a moment posing grandly and then began her well-rehearsed presentation.

The audience was captivated by the rapid succession of schmaltzy slides: the rainbow coalition of children on the jungle gym, the two children pushing the disabled child in a wheelchair, and the handsome male teacher assisting an enraptured group of girls in a science lab. Helen didn't recognize any of the children or the teacher and wondered if the pictures came from some online educational image provider. She wouldn't put it past Pamela. Next up was a chart that allegedly diagrammed the student-to-teacher ratios, broken down by subject and grade, with dollars spent per child as a percentage of total tuition. Who cared that it was incomprehensible? It looked convincing. Pamela then asked the audience for questions, and a dozen hands shot up.

"Many of us will be sending our children to school for the first time and are concerned about their ability to separate. How does The School handle this transition?" a mousy woman standing in the back of the room asked.

Pamela knew the type: one of the "mothers who care"—so much that she had never spent a night away from her child, believed in the family bed, and was still nursing her four-and-a-half-year-old.

"One of our primary criteria in making admissions decisions is school readiness. *Your* readiness." The audience laughed as Pamela looked directly at Miss Mousy.

"This was not said in jest," she added sternly. "If we have any sense that you're not ready for school, then we're not interested in your child coming here." The audience giggled nervously, still not sure if she was serious.

"When it comes to separation, your children are taking their cues from you. I find that 'letting go' is usually more of a problem for the parent than the child. We provide a safe, inviting learning environment. It is up to you to model a positive attitude and give your child the message that you approve of this new place. If you cry, your child will cry. If you express enthusiasm, your child will, too. A smooth separation is up to you. Next question." She pointed to the slicked-back hair in the third row, a man who still thought *American Gigolo* was a great fashion moment.

"Could you speak on the subject of homework? The School has a reputation for having a heavy load in the early grades. What can we expect?"

She got this one every year. "Homework begins in first grade, with a fifteen-minute daily assignment, and increases by fifteen minutes each year thereafter. I personally monitor each teacher to make sure their assignments do not exceed that limit."

The parents whispered amongst themselves, counting on their fingers in an attempt to calculate the total time required of their homework-resistant children by the time they reached eighth grade.

What a crock, thought Helen, who knew without counting that Zoe was spending at least three hours a night on homework by seventh grade.

Another father asked, "How involved should the parents be in the homework?"

Helen found it odd that the fathers were asking about homework. Since when was Dad the designated homework monitor? Certainly not in her house. Probably just a ploy to appear involved.

"Let's just say, the minute you ask your child, 'How did *we* do on the math test today?' you're too involved," was Pamela's response every year.

That always got a big yuck. Next question.

"What are the expectations regarding fund-raising. Will we be hit up the minute we are admitted?"

Yup, thought Helen. She knew that a solicitation letter went out within a matter of weeks after The School received a signed contract and deposit.

"I hate to think my development office is doing any hitting—it's not permitted in school," Pamela tittered. "We strive for one hundred percent participation but make no demands as to amount. A small gift is as highly valued as an enormous gift." As if this group believed that.

"Could you speak for a bit about admissions out? What is your track record for getting all the graduates into the top high schools? I think it's safe to say that if we send our children here we're counting on that. Is that a fair assumption?" Mr. Belzer asked aggressively.

Sara singled them out of the group just in time to see the wife squeeze his knee and thought, *These two are painful to watch. Their love life must be really unpleasant. But then, who am I to criticize their love life? At least they have one!* Witnessing so many couples at their absolute worst had made Sara extremely cynical about the state of marriage, and she partially attributed her single status to this. She longed for a child of her own but was so repulsed by the behavior of so many of the couples she interviewed every year that it was hard for her to imagine entering into holy matrimony. After meeting Tally Easton, she wondered if maybe she should give some serious consideration to joining MOTBOB.

Pamela was prepared for the Belzer question. It, too, came up every year but, in the last few, had taken on a new level of urgency.

"Our top students go to the top ten high schools; others to second-tier schools; some even go to public school." There was rumbling in the room as parents readjusted both their positions and their expectations. "I can safely say that *every* child who graduates from The School goes to high school," Pamela added.

Oh, well put, Rothschild, Helen mused.

"What is The School's philosophy regarding learning differences? Do you have support for children with special needs?" asked Flora, the former nanny, now stepmother, of the Barton twins, who, Sara noted, was sitting alone.

"'*Vive la différence*' is my philosophy," Pamela proclaimed.

Oh, God, thought Sara, *here she goes.*

Pamela continued. "Children learn at their own rates, in their own ways. We respect those differences and support them . . . to a point. There may be a time when we may recommend a specialist for your child, but that would be a last resort. Most learning problems are manageable in-house—ours, not yours"—(titter, titter)—"and are often the result of laziness on the part of the child. A swift kick in the pants is often all that is needed."

The audience was hushed. They would have liked to believe this, but it certainly didn't jibe with much of the current literature. They all knew someone whose child was receiving help for some learning problem or another. But wouldn't it be nice if she were right?

Pamela wrapped up her presentation. "I invite all of you to stay for refreshments, which were made especially for you by our fourth-graders, who are studying the food chain. And feel free to introduce yourselves and chat with some of the members of our close-knit team," and then she introduced each one by name. "And make sure you meet Helen Drager, the president of our intrepid Parents' Association. She can tell you all our dirty secrets, tee-hee."

Nothing would give me more pleasure, thought Helen as she caught Sara's eye and shot her a sly sneer.

Sara spotted Clarissa and Benjamin Whyte, and just as she was about to say hello, Pamela appeared out of nowhere and, steering both by the elbows, gushed, "I'm just dying to show you the Jubilee cheese tray that Fiona Baggbalm sent me. You remember Fiona . . ."

Helen was cornered by the Swansons, who were bubbling over with excitement about Miranda's budding ballet career. They couldn't wait to tell someone that they had received a callback for a second audition for *The Nutcracker,* the pinnacle of achievement for a toe-shoe-and-tutu-toting mother.

"Should we let Ms. Nash know about this, or will you?" Mrs. Swanson inquired.

"I'll take care of it," Helen answered, as if it mattered after Miranda's swan dive last month.

"How many children do you have in The School?" Mrs. Swanson asked. How novel! An applicant who was interested in talking about a child other than her own!

"Just one. Zoe. She's in eighth grade, so this is our last year here."

"So you're involved in admissions now, too. How's that going?" Mr. Swanson asked.

"I'm sure it's the same for us as it is for you. Challenging. But we'll all get through it," Helen answered calmly.

"But you've got the added advantage of the head of School as your advocate," Mr. Swanson countered.

Not sure that was an advantage these days, Helen merely responded, "Of course. But all students at The School have Pamela behind them."

"At least you don't have to worry about your daughter doing something along the lines of what Miranda did," Mr. Swanson joked as his wife blanched, mortified at his reference to her worst nightmare.

"No. I don't worry that she will do *that*," Helen laughed. "But believe me, teenagers find plenty of other ways to express their anxiety," she added, rolling her eyes. Like go on a hunger strike à la April Winter, or some other equally self-destructive trick.

As Sara was busy nodding along to the Belzers' assertion that Sam's KAT scores would undoubtedly reflect his high level of intelligence, and telling Mrs. Yu that Daniel would be more than welcome to bring kimchee to school for lunch, Helen quietly slipped out the side door.

Arriving at The Bucolic Campus School for their tour and interview, it was hard for the Dragers to believe that this verdant sprawl was only a short drive from midtown Manhattan. The campus achieved a dynamic synergy between innovation and tradition through the harmonious coexistence of its neo-Gothic and modern buildings. Admirers called the school Oxford on the Hudson, in reference to its superb academic reputation. Critics called it The Bucolic Country Club, in reference to its enormous athletic facilities, far exceeding those of any other New York City school. In both respects, the Dragers were awed.

As they visited the brightly lit classrooms, they were struck by how studious the students appeared and how many seemed to be genuinely engaged in the Socratic method of learning, with teachers who taught with greater passion than they had seen elsewhere.

TEACHER: Claudia, how would you describe Charlemagne's foreign policy?

CLAUDIA: Ambitious. Ruthless. Inhumane.

TEACHER: Jacob, what do you think motivated this policy?

JACOB: He would say Christianity. I would say greed.

TEACHER: Christina, do you see any similarities between what

Charlemagne was doing in AD eight hundred and twenty-first-century world events?

CHRISTINA: Recent U.S. foreign policy, perhaps.

TEACHER: Perhaps. Hannah, would you agree with that statement?

"Now, that's teaching," Michael whispered as they snuck out to visit the art complex, an enormous new building containing multiple theaters, music studios, photographic darkrooms, video editing facilities, and anything else a creatively motivated student could possibly desire. The Dragers spent a particularly long time in the music department, in conversation with a delightful faculty member who spoke with equal zeal about Prokofiev, Charlie Parker, and Liz Phair. They were particularly impressed with the schedule of performances and were excited by the prospect of Zoe's getting caught up in the stream of cultural activity.

But it was the student body that impressed them the most. The kids looked clean-cut and healthy, in clothing and jewelry that unequivocally passed parental muster, and makeup that didn't require modification by a spittle-soaked, tissue-wielding mother. Tattoos and multiple piercings were the exception rather than the rule, and only a handful of students displayed the adolescent angst that Helen and Michael had come to associate with high school students over the past two months.

All three members of the Drager family simultaneously reached the same conclusion: that they at last had found the ideal school for Zoe. The question was, would The Bucolic Campus School think Zoe was the ideal student?

They were sitting in the reception area of the admissions office, quietly speculating about Zoe's chances, when they heard a burst of laughter emanate from the director's office. They looked at each other quizzically. The door opened, and a pleasant-seeming couple with their well-groomed son emerged and smiled at the Dragers, who, unaccustomed to such friendliness among competitors, were momentarily caught off guard.

Vincent Gargano, a Robert De Niro type (with the twenty pounds he gained for *Raging Bull*), barreled into the reception area.

"Nice to meet you folks." Mr. Gargano extended hearty handshakes all around. "Come with me kiddo," he said as he escorted Zoe into his office.

As Michael and Helen waited patiently, each with a book they were pretending to read, they periodically heard a peal of Zoe's laughter, a low rumble of voices, and another peal of laughter. Michael gave Helen a thumbs-up, and she responded with two thumbs-ups.

Twenty minutes later the door again opened, and out came a beaming Zoe with a jolly Gargano bouncing right behind. "Dad, you won't believe what Mr. Gargano has in his office!"

No, Michael couldn't imagine. Playstation Mega 6.1? A bevy of lap dancers?

"So your magnificent daughter tells me you're a Knicks fan," Gargano said from his office doorway.

My daughter, magnificent? Helen wondered if she had heard him correctly.

"Since I was about thirteen." Michael grinned broadly. "Been a season ticket holder since 'eighty-five–'eighty-six."

"Ewing's rookie year!" Vinnie enthused. "Then you gotta come on in and check *this* out."

One entire wall of Gargano's office housed a built-in floor-to-ceiling bookcase, which served as his own personal shrine to the New York Knickerbockers. Michael had never seen anything like it, besides the time he took Zoe up to Springfield, Massachusetts, to the Basketball Hall of Fame; Helen was surprised to see so much sports paraphernalia in the hallowed halls of this impeccably maintained academic institution. There were team pennants, authentic game-worn jerseys, autographed balls, and at least twenty photographs of Gargano standing courtside next to several gargantuan pituitary cases. Occupying its own place of honor in the middle shelf was a perfectly minted set of twelve bobble-head dolls. Each plastic figure was molded and painted in the exact likeness of a member of the 1969–70 World Champion Knicks basketball team. Michael was in his element.

Do not covet thy admissions director's collectibles. Michael tried to remind himself of whatever Commandment he was breaking. *Or was it, "Thou shall not worship false idols"?*

"So, Mike. How many can you name?" Gargano gently elbowed Michael in the ribs.

"I don't believe this!" Helen moaned under her breath. "A sports trivia entrance exam!"

"Piece a cake. No problema," Michael replied, not at all daunted by the challenge.

Helen was impressed with Michael's social dexterity. He usually hated being called Mike, Mikey, Big Mike, and normally made no bones about putting an offender in his place.

Come on, Michael. You've been training for this moment for thirty years, she silently cheered, like the pom-pom shaker she never thought she would become.

Michael started with the easy ones first. "Reed, Frazier, DeBusschere, Bradley, Barnett, Jackson . . . Riordan, Donny May, Cazzie, Nate the Snake Bowman, Stallworth, Bill Hosket, and . . ." He paused at the bobble-head in the number 16 jersey, causing Helen a moment of fret. "And John Warren."

"Way to go, Big Mike." Vince high-fived Michael. "Most people think it's Monroe."

"They're probably Nets fans! We didn't trade for him until 'seventy-one, and he wore number fifteen."

"Yeah, but not until 'seventy-two." Vince threw him a curve. Apparently, the exam was still not over. "What number did Earl wear before he switched to fifteen?"

"Thirty-three," Michael said without blinking, "After Cazzie got traded to the Warriors. Then Sly Williams wore it, and after that Patrick."

Gargano whacked Michael's shoulder with admiration. "Your husband's pretty good," he said to Helen.

"Thanks. I think so." She smiled. "And my daughter thinks so, too," she said, valiantly trying to turn the discussion to Zoe.

"Zoe is a terrific kid. Tell me about her." Gargano pulled up a few chairs and kicked off the interview with a series of thoughtful questions about Zoe's strengths and weaknesses. He couldn't have been more engaging and positive, and after twenty minutes of this, the

Dragers left with the impression that Zoe's acceptance was a foregone conclusion.

In the taxi on the way home, Helen laughed. "If Zoe gets in, I promise, you can get DirecTV, and I will never bust your chops about watching basketball ever, ever again."

"I won't get in! Ms. Rothschild said I have no chance of getting in to The Bucolic Campus School." Zoe was in tears. She had been stoic until they had left the campus, but once out of range, she broke down.

Helen, putting an arm around her, said, "I came away with a really good feeling about this school. Let's think about what we can do to increase our chances. I told you about Sir Basil being on the board and writing a letter. That will help. We can write a first-choice letter if we decide—I mean if *you* decide—it's your first choice. That might help. Your SAPS scores *will* be good. Bertha assures us. And Daddy certainly passed his test with flying colors."

Like that matters, Zoe answered silently.

That night, after Zoe went to bed, Helen sent Pamela an e-mail.

Pamela,

We all LOVE The Bucolic Campus School <u>and</u> Vincent Gargano. I'm sending him a thank you note right away. Will you be speaking with him? Let me know what our next steps should be.

Helen

"Michael. In the note to Gargano I think I should reference basketball just to make sure he remembers who we are. Give me an arcane little question for him."

"I don't know . . . How about, ask him what Knick players have worn number fifteen since Earl retired."

"Earl Monroe is retired?" Helen asked. "Is he in assisted living?"

* * *

While Sara was in her office reviewing the Dondi-Marghellettis' application before their eleven o'clock interview, Brandi buzzed to tell her that Lydia Waxman was on line five.

"Sara, how's it going?" Lydia asked at a fast clip—not one to waste anyone's time.

"Uhhch," Sara responded with the guttural sound she had heard Helen frequently use when referring to something distasteful.

"Just touching base on the Easton application. Tally just called me with a novel idea! She has offered to emcee a special Thanksgiving Day assembly in honor of all of The School's turkey-baster children."

"Do we have any?" Sara asked incredulously.

"According to Tally, several members of MOTBOB have children who attend The School," Lydia answered with the flippancy of someone who has a direct link to the world of celebrity gossip.

"She would know. But regardless, the answer is NO." Sara was appalled at the suggestion. "Besides, the older children are going to be serving a turkey dinner to their elderly friends from the senior center."

"Octogenarians! Excellent! They're one of Tally's largest targeted demographics." Lydia pulled out all the stops. She worked hard for her clients.

"Lydia, I'm not interested in using The School's community service program to boost Tally's ratings. If and when Montana Easton is enrolled at The School, we can consider Tally's generous offers. Not before."

"So you're saying that when Montana is enrolled—"

"Gotta run." Sara cut her off and hung up as Brandi stuck her head in to tell her that the Dondi-Marghellettis just called to reschedule their interview. Apparently there was a baggage handlers' strike at Malpensa, and they were stuck in Milan. That was good news. It bought her an hour. Brandi buzzed to tell her Helen was on line one.

Helen was in better spirits than Sara had heard her in for quite a while. Apparently they had had a very positive experience at The Bucolic Campus School yesterday.

"Yeah, it's a great school. If I could come back as a fourteen-year-old, that's where I would want to go," Sara responded with unmitigated enthusiasm, relieved that the Dragers had at last found a school they were excited about. Helen had become fairly high-maintenance lately, with her weekly tales of admissions travails, sharp critiques of all the schools, and complaints about her fellow bounty hunters.

"Then why is Pamela so negative on it for us? She acts like Zoe doesn't have a chance in hell of ever getting in," Helen complained.

"Because she has no influence there. Gargano won't even take her calls," Sara began.

"Why the hell not?" Helen interrupted angrily. "Sorry, I didn't mean to attack you."

Sara let it pass. "A few years ago she twisted his arm to accept one of her students, against his better judgment. Remember Andrew Procter?"

"The asshole all the kids called 'the proctologist'? The one who was suspended for putting cat turds in Miss Kohler's mailbox?"

"That's him, the little shit. Pamela totally fabricated his teacher recommendations and whitewashed his school record. Even though his SAPS scores were lousy, she painted him out to be a hardworking overachiever from a very wealthy family. She really did a snow job on Gargano and even implied that the father was a Procter of Procter & Gamble."

"I always thought that he was. I guess her propaganda worked."

"Well, he isn't. When Andrew got to The Bucolic Campus School, he was a washout from day one. They finally expelled him last June. Pamela's credibility with Gargano is shot."

"Oh, great." Helen was leveled by this news. "So why did she push for the kid when she knew he wasn't playing with a full deck?"

"Because his parents own a horse farm in Bedford where Pamela mucked about on weekends. They desperately wanted Andrew to go to The Bucolic Campus School, and Pamela promised she would get him in, knowing full well he couldn't cut it. You know how it goes with her—kid pro quo."

"Talk about moral bankruptcy. So where does that leave us, now that we've all gotten our hearts set on The Bucolic Campus School?"

"Just stay calm. If Zoe's the right fit, Gargano will figure it out. From what I hear, he's a straight shooter. Just keep Pamela out of the loop."

"Oh, no, I already sent her an enthusiastic e-mail." Helen immediately regretted her efficiency.

Uh-oh, bad move, thought Sara, but decided against upsetting Helen further. "Don't worry. She'll most likely ignore it. She's occupied with other things these days."

"Like what? What could possibly be more important?" She was getting shrill again.

"I've got to take this call. I'll call you later." Sara hung up.

Zoe arrived at the Cashin residence promptly at noon to spend the afternoon studying with Catherine. After a snack of frozen decaf mochaccinos and homemade macadamia nut chocolate-chip cookies, compliments of the Cashins' luscious blond au pair, the girls ascended to the third floor.

Catherine's three-room boudoir was the ultimate teenage girl's fantasy. An artfully scored suite of pinks and greens, it was composed of unmatched but ingeniously coordinated patterned fabrics, wall coverings, and window dressings. Florals, plaids, dots, and stripes were cleverly mixed to create an abounding cheerfulness that even spilled over into the bathroom and walk-in closets. But in addition to all the froufrou, no modern technology was spared; it was all just well concealed within custom-built cabinetry, retrofitted armoires, and curtained alcoves. The décor achieved a perfection that qualified it for a six-page spread in an upscale shelter magazine with the headline: SWEET DREAMS: A DEBUTANTE'S DREAM SUITE.

The family dog was curled up on a lime-green floral sofa surrounded by a collection of needlepoint throw pillows stitched with epithets like "Life without poochies? Don't even think about it!" and "What part of 'Woof,' don't you understand?" The Siamese cat, Mai Tai, was peacefully stretched out on the candy-cane-pink window seat, her steady purr in concert with the whir of the central air purification system that provided just the right level of white noise to obliterate the sound of the bustling city outside.

On seeing Catherine's dream suite for the first time, Zoe wasn't sure whether the strong reaction she felt was more awe or envy. The Cashin home seemed like a castle out of a fairy tale. But on the other hand, Catherine seemed in many ways just like her and her less affluent friends: no happier, no more self-assured, no better off socially. Did having so much money mean that life for Catherine was any easier? It didn't seem to be. She still had to study for the SAPS, she didn't have a boyfriend, she had a few zits, and she had fights with her dad (at least she said she did). *And* she had lost her mom.

"Let's get to work. We left off on the 'Ps.'" Catherine opened her vocabulary notebook and began.

"Pecuniary?"

"Having to do with money," Zoe answered without hesitation.

"Pretentious," Zoe read, as they took turns quizzing each other.

"Making an exaggerated show," Catherine answered.

"Philanthropy?"

"Donating, giving."

"Prurience?"

"Having lustful thoughts."

"I love this one. Priapic?" Zoe said, stifling a giggle.

"Oh, I know that. Ummm, phallic, resembling a phallus. Right?"

While her daughter was working on vocabulary in the ivory tower of the enchanted castle, Helen was ten blocks away, doing research at the museum. Scheduled to pick Zoe up at five-thirty, she packed up her notes and headed south. Catching a glimpse of herself in a shop window, she decided she looked a bit disheveled and would benefit from a fluff-up before making an appearance at the Cashins'. She popped into an overpriced Madison Avenue pharmacy/cosmetic emporium and began poring over a rack of lipsticks, sampling shades on the back of her hand.

"May I help you?" asked the frosted-haired saleswoman named Rena, her foundation forming tiny fissures as she spoke.

"I need a new color. Something . . . hmmmm . . . in the terracotta family . . . but not too orange," Helen responded, gaze fixed on the lipstick, careful to avoid eye contact.

"Let's try this one. May I? It's called Sienna Swinger." Rena wiped the colored tip with a tissue and gave Helen's taut lips a smear.

Pretending it was the furthest thing from her mind, Helen accepted the invitation to sit in the tall chair while Rena applied a light layer of powder, a whisk of blush, a swipe of mascara, and a dash of eye shadow.

"So, let's see. I used nude cream powder, hint of blush, cobalt sky eye shadow, Aubergine mascara. Look how great your eyes look." She held up a mirror, and Helen nodded in approval. "And Sienna Swinger on the lips. That comes to two eighty-eight forty-two, with tax. Will that be cash or credit card?" Rena was busy stacking all the costly little boxes into a neat pile on the counter.

"I'll just take the lipstick. How much is that?" Helen replied.

"Twenty-two fifty," Rena replied acridly as the San Andreas fault appeared on her brow.

"I'll pay in cash," said Helen as she counted out the exact change and scooted out the door. She hated to cheat Rena out of a commission but rationalized her meager purchase on the grounds that she often did work on spec, too.

She arrived at the designated street, an elegant block lined with the kind of graceful limestone maisonettes that normally house consulates, institutes, or the heavily shaded offices of esthetic plastic surgeons. Arriving at number 17, she was surprised to find only one doorbell, mounted on a shiny brass plaque, engraved in cursive: "Cashin."

Wow. Single-family dwelling, she mused as she pressed the buzzer. The immense door automatically swung open.

Anticipating a stiff greeting from someone named Jeeves, she was surprised; framed in the massive entryway was the ruggedly handsome Phillip, who, in brown corduroy pants and plaid flannel shirt, looked more Marlboro Man—nonsmoking, of course—than money manager. But the backdrop of the enormous foyer, with its checkerboard floor of black and white marble, sweeping Sleeping Beauty staircase, and refined grouping of French eighteenth-century Boulle settee and end tables, betrayed his true identity.

Holy shit! Is that a Monet? Helen wondered as she caught a glimpse of a lily pond over Phillip's right shoulder.

"The girls are just finishing up. Can I offer you a glass of wine?" he cordially suggested.

Helen glanced at her watch. "Sure, sounds lovely." She tried to act nonchalant as she followed him up the million-dollar staircase to the sitting room on the second floor, home to several more significant paintings and exquisite pieces of important furniture. This was, without question, the most spectacular New York residence she had ever set foot in, and she had been in some doozies.

"The girls seem to have had a productive afternoon without our Birdie," Phillip said lightly as he poured them each a glass of very old Bordeaux.

"Don't tell Bertha that; she'll charge us!" Helen replied as he handed her the gossamer-fine crystal. "Cheers." She raised her glass and looked straight at her host.

"Cheers," Phillip replied, holding her eye for a few seconds longer than the moment prescribed. She looked away.

"Wonderful painting." She wandered over to the sublime still life above the Louis XIV curly maple bombé. A Cezanne! She restrained herself and managed to act as though an encounter with a major impressionist painting in a private home were a common occurrence.

"Eighteen ninety-four. I've always thought it was his best year," she stated quietly but with the authority of a true connoisseur. Phillip nodded, clearly impressed. "Have these paintings been in your family for generations, or are you the collector?" she asked, fully aware of the multiple subtexts buried in this question: aristocracy or nouveau riche? Self-made or inherited wealth?

"My mother was the collector. She spent a lot of time in France while my father was still alive, mostly as a way to escape their marriage. She bought art to compensate for the pain he caused her by having serial affairs. I was their only child, so I inherited the paintings."

As Helen was speculating whether Phillip had also inherited his father's zipper problem, he asked, "Have you finished all of your interviews?"

"We had the last one last week. At The Bucolic Campus School. That is, unless we get an application from The Very Brainy Girls' School. Ours still hasn't come," she replied matter-of-factly. She continued to be perturbed by this but, still considering him more a competitor than an ally in the admissions arena, didn't share her frustration.

"Odd," he murmured, and changed the subject. "The girls asked me if they could get together over the weekend. Would you consider going to a few galleries with me while they hang out here? I would love to take advantage of your expertise and look at a few shows with you."

She was completely taken aback by the date-ish sound of his proposal, but fortunately, at that moment Catherine and Zoe came racing down the stairs, the floppy dog following behind. Zoe exuberantly threw an arm around Helen, nearly knocking the wineglass out of her hand, while Catherine demurely snuggled up to her father. Despite the fact that she came within millimeters of spilling a 1945 Mouton Rothschild (no relation) on an eighteenth-century Savonnerie carpet, Helen was thankful for the girls' intrusion, as it freed her from having to respond to Phillip's invitation. It may have been a casual suggestion on his part, but from her married perspective, it was a perplexing offer.

She smiled and thanked him for the glass of wine while the girls engaged in a melodramatic farewell.

On the walk home Zoe talked nonstop about the perfect Cashins and their flawless domestic arrangement.

Helen cleared her throat before asking, "I may be off base here, Zoe, but the fact that Catherine's mother died recently . . . doesn't that put a little damper on things?"

"If anything, the opposite," Zoe replied, knowing it was hurtful the minute she said it.

Helen *was* hurt and told her so.

"Just kidding, Mom. God, you're sensitive."

You're right, she thought, *I am.* "How did the studying go without Bertha?" Helen returned to a safer subject.

"We got a lot done. Catherine's really smart. Smarter than I am."

"You're very smart, too. Do you and Catherine discuss the schools you're applying to?"

"What do you think? Of course."

"Where do you think she wants to go?"

"She seems pretty set on The Very Brainy Girls' School. She kind of acts like it's a done deal."

"Hmmm," was all Helen said. She decided there was nothing to be gained from informing Zoe that the Cashin fortune would undoubtedly secure Catherine a place at whatever school she chose.

"I can't wait to tell Dad about their kitchen. Remember when we got the tour of the kitchen at Alain Ducasse? Well, triple that. And they have every gizmo and gadget you can think of."

"And staff, too?" Helen asked.

"Only two. Of course, besides Inga, the au pair."

"Of course."

"And their dog! Don't you think Stella is the cutest?"

"She is cute. What kind of dog is she?"

"A goldendoodle."

"A what?"

"A cross between a golden retriever and a poodle," Zoe explained.

"Talk about gilding the lily. What's wrong with just a plain old poodle?" Helen joked.

The phone was ringing as Helen unlocked the door to their apartment. She threw down her bag and grabbed it on the fourth ring.

"Vince Gargano at The Bucolic Campus School," the voice at the other end announced brusquely.

Helen gulped and then gushed, "Hell-o! How are you?"

"Fifteen is a trick question," the voice at the other end barked. "Right?" he demanded.

"I guess," she stammered.

"Whad'ya mean, ya guess? You wrote the letter?" he replied gruffly, and then chuckled.

She laughed nervously, finally remembering what this was about. "I'm sorry I don't know the answer. Michael added the question."

"Of course he did. Tell him the Knicks retired number fifteen for Monroe in March, nineteen eighty-six, and then retired the number again in March 'ninety-two for someone else, okay? And ask him who and have him give me a call," Vinnie demanded, and hung up.

Helen was shaking as she quickly tried to get the question down on paper before it slipped her mind. A call from the head of admissions of their first-choice school had to be good news on some level. At least they had made a connection, even though it was a tenuous one and had nothing to do with their child. She called Michael and, not finding him in his office, left a message, with details about Vince's call.

Zoe was in her room, getting started on the hours of homework she claimed to have, as Helen was sorting through the mail. She tossed all the junk, stacked a few magazines on the hall table, put bills in a pile, and then, curiously, opened the anomalous hand-addressed envelope—a personal letter these days was such a rarity. In it was a copy of the letter of recommendation that Sir Basil had written to The Bucolic Campus School, allegedly on their behalf.

Dear Mr. Gargano,

As a member of the Board of Trustees, I am writing to recommend a highly qualified applicant to The Bucolic Campus School. I must begin by saying that although I do not personally know the student, Zoe Drager, her mother is a close colleague and friend for whom I have the utmost respect.

I first met Helen Drager eighteen years ago when she was a researcher for the Hilden-Bonfiliac Collection where I was, at that time, chief curator. Helen was referred to me by my dear friend, Reginald Sinsabaugh, the then Professor Emeritus of the École des Artes Decoritivs in Reims, who was working with me on an exhibition of Sevres porcelain. Helen had previously studied with the late, great German Expressionist scholar, Ursula Heinengröder at the University of Berlin . . .

"Urrggg . . . ," Helen growled. "Why did I spend half an hour describing Zoe and all her attributes? This man is incorrigible. And useless!"

That night Helen read Michael Sir Basil's letter, the conclusion of which read:

Helen is highly intelligent, full of wisdom and common sense and of the highest moral character. Some of these traits must have found their way to her daughter. I am sure that you will give every possible consideration to offering a place to Zoe, if there is one available for her.

"At least it ends well," Michael, the optimist, responded.

"If your cousin Vinnie is willing to wade through the dunghill to get there. By the way, did you talk to him today?"

"Online. After I got your message, I e-mailed him. He IM'd me and we had a good ten minutes of quality cyber-bonding."

"Excellent. What did you talk about? Zoe, I hope."

"Actually, Zoe never came up. We were talking about how many Knicks players have had the same last name as U.S. presidents."

"Michael!" Helen was exasperated.

"What? Not counting the four Confederate Davises, he got six of eight—all he missed was Tom Hoover and Greg Fillmore."

"So where do things stand with us now?"

"He's supposed to get back to me with how many points Bill Bradley's scored in his college career."

"That's Bill Bradley the former presidential candidate, right?"

"Yup."

"Where did he go to college?"

"Princeton."

"Well, there's the in. There must be a way to use Princeton as a way to lead the discussion to Zoe." She wasn't sure how, but that was Michael's problem. "Otherwise, there's not much point in continuing to play this game."

"Okay, okay." He was starting to feel put-upon, now juggling two admissions directors. "Don't forget, I'm also working Frampton. The audition is coming up soon. Do you think we should have Zoe there? That way Justine can get to know her better."

"No way! Keep Zoe as far away from that as possible," Helen said adamantly. The audition was beginning to resemble a Camembert cheese. When the idea was fresh, it was just barely palatable; as time went on, it was becoming hard to stomach. She was almost ashamed to admit that it was her idea in the first place.

"Okay, okay," he agreed.

"But I get a sneak preview of the audition tape," Helen added lightly.

"Who knows? She may be brilliant."

"Ten to one she's not."

After a late dinner, both Michael and Zoe retired early, leaving Helen alone on the living room couch with a thick novel and a cup of tea. All evening she had looked forward to having some time to herself to think about Phillip.

As she drifted into a dreamlike state, she felt a vaguely familiar tingle, a sensation she had not felt in years. Her book fell to the floor as her recollection of the afternoon encounter assumed a cinematic quality. She replayed the scene over and over, searching for meaning in every gesture, in every word. *This is feeling like a PG-13 movie,* she thought abashedly. *I guess I'm safe as long as it doesn't become an R.*

In the twenty monogamous years that she and Michael had been together, Helen had rarely entertained thoughts of being with another man, except for the usual movie-star fantasy, like the George Clooney phase she went through after seeing *Ocean's Eleven.* Occasionally she met a man she found intriguing, but he invariably turned out to be either married or gay or both. Phillip was the first attractive man she had met in years who was neither. Not only was he available, he was also emotionally accessible and, to top it off, intelligent, sophisticated, cultured, and sexy as all hell. And the fact that he had one of the most extraordinary private art collections she had seen in years didn't hurt either.

What should I do about this weekend? she asked herself. *Since I'm sure he has no interest in an involvement with a married woman, and I have no intention of this going any further, is there any harm in spending a few hours with him on Saturday?*

"Helen, are you coming to bed?" Michael sweetly called out from their bedroom.

"In a minute. I just have a few more pages till the end of the chapter."

Gathering her files, Sara slowly and deeply inhaled and exhaled, attempting to relax before heading upstairs for the monthly "state of admissions" meeting, a tradition that was established years ago by Pamela and that today, for the first time, would include Felicity.

Deeply immersed in one of their little colloquies, Felicity and Pamela hardly acknowledged Sara's arrival until she rustled her papers and cleared her throat. They finally looked up as she seated herself, making an effort to sit up straighter than usual.

Skipping all pleasantries, Pamela demanded, "How many applications have we received to date?"

Sara assumed that Felicity's preoccupation with her split ends was an indication that she had no interest in the numbers, so she shifted the angle of her chair to face Pamela and addressed her report directly to her.

"As of yesterday we have received six hundred and two applications. We currently have forty-eight openings in Kindergarten, so my thinking is that we should accept sixty, assuming we can count on our usual eighty percent yield. About four hundred of the applications are from reasonable families with well-qualified children. That number is so large, it will make the selection process incredibly difficult. But the bigger dilemma is what to do about the unprecedented number of sibling applications we've received this year. There are thirty-seven. I don't see how we can accept all of them, but it's very tricky to decide which to reject."

"Who are some of the families applying with siblings?" Pamela asked. This was information she should have known.

"Newman."

"Accept."

"Fontaine."

"Accept."

"Moore."

"Reject. One Moore is more than enough."

"Nicholas is graduating this year. We'll only have one Moore if we accept Nina."

"Absolutely not. I couldn't take nine more years of Neal Moore's whining."

"He is a kveck," Sara concurred.

Pamela scrunched her nose. "Do you mean kvetch?"

"Right," Sara stood corrected.

"Please don't speak a language you are not proficient in. I get enough of that from this Kermit." She pointed her thumb at Felicity.

You should talk, Madame Pompadour, Sara thought.

"So our current policy regarding sibling acceptance is what?" Sara asked, wanting some clarification.

"Case by case. Make sure you run each one by me. By the way, I will have final approval on all acceptances, not Felicity."

"So, Felicity, your role in admissions is . . . ?" Sara inquired delicately. She found it offensive that Pamela talked about Felicity as if she weren't in the room.

"Negligible," Pamela finished the sentence. "She's still learning. And by the way, I will need at least three slots to fill at my own discretion. Preferably five."

That was a big number. Sara took a deep breath and then exhaled with a force that was packed with exasperation. Felicity stopped fiddling with her hair just long enough to shoot Pamela a what's-her-problem? look.

"And then there's the question of what to do about Tally Easton," Sara broached the ever delicate celebrity issue.

"What's the question? We accept Wyoming," Pamela responded definitively.

"It's Montana," Sara corrected, and realized it was a mistake to have brought it up. She decided it would be best to postpone making the Easton decision for as long as possible.

"Pamela. While I've got you. I got a call from the music director of The Public School. She has invited our choral group to partner with her choral group for a holiday performance."

"The Public School? Our chorus performing with a public school's? Why would you even consider that?" Pamela acted as though Sara's proposal were as absurd as if she had suggested that The School hire a white supremacist to chair its diversity committee.

"Because they have one of the best music programs in the city, and an award-winning choral group. She's proposed that over the next month we combine our two groups, have a few rehearsals, and perform together during the holidays. I think it's an excellent opportunity for us," Sara soldiered on.

"Can't you arrange the same sort of thing with a more reputable school? The Fancy Girls' School, for instance?" Pamela inquired.

"No. I can't. This is part of a pilot program that was initiated by the mayor's office. They're interested in fostering partnerships between public and private schools and chose The Public School and The School because of our outstanding music programs. The mayor has asked the combined group to perform at Gracie Mansion during the holiday season."

Sara knew all along that this would be the part that would hook Pamela, but got a certain pleasure out of luring her in slowly.

"Well, all right, then," Pamela agreed, feigning reticence. "Since it is such an unorthodox partnership for The School, I think it best that I be the one to inform the parents of the choral members."

At that moment, Margaret barged breathlessly into Pamela's office. "April Winter has fainted on the volleyball court. We called nine one one, and an ambulance is on the way."

"I keep telling Dana she *has* to get some breakfast into that child," Pamela responded casually. Taking her cue from her mentor, Felicity remained immobile as Sara dashed out, following Margaret back to the gym.

The students were nervously standing around in their gym uniforms and sneakers, relieved that they weren't the one on the floor getting mouth-to-mouth resuscitation from Ms. Nash. Sara had her CPR and Red Cross emergency certification and was just the person one would want to have on board one's lifeboat in the event of a shipwreck.

When the ambulance arrived, most of the kids backed up to clear the way, but a curious few stuck close to the action, anxious to see what would happen.

Pamela waltzed into the gym just as the gurney was wheeling April out, her face covered with an oxygen mask, two emergency medics in bright orange jumpsuits flanking her sides. With a morbid desire to pick up some titillating detail they could pass on to their friends, a few students trailed behind.

"Pamela, why don't you go in the ambulance? I'll call the Winters and then follow in a cab," Sara suggested.

"No, you go in the ambulance. I should stay back and make sure the children are all right," Pamela insisted. "They must be shaken up."

"Fine," Sara snapped, and hopped into the vehicle just as the siren began to wail.

Sara ended up spending the better part of the morning in the emergency room, where she remained with April until the Winters arrived. Both Dana and Patrick responded to their daughter's predicament with more anger than compassion, blaming her for skipping breakfast and not getting enough sleep the night before. Sara stood to the side as the resident psychiatrist explained to them that April was dangerously underweight and exhibited multiple symptoms of depression, but the Winters continued to insist that her problems were nothing serious.

After the third time that Dana sharply asked, "Where the hell is Pamela?" Sara decided it was time for her to leave. There was nothing more she could do for them, and she was beginning to feel unwelcome. Also, she had an interview scheduled in forty-five minutes that she really shouldn't miss.

On her way back to The School, Sara thought about how tragically April's adolescence was unfolding. As if the external pressures weren't enough, she had her parents' expectations to contend with as well and was literally being pushed to the brink of collapse. She remembered that there had been early signs of April's instability, when in first or second grade, she had pulled out all her eyelashes. Sara recalled thinking at the time that Pamela was irresponsible for not recommending psychiatric help to the Winters before the problem worsened.

Sara was grateful that in Kindergarten admissions the children were relatively oblivious to the external turmoil, and that sensible parents made every effort to shield their children from it. But there were always a few cases in which the parental hysteria filtered down, laying early groundwork for this type of anxiety-related disorder. She hoped that Helen wasn't exerting undue pressure. She would hate to see Zoe suffering like April.

At three-thirty that afternoon, Helen arrived at The School to take Zoe on a prearranged shopping expedition. As they traveled downtown, Zoe poured out all the gory details of April's collapse.

"We were in the middle of a volleyball game. She was on my

team. Ethan Weill whacked the ball really hard and it zoomed right over April's head. She jumped up to get it, missed, and then sort of crumpled on the floor. We stopped the game; Mr. Buff ran over and turned her over and she looked dead. But she was breathing. Marissa ran upstairs for help; I ran and got water while everyone else was just standing around looking panic-stricken. Sara came in and was giving her CPR when the ambulance arrived. I guess she's at the hospital now."

"Did she regain consciousness?" Helen asked.

"Not before she was taken to the ambulance."

"That's serious."

"No kidding. And, Mom, all the kids are saying that if she misses too much school she might not get into high school."

"Sweetie, if April's health is in jeopardy, treating her physical problems has to take precedence over everything else in her life," Helen explained gently.

"And what if she can't take the SAPS?"

"Zoe, none of that matters if she's sick. She's had problems for years that have gone untreated. The stress of admissions has exacerbated them, and hopefully now, the Winters will be forced to face reality and get her help. Her education may have to be put on hold for a while."

Zoe listened intently, thinking about whether what her mother said supported or disputed what some of the kids at school were saying today—that April was on the verge of committing academic suicide.

Their destination was SoHo—Manhattan's answer to the shopping mall. The cobblestoned former industrial district, lined with dignified cast-iron buildings, had over the past ten years been transformed by developers from a bohemian neighborhood into a retailer's paradise. Now it was home to every store in the lexicon of teenage shopaholics and on the weekends was overrun by tourists on the prowl for urbane consumables. And as far as Zoe was concerned, it was *the* place to shop.

The search for the perfect jeans and hooded sweatshirts was an activity they both enjoyed. Helen got vicarious pleasure from seeing her daughter look adorable in virtually everything she tried on, while

Zoe was glad to be the beneficiary of her mother's discerning eye and credit card largesse. After a fruitful hour at Zoe's current favorite store, Betwixt, Between and Beyond, they stopped for a break at a trendy snack bar, popular for its vast selection of panini.

"Mom, tell me about your boyfriends before Daddy," Zoe asked out of the blue.

Helen paused for a moment, wondering what sparked this question. She hesitantly began a shorthand version of her premarital love life, careful to avoid any mention of one-night stands and zipless fucks—not that there were many, but there were enough to edit when speaking to a teenaged daughter.

"So you were a virgin when you met Daddy?" Zoe inquired curiously.

"Uh, not exactly," Helen hedged. "But that's not important. The important thing is that we've been faithful to each other since we got married."

"Aren't you ever tempted? You know, by other men?" Zoe asked. Helen couldn't help but wonder if there were subconscious or, for that matter, conscious thoughts of Phillip Cashin motivating Zoe's query.

"Rarely. But neither of us would ever compromise our relationship or our family by doing something foolish," she stated definitively, for her own benefit as much as Zoe's. They both fell silent and nibbled on their prosciutto and mozzarella sandwiches, Helen wistfully thinking of missed opportunities, Zoe deciding which of her new outfits she would wear the next day.

When they returned home that evening, they listened to the numerous voice-mail messages that had accumulated in their absence, all related to April Winter's hospitalization. Zoe excitedly returned the calls from her friends, anxious to get filled in on the most recent developments, and later that evening, Helen reluctantly returned Dana's call.

"As president of the Parents' Association, I thought you should get a heads-up on the situation," Dana began what was clearly going to be a drawn-out saga. Helen took off her shoes, put up her feet, and quietly plugged in the hands-free headset so she could sort through the mail while Dana yammered.

"April experienced a momentary black-out in gym class at ten thirty-seven this morning and was rushed—by ambulance, I may add—to the hospital. Sara Nash accompanied her in the ambulance, although I would have expected Pamela to. You know, she and April have such a special relationship. Not only did Pamela not go to the hospital, she left The School for the ENTIRE day, leaving no number where she could be reached. Later in the day, when I called The School to speak with her, Margaret tried, as usual, to cover for her. She actually burst into tears when I cross-examined her, and still wouldn't tell me where Pamela was."

"It's now ten p.m. Have you heard from Pamela yet?" Helen agreed that Pamela's not calling was unconscionable, but it was hardly out of character.

"Not a peep. Patrick is furious and, after speaking to John Toppler, is talking about a lawsuit. But I think we should proceed a little more slowly. You know, learn the facts first. Then we can discuss legal action."

"Good idea." Helen was having trouble imagining what the charge would be. The School had responded to the emergency in a responsible manner. Pamela's lack of common courtesy? Rude, yes, but hardly a crime. As far as Helen was concerned, if anyone should be accused of a crime, it should be the Winters. The crime was called negligence.

"But more importantly, Dana, how is April?"

"Fine. She's fine," Dana answered too quickly.

"Is she home now?"

"They want her to spend a night or two there, for, er, observation," Dana said evasively.

Psychiatric, thought Helen. "So what can I do to help?" she offered sincerely.

"There's a PA meeting tomorrow morning. I would like to discuss the incident. So I thought I would call you tonight so you can put me on the agenda," she demanded rather than asked.

"You know, the agenda is always approved by Pamela before each meeting. Unless I can reach her tonight, I'm afraid I can't do that. However, I have no objection to your bringing it up at the end of the meeting in the open forum," Helen volunteered.

"I'll be there. But, uh, Helen, do you think I'm overreacting? I mean, I'm not sure it's exactly a good time to, you know, cross Pamela." Dana began to backpedal.

"Why is that?"

"You know, admissions," she whispered.

"Dana, you have a legitimate gripe. One thing has nothing to do with the other," Helen responded, but she knew damn well the two were intertwined. "So, I'll see you tomorrow at the meeting," and she hung up.

As she was leaving for school the next morning, Zoe asked her parents if she could visit April in the hospital after school that day.

"That's a nice idea. I know you and April haven't really been close friends for a while, but I'm sure she would really appreciate it," Helen said encouragingly.

"I think so, too. It was Julian's idea. He thought since she's in most of our classes, we could fill her in on what she's missed. You know, the homework and stuff."

"Home by six, though. You have that history paper due."

Helen arrived at The School to find a larger group than usual assembled in the multipurpose room. Normally about a dozen room parents attended the monthly PA meeting, but today there were close to twenty. All it took was a little drama to mobilize the troops; add to that a looming combat, and the entire stroller brigade came out in full force.

As the parents hovered around the coffee urn and Danish pastry, rehashing the story of who did (or didn't) do what during April's crisis, in waltzed Pamela Rothschild.

"Dana, dear, I am sooo sorry about April. I so wanted to get over to the hospital, but I could not for the life of me get out of my meeting. I was stuck in a room all day with the heads of the top ten city high schools discussing admissions," Pamela emoted histrionically.

A surge of whispering filled the room; the Rothschild worshippers murmured supportively; the skeptics raised their eyebrows and subtly sneered. Dana fell somewhere in between. Although even *she* was beginning to have niggling doubts about Pamela's integrity, she forced herself to brush them aside.

Helen called the meeting to order. "The first item on the agenda is the upcoming book fair. Cheryl, could you give us a progress report?"

"We've received donations of over five hundred new and used books for the fair. We're very long on fiction, so we're looking for more nonfiction—how-to's, cookbooks, travel guides, self-help, etcetera."

"I could ask Michael if the Cooking Network could donate some cookbooks," Helen offered in an effort to get the ball rolling.

"My sister just published *Children's Etiquette for the Millennium.* Maybe I could get her to donate a few copies," Lauren Toppler volunteered.

"I can name six families who should buy that book," Pamela tittered. "I have just received a box containing a dozen copies of Tally Easton's new book, *How to Tell Your Child that the Stork Is a Kitchen Utensil.* I'm sure there will be a few customers for those." There was murmuring in the room. Did that mean Tally's son would be admitted?

"Good. Anything else on the book fair? No. Okay. Next item on the agenda is the Holiday Festival. Janine, how is the bake sale shaping up?"

"I'm happy to report we have a long list of participants. At least forty people have volunteered to bake. The list of goodies includes petit fours, baklava, biscotti, a tarte tatin, three Boxing Day puddings—thank you, Pamela—a charlotte russe, pain au chocolat, red bean buns, and something called lou-kou-ma-des," Janine recited.

"Sounds Greek to me," someone in the back of the room joked. Fortunately, Irena Kaztanakas was not at the meeting.

"No sprinkle-covered Christmas cookies or red-and-green cupcakes?" Helen asked sarcastically. Apparently not for this melting pot of a parent body.

It was Pamela's turn to hold forth. "I have some exciting news regarding the Holiday Festival. Through my relationship with the mayor's commissioner of culture and my very close friendship with the music director at The Public School, I have come up with an innovative plan to combine our two choral groups. After several rehearsals, the group will perform during the holiday season at both schools and at Gracie Mansion. It is a once-in-a-lifetime opportunity for our chorus to expand its repertoire and its reach. This kind of community partnership has been a long-term goal of mine, and I am grateful to my colleagues in the public schools for agreeing to participate," Pamela explained with such conviction that she even had herself believing it had happened this way.

Helen thought this sounded like a great coup, and wondered why Sara hadn't mentioned it. Maybe it was news to her as well.

"Thank you, Pamela," Helen said solicitously. "The last item on the agenda is the annual fund-raising auction and gala, which will take place on February ninth. I know the committee has been working very hard on soliciting items from the entire community, and from what I have heard, they have an exciting evening planned. Denise Doyle-Gillis, our auction chair, will give us an update." Helen ceded the floor to Denise.

Denise boasted an MBA, a law degree, and a host of managerial and organizational skills. When her first child was born, she redirected all her energy into being a full-time mother, the kind who micromanaged her children's lives and shuttled her family in a Volvo station wagon bearing a bumper sticker that read, "Got breast milk?" The downside was, Denise could be bossy and possessed a self-assured stubbornness that made disagreeing with her almost impossible, and as a result, many of her committee members regularly griped about her abrasive and dictatorial style. But Helen recognized Denise's take-charge attitude as an asset and was thrilled to have her chair the auction committee, thereby allowing her to distance herself from this event. She had no time for that this year.

Denise took the floor. "The theme for this year's gala is 'A Night to Remember.' The Newman family has generously underwritten the cost of renting the magnificent party boat the *Spirit of New York*, which will sail around Manhattan for about four hours. In every way possible, we hope for the evening to feel like a glamorous cruise. The invitation will be designed to look like a boarding pass; the wait staff will be dressed in full dress whites; the decorations nautical and the sea breeze plentiful."

"Our goal is to raise three hundred thousand dollars. For those of you who are new to this, let me tell you how it works. The auction catalogue will contain approximately fifty items that have all been donated to The School. The donor of each item will establish its value so that when the sale begins, the auctioneer knows where to start the bidding. If all goes accordingly, there will be several people interested in each lot and the bidding will raise the sale price of the item way above its value. The auctioneer will accept bids in increasingly large increments as the sale price increases. Does everyone understand?"

"What was the highest-priced item last year?" a new parent asked.

"I think it was the walk-on part in a Woody Allen film. That went for eighteen thousand. Right, Helen?" Denise answered.

"I think that was tied with the sixth-graders' stained-glass window," said Helen.

"Oh, I remember that. It was spectacular. The battle scene from Thucydides' Peloponnesian War."

"Denise, can you tell us what some of the highlights will be this year?"

"Let's see, there's the week in Tuscany at a Medician villa for eight to ten people, cook and child care included; lunch with a Hollywood agent, who will read and critique a screenplay; a parking space in front of The School. There's no limit as to how high that could go. And there are many of the always-popular classroom projects. One of this year's more spectacular is the ginkgo-wood canoe carved by the seventh-graders out of the tree that fell in front of The School during Hurricane Doris. Oh, and I can't forget the four-day weekend at the Winters' Telluride ski chalet. Is that confirmed, Dana?"

"I'll have to get back to you on that," Dana replied curtly. Denise looked annoyed as she scribbled a question mark on her list.

"And of course, The School's famous six-course Provençal dinner for twelve prepared by our own Pamela Rothschild!" Like a game show host, Denise ratcheted up her voice with each item.

Compliments of Le Bon Take Out, Helen said to herself. She knew for a fact that Pamela cooked none of the food she pawned off as her own at her celebrated dinner.

"Who will the auctioneer be this year?" someone asked.

Pamela responded instantly. "The same as last year—I got us Alasdair MacIntyre from Christie's," once more taking credit for something she didn't do. Through a friend at the auction house, Helen had been able to convince Alasdair to return—a minor miracle after the humiliation he suffered last year when an inebriated parent repeatedly badgered him about what he was wearing under his kilt.

"Can we ask him to wear a royal naval officer's uniform this year instead?" Denise asked, anxious to maintain her theme throughout.

Helen, sensitive about wasting time, let it pass. "We still need volunteers for all of these events. Please, everyone let the committee chairs know what you can be counted on to do. Before we finish up, is there any new business?" Helen asked, looking directly at Dana Winter.

Dana began, "I want to thank everyone for the outpouring of support I have received since my daughter's, ahem, accident in gym class yesterday. I am happy to report she's absolutely fine. The diagnosis is a teensy-weensy case of anemia, and she'll be back at school next week. Several members of The School staff performed admirably, and I am grateful to those individuals." Her sphincterlike lips tightened into a constipated grin. Pamela's saccharine rat-on-me-and-April-gets-in-nowhere smirk wasn't lost on Helen, who thought that there was no doubt—these two understood one another completely.

Brandi was out at a chiropractor's appointment that morning, leaving Sara alone to field calls from the dozens of applicant parents who, looking for ways to distinguish themselves from the pack, phoned with flimsy queries.

MS. FIFE: I just wanted to make sure you got our thank-you note.

SARA: Yes, I did. Thank you.

MS. FIFE: You did realize Lukie wrote it himself, didn't you?

SARA: That was pretty clear.

MS. FIFE: Had we told you that he does calligraphy?

SARA: *You call that calligraphy? Who are you kidding?* No, I don't believe you had mentioned that.

MS. WONG: Did you get a chance to listen to the recording of Timothy's piano recital?

SARA: Not yet.

MS. WONG: I think you'll enjoy it. That is, if you like Beethoven sonatas.

SARA: I do generally enjoy Beethoven. Particularly when it's played well.

MS. WONG: Timothy's teacher said he's ready for the Junior Philharmonic.

SARA: Really. Who's his teacher?

MS. WONG: Mr. Wong.

SARA: Oh.

Thankfully, Brandi finally arrived, relieving her to attend to her interview with the thrice-rescheduled globe-trotting Dondi-Marghellettis.

"I'm glad to finally meet you." Sara warmly shook their hands and ushered them into her office.

Fashionisti personified, the couple were dressed and accessorized head to toe in haute couture. Despite the chilly November weather, he was sockless in alligator loafers, and she was bare-legged in open-toed mules. Her delicate feet and tan legs were those of a woman half her age. And was that a toe ring? How risqué! Even their eyewear approached new heights of chic: his blue and architectonic, hers magenta and feline.

I would look like a complete dork in those glasses, Sara thought. But it was their lustrous dark hair that Sara admired most as she reached up and stroked her own coarse, dry locks. *There must be something to that Mediterranean diet,* she thought, and began the interview.

"You are quite a peripatetic family, aren't you?"

"Si, si molto peripatetico," Livio laughed warmly, flashing his dazzling teeth. "We like very much to travel."

Great smile, she thought. "Do you see yourselves settling in New York now that Aurora will be starting kindergarten? We wouldn't want her to enroll at The School if you don't intend to stay here, at least for a while." She spoke more slowly this time, not sure about their English.

"No, no, of course not," Guiliana responded at a fast clip to demonstrate her fluency. "We have just purchased the Palazzo Hotel on Fifth Avenue. Livio and the children will live there, and I will do most of the traveling alone. Livio loves New York, even more than Roma," she added enthusiastically.

So he's a stay-at-home husband? wondered Sara. *Or is it a stay-at-hotel husband?*

"New York *con i bambini* is verry gooood," Livio added.

"Tell me about Aurora," said Sara.

"Ahhh, Aurora," Livio began in the tone of a completely smitten and overindulgent father. "*Mi angela.* The sweetest girl to ever walka de earth."

Guiliana, the pragmatist, knew that wasn't a good answer, and added, "She is bright and creative. Warm, loving, and, oh, happy as can be. Extremely sociable as well. The moment anyone meets her, it is love at first sight. When we go to Milano, Capri, Genova, Portofino . . ."

Sounds like the complete line of Pepperidge Farm cookies, Sara thought.

"Tell me a little about Aurora's language skills," Sara probed, concerned that with the parents' predilection for peppering their English with Italian, Aurora might not be conversant enough to communicate with her peers.

"She is absolutely trilingual: Italian, French, and English," Guiliana answered.

"She speaka Italian *a casa,* with mama, papa, and baby Bruno. She learna de French froma de concierge. And English, well, she speaka English with you." Livio smiled broadly and gestured with both hands, palms up, as though offering his firstborn to Sara, which, in essence, he was.

Between Livio's charm, Aurora's excellent language skills, and Guiliana's direct manner, Sara ended the interview with a positive view toward the Dondi-Marghellettis, assuming that Aurora performed well on her interview and KAT. Pamela would be pleased. She had a long-standing desire to enroll a child of hoteliers, for reasons both personal (vacation freebies) and fund-raising (auction donations). And then there was Simone Savage, who was pushing hard for both this family and the Von Hansdorffs. Sara already knew she would accept only one, and with all else being equal, the choice between the uptight Austrians and the happy-go-lucky Italians was a no-brainer; why opt for Sturm und Drang when she could have la dolce vita?

So far, April's only visitors had been her parents, who had been hanging around, wringing their hands and coaxing her to eat, as though all that was needed to restore her to good health were an infusion of calories. Throughout the day they had taken turns venturing out on foraging missions, each time returning with baskets of fruit, boxes of fancy chocolates, and platters of sandwiches, all of which had so far gone untouched.

Later that afternoon, when the Winters were finally called into a meeting with the docs and shrinks, and Julian and Zoe arrived unannounced, April seemed genuinely pleased, telling them how relieved she was "to at last get a break from the parental unit and their tedious attempts at force-feeding."

Like most normal kids, Julian and Zoe were ravenous after a day at school, and at April's urging, they gorged themselves on her assorted goodies. She secretly planned to pretend to her parents that she had eaten all the food while they were away, thinking that would get them off her back.

Zoe was disturbed by April's appearance. The hospital room's harsh fluorescent lights highlighted her waxy skin, colorless, thin hair, and grayish teeth. Her collarbones protruded angularly from the open neck of the pale-blue hospital gown, and her scrawny arms lay lifelessly by her sides, barely able to support the intravenous needle attached at her wrist. It was hard to believe she had even been standing upright on the volleyball court just yesterday.

As they ate and drank, Zoe and Julian made a concerted effort to cheer April up by recounting the events of the day.

"Heather and Kevin broke up during lunch," Julian offered.

"Wow, really. They've been a couple forever," April responded, the flatness of her voice belying the feigned interest she professed.

"Yeah, since, like October," Zoe agreed.

"Oh, we have to tell you about history class today," Julian said, trying hard to come up with a humorous tidbit that might amuse her. "Mr. Heller was lecturing about the Roman Empire. Every time he mentioned Julius Caesar he looked at me and accidentally said 'Julian Caesar.' Michael Connor passed a note to Bobby Lehane that said: 'Heller's got a hard-on for Toppler,' and Mr. Heller intercepted it. He was so freaked out, he dismissed the class."

"I feel bad for him," April sympathized with the teacher, not finding the story at all amusing.

"You're right. That was really mean of Connor," Julian answered, sorry he brought it up.

"Oh, did you hear that John Bushman was suspended yesterday?" Zoe changed the subject.

"No, what happened?" April looked worried.

Zoe pressed her knee against Julian's. This was hard work. She forgot how humorless April had become in the past year or so.

"He stole a copy of the algebra test, made copies, and then tried to sell them. Marissa squealed on him and he's out for the rest of the week," Zoe giggled, but April looked upset.

"It's not like it's the first time Bushman's been suspended. Remember the time last year when he came to the seventh-grade dance blotto?" Julian and Zoe laughed, and April stared.

"When do you think you'll be back in school?" Zoe inquired, tired of trying to be entertaining.

"It depends. The doctor from the psychiatry department told my parents I should go to a residential program for a few months, but since they refuse to accept the fact that I have an eating disorder, I don't think that will happen. The emergency-room doctor told them

I fainted from anemia, which is true, so all they're interested in discussing is how to raise my iron levels."

"Well, you know what they say: de Nile is not just a river in Egypt," Julian quipped. Zoe forced a laugh, but April didn't crack a smile.

"I'm a little scared about what will happen if I go home," April confessed in a voice so low Zoe had to lean over the bed to hear her.

"What do you mean?" Zoe asked.

"My parents are pressuring me so much about high schools, and with the SAPS coming up next month, I just feel like I might freak out completely," she quavered, and started to sob.

Julian took her hand and stroked it. "Believe me. When it comes to feeling pressure from parents, I can totally relate."

Zoe watched Julian with admiration, realizing he had a much better handle on this than she did. Her parents could be pains but were nothing compared to the pressures these two were dealing with.

"Maybe you should tell them you can't handle it and need some therapy. If you don't get in anywhere, you can always spend an extra year at The School. A few kids have done that in the past," Julian suggested.

"My parents would sooner I die," April whispered, turning her gaze towards the wall.

"I don't know. The school stuff just seems so irrelevant if you're sick," Zoe offered, remembering what her mother had said.

"April, you're skeletal. You weigh less than eighty pounds. You can't be expected to go through this now. The pressure is intense," Julian added emphatically.

"How are you guys handling it?" April whimpered, tears welling up in her eyes.

They looked at each other before answering. "Depends on the day," Zoe answered. "It's a roller coaster. I have a good interview, like last week at The Bucolic Campus School, and I get psyched and think it's going to be fine. Then I take a sample SAPS test and do poorly and think there's no hope."

"Mine is a lesser-of-two-evils situation," said Julian. "First I visited Extrover Academy and felt like a yeshiva boy at a Cape Cod clambake. And my gay-dar registered a total zero—not one queer on campus. Then my dad tells me he's getting his partner to push for me at Mannington—you know, the school that put the 'M' in 'machismo'—and I get totally suicidal," he said, and then immediately regretted his choice of words.

"Well, my mother is *fixated* on The Fancy Girls' School. Ms. Rothschild said they have only one opening, but my mother is convinced they will accept me 'cause we went to some pathetic cooking school last summer that's owned by their fat-ass admissions woman," April explained.

Zoe was startled. She'd been considering The Fancy Girls' School as well and hadn't known there was only one opening. But if April dropped out of the picture, the spot could conceivably be hers. Zoe was ashamed she'd let such an evil thought even enter her brain, especially at a time like this. She leaned over and gave April an impulsive compensatory kiss on the cheek as she wished her a speedy recovery.

"What a surprise!" Dana Winter squealed as she returned to find April with her friends.

"We were just leaving," Zoe said, anxious to avoid conversation with the nosey Mrs. Winter. " 'Bye, April. Take care."

As Zoe and Julian were walking home, they ran into Zachary Harmon, a normally laconic friend of Julian's from camp who was a freshman at The Bucolic Campus School. The three stood and chatted for a few minutes and, of course, talked schools. When Julian told him that Zoe had applied to his school, he suddenly became highly animated.

"The Bucolic Campus School kids have the most awesome parties. Too bad you weren't there in seventh grade for the Bar Mitzvahs. Julian, did I tell you about Jake Moskowitz's? His was the one at the Trump Lloyd Towers. There was tons of caviar, a sushi bar, a crepe station, a deli counter, hot dog stands, a Slurpee machine. It was like, you name it, they had it. They had a live band *and* a DJ. There were fortune-tellers, an amazing magician, face painting, a casino, all kinds of video games. Some of us snuck in some booze and got totally wasted. It went on until like two a.m. It was totally awesome."

"Sounds like a blast," Zoe responded sarcastically. She was both offended and intrigued by the concept of these lavish parties. The most extravagant Bar Mitzvah she had ever attended was Ben Wachtel's black tie at Tavern on the Green. But it didn't begin to approach that level of coolness, especially because her parents had attended, too.

"But you'd be there for the sweet-sixteens! They're supposed to be stellar," Zachary added.

"Can't wait," Zoe said flatly.

Both Michael and Helen were at home to witness Zoe's stormy entrance. She threw her coat and backpack on the floor of the living room, dove onto the sofa, buried her face into a pile of throw pillows, and started to whimper, quietly at first, and when no response was forthcoming, upped the ante to full throttle. Helen glanced at Michael and, with a mere raise of an eyebrow, asked "Whose turn?" and he pointed to her. She went over to the sofa and slowly rubbed Zoe's back. The heaving sobs gradually subsided, and Zoe sat up and wrapped her arms tightly around her mother, reminding Helen that despite all signs to the contrary, Zoe was in many ways still her little girl.

"Was it upsetting to see April?" Helen asked gently as she stroked Zoe's hair.

"No. Yes. But that's not the problem. The problem is a jerk named Zachary Harmon."

Both parents logically jumped to the same conclusion about Zachary, but while Michael was instantly ready to hire a hit man, Helen was all ears. So that when Zoe caught her breath long enough to tell them about the orgiastic Bar Mitzvahs, Helen was able to respond constructively while Michael was still talking about going to the mat with Zachary for making his daughter cry, regardless of the actual reason.

"So you're upset because you think this means that all the kids at The Bucolic Campus School are decadent party animals?" Helen asked gently.

"That and lots of other stuff. I just keep thinking that there's no school that's right for me. Or that will accept me," and the sobbing began anew.

"Sweetie, you know that's irrational. Everyone finds a place that's right for them. One boy's report on one outrageous party shouldn't color your whole opinion of The Bucolic Campus School. That might not be your crowd, but I'm sure there are plenty of kids there who are more your type. C'mon, you're smarter than that. Let's stay focused on making sure you do everything possible to get into *all* of the schools, and then you'll be in the position of having a choice."

"Talk about pressure," Zoe said, wiping her nose on her mother's shoulder, reminding Helen of all the years she had unknowingly walked around with stains on her shirt when Zoe was a regurgitating infant.

"Mom didn't mean it that way. She meant that if you can possibly manage to maintain a positive attitude, we'll all feel better throughout this process."

"No, I didn't," Helen said angrily. "I meant that Zoe needs to work as hard as she can for a few more months to get what she wants. It's not about making us all feel rosy; it's about directing her energy in a positive direction. Once she gets in, then she can decide where she wants to go. Zoe, it's not worth getting worked up each time you meet some jerk or hear some scuttlebutt."

Both Michael and Zoe were silenced by Helen's harsh directive. A few seconds passed, and then Zoe picked up her backpack, dragged it by the straps across the floor to her room, and closed her door, not quite slamming it, because that violated house rules, but loudly enough to make her point. Helen exhaled audibly, and Michael scratched his receding hairline.

"That time of month?" he inquired.

"It's mine, so it must be hers, too. It's a cruel god that synchronized our cycles."

"I'm glad I'm going away this weekend."

"You are? Where?"

"I told you months ago. It's the annual staff retreat in the Berkshires, remember?"

"I forgot. That will be nice for you," she said falsely, registering her momentary feelings of resentment.

* * *

Later that evening Helen lightly knocked on Zoe's door and found her hunched over the computer, still at work on her history report, "Why There Were No Female Gladiators in Ancient Rome."

"Do you need help finishing up? I could proofread for you," Helen offered.

"No, thanks."

"Do you have any tests tomorrow?"

"No."

"Are you hungry? Can I get you a snack?"

"No, thanks. I just want to finish and then go to sleep."

Helen was exasperated but, not one to go to bed with unresolved anger, stood behind Zoe and massaged her shoulders.

"I heard some good news today about the choir." Helen told her what she learned at the PA meeting about The Public School.

"Cool."

"Has Sara told the group about it?"

"Uh-uh."

"So you never got to tell me, how is April?"

"Depressing."

"Do you want to talk about it?"

"Not now, Mom. I've got to finish this paper," Zoe answered impatiently.

"You're right. I'm sorry. Just one more thing. What are your weekend plans?"

"Catherine Cashin invited me over. We'll do some test prep and then hang out. That is, if it's okay with you." Zoe's method of making up with her mother usually entailed a kind of deferential rapprochement.

"Fine. Just fine. Good night, sweetie."

"Night."

Helen buried herself in paperwork. She got out the application-tracking spreadsheet and updated the status column.

SCHOOL	PHONE #	DIRECTOR OF ADMISSIONS	STATUS
The Fancy Girls' School	674–9876	Justine Frampton	Michael to schedule audition
The Progressive School	563–9827	Soledad Gibson	Sent thank you (no thank you) note
The Bucolic Campus School	475–8392	Vincent Gargano	Michael bonding with V.G.
The Safety School	498–5937	Shirley Livingston	Sent thank you note
The Very Brainy Girls' School	938–8475	Eva Hopkins	STILL waitlisted for application!! Called again. No progress.
The Downtown School	483–8473	Taisha Anguilla	Gave up

She then checked her e-mail and found two from Pamela.

Helen:

I spoke with Vince G. at The Bucolic Campus School. He and I are VERY close. He said that they have only a few openings and will have to be ULTRA selective this year. He has no memory of you or Michael but said Zoe "seemed like a decent kid." He said, "Pamela, for you, I will take a second look." So, you shouldn't get your hopes up, but I will keep on pushing.
What's new with you and Justine Frampton?

The second e-mail from Pamela was addressed to the parents of the eighth-grade students.

To All:

A few reminders as we move forward through the admissions process.

1. Everyone must give all recommendation forms to my assistant by the end of next week. We have many forms to process and need as much time as possible to assemble a superlative package on your child.
2. Do not, I repeat, DO NOT, solicit outside letters of recommendation for your child. As we say in admissions, "The thicker the file, the thinner the applicant." You don't want your child to be perceived as thin, do you?
3. Declare your first choice school to me, AND ONLY ME, as soon as possible. This information will remain confidential, to be used at my discretion.
4. STOP comparing notes. I'm TIRED of parents coming to me saying "he said . . . she said . . ." No one is served through rumor-mongering. M.Y.O.B.
5. Lastly. Trust me. It will all work out.

Helen rubbed her eyes, rested her head in her hands, and stared at the screen. Between the strain of keeping pace with Zoe's mood swings and navigating Pamela's mental minefields, Helen had lost all sense of equilibrium. This emotional roller coaster reminded her of the way she felt at twelve years old, careening out of control on the Coney Island Cyclone, screaming at the top of her lungs for the ride to stop. That same nausea and dread visited her now, causing her heart to race. She wondered if this was what a panic attack felt like.

As Sara and her choral group entered single file through the metal detector, they were given the once-over by the The Public School security guard and asked to present I.D. before they were permitted access to the auditorium for their first rehearsal.

The imposing cinder-block building reminded Zoe of pictures she had seen of industrial buildings in formerly Communist Eastern European cities with impossible-to-pronounce names like "Walbrzych" or "Plzen." And like Zoe's image of these gloomy foreign places, The Public School felt mysterious and alien, with a sense of lurking danger in the locker-lined halls and dimly lit classrooms.

While The School had lace curtains, The Public School had metal security bars. While The School smelled of ammoniated cleansers and floral-scented air fresheners, The Public School smelled like a mildewed mop. While The School had Miss Lulu, the seventy-eight-year-old receptionist who had held the same job for twenty-seven years, The Public School had armed Officer Braxton. While The School had a rooftop garden and playground, The Public School had a crumbling asphalt surface and a broken basketball hoop. But The Public School did have a Steinway grand, a lively accompanist, and a *full-time* choral director, which was more than they had at The School.

Elizabeth Marcus and Sara Nash greeted each other warmly as the two camps of students eyed each other warily. The School's choral members were predominantly Caucasian; The Public School's were not. But that was hardly an issue for any of these New York children, for whom diversity was more than a buzzword—it was one of the stated goals of many of their parents when they chose to commit to an urban life.

The schism between the two groups was primarily stylistic. When preparing for their first meeting, Sara had given her group strict dress code guidelines and even went so far as to require each of her students to wear khakis and white shirts. As soon as they arrived, she realized she had erred on the side of unnecessary caution. Her kids looked (and felt) like a Republican youth group in contrast to the Red Diaper babies of The Public School, most of whom were dressed in much cooler stuff. There were boys in he-man-size jeans that hung so low that the crotch was near their knees. And girls in tank tops that revealed both bra straps and belly buttons, with hip-hugger pants so south of the navel that an unruly pubic hair was visible here and there.

Sara and Elizabeth acted quickly to remedy any sense of divide in the room by having their students introduce themselves one by one to the group, alternating between the schools.

"Hi. My name is Nicholas Moore. I play computer games, except our computer's been broken for a while, read sci-fi, and sing. Duh, why else would I be here."

"I'm Shanika Thomas. I'm five eleven. I play center on the basketball team, I write poetry, and I'm a kick-ass rapper. The kids all say I rock."

"My name is Marissa Doyle-Gillis. I'm a member of the tristate junior gymnastic team, the Junior Junior League, a Model UN delegate, winner of The School's spelling bee for four consecutive years . . . What else can I tell you about myself. I have a 3.85 grade point average, I was nominated for the New York State—"

Sara interrupted. "Thank you, Marissa. Let's keep our introductions brief. Next?"

"I'm Jorge Ortiz. I play shortstop on the baseball team. I'm eighth-grade class vice president and I'm a straight-A math student. That's why my nickname is 'the Wiz.' "

"I'm Julian Toppler. I love Broadway musicals, the Miss America Pageant, and everything Judy Garland ever did."

The Public School kids raised their eyebrows, but to The School kids he was just Julian, someone they knew they could always count on for a laugh.

"Hi, I'm Max Kupka. I love to sing in choral groups. I come from a family of violinists, so I guess you could say music is in my blood."

Elizabeth whispered to Sara, "His parents immigrated from Prague, where they were both principal violinists in the national symphony. He's a really special kid."

"Hi. I'm Zoe Drager. I also love to sing with a choral group, and that's why I'm really happy that we have formed this alliance with The Public School."

Sara smiled. *Leave it to Zoe to say just the right thing.*

By the time all students had their turn, everyone was laughing and more or less relaxed and, following the director's instructions, fell into choral formation and began singing a few tunes. At the end of the rehearsal a few students were called up to speak with the directors and were assigned solo parts. Zoe was picked to be one of the soloists, as was Max Kupka.

Zoe thought that Max was really cute. With curly brown hair, pale-green eyes, and unblemished skin, his looks were as close to cherubic as was possible in a fourteen-year-old verging on puberty. His voice was about to crack, and his moustache was about to sprout, but until that happened, to Zoe he was Eros incarnate. In faded blue jeans, navy V-neck sweater with a white T-shirt beneath, and round horn-rimmed glasses, he was, as Sara described him later to Helen, "delicious."

Zoe was sure he hadn't looked twice at her until, at the end of the rehearsal, when they were standing together waiting for the director to give them their sheet music, he said, "Zoe, right?"

"Yeah?" She was both unsure how to respond and thrilled that he remembered her name.

"Hi," he said, and put out his hand to shake hers.

"Max, right?" she asked, and shook his shyly. He smiled.

He is A-dorable, she thought, putting the emphasis on the A, as she had heard Julian do many times when talking about a boy they both thought was attractive.

Ms. Marcus handed them each their music.

"See you next week," Max said casually.

"See you," she answered, melting.

When Sara's group returned to The School, she handed out the rehearsal schedule and congratulated her children on their good behavior. They discussed the selections for the program, and before dismissal she added, "By the way, there will be no dress code for future rehearsals. My mistake."

"I see you do know how to fold," Helen teased Michael, who was packing for his office retreat in the Berkshires. "Is there some way I could get you to do that on a daily basis?" She was tired of being the family laundress and complained about it regularly.

"Helen, my appearance this weekend is important. I'm in management. I have to look the part."

"And *I* do six loads of laundry a week, drop off and pick up your shirts from Hip Fong's, and schlep suits to and from the dry cleaner so that you look the part every day."

"What's bothering you? You've been so bitchy lately."

"I'm sorry. I'm just feeling really drained. I'm so sick of the admissions crap. I can't *wait* until it's all settled. I hope a relaxing weekend will help."

"I'll be away. Zoe will undoubtedly have made her own plans. So you can do whatever you want. See some friends. Go to the movies. Get a massage. Spend the weekend in bed."

The following morning, Helen was awakened by the tinny sound of rain pounding against their bedroom air-conditioner, the start of a weekend that was forecast to be dreary with scattered showers. Michael was out the door by seven, Zoe was still asleep, and Helen was enjoying the luxury of lingering in bed. She loved a rainy day, especially when there was nothing she *had* to do. If she were feeling industrious, she would devote the day to the activities of daily life that never seemed to get done during the week, like mending, closet cleaning, checkbook balancing—the list was endless. And she was also toying with being virtuous and checking out the new class at her Pilates studio called Willpower and Grace, which everyone was raving about. And there was the new Almodovar . . .

"I hope it's the way you like it." Zoe wandered in sleepily, her offering of coffee in hand.

Helen was touched. "Just the fact that you made it means it'll be good. Thank you." She stretched out her arm, inviting Zoe to tuck into bed with her.

Zoe curled up and started to twirl a lock of her mother's hair, a habit she developed as a nursing infant and still sometimes unconsciously did. Helen was blissful.

"What are you doing today, Mom?"

"This. Can we just stay like this all day?"

"No way," Zoe laughed. "I'm due at Catherine's at noon. We're planning to study for a few hours and then hang out. She invited me to sleep over. Can I?"

"I don't know. With Daddy away I thought you and I might do something together tonight. What do you think?"

"Okay," Zoe answered with a hint of disappointment.

"I'll take you over to the Cashins' and then go to a few galleries in that neighborhood. There're a bunch of shows I need to see." Helen suddenly decided how she was going to spend the day. What she hadn't decided was whether she planned to do it alone.

When they arrived at the Cashins', they were greeted by both Phillip and Catherine, just back from their Saturday morning indoor tennis lesson. They looked ready for Wimbledon in his-and-her classic white cable-knit sweaters with navy and burgundy stripes at the neck and wrists. With their long legs, their obvious athleticism, and what probably amounted to thousands of dollars in lessons, they could probably take at least a few games off their opponents at any club they chose. Helen predicted that within a few years, Catherine would be the captain of The Very Brainy Girls' School's varsity tennis team.

When Inga the au pair announced lunch, there seemed to be a general assumption that Helen was staying, so she followed them all up the stairs to the second-floor dining room, where a smorgasbord was laid out across an enormous Swedish Biedermeier table. Several other equally stunning and rare pieces of Gustavian furniture were scattered throughout the well-proportioned room, but it was the unusual series of landscape paintings that caught Helen's eye.

"Vilhelm Hammershoi?" she asked.

"You know Hammershoi?" Phillip asked, surprised.

"I'm really only familiar with his still lifes. Mid eighteen-eighties?" she asked.

"Wow, you're good. Eighteen eighty-six," he responded.

"Despite their frigid reputation, I've always thought the Scandinavians were masters of the art of gracious living," she added as she admired the other magnificent pieces in the room.

"Margot was Swedish," he said. She wasn't sure if he volunteered that information to support her statement, but not wanting to follow up with a question about his deceased wife, she let it drop, while he busied himself pouring drinks.

Against her better judgment, Helen accepted Phillip's offer of an aquavit and then passively nodded when he poured her a chaser of Danish beer. Zoe, taking her cues from Catherine, was occupied balancing a filet of pickled herring on a slice of buttered pumpernickel bread and politely tasting a forkful of beets in sour cream.

"She always refuses borscht at our house," Helen joked. But she was proud of her daughter's ability to mingle comfortably with high society and chalked it up to one of the hidden perks of a private school education. If not to the manner bred, at least she had learned how to break bread in the proper manner.

The girls finished eating and excused themselves to go upstairs, leaving Helen and Phillip alone with the remains of their briny lunch. They sat in silence, Phillip sliding his finger around the rim of his glass, Helen creating a circle of stray peppercorns on the linen tablecloth. For the first time in the brief period they had known each other, they were at a crossroads, where Helen found herself wondering whether their situation was merely a logistically mandated outgrowth of their daughters' burgeoning friendship or whether it possessed a life of its own. Phillip broke the silence.

"I need to run over to a gallery on Madison this afternoon where I have a couple of pieces on hold. Would you mind going over there with me? I would love to get your opinion on these things."

"Sure. I'd be happy to," Helen answered, relieved to have an escape plan and curious to know what "things" he was considering.

When they informed their daughters of their plan, Catherine scarcely looked up from her notebook and murmured sweetly, "See you later, alligator," as Zoe added in a querulous tone, "In a while, crocodile." In a masterfully subtle act of role reversal, Zoe shot Helen a wickedly fake smile and a squint of an eye that befitted an overbearing Jewish mother and seemed to say, "Go. Adulterously gallivant with your Mr. Wonderful. See if I care."

The rain had become torrential, but anxious to escape the awkward situation, they agreed to brave the storm. Phillip had an enormous umbrella, the kind used by golf caddies to shield their clients when caught in a deluge on the sixteenth hole, and proposed that they take just the one. As Helen's was a junky folding number she had bought from a Nigerian street vendor for a few dollars, she agreed.

The short walk to Madison Avenue entailed a certain amount of puddle jumping, but chivalrous Phillip was on hand with a steadying arm each time they made a leap. At one point a huge gust of wind forced the umbrella to the ground, subjecting Helen to a momentary drenching that left her hair and face dripping wet. Recovering his balance and positioning the umbrella back overhead, Phillip spontaneously touched Helen's cheek and wiped away a few drops.

"I find you incredibly attractive." His gaze held hers.

Before she could respond, he was kissing her on the mouth, softly but with enough passion that there was no question as to its meaning. Returning the kiss, she murmured, "And I you."

But so what? she wondered. *This means nothing, right?*

"You are so beautiful. I haven't had any feelings for a woman in such a long time. It's like I've been sleepwalking. I didn't know if I would ever feel this way again. I must thank you."

"You're welcome. I guess you could say I'm your wake-up call," she said, looking straight into his eyes. It had been so long since she had felt this way, too. It was not just the kiss. She and Michael kissed all the time: hello, goodbye, as stage one to foreplay. But not like this—kissing for kissing's sake—complete with eye contact, tender strokes, *and* compliments from the most gorgeous and interesting man she had met in years. Oddly, it was not the thought of Michael that was preventing her from melting into his embrace; it was the "don't do it, Mommy" look that Zoe had given her as they were leaving the Cashin mansion. Or was she projecting? Either way, whether it was coming from Zoe or her own unconscious, which, given their shared DNA, were almost one and the same, she read the message loud and clear.

"A wake-up call. That's funny," he smiled. "We haven't even slept together."

"No. And we probably won't," she responded softly.

"That's disappointing," he answered, kissing her again.

Extremely disappointing, thought Helen.

"But understandable under the circumstances," he added in a gallant display of his moral backbone.

Oh, God, he's perfect, she thought.

"Here we are," he said as he held the door for her. He closed the umbrella and stuck it into the waiting brass stand in the entrance of the Gallery Nouveau Russe, where the contemporary glass that Helen had reviewed last month was still on exhibition. No sooner had they shaken the excess water from their hair and sleeves than Josh Kirov darted towards them.

"Mr. Cashin," he gushed. "I didn't expect you to come out in this weather."

"I knew it was the final day of the show, and I had promised to take one last look."

"Of course. We're holding three pieces for you. And Helen! Are you two together?"

Careful to dispel any notion that they were *together* together, she responded, "Our daughters are friends, and Phillip knows I have expertise in this area, so he asked me to come along."

"Oh! So you're doing some art advisory work these days?"

"Just in a friendly capacity," she answered. Josh was visibly relieved that he wouldn't be having to offer her a commission.

As Josh guided Phillip around the exhibition, Donald waved and then beckoned Helen to the back office.

"I didn't know you were friendly with Phillip Cashin," he whispered, sounding far too impressed for her taste.

"There are lots of things you don't know about me, Donald," she whispered, purposely sounding mysterious.

"Phillip Cashin is major," he replied. "Hubba hubba," he added, crassly moving his pelvis forward and back, which, with his love handles, looked more latter-day Elvis than the Ricky Martin effect he sought.

"Major how?" she asked. She knew exactly what he meant, but didn't want to miss an opportunity to learn more about Phillip.

"Oh, you know, major moolah, major collector, MAJOR good-looking—but I hardly have to tell you that, do I?" he snickered. "And MAJOR ladies' man, but I probably don't have to tell you that, either." Donald was giddy.

"He was major married until last spring, you know," she added bluntly, jumping to Phillip's defense.

"That's common knowledge, sweetheart. But it doesn't mean bubkes," he responded knowingly.

Doesn't it? she wondered. He certainly didn't seem the type to cheat on his wife.

"Helen, could you come look at these? I'm trying to decide which to get as a gift for my mother-in-law for her seventy-fifth birthday," Phillip called from the gallery. She walked over and examined the three pieces under consideration.

"Hmmm. For mother-in-law . . . Definitely not this one. Too sexy," she said, pointing to the green one with the ripe-fig-pink interior. "This one is a bit too edgy," she said, holding up the jagged ruby crystalline piece. "This third one has a lot going on. It's very complicated. Would that suit her?"

"She is complicated. As is our relationship. But which is your favorite?" he asked her.

"I like the green one," she answered without hesitation.

"The forbidden, libidinous one," he teased.

Josh and Donald exchanged glances.

Phillip spent a few more minutes contemplating the objects, picking each one up, running his hand over the surfaces, and then carefully placing them back on the shelf. Since each piece was priced at around twelve thousand dollars, it was not unreasonable for him to take his time.

"I can offer you a twenty percent discount if you take all three," Josh offered, hoping to consummate the sale today.

"Thanks Josh. I'll call you on Tuesday. I have to sleep on it," he answered distractedly.

Josh looked defeated. Helen, still bristling from Donald's tacky comments, was glad that Phillip resisted the aggressive sales tactics. Now she just wanted to escape before one of them began the deadly admissions conversation.

Too late. "Mr. Cashin, where is your daughter in school these days?" Donald inquired as they were buttoning their coats.

"She's at The Community School. But it only goes through eighth grade, so we're in the process of applying to high schools."

"We're in the same boat," Josh replied, trying to delay the departure. "Except we have twins. You know we have twins, don't you?"

Not waiting for Phillip's response, Helen walked out the door. He dutifully followed right behind. Since the rain had let up and they were no longer compelled to huddle closely under the shared umbrella, Helen made a point of maintaining a polite distance as they walked.

"I can't set foot in that gallery without having a conversation about schools. I have to remember not to go in again until after February," she said to explain her annoyance.

"I wouldn't have minded talking about schools," Phillip responded, not understanding why she seemed so perturbed.

"Well, I would. I've already done that with them, and ever since then they have been bugging me about using my influence at The School to get their twins in."

"And you're not comfortable doing that?" He seemed genuinely bewildered.

"No! I'm not!" She looked at him incredulously. "Would you do that for them?"

"Maybe. But they didn't ask me."

"Consider yourself fortunate," she replied shortly.

"It's not such a big deal to make a phone call."

"Whose side are you on?" She realized she sounded ridiculous the minute she asked, and then struggled to amend her comment. "I mean, you're just so relaxed about the whole admissions thing. How is that possible?" she asked, implying that he was at fault for not displaying sufficient angst.

"I just know it will all work out. Besides, worrying about it is not going to help."

"And you're probably used to always getting everything you want," she said sharply.

"Not always. Like now," he said softly, taking her in his arms again for a kiss. This time she turned away. "I'm sorry, Helen. I'll stop pushing."

Don't stop, she thought, and stepped away, relieved to see they had reached his house. She refused the invitation to come in, and they agreed he would send Zoe home in a cab after dinner.

"Thank you. I had a lovely afternoon," she said awkwardly. "Lovely afternoon" seemed such a flimsy choice of words to describe their time together.

"I should thank you for lending me your eye," he replied, but despite his warm tone, his words also sounded superficial. The awkwardness of the moment passed when Helen leaned over and gave him a friendly goodbye kiss on the cheek and quickly departed. As she reached the corner, she turned around and saw he was still standing in front of his house. But she didn't wave.

By the time Zoe returned from the Cashins', the rain had started up again, and the night was colder than predicted. They agreed that an evening at home was preferable to going out, and changed into pajamas, made a pot of hot chocolate, and set up a game of Scrabble on a lazy Susan on the bed.

Competitive by nature but mindful of the fact that Zoe was not, Helen restrained herself from playing the cutthroat game she would normally have, had her opponent been anyone other than her daughter. But she made sure to keep the game lively nonetheless.

" 'Quart,' for thirty-six points." Helen both put the "Q" and the "T" on triple-letter squares.

Zoe took her time and then laid down a "Z" to make "quartz," and then built "glaze" horizontally, for forty-four points. She won the game.

"Excellent. I love playing with you. It's a win-win for me. I'm happy when I do well in the game, but even happier when my daughter wins."

"Catherine said her dad says the same thing when they play tennis. He's ecstatic if she wins a few points."

"I guess it must be one of those universal parental responses."

They were both quiet as they scooped the tiles into the drawstring bag and packed the board and racks into the box.

"What do you think of Phillip Cashin?" Zoe asked. Helen took her time answering, knowing how carefully Zoe would be listening.

"I think he's handsome, rich, charming, and very spoiled. He's a man who's used to getting his way. What do you think of him?"

"He's obviously rich, handsome, and charming, but I think he's kind of depressed. He's not nearly as much fun to be around as Daddy," she said pointedly.

"That's very astute of you. He's pretty serious," she agreed, understanding that Zoe was asking for her to be critical of Phillip. "It's really important to have fun in a relationship. For me, a sense of humor is key."

"For me, too," Zoe agreed with a certitude that Helen found endearing. She was pleased that Zoe's perceptions about men were filtered through her experience with Michael. Helen knew that the father generally represented the ideal against which all the men in a girl's life were judged.

"I met this really cute kid at The Public School the other day. His name is Max Kupka. I think he probably has a good sense of humor."

"I love his name. Tell me about him."

"He's very cute, has a great voice, and was really friendly at the rehearsal. He even remembered my name after hearing it only once. That must mean something, don't you think?" Zoe asked.

"Absolutely. So you'll see him again next week, right?"

"I think so," Zoe answered. "We rehearse again on Thursday. He has a solo part, too, so I'm hoping we might even have a few extra practices together."

"That would be nice. You might get a chance to talk a little if that happens. Get to know him a little better."

"Yeah," Zoe replied dreamily.

Helen was touched by her daughter's unfettered enthusiasm for a boy she barely knew, and she supported it wholeheartedly, thinking that Zoe was probably ready for a little romance. But in the depths of her maternal psyche, she had to admit she was a tad envious of Zoe's youth, innocence, and, even more, her freedom. Ah, to be fourteen.

DECEMBER

December was the cruelest month for those who worked in the trenches of the New York City private schools' admissions offices. While the applicants were busying themselves with their holiday plans, the admissions directors were working sixty-hour weeks reviewing test scores, fulfilling requests for eleventh-hour applications from desperados who had missed all previous deadlines, notifying applicants about missing materials, scheduling last-minute interviews, and dealing with whatever other unanticipated problems developed along the way.

Sara was completely absorbed in reading the KAT reports, which were filtering in at a rapid clip. She was particularly intrigued by Sam Belzer's. It bore out what she had suspected all along.

> CONFIDENTIAL
> Student: Sam Belzer
> Age: 4.9
>
> SELF-CONFIDENCE:
> Sam refused to greet the examiner. He was resentful and

hostile when asked basic questions. Refused handshake and avoided eye contact. Poor posture. General lack of confidence.

UNDERSTANDING OF TASKS:

Did not listen carefully to directions, so consequently failed to grasp expectations. Was anxious when moving from activity to activity and grumbled "I don't work for you" when asked to sit, and "Who died and made you God?" when asked to draw a triangle.

LANGUAGE SKILLS:

Sam demonstrated some outstanding verbal skills. He has a wealth of information about the world and broad knowledge of facts. But when it came to answering direct questions about himself, he floundered. He has poor social judgment and lacks common sense for everyday situations. Formulated lengthy, complex definitions for words. Relationship between thoughts and words is interesting. When asked to complete the rhyme "Hey diddle diddle . . ." he responded, ". . . the cat made a piddle."

VISUAL-MOTOR SKILLS:

Alertness was erratic. At times Sam was engaged, e.g., when stacking blocks. But when asked to sequence pictures he was confused by the request and threw them at the examiner. When asked to identify the missing element in a picture, his response was "That's a stupid question."

MOTIVATION:

Selective.

OVERALL IMPRESSION:

Sam is a troubled young boy with distinct disdain for authority. This examiner recommends family therapy, as Sam's problems appear to be parental in origin.

Poor Sam, thought Sara. *If I didn't think his parents would be a total pain in the ass, I might actually be inclined to accept him. He needs all the help he can get.* She was interrupted by Brandi, who, announcing that Simone Savage was on the phone, placed the Greta Von Hansdorff and Aurora Dondi-Marghelletti reports on her desk and transferred the call.

"Sara, dahling, how are you?" Simone greeted her unctuously.

"Just fine, Simone, and you?"

"Pins and needles. I always get tingly when the KAT reports start to come in. It's very exciting, don't you think?"

"'Exciting' is one word for it. So can I assume you're calling to discuss your two candidates?"

"Of course, dahling, and you have to agree, two more shining stars have never passed through your galaxy, have they?"

"They are both bright. Let's see . . ." She opened Greta's file first. "Picture completion, ninety-ninth percentile; block design, ninety-eighth percentile; object assembly, ninety-ninth percentile; arithmetic, ninety-seventh percentile; vocabulary, sixty-fourth percentile. Pretty impressive. But I'm concerned about the vocabulary score. Let's see what the examiner's report says about her language skills."

Sara read from the report, "'Greta was extremely reserved and would only speak when spoken to. Her shyness borders on aberrant and indicates a certain degree of repression. It was difficult to accurately measure her vocabulary and language skills as she was unwilling to use either in the presence of the examiner. She did sit up straight, made good eye-contact and followed directions precisely, indicating good comprehension.'"

"She sounds like a teacher's dream, wouldn't you say, dahling?" Simone offered optimistically.

"Quite the contrary. At The School we encourage our students to communicate openly. I hate to break it to you, Simone, but I think that Greta is not a good fit," she said. "Not a good fit" was commonly understood in admission's parlance to mean "no go."

Simone was not pleased with Sara's assessment but, being the consummate operator, immediately switched gears and went to bat for her second candidate. "The Dondi-Marghelletti child. Now *she* is special, is she not?" Implying that if Sara rejected Greta, she couldn't not accept Aurora.

"She is an attractive candidate," Sara responded flatly. Since all parents perceived their children to be "special," any enlightened educator understood the emptiness of the "S" word.

"Let me take a look at her report. Hmmm . . . 'Picture completion, ninetieth percentile; block design, ninety-fourth percentile; object assembly, ninety-fifth percentile; arithmetic, eighty-fourth percentile; vocabulary, ninety-ninth percentile. Quite good." She was favorably disposed but not ready to give Simone the verbal commitment she so wantonly craved. "Let's see what the examiner's overall impression was." And she read, " 'Aurora is a highly personable child. She is warm, friendly and strives to please. She communicates successfully in three languages and makes seamless transitions between all three.' "

"Quite a cunning linguist, wouldn't you say?" Simone tittered.

Sara laughed. "I will do everything I can to find a place for her"—tossing Simone a small bone on which to gnaw.

"Lovely, Sara, dear. I'm sure you will do your best," Simone said, meaning, "I'll take that as a yes."

In the twenty years that he had been employed in television, Michael had never approached an audition with this much dread. As if the whole production were not convoluted enough, it was now further complicated by two ironic twists: the network executives had unanimously decided that Provençal cooking was the next big thing, and Michael's direct boss, Xavier, was inexplicably gung ho about casting Justine Frampton in the starring role. All of this meant that rather than the standard ten-minute taped audition, Michael was producing a full-blown thirty-minute pilot, currently titled "La Cuisine de Justine."

As corporate interest in the show mounted, it seemed as though the care and feeding of Justine's ego grew proportionately. Even Michael's consistent and dependable crew was reaching its breaking point and had begun, behind his back, to question his motives. From what they were seeing, this Frampton woman was one taco short of a combination plate, and they couldn't understand why their normally levelheaded boss had become her champion. On Michael's orders, they had all put in overtime to fulfill Justine's endless litany of demands. Roland, the production assistant in charge of procurement, was aghast at the specificity of Justine's shopping list and her recalcitrance when faced with his suggestions for substitutions. When he proposed the more readily available *fleur de sel* in place of the impossible-to-find *sel gros,* she dug in her heels and insisted on the latter.

"C'mon. Salt is salt. She'll never know the difference," Roland said when presenting the problem to Michael. Fully expecting him to agree, he was stunned when Michael blew up. "Get her the *sel gros* even if it has to be shipped overnight from Morton's-sur-la-mer or wherever the fuck it grows." Roland had never seen him this short-fused.

The same went on with the kitchen equipment. Justine insisted upon an earthenware *tian* from Roussilon for her gratinée after rejecting the French ceramic casserole that was the network standard, because she thought it looked "peasanty." Forget about their sturdy garlic press and pepper mill; she claimed she couldn't possibly function without *"le presse ail and le moulin à poivre,"* which were available only in Paris. And she declared that the network's restaurant-quality four-burner cooktop was insufficient, and demanded six burners and the installation of a new, super-turbocharged exhaust fan because, as she put it to Michael, "You wouldn't want me coughing from smoke inhalation during the taping, would you?"

The poor stylists were under even more pressure—getting the horsey Frampton to resemble anything close to a telegenic television chef was tantamount to transforming Chef Boyardee into Wolfgang Puck. There were numerous meetings that seemed to go on for hours, at which three professionals debated the pros and cons of the various hair and makeup alternatives. Unable to reach a consensus, Michael was called in to make the final decisions on all that and everything else.

"I've called all over town and I can't find the warm-toned klieg light that Frampton is demanding we use," the usually mellow lighting technician lamented. "She's claiming it's the only light that will 'do justice to her subtle skin tones.' Her skin tones are anything but subtle. I think we'd be much better off with diffused lighting. Don't you?"

"Real chefs don't wear toques," the wardrobe mistress insisted impatiently. "Michael, I'm telling you, don't give in on this one. She'll look like the Pillsbury Doughboy if you do."

"Say no more." He held up his hand as if he were stopping traffic at a four-way intersection where, if a head-on collision occurred, he would be the one to blame.

In the middle of this Armageddon, his assistant, Charlotte, announced that Justine was on line one. He took her call immediately.

"Michael, I want to make a last-minute change," she told him.

"Yes?" He braced himself, afraid to hear what was coming.

"The lamb should be boned," she stated authoritatively.

"But we've already received delivery on sixteen legs of lamb on the bone, and we're taping tomorrow. I don't think that's going to be possible. And you've worked so hard to finalize your recipes," he added hastily.

"Yes, yes. It was just a thought. But if I had my druthers I would rather do the butterflied leg of lamb. It's easier to carve and tends to be . . ."

Charlotte stuck her head in the door and whispered, "Vincent Gargano on line four."

Triage! The admissions director from two of Manhattan's most prestigious schools were calling him, both for absolutely ludicrous reasons, and he had to quickly choose between them.

Michael moaned and cut Justine off. After all, The Bucolic Campus School was currently their first choice. At least, he thought that had been the case this morning.

"Yo, Vinnie. What's up?" Michael switched gears.

"Were you at the Knicks-Magic game last night?" Vince asked.

"Yeah, man. McGrady really lit it up."

"So how are your new seats?" Vince hinted.

"Great. Section one eleven, Row B. After ten years in the green seats I never thought we'd get an upgrade," Michael replied. "We should catch a game together one night."

"That would be great, man," Vince replied enthusiastically.

"That is, unless you're too busy with work," Michael answered, remembering Helen's orders to steer the next conversation with Vince in an admissions-related direction.

Unfortunately, his effort was suddenly derailed by Charlotte, who stuck her head in and whispered, "Frampton again on line three. She sounds agitated." He momentarily put Vince on hold.

"Tell Frampton to *please* get here as early as possible tomorrow and we will discuss whatever it is then," he hissed to Charlotte.

"Yo, Vinnie, sorry." There was an ominous dial tone at the other end.

The next morning, not as early as Michael had hoped, Justine Frampton was on the set, and the cameras were ready to roll. There were just a few last-minute details to iron out, her appearance being the primary one. She had insisted on wearing a white chef's jacket with her initials embroidered in red over her left breast, but given her double D cup, the monogram was oddly angled and nearly impossible to read, and the wardrobe mistress was dashing about trying to find a substitute. After a lengthy discussion, Justine finally relinquished the toque, and now the hairstylist was desperately trying to restrain her unruly hair and keep it off her face and out of the food. Every few minutes Michael ordered the makeup artist to dust Justine's face with powder. "We absolutely can't have her dripping sweat on the set," he whispered. "And make sure her moustache doesn't show."

The network cooks had been in the kitchen since the early morning and finally announced that all the prep work was complete. Behind the set stood eight legs of lamb in various stages of preparedness, from raw to fully cooked. One was oven-ready, smeared with herbs and garlic; another was in the oven, sizzling away. One was already carved and plated. There were several dishes of fully cooked potatoes gratinée, others partially prepared, and dozens of whole peeled potatoes and piles of potato slices. The ratatouille was set up in much the same way, with the whole raw vegetables, the sliced and diced vegetables, and the final product ready to serve. The kitchen counter was packed with dozens of little glass bowls that contained every ingredient on Justine's lists, including minced garlic, chopped rosemary, ground mustard seed, shredded basil leaves, diced onions, and, of course, *sel gros* that arrived that morning from somewhere in France. All that was missing were Justine's skilled hands and magic touch.

"Ready on the set?" Michael asked the entire crew.

"Ready," they all replied.

"Ready," Justine spoke confidently as she cocked her head and looked kittenishly at camera one.

"Four, three, two, one, action! Take one!" Michael ordered, and the cameras started to roll.

For the next thirty minutes and twenty-two takes, Justine Frampton lurched around the kitchen like a hyperactive four-year-old in desperate need of a nap. In a gyroscopic frenzy, she spun from the counter in the foreground to the sink at stage right to the oven at stage left, while the two cameramen moved frantically to hold her in frame, and the sound technician scrambled to keep her on mike. She never stood in one spot for more than a few seconds, and as a result, her enormous rear end was bouncing in frame throughout much of the taping.

Moving at a speed no one would have thought her capable of, she went from demonstrating the proper way to season the lamb to stirring the ratatouille, to peeling a potato, to zesting a lemon, to chopping rosemary, all the while talking coherently about the virtues of sea salt. As she whipped back around to pat the half-dressed lamb, one of her globular earrings fell into the simmering zucchini, and then, not missing a beat, she reached her bare hands into the steaming pan, fished it out, and clipped it back onto her ear.

On take fourteen, the lamb was finally in the oven, and she began madly slicing potatoes with a frighteningly large cleaver. The crew in the control room gasped as she nicked her left thumb, instantly staining the white tubers a deep shade of crimson. She casually wrapped a towel around her bleeding finger as she made an off-color joke about passing the potatoes off as beets. Everyone in the control room laughed except for Michael, who was far too distressed to see the humor in any of this. Once the towel was totally soaked through with her blood, she tossed it on the counter and used both hands to demonstrate seeding a tomato. She then grabbed the same towel to swab the tomato juice that was running down her arms and, still with the very same towel, wiped a platter onto which she then plunked a tangle of grilled peppers. As someone in the crew made a crack about the health department, Michael covered his face with his hands and muttered something about his wife.

Less than thirty seconds later, arms flailing as she lunged across the counter in an effort to catch a runaway bloodstained potato, Justine knocked over a measuring cup full of olive oil, splattering it in all directions as it fell to the floor. Wiping her hands across her now lubricated chest, she quipped, "Good thing I always insist on extra-virgin."

Meanwhile, smoke was billowing out of the oven due to the untended, grease-spattering lamb; the pot of potatoes was boiling over, raining puddles of starchy water all over the stove; and the sizzling vegetables were now crisp and starting to burn. She picked up a piece of charred eggplant with her bare fingers, shrieked, threw it on the floor, and dashed to the sink. While running her hand under cold water, she asked her audience, "Don't you hate when you burn yourself? It's almost as painful as passing a kidney stone."

At the end of the taping, against a backdrop of bedlam, Justine proudly presented a camera-ready Provençal meal as if she had effortlessly made it all herself. But what was most remarkable about the entire performance was that despite her oil-stained smock, bleeding thumb, burned finger, and disheveled hair, miraculously, she never broke a sweat.

"Cut," Michael ordered from the control room, and the crew spontaneously started to applaud. As he glanced under his arms and saw two large, wet, circular stains, he didn't know if he should laugh or cry.

On the first frigid day of the year, Helen was busy assembling a bag of snacks for Zoe to take to the SAPS testing center. As she spread a slice of whole-wheat bread with peanut butter, she thought back to the many sandwiches she had packed for Zoe over the years. Every time there was a field trip, a picnic, a plane trip, or a lousy selection on The School's lunch menu, Helen had packed a brown bag for her daughter. She felt a certain melancholy as she realized that those days had become fewer and farther between, and that before she knew it, Zoe would be living somewhere else and packing her own lunches.

"Mom, what time do we need to leave?" Zoe shouted from her room.

"The test is at one, so let's leave at noon. That should give us plenty of time," Helen answered as the phone was ringing.

"Hi, Mom. Just calling to see how she's doing this morning. Staying calm, I hope," Bertha Kauffmann sounded uncharacteristically tense. She had a lot riding on this, too.

"It's kind of you to call, Bertha. And yes, she's fine. She got a good night's sleep and is ready as she'll ever be."

"She'll do great. Lemme speak to her a minute," Birdie demanded.

Zoe picked up the extension in her room.

"Hey, sweetheart. Listen. Three of my students took the test yesterday and called to tell me the essay question. This year they're using the old 'what's your favorite book, and why?' Remember what we talked about. Form is more important than content. What book did we decide on for you?"

"Of Mice and Men," Zoe answered.

"Right. Good. Just don't go into your theory about the sexual overtones of Lennie and George's relationship. You may think it's interesting, but you don't wanna risk offending your reader. Okay, doll?"

"Okay. Thanks for letting me know the question. That will help a lot. Oh, Bertha?" Zoe lowered her voice so her mother couldn't hear. "Do you really think I'll do okay?"

"Absolutely, sweetheart. I'm banking on it," she answered. Zoe missed the double entendre. "Call me the minute you get outta there."

"I told my parents that either I come alone or I won't come at all," April Winter explained to Helen and Zoe when they arrived at the test center. "They've been driving me crazy since I got home from the hospital. I can't stand their hovering. My dad actually came into my bedroom and sat down on my bed last night, just 'to talk' "—she quoted with her two bent fingers. "How gross is that?"

Helen took this as a signal for her to leave. "I'll be back for you at four. Here's something to eat at the break," she said as she handed Zoe the bag. "April, did you bring a snack?"

"No. I don't need anything," she answered wanly.

"Zoe has plenty for two. You should both eat something at the break. Brain food." She gave her daughter a big hug and whispered, "Good luck, sweetie. Just give it your best. I love you." As she left the building, she saw Julian Toppler stepping out of a black town car, in a long coat and dark glasses. Very *Sunset Boulevard.*

I doubt if the SAPS proctor is ready for this close-up, Helen laughed to herself.

In response to an urgent e-mail sent by Lisa Fontaine late the previous night, Helen had agreed to meet her for lunch while Zoe was taking the SAPS. In the taxi on the way to the restaurant, Helen speculated on what the highly confidential school matter Lisa referred to in her e-mail could be, and decided that it most likely had to do with the financial crisis she had alluded to a few months back.

When Helen arrived at the small Lexington Avenue café, she found Lisa in a corner booth, engaged in a heated cell phone conversation. Lisa gestured for her to sit and held up a finger to say she would be just one more minute, leaving Helen in the impossible and awkward position of pretending not to listen.

"Did you speak to our attorney?" Pause. "What kind of lawsuit? No way, keep John Toppler away from this. I mean it." Pause. "I'll call you later. I'm with her now.

"I'm sorry, Helen. Thanks for meeting me on such short notice. Let's order something to eat. I'm ravenous."

As soon as they had ordered a ladies' lunch of salads and sparkling water, Lisa began.

"The board received the auditor's report last night, and the news was very distressing. I hope you're ready for this," she said, and cleared her throat dramatically. "During the course of the last three months—that's the first quarter of The School's fiscal year—Pamela has withdrawn something in the neighborhood of two hundred thirty thousand dollars from The School's primary cash account. Much of it was in the form of funds wired to an account in her own name. That's money above and beyond her salary, of course. In addition, some was wired into an account that we have learned belongs to Felicity Cozette. There was a large sum wired to that cooking school in France that belongs to Justine Frampton of The Fancy Girls' School, presumably for Pamela and Felicity's visits last summer, and a deposit for next summer. There was money wired to a real estate company in the Caribbean for a vacation rental this month. The list goes on. On top of all that, she's submitted receipts for reimbursable expenses for the quarter to the tune of twenty-three thousand, four hundred and fifty dollars, which far exceeds her T and E budget for the entire year!" She paused to take a bite of her salad.

"Those are huge numbers. How did she possibly think she could get away with this?" Helen gasped.

"Delusions of invulnerability? Inflated sense of entitlement? An uncontrollable self-destructive impulse? What do you think?" Lisa asked.

"Mental illness?" Helen ventured. "I'm serious. I think she's really sick. She's lost what little sense of reality she had."

"And in the process of losing her mind, she's committed prosecutable criminal acts," Lisa added. "At this point the board's job is not to figure out why she's done this but to decide what to do about it. And clearly, that decision must be made with the utmost sensitivity. The bottom line is, we have to act in the best interest of The School. The board asked me to get your input on this, the feeling being that as president of the Parents' Association, you would have a good read on what kind of response we can expect to get. However it plays out, it will be explosive. But we need to have a plan in place before anything leaks. You and I both know that the board's a sieve."

"Can you give me some idea of the board's thinking on how it would like to proceed?"

"Big debate. Many trustees want her fired immediately. Someone even suggested she be arrested and led out in handcuffs. Personally I think that's a little extreme. Others want to allow her to stay until winter break, which is only two weeks from now, and announce at the Holiday Festival that she's not coming back in January. At that point we would begin legal action, if that were still considered necessary. We're meeting again tonight to make a decision. What do you think?"

"It's a tough call. Either way, you drop a bomb like that and you can expect some heavy fallout." Helen's mind was racing as she weighed the options. "But maybe the board shouldn't act so quickly. I mean, what about due process and 'innocent until found guilty'?" Helen asked. She couldn't have cared less about Pamela's civil rights. She was just angling for a stay of execution until after February 12.

"Helen, there's no question that she embezzled large sums of money. The decision to terminate her was not made lightly. It was the result of a thorough investigation. Believe me, everyone wanted to give her the benefit of the doubt. There's just no more doubt at this point, and it's time to give her the axe. The only question is when."

"Oh," was all Helen could think to say to that. "What about an interim head of School? That'll be the first question everyone will ask. Who will be running the show?"

"If the associate head is cleared of any wrongdoing, which is a big if, it will probably be her," Lisa answered.

"Felicity?" Helen was stunned. "She has about as much business heading The School as Marcel Marceau has chairing the linguistics department of the Sorbonne."

"Helen, I'm on the same page as you are on this. But it's not my decision. The School's bylaws stipulate that in the event of the head's sudden departure, the associate will assume the role until a full search is conducted. If for some reason the associate can't serve, the next logical choice is Sara Nash. But the board is concerned that she has no classroom experience. Plus, she's up to her ears in applications, and until she's done with admissions, it will be difficult for her to find the time to do anything else. Another possibility is to hire an outsider as an interim head. But as you can see, there's no ideal solution. It's a god-awful mess," Lisa said wearily. "Trust me, Helen, there have been moments when I've been tempted to walk away from the whole thing—pull my kids out of The School and resign from the board."

"Where would you go? The kids have to go to school."

"That's the problem. We're all stuck."

"I don't mean to sound egocentric, but can I ask you a question?"

"Of course. We all have our own concerns. What's yours?"

"Has the board considered how this change might affect the

eighth-grade admissions process? We're sort of in the thick of it, and January is a crucial month. How will we manage?"

"That hasn't been discussed. I'll make sure to bring it up at the next meeting. Let's see, who are the other board members with eighth-graders?"

"I can only think of two: one who summered in Provence, and John Toppler," Helen answered.

"I guess neither of them can be relied on to be of much help. They each have their own set of issues, don't they?"

"I would say so," Helen replied tersely.

"Anyway, since there are bound to be repercussions to tonight's board meeting, I thought you should know where things stand," Lisa said.

"Thanks," Helen replied, not sure for what. "The good news is, the eighth-graders can stop racking their brains about what kind of charm to get for Pamela's stupid bracelet," she joked nervously.

Lisa's cell phone chimed the first ten notes of "Taps," and Helen returned to the testing center.

"Guess what? I got an eight o'clock reservation at Booboo tonight. I can't wait to take my two favorite gals to dinner. See you there," the upbeat voice mail message from Michael greeted them when they returned home late that afternoon. Helen hadn't heard him this ebullient in a while and assumed he intended the dinner to be a celebration in honor of Zoe's completion of the SAPS.

She returned his call. "What a nice idea. But unfortunately, Zoe's made plans to go over to the Topplers'. Julian has put together some sort of impromptu get-together," Helen replied regretfully. She had been disappointed when Zoe told her the plan, for she, too, had hoped they would all spend the evening together.

"Then I'll just change the reservation to two," he said with no discernible loss of enthusiasm.

"Really? You want to go anyway? We could do a dinner out tomorrow night with Zoe if you want."

"No. It wasn't easy to get the reservation. Let's go tonight. We have a lot to talk about," he replied cryptically. That tone always made Helen nervous. "Meet me there at eight. Love you."

"Me, too."

"Wow, Dad must have used some muscle to get a table there," Zoe said, aware that Booboo was one of the hottest places in town and normally booked up months in advance. "But Julian's should be fun."

"Who's going to be there?" Helen inquired.

"The usual cast of characters. And . . . a few extras," she added cagily.

"And who might those be?"

"Catherine Cashin is coming. Julian told me to invite her. Oh, and a few kids from The Public School."

"A certain Max, perhaps?" Helen teased.

"How'd ya guess?" Zoe smiled.

"Oh, mother's intuition," Helen laughed.

Booboo was packed with customers—four deep at the bar and a dozen or more surrounding the front desk—trying every trick in the book to secure a table. Booboo's rustic Italian fare was the talk of the town, and ever since the New York food critics awarded it three stars, diners were clamoring for a chance to sample the quail tongue ravioli and the pork belly lasagna, two of Booboo's signature dishes.

"Mr. Drager?" the maitre d' greeted them. "Your table is ready."

Emerging from the crowd, Helen enjoyed watching heads turn to see who had made the cut. It didn't even matter that when they ascertained it was no one famous, they resumed their conversations.

"You look lovely tonight," Michael said warmly, admiring Helen's bright-pink Chinese jacket and simple orange silk shift. She had worked hard to get the two red-lacquered chopsticks to hold her hair in a French twist and was glad Michael had noticed.

"Thank you. You look pretty handsome yourself," she responded. "Who'd you have to sleep with to get us this table?" she joked affectionately.

"You underestimate my importance in the culinary world," he replied.

"So the screening wasn't a total disaster?"

"Let's get some wine and then we can talk about it," he answered.

With great fanfare the sommelier presented a wine list as thick as the Poughkeepsie phone book.

"Can you recommend a good Barolo?" Michael asked, impatient to tell Helen his news.

"Try the nineteen ninety Villa Settimo. It's big and fat, has a distinctive fruity bouquet, a flinty undercurrent, and a hint of old leather. I think you'll find it to your liking," he stated.

"Fine," Michael replied, not bothering to check the price.

"I don't usually go out of my way to drink old leather, but I guess I'll make an exception tonight," Helen said after the waiter departed.

The sommelier returned with the selection, and after the interminable ritualized decanting procedure was completed, the Dragers finally each held a goblet of wine.

"Cheers," Michael toasted.

"To Zoe. She seemed pleased and relieved after the test today. I know I am."

"When do we get the results?"

"In three days. We paid extra for express service."

"I'm sure she did just fine." Michael was sanguine as usual.

"She felt that she did her best. That's all we can ask of her," Helen replied, making a concerted effort to finally relax. It seemed pointless to worry about the scores now, especially since there were other things to fill that void, like today's chapter of *The Perils of Pamela,* for starters.

"I also want to make a toast to my wife. The creator of the Cooking Network's new hit show, *La Cuisine de Justine*!" he announced grandly.

"Not funny," she said dryly.

"May I tell you about tonight's specials?" their waiter interrupted. Not waiting for an answer, he launched into a protracted recitation.

"And our last special this evening is the tripe, which, if you like it, is magnificent. It's prepared in a bone marrow reduction, with assorted Willamette Valley root vegetables, and finished with a veal demi-glace and a dollop of wild dandelion pesto."

"Aren't all dandelions wild?" Helen smiled at Michael as she asked the waiter.

"I'll have to ask the chef," he replied humorlessly, and strode off.

"So where were we? You were about to tell me what happened at the screening this morning." Helen had been anxious all day about Michael's meeting.

"Are you ready for this? The network execs flipped over the tape. They see it as a brand-new genre of program—a comedy cooking show. Xavier has somehow convinced himself it's sheer genius. He's been describing it as Julia Child meets the Three Stooges. He thinks it has huge potential and wants me to develop it as a series."

"Michael, that's extraordinary. What a coup! And to think the show began its life as a capricious escapade."

"You've been spending too much time quizzing Zoe on her word lists," he joked.

"You'll see. It'll pay off when she scores a ninety-nine percent on vocabulary," she retorted. "So what are the next steps on the show?"

"The first step is to begin negotiations with Justine. That could be tricky. I don't think she thinks of herself as a comedienne. Do you?"

"Definitely not. She strikes me as someone who has zero sense of humor, particularly when it comes to herself."

"So the question becomes, how to present the concept in a way that will appeal to her."

"Want my advice?" she offered.

"Of course," he answered warily.

"The best way to catch flies is with honey. Flatter her. Convince her that she's on her way to becoming a star and you'll have her eating out of your hand. She won't care if the show is a comedy or a tragedy."

"I honestly think it's a bit of both," Michael responded, not wholly convinced this strategy would work.

"Hello, Michael. Reality check. Remember why you're doing this. You don't have to go all the way to contract. You just need to string her on until early February. That's two months from now. Once Zoe is accepted at The Fancy Girls' School, or at any school, the show can fizzle out, like so many of the proposals that float around the network."

"Along with my career." He was becoming agitated. "Helen, I think you're missing the point here. *La Cuisine de Justine* has taken on a life of its own. I spent a small fortune producing the pilot, what with all of her ridiculous demands and our overtime costs. The network expects a return on that investment. The fact that they loved the pilot is a huge relief. Now I've got to deliver a viable program."

"Would you like to order now?" The waiter was back and wasn't going to take no for an answer. He was hoping to turn over the table at least one more time tonight.

"I'm a sucker for innards," Michael said, and ordered the calf's liver cannelloni.

"Good choice," replied the waiter.

"And I'll have the brains," Helen ordered.

"Also a good choice," the waiter replied, and went back to the kitchen.

"Do you think they would ever tell you if it wasn't a good choice?"

"Definitely not. So I have some news, too." As Helen told Michael the story of the accounting scandal, he shook his head from right to left and muttered, "Jeesssuuusss" numerous times.

"That's outrageous. Way beyond anything I would ever have imagined her capable of. So what do you think the board will do about a new head?" he posed the question that had consumed her attention all afternoon. She laid out the three options.

"Felicity! No way! It seems pretty obvious that she's an accessory to the crime, or certainly guilty by association. Not to mention, totally unqualified. I'm sure the board will come to that conclusion pretty quickly. What about Sara? Would she do it?" Michael asked.

"I'm not sure. She's got a lot on her plate as it is."

"And then the question becomes, do you think she's capable of doing the job?"

"She's ten times more capable than Pamela!" Helen replied defensively.

"Helen, she's your best friend. Do you really think you can be objective about this?" Michael asked gently.

"You're right. I'm not sure I can be. And between us, I do have one selfish concern. I'm not convinced she can be of much help to us on admissions. She's a major figure in the kindergarten world, but she's not wired into the key players in the high school admissions offices. And who knows about the third scenario. An outsider would be a complete wild card. In any case, I think we can pretty much assume we'll be flying solo on admissions from here on in."

"It seems to me, we've managed pretty well so far with very little help from our pilot, Pamela," Michael expressed with annoyance.

"But it's the final stage that's critical. It's the time when the heads of school make the secret deals with the admissions directors. It's when all the wheeling and dealing takes place."

"Between wheeling with Frampton and dealing with Gargano, I feel like I've practically majored in wheeling and dealing this semester," Michael exclaimed.

"And you deserve extra credit for that," Helen teased, and kissed him on the cheek.

Finishing up the last of her appointments for the day, Sara logged on to check her e-mail.

Hey,

It's been a few days since we've communicated. Anything new at The School?

Helen

PS. When is the next rehearsal with The Public School? Zoe seems excited about the program.

Sara was dying to ask Helen what she knew about all the ominous-looking gray-suited accountant types who had been wandering in and out of the business office for the past few weeks. They had last been seen carting away boxes of computer records and confidential-looking files, creating a nervous stir among the members of the administrative staff. But she knew it would be indiscreet and unprofessional to mention this.

Helen,

Same old, same old. I'm swamped with applications so I'm mostly confined to the Admissions Office. Except on rehearsal days, which I look forward to fanatically. Next one is this afternoon. Zoe will be practicing her solo then. Why don't you pop in at the tail end of the rehearsal and hear her sing?

Love, S.

Helen was also desperate to talk to Sara about the unfolding drama at The School, but her e-mail suggested she wasn't privy to recent developments, and Helen knew that she shouldn't be the one to tell her. Moreover, she was under strict orders from Lisa Fontaine to maintain absolute secrecy (spousal dispensation went without saying) and would have to wait until after the Holiday Festival to discuss it. But if Sara let on that she knew *something*, that would free her to break the code of silence, and she found herself hoping that would happen.

Helen closed her e-mail box, turned off the ringer on the phone, and went to work on the article that was due at the magazine by the end of the week. It almost seemed like a luxury to devote her full attention to professional matters and temporarily close the door on those related to school. Her current writing assignment, an article entitled "Sentimental Education: Do Art Schools Produce Successful Artists?" required extensive research as well as critical thought, and she enjoyed the sense of escape that such deep concentration provided.

By the afternoon, satisfied that the piece was finally complete, she logged on to the museum's database in search of an image to illustrate her article. She had a painting in mind—a sumptuous abstraction by the self-taught Eva Ormolu, called *Deception*—and was pleased that she was able to locate it easily. Learning that a reproduction of the painting could be obtained from the museum for a small fee, she copied down the pertinent information and, while doing so, noted the provenance of the painting: "Gift from the Collection of Phillip and Margot Cashin." Of all the thousands of paintings she could have chosen, there was something spooky about this coincidence.

With half an hour to spare before the choral rehearsal, Helen logged on to Google and typed in Margot Cashin. Several entries appeared, and she selected the one listed as "Obituary." Not surprisingly, it was a sizable piece and included a photograph of the deceased. Helen was ashamed at the tingle of pleasure she experienced on discovering that Margot was not the great beauty she had imagined her to be. Based on some deeply ingrained stereotypes, Helen's working image of Margot had been that of an Ingrid Bergman type, an educated man's Nordic trophy wife. As a result, she was thrown by the plainness of the woman's face—it just didn't jibe with her preconceived notion of Phillip's wife. Was it her imagination, or did Margot look slightly deranged? She read the obituary with great interest.

> Margot Cashin, a well-known figure in the world of Scandinavian philanthropy, died yesterday at her home. The cause of death is not known.
>
> Margot Cashin was born Margot Birkenstock in Stockholm, Sweden. With her parents, Lars and Ingrid Birkenstock, she immigrated to the United States as a young child. Her father was the cultural attaché to the Swedish consulate, and her mother currently runs an agency that places Swedish au pairs with New York families.
>
> Ms. Cashin attended The Fancy Girls' School in Manhattan and Mount Holyoke College.
>
> Ms. Cashin was a trustee of the Fund for a Kinder, Gentler World, a founding member of 101 Great Danes, a trustee of the Swedish Massage Institute, president of the First Finnish Finishing School, and a member of the board of trustees of The Very Brainy Girls' School in Manhattan.
>
> She is survived by her husband, Phillip Cashin, and her daughter, Catherine.

Margot Cashin was a trustee of The Very Brainy Girls' School and attended The Fancy Girls' School! No wonder Phillip is Mr. Mellow about admissions. Catherine is a legacy at one school and the daughter of a trustee of another! She's in like Flynn in at least one and probably both. They hardly need to apply, they're so VIP. Why did they even bother with Bertha Kauffmann? I bet she could have skipped the SAPS altogether and still gotten in. Meanwhile, he's say-

ing things like "I share your pain." He never shared my pain! He has no idea what my pain is about. What a shmuck! she fumed. As she stormed out of the apartment, she took great pleasure in slamming the door, free to break their cardinal house rule since no one was home to notice.

As Helen approached The School's auditorium, she heard a clear, mellifluous voice singing "Greensleeves."

What child is this? she wondered as she opened the door soundlessly, tiptoed in, and took a seat in the back of the room. The chorus was seated quietly on stage, listening intently while a pubescent Adonis, who Helen hoped was named Max, practiced his solo.

"Thank you, Max, that was lovely," Sara said as he finished the piece.

Yes! Helen cheered to herself. *Good choice, Zoe.*

Max grinned as the group applauded, and then it was Zoe's turn. Helen's heart raced nervously any time her daughter was on stage; she suffered from the common maternal syndrome known as "performance anxiety by proxy." As Zoe sang a bluesy rendition of a maudlin Christmas favorite, Helen beamed, proud that her daughter had the talent to successfully reinterpret such a stodgy old classic. As Zoe finished and the group applauded, Helen found herself welling up with tears (another symptom of the syndrome).

The rehearsal was over, and as the kids were gathering their belongings and making their usual ruckus, Helen approached Sara and wrapped an arm around her shoulder.

"They sounded terrific," she said enthusiastically, giving a squeeze.

"Your daughter rocks, don't you think?" Sara smiled appreciatively.

"Absolutely. And that Max has quite a voice," she said, and then, cupping her hand around Sara's ear, whispered, "plus he's cute as a button."

"I think Zoe thinks so, too," Sara whispered back.

"I think you're right," she replied, following Sara's gaze to the far side of the room, where Zoe and Max were conversing in a corner. Even from twenty feet away, Helen could see that Zoe was smitten.

"It's good to see you. I've been desperate for a Helen fix lately.

I'm in dire need of a good long shmooze," Sara confessed. "I got it right this time, didn't I?" Helen laughed, and then wondered if Sara's need to talk meant that she knew something.

"I would love to get together soon. What's your schedule like?"

"Nuts. Between admissions and the holiday choral rehearsals I don't think I can commit to anything before the break. Are you around during the vacation?"

"Zoe will be off building houses in Cuba with Huts for Humans, which means Michael and I will most likely be staying home. Her trip is probably all we can swing," Helen replied.

She and Sara had often joked about the elaborate holiday vacations taken by many families in The School and how, in January, there was never any question where they had been. There were the skiers, identifiable by the lift tickets dangling from parka zippers, many of whom also came back hobbling on crutches. There were the island hoppers, identifiable by their beaded cornrows, an affectation Helen found particularly offensive on Caucasians and blamed on Bo Derek. But the worst were the international shoppers, identifiable by the Fendi and Prada they bought in Italy, where they allegedly went for cultural enrichment but in fact spent most of their time raiding designer outlet stores, where the current must-haves could be bought at a fraction of their retail price.

"How about you? Do you have any plans?" Helen asked.

"I was hoping to take a few days up at the yoga retreat, but it's looking like I'll actually have to work through most of the vacation," Sara replied.

Hmmmm, Helen thought, and wondered whether that meant she was involved in the transition, and if so, how.

"So let's try to spend some time together then," Sara added.

"Perfect," Helen replied. By then they would be free to talk openly and finally break down the awkward barrier that had been building all semester. "I'll look forward to it. Gotta get going. I hear homework calling."

As Helen and Zoe walked home from the rehearsal, it was as though they had reversed roles; Zoe was giddy and loquacious, Helen terse. Helen's usually exemplary posture was slack; Zoe, walking on air, held her head high.

"Isn't Max adorable? I think he's soooo cute. Don't you think he has an amazing voice? Don't you love his glasses?" She didn't wait for her mother to answer. "He's going to come with me to Catherine's party on Saturday night."

"What party?" Helen asked abruptly.

"I told you about it the other night. Or maybe I told Dad. Anyway, she's having a bunch of friends over from her school and invited me and Max."

"Will her father be home?"

"I guess. I didn't ask," Zoe answered.

"You know the rule. You are not allowed at a party at a friend's house unless there's a parent present. Will you please call Catherine and find out?" Helen requested more sternly than the situation called for.

"Why don't you call him? It's not like you don't know her father," Zoe shot back. Helen thought she detected a hint of sarcasm.

"All right. I will," Helen answered as they arrived at their building.

"You know what?" Helen softened her tone. "I think it's been three days since you took the SAPS. Here, hand me your backpack," she offered, slipping the straps off Zoe's shoulders, her arms straining under the weight. "Why don't you check the mail?"

Having closed the mailbox, Zoe stuffed the envelope that had arrived from the testing service into the pocket of her jacket.

"I get to look at it first," she announced.

Helen, having come up with no rational reason to disagree, rode up the elevator in silence, heart beating nervously, annoyed but also impressed by Zoe's self-control; she would have torn the envelope open right then and there. The minute they entered the apartment, Zoe went into her bedroom and closed the door while Helen busied herself by emptying the dishwasher. A few minutes later Zoe emerged and, expressionlessly, handed Helen the report.

Vocabulary	88 percentile
Reading	86 percentile
Reasoning	87 percentile
Mathematics	74 percentile

As Helen stared thoughtfully at the numbers, Zoe watched, eager for some sign from her mother indicating whether or not she thought the scores were satisfactory.

"It looks good to me, sweetie." Helen carefully meted out the flow of praise. She wanted to respond positively, but not with false overenthusiasm. The results were not the resounding success she had hoped for, but were by no means disastrous; they fell somewhere in between, neither here nor there.

"How do you feel about it?" Helen asked gently.

"I'm not thrilled. But I guess it's okay. I don't know . . ." Zoe was obviously confused, too.

"Why don't you go call Daddy and tell him. Use the phone in your room. I have a few calls to make."

This was one of those moments when she wished there were an admissions god—a higher authority she could count on to tell her that everything would be all right. It should have been Pamela, and in past years, at least according to those who believed in her omnipotence in the realm of admissions, it was. But now that Helen knew for a fact that Pamela had lost all contact with reality, there was absolutely no solace to be gotten from a conversation with her.

"Bertha. I'll call Bertha. She's the next best thing to a god," Helen decided. She got her on the first ring.

"Birdie. Hi. It's Mom."

"Mom who?"

"Sorry. Drager. Helen Drager. We just got Zoe's scores."

"And? Are ya celebrating?"

"Not exactly. I'm not quite sure how to react," and Helen read her the results.

"An 83.75 average."

"You figured that out quickly," Helen admired.

"It's my business, Mom. These scores aren't bad at all. They're what I call cliff-hangers."

"I was hoping maybe you'd shoot off some facts and figures, like what the average scores are for students accepted by the schools we've applied to. Something we can hang some hope on." Helen was practically pleading for some reassurance.

"Three years ago I could have given you that. These days, all bets are off. The schools are so inundated with applications from high scorers that it's impossible to know what the cutoff points are. There's no way to predict. As the saying goes, it ain't over till the fat lady sings."

"Oh, great," Helen replied sarcastically. "So I take it, by the 'fat ladies' you're referring to the admissions directors?"

"You got it, sweetheart," Bertha concurred.

Talking to Bertha provided no comfort. All she wanted was someone to tell her it would all work out, that is, someone other than Michael, who, when it came to Zoe, had no capacity for objectivity.

"Mom, I talked to Dad and *he* was really pleased when I told him the scores," Zoe announced, leaning against the frame of her bedroom door.

With nothing to be gained from disagreeing she replied, "That's great. I'm glad Daddy feels that way. He usually has a pretty good sense of things."

"Yeah, I really trust his judgment," Zoe said resolutely. "I have tons of homework," she said, returning to her room, and then over her shoulder she added, "And don't forget to call Catherine's dad. I *have* to go to her party on Saturday."

The Dragers had a rule that Zoe was required to provide them with details of her evening plans, specifically, at whose house, until what time, and verification that at least one parent would be home. This seemed to be an established practice among most of Zoe's school friends, and it was not uncommon for the parents to call one another to confirm that the plans had met with everyone's approval. But recently, keeping tabs on Zoe was not so simple, as her social circle was expanding to include kids from other schools, who lived in other parts of the city and moved around more freely. And with these new friends came new parents, most of whom Helen had never met. Like Max's, for example.

A party at Catherine's posed a different problem; after their romantic interlude, she was afraid that Phillip might interpret a call from her as an overture. And even though a part of her was still bristling over his wife's pedigree, there was also part of her that was excited by the thought of speaking with him.

As she dialed the number, her pulse quickened.

"Hello, Phillip? This is Helen Drager," she stated plainly, careful to keep her voice emotionally void.

"Helen, hi! I'm so glad you called," he answered so warmly that he instantly melted the anger she had been harboring all day.

She was unsure how to respond. Fortunately, he continued.

"I'd been thinking about you all day. I just finished reading your article, 'Cocktales.' I thought it was brilliant."

"You mean British brilliant or *brilliant* brilliant?"

He laughed. "*Brilliant* brilliant, which by my standards is a compliment. Unlike some people, I don't use the term loosely."

"Well, then, thank you," she softened.

"I thought the analogy you drew between the violence of the cockfight and the competitiveness of contemporary society was very insightful. You also raised a few psychological issues that have been on my mind lately."

"Really? Like what?"

"Oh, like the universality of aggressive male behavior, for starters. I'm afraid I could be accused of that at times."

She was silent as she wondered, *Hmmm, does that make me a cock-tease?*

"But how have you been?" he fortunately changed the subject. "I miss seeing you now that the SAPS are done. Did it work out well for Zoe?"

"Pretty well. How about Catherine?"

"She did all right." He was equally ambiguous.

"I'm sure her scores won't matter," Helen said abrasively. Phillip either chose to ignore her innuendo or missed it entirely.

"I would love to see you some time soon, but I'm not sure how," he said gently. "I realize there are, uh, complications."

She supposed "complications" meant "your marriage." But despite the "complications," the sound of his voice triggered a longing.

"But you called me," he said.

"So I did. I gather there's a plan afoot to have a bunch of kids invade your house on Saturday night. I just wanted to make sure you had approved before I gave Zoe permission to go."

"Of course. For weeks I've been encouraging Catherine to have a party. It will be the first time since her mother died that she has asked to have a group of friends over. I thought it would be good for her."

"I also wanted to make sure that you plan to be there," she said.

"Absolutely. Will you join me? You're probably more experienced with this sort of thing than I am."

"I don't think that would be a good idea. First of all, I've had almost no experience chaperoning boy-girl parties. And second of all, Zoe would kill me. But could I ask you to do me a favor?"

"Anything."

"Would you mind keeping an eye on her for me? Apparently, she managed to get Catherine to invite the new man in her life. A boy named Max. He's her first serious crush, and she's very excited about the prospect of seeing him at the party."

"Do you approve of this Max?"

"He seems like a decent kid, but who knows? I've only met him briefly. If you could just let me know if it looks like things between them are going too far, I would be highly appreciative."

"What's your idea of too far?" he asked provocatively.

As far as we went? she thought, and then said, "I'll leave that up to you to decide."

Having been summoned to Pamela's office, Felicity teetered in on three-inch stiletto heels. Much to Margaret's amazement, she was braless, her skintight white spandex sheath leaving nothing to the imagination.

"Felicity, *ma chérie*, come, sit, make yourself comfortable, if it's possible in that getup," Pamela welcomed her. "I have some very exciting news to share with you. After our trip to St. Barts, I'm thinking that I might not be returning to The School."

Tears welled up in Felicity's eyes. "How can zat be? I don't understand!" she cried.

"I have been positively hounded by headhunters in the past few months, and they are all telling me I am in great demand. The time is right for me to make a move. There are several offers on the table, all of which are once-in-a-lifetime opportunities, and I am under tremendous pressure to make a choice immediately. You can't imagine how conflicted I am. The minute I make a decision, you will be the first to know. The board is being so understanding. They've always known that my days here are numbered, that I am destined for greater things, so they have kindly agreed to release me from my contract as soon as need be," Pamela improvised mawkishly.

"*Mon Dieu!* What will I do?"

"You will carry on here. I need you to head The School. If you don't, they will get that awful Sara Nash to do the job. That would be ruinous. I couldn't bear to see that happen to our beloved school."

"But I can't head Zee School. I don't know the first thing about how to run zis place," she whimpered, and wiped her nose with the back of her hand.

"It is only temporary, until they hire someone new. If you don't step up to the plate, then Nash will, and if she becomes the interim head, there is a good chance they will make her permanent. We can't take that chance, can we?" she said in the imperious tone she reserved for such portentous speeches.

Felicity looked confused. "Why not? I don't see why zat would be so bad."

Pamela picked up her riding crop and twitched it menacingly close to Felicity's face. "Because, *mon enfant,* she is . . . she is . . . ," she sputtered, "an opportunistic, granola-eating, two-faced New Age admissions wonk! She doesn't know the first thing about running a school!"

"And . . . I . . . do?" Felicity quaked.

"You have been my protégé for what? Three months? You have had the distinct advantage of learning at the foot of a master. That counts for a lot." She paused. "Well, something anyway." Pamela's brio gave way to defensiveness.

"Three months, eet is not so long," Felicity suggested.

"Deal with it. Find the courage to act authoritative for once in your life. And by the way, that oh-la-la getup won't cut it in the oval office. You may act twittish, but take it from me: dress British. It will enhance your image immensely. And while you're at it, your roots could use a touch-up," she advised, and with a flick of her wrist, she shooed the pouting Felicity out the door.

* * *

"Have you seen the December issue of *Tally Ho*?" Brandi cried, running into Sara's office while brandishing an open magazine.

"No. I haven't been to a nail parlor recently. That's the only time I see it. Why?" Sara replied.

"You're gonna hit the roof when you read this," she predicted, plunking the glossy magazine on Sara's desk. The cover featured a full-body shot of Tally Easton in a floor-length, black-belted crimson velvet gown, trimmed at the neck and wrists with white fur, no doubt intended to be some sort of feminist commentary on the patriarchal institution of Santa Claus. Impishly peeking out from behind her immense red skirt was Santa's little helper, an elfin Montana Easton decked out in green velvet.

Sara opened the magazine to the page marked by Brandi with a yellow sticky tab and read Tally's monthly column, "Tally's Dallies."

> My dear Sisters and Mothers,
>
> As you know, I believe that the greatest gift we can give to our children is the gift of a good education. So it is with enormous joy that I begin this holiday season. I have just received news that my little gobbler has been accepted into next year's Kindergarten class at The School, one of the best New York has to offer. I encourage each and every one of you to celebrate the yuletide season as I have, by giving your children the greatest gift of all—the gift of learning.
>
> And don't forget, if you are a member of MOTBOB, do as I do every year—thank the blessed baster who delivered our darlings to us.
>
> Godspeed,
>
> Tally Easton

"I think I'm going to be sick!" Sara yelled, and threw the magazine across the room, hitting a hanging fern so hard that Brandi had to dash over to steady it before it crashed to the floor.

"What about it is making you sick? The style or the content?"

"Both. But I can hardly hold the style against her, can I? It's classic, sanctimonious Tally. The content, on the other hand, confirms what I've been suspecting for months. Pamela has WAY overstepped her boundaries. She's lost what little sense of morality she ever had. The woman has come unhinged!" Sara raged. It was the closest Brandi had ever seen Sara come to a full-blown temper tantrum, and she thought her boss needed a belt of whatever the New Age version of a drink was. Tension-tamer tea? Kava kava? Or better yet, a ginseng martini?

"What can we do about it?" Brandi questioned, ever the dutiful assistant.

"Absolutely nothing. I can't call Tally and tell her it's a no go. It's too late for that. But I will call Lydia Waxman and see what she knows about this. Could you get me her number, please?" Sara asked, having calmed herself a bit. Lydia took Sara's call immediately.

"I take it you're calling because you've seen the December issue of *Tally Ho*?" Lydia began. "Tally is so thrilled that Montana will be coming to The School that she couldn't contain herself. I hope it's not a problem."

"It is a problem, Lydia. A huge problem," Sara declared angrily, disgusted by Lydia's sycophantic willingness to overlook Tally's egregious behavior solely on the basis of her celebrity status. "What I want to know is how Tally's acceptance was communicated. I can only assume it came from Pamela. Did you get those two together?" she demanded.

"Well, I guess you could say so. I called Pamela after you rejected Tally's generous offer to help with The School's Thanksgiving activities. I felt you were, how shall I put it . . . slightly out of your league, and that it was my duty to my client to make Pamela aware of the offer. During that conversation Pamela gave me the good news on Montana's acceptance."

"I consider that a serious breach of our relationship, Lydia. You should know by now that (a) I've never been a celebrity chaser, and (b) I find that kind of backroom dealing highly offensive. So you can tell any of your so-called clients that from now on, if they're interested in applying to The School, they are better off doing so on their own." And she slammed the phone down.

Brandi waited until Sara had caught her breath and stopped pacing before she announced that Lisa Fontaine was on line two. She knew that Sara had to take this call.

"Sara, the board would like to meet with you on Monday evening. Could you make it at seven?" Lisa proposed curtly.

"Of course," Sara answered automatically, even though Monday was the night her meditation group met. She hesitated a moment and then continued, "Uh, could I ask what the meeting is about?"

"I'm not at liberty to discuss it with you in advance," Lisa replied guardedly.

Sara's first assumption was that the meeting was related to the *Tally Ho* article, and she could well imagine the board blaming her. But, if that were the case, Lisa would most likely have discussed it on the phone, since it hardly warranted the attention of the full board. Then she realized it was more likely related to the recent activity in the business office. She had become friendly with one of the accountants, expecting that he would eventually reveal the purpose of the investigation. But he proved to be tight-lipped, and all she could glean from a few of his remarks was that there was an unexplained deficit on the balance sheet. That was hardly a surprise given Pamela's profligate attitude towards spending. If Sara were so inclined, she could certainly drop some hints to the accountants about where they might look for missing funds, but decided against doing so on the grounds that her participation in Pamela's downfall was bad karma.

"You're not yourself tonight. Is anything wrong?" Helen asked Michael, who had arrived home from work that evening in an odd mood.

"No. Nothing's wrong."

"What was your day like?"

"The usual."

"Michael!" Helen said with annoyance. "You're acting like Zoe on a bad day. What is it? Negative ratings on *Epicurean MD*?"

"No, actually, that's one show that's doing well."

She let it go until after dinner, when Zoe was in her room doing homework and they were cleaning up the kitchen.

"Sorry if I seemed distracted," he began. "I just didn't want to discuss it in front of Zoe. It's sort of a good news/bad news situation. The good news is, *La Cuisine de Justine* is alive and well. Justine is going to France for the winter break and suggested that we join her to scout the locations. The bad news is that 'we' has turned into Xavier and me. Suddenly he's all over the project and wants to be involved in every step."

"That's not so bad. I like his wife. The four of us would have a good time."

"The other part of the bad news is that the wives are not invited. He thinks the two of us should go alone."

"What! That's ridiculous. What kind of grinch takes a trip to Provence during the Christmas holidays without their family?"

"Xavier. And I'm stuck going with him."

"Oh, poor you," she said angrily. "So while Zoe's in Cuba and you're in France, the little wife stays home alone? That really sucks, Michael, and you know it."

"You're absolutely right. You have every reason to be angry," he said in complete agreement, as though that would help to placate her. Instead it infuriated her.

"Easy for you to say! You'll be feasting on coq au vin and boûche de noël in Cap Ferrat while I'm forcing down overcooked flanken at your parents' retirement home in Piscataway. I hope you gain ten pounds!"

"Helen, this is a business trip. Presumably we'll be working."

"Real hard, I'm sure," she said bitterly. "How come Justine isn't spending the winter break in New York finishing up the last of the admissions business? I know Sara's going to be."

"Maybe she's already finished."

"Well, if that's the case, all I can say is, if Zoe hasn't made the cut, Frampton is dead meat."

"She has to accept Zoe since we've given her exactly what she wanted. There *is* a certain social contract she is obligated to honor."

"Whose rules are those?" Helen questioned.

"The rules of the favor bank."

"I've got news for you. The favor bank isn't insured," she sneered.

"Helen, I think you're forgetting how we got into this mess in the first place. You can't blame me for having to go on this trip."

"Who else am I going to blame, if not you?"

"Blame Xavier or, if it makes you more comfortable, blame Justine."

"Is there some way I can justify blaming Pamela? I would actually get pleasure out of doing that."

"Sure, blame Pamela. Good idea. If she were doing her job, we wouldn't be in this ridiculous situation to begin with."

"Okay. It's her fault," she said, and stroked his cheek. "I'm sorry. You've been such a great sport about this whole thing. I do love you for that." She gave him an affectionate hug.

"Look. Don't feel obligated to see my parents during the holidays. Zoe will be away. Why don't you go to a spa. That Pilates place you've been reading about. Let me treat you to that," he offered kindly.

"Thank you. That's sweet. I'll think about it," she whispered forgivingly. "Let's go to bed."

As they were undressing, he asked, "So what are our weekend plans?"

"Zoe and I have a date to go to the museum tomorrow to see the new photography exhibition. Why don't you join us?"

"I'll pass. The Knicks are playing the Bulls."

"Say no more."

"And what about the evening? Do we have plans?" he asked.

"Zoe is going to a party at Catherine Cashin's, and we have a long-standing dinner date at the Doyle-Gillises'."

"What dinner?"

"I'm sure I told you about it weeks ago. Denise is having us to dinner with the Topplers to do some brainstorming about the auction. She's hoping to get John to come up with some big-ticket items for the sale. It'll be interesting to see her in action. You know how tenacious she can be."

"That I do. She's been calling me every week about getting the network to put together a day with a chef or a guest appearance on one of our shows. I told her I would see what I can do, but it's the last thing I need right now," Michael complained.

"She won't let you off the hook until you do. You're better off doing it sooner than later and saving yourself the aggravation of getting a call from her every week. Put Charlotte on it."

"Good idea," he replied. "What's Denise's husband's name again?"

"Richard."

"He's a passive fellow, isn't he?"

"He lets her run the show."

"Do you think people say that about us?"

"It's true, isn't it?" she teased, and climbed on top of him.

Helen interpreted Zoe's enthusiasm about their outing to the museum as a sign of maturity. It wasn't long ago that getting her daughter to agree to a museum visit required bribery, usually in the form of a purchase at the museum shop, where they would spend what felt like hours debating between the hieroglyphic rubber stamp set and the make-your-own-Moroccan-jewelry kit, either of which would ultimately provide about twenty minutes of entertainment before being relegated to the top shelf of the hall closet.

After leisurely meandering through the great hall, they arrived at the exhibition—a blockbuster retrospective of one of the more popular portrait photographers of the twentieth century—where they took their time, pausing in front of each portrait to discuss the subject and the esthetic merits of each composition.

"She looks so sad," Zoe said thoughtfully in front of a portrait of Marilyn Monroe. "What a hopeless romantic."

"That's such an intelligent observation. I would never have thought to describe her that way, but I think you're right. She was a romantic," Helen agreed encouragingly.

"I feel like I have a whole new appreciation for photography now, Mom," Zoe answered.

"Really? Why's that," Helen asked.

"Because now that I'm older, I have so much more experience with people. You know, I think I've even learned a little about the opposite sex," Zoe replied earnestly.

Helen was touched. "I assume you're referring to Max?"

"Uh-huh," she answered dreamily.

They continued down the row of photographs.

"Doesn't this look sort of like Daddy?" Zoe said, pointing to a portrait of the young Marlon Brando.

I wish, thought Helen, but realized that it was important to give Zoe positive reinforcement, and if Zoe thought her dad looked like Stanley Kowalski, more power to her. "A little," she conceded. "I beg of you, just don't say that portrait of Dame Edith Sitwell reminds you of me." She pointed to the photograph of the patrician, hawk-billed poetess.

"She sort of does," Zoe giggled.

Helen moaned.

"Just kidding, Mom. But you have to admit, this guy looks a lot like Max," Zoe said, pointing to a portrait of Montgomery Clift.

"Hmmm, you may be right. I've only met Max once, so I don't have a strong mental image of him yet. But I hope I will get to spend some time with him soon."

"Mom. Can I tell you something?"

"Of course. You can tell me anything."

"Promise you won't get mad?"

"I can't promise that, but I promise I will listen to your point of view first."

"Okay. I don't think I want to go to Cuba, 'cause I don't want to be away from Max for two weeks." Zoe spoke quickly and then waited anxiously for her mother's reaction.

"Zoe, that's crazy!" Helen responded emphatically. "Think about it this way: if your relationship has any future whatsoever, then what will two weeks apart matter? And if Max cares about you as much as I think he does, then he would never want you to give up such a great opportunity. He'll be here for you when you get back, and if he's not, then that proves he wasn't worthy of you in the first place. Don't you think?"

"I guess so," Zoe replied tentatively, not sounding one hundred percent convinced.

"And if you're looking for more concrete reasons as to why you have to go, I can give you two. One, it's already paid for and it's probably too late to get a refund. And two, you need the community service credits in order to graduate from eighth grade," Helen said didactically, and took a step backwards, almost falling over the stroller that had stealthily crept up behind her.

"Oh, I'm so sorry," she said as she regained her balance. The formidable two-seater held a boy and a girl who, to her, looked far too old to be strapped into a stroller. Pushing the behemoth load was Donald Roman. Josh Kirov was standing a few feet away, struggling to get a glimpse of James Dean through the crowds.

"Oh, Donald! These must be your twins!" Helen greeted her colleague.

"Alexi and Anna, say hello to Mrs. Drager," Donald commanded with the authority of a wet noodle.

Predictably, given the presence of a pacifier in both children's mouths, she received no reply. The poor twins were additionally constrained by their suffocating and impractical (dry cleaning required) blue (his) and pink (her) snowsuits and an overabundance of color-coordinated hats, scarves, mittens on strings, and embroidered suede snow boots.

The sight of their flushed cheeks and sweaty brows produced a sympathetic hot flash in Helen and an unconscious impulse on Zoe's part to squat down and help the struggling Alexi to loosen his scarf.

"It looks like someone might be a member of the babysitters' club," Josh giggled as he planted two air kisses on the void between Helen's shoulders and ears. "This must be your daughter. What's your name?" he asked Zoe so patronizingly that he might as well have ended the sentence with "little girl?"

"Zoe, meet Josh Kirov and Donald Roman. They're the two dealers who own the Gallery Nouveau Russe on Madison Avenue. I'm sure you've been there with me," Helen made the introduction.

"And how is your client Mr. Cashin?" Josh asked with a nod-nod-wink-wink.

Zoe shot a glance in her mother's direction.

"I told you, Josh, he's not my client. And you well know, I'm not in the art advisory business," Helen responded curtly.

"Well, he certainly seemed interested in your advice." Donald jumped in and tried to lighten the tone.

"Cash in, cash out," Josh quipped.

"Ka-ching," Donald added, imitating the sound of a cash register.

Helen was momentarily flustered and then furious. She was adamantly opposed to discussing Phillip (although curious to know which glass piece he did end up buying) in front of Zoe, who at this point was visibly perturbed. She quickly changed tack and asked them about the only thing that she knew interested them more than gossip.

"How are you two progressing with the admissions process?" she asked with studious concern. As she expected, the floodgates opened.

Jabbering in concert, Donald and Josh took turns plowing their wide load through the museum corridors, unwittingly forcing everyone in their path to jump out of the way.

"We can't decide if we should hold out for one school that will take both, or send them to different schools."

"In which case, the question arises, should they each go to a single-sex school?"

"They say girls benefit more from single-sex schools than boys."

"Only some of the studies support that. I've read the opposite point of view as well."

"Donald likes a more nontraditional approach than I do."

"No, I don't!"

"You said you liked The Progressive School."

"No, I didn't!"

"You said you felt comfortable there."

"I was comfortable, but I didn't think our children would necessarily do well there."

"So sue me. I stand corrected."

"The School will probably take one but not both."

"Well, we hope so, anyway. Have you heard anything from Sara Nash about our chances?"

Fortunately, Helen wasn't given a chance to answer.

"It's considered the best place in the city for the elementary years, but then we have to worry about high school the entire time we're there. That would kill me."

"We should be so lucky."

"What's that supposed to mean?"

"Just joshing, Joshie."

"Oy. Helen, this is what I put up with every day."

And on and on. Finding the Donald-and-Josh performance hilarious, Zoe had enough social grace to stifle her laughter, while Helen just longed to escape. Finally, they arrived at the museum exit, and as they were saying their goodbyes, Helen, unable to restrain herself, blurted, "If you want some motherly advice, lose the stroller. Your children could use a little freedom."

The two men looked stunned. It had never occurred to them to venture into the world with their children free to move about. It seemed so risky, so dangerous, so inconvenient.

"Joshie, Helen's right. Let's go right now and buy a couple of those leashes they make for children."

"*Hopeless,*" thought Helen as Zoe elbowed her in the side.

As soon as they were alone, Zoe had Helen in stitches with a dead-on impersonation of the two high-strung fathers, including a nearly verbatim playback of their dialogue. Suddenly, remembering the part about Phillip, she became solemn.

"What was that about Catherine's dad?" Zoe asked.

"Sometime last month, Phillip had asked me to go to Donald and Josh's gallery with him. He wanted my advice on a purchase. That's all."

"I didn't know you did that. Does Daddy?"

"I don't report to Daddy on everything that I do," she said sharply, and then immediately regretted sounding so defensive. "I mean, I just made a quick trip over to the gallery with him the day you and I had lunch at the Cashins'. Remember that day? The whole thing was so insignificant that it never even occurred to me to tell Daddy about it. It was nothing."

"Josh and Donald made it sound like it was more than that."

"That's because to them it was. Phillip Cashin is an important collector, so for them it's a big deal when he comes to their gallery and buys something."

"Oh."

"Look, sweetie! Aren't those the jeans you've been looking for?" Helen deftly steered them towards the window of a very trendy shop. "Let's go in and see if they have your size," she offered, convinced that her diversionary tactic was no worse than offering a bottle to a crying infant. The desired outcome was the same—silence the child and rescue the mother.

* * *

Michael was pacing in front of the television with the phone glued to his ear, shouting, "Did you see that? Did you see that sixty-five-footer at the buzzer? Look, look, they're doing an instant replay. Whoooo, can you believe it?"

Having just returned from their outing, Zoe was in the kitchen making a sandwich, and Helen was casually leafing through the mail. Two envelopes immediately caught her eye: one from The Bucolic Campus School and one from The Safety School, both addressed to "The Parents of Zoe Drager." She tore open The Bucolic Campus School's first, and out fell a form letter with the heading "Notification of Incomplete Application" and, handwritten underneath, "Missing: head of school's Recommendation." The envelope from The Safety School contained the same kind of notice.

"That worthless bitch!" she exploded as she threw the letters on to the couch next to Michael, who was still clutching the phone and riveted to the game.

"Vinnie," he mouthed, and pointed to the receiver. Helen picked up the notice from The Bucolic Campus School and held it in front of Michael's face. He read it and shrugged, as if to say, "What am I supposed to do about it?" and then went back to yelling into the phone about somebody's jump shot.

"Zoe, I need to use the phone in your room," she said with urgency.

"What's the matter, Mom?" Zoe asked fearfully.

"I'll tell you in a minute," she said as she closed the bedroom door.

She tried Sara first at home but got no answer. She tried her at The School, and Sara picked up.

"You're not gonna believe this, but Pamela has failed to do the one simple thing we've counted on her to do for us."

"What's that?"

"The only thing she HAD to do. If she did nothing else this semester, this was the one thing we needed her to do."

"WHAT?"

"The head-of-school recommendations!"

"Helen. Calm down. We'll get them written," Sara said with a calm that belied her own panic. If Pamela had let these two fall through the cracks, how many others were in the same boat?

"How? How the hell will they get done?" Helen demanded. "It will be impossible to get them done now." Helen stopped herself before adding, "Now that Pamela is a lame duck."

"They will get done if I have to write them myself and get Pamela to sign them, okay?"

"I've had it with her."

"How do you think I feel? I have to work with her," Sara said angrily.

"I'm sorry for dumping on you. I just needed to vent," Helen said conciliatorily.

"You know I'm always here for you. But I have to tell you, Helen, I'm getting really tired of being on the receiving end of all your anger. Your negativity is starting to rub off on me. I can't take much more of it," Sara declared with a vehemence that surprised them both.

There was a momentary silence on both ends.

"I'm sorry," Helen muttered. "It's just that I really don't know where else to turn."

"I'm sorry, too. But let up a little. Somehow it will all work out," Sara said. "Listen, I'm tied up all day Monday, but let's talk Tuesday morning and we'll figure out a game plan for getting the recommendations done, okay?" she proposed, hoping that by Tuesday she might have something concrete to offer.

"Sounds good. Thanks again. I really appreciate your being there for me. I hope you have a good weekend."

"You, too," Sara signed off curtly.

Helen wearily wandered into Zoe's room, lay down on her bed, and with heavy eyes observed her daughter as she dressed for Catherine's party. Zoe settled on black velvet jeans and a bell-sleeved peasant blouse, both perfectly suitable to a party at the Cashins'. It was only when Zoe applied her makeup that Helen weighed in with "Not too much. That's a little too dark. A little lighter, sweetie."

Last, in a moment of weakness, Helen agreed to let Zoe borrow her garnet chandelier earrings, the antique pair she had inherited from her mother and that were currently all the rage.

"You have to promise me, you will *not* take them off," Helen said seriously.

"I promise," Zoe agreed.

"I mean it," Helen repeated sternly.

"Dazzling," Michael said as Zoe emerged from her room. "If I were Max, I wouldn't let you out of my sight the entire night."

"You're so corny, Dad," Zoe said as she kissed him on the forehead. "So you'll pick me up at midnight, right?"

"Wrong, Cinderella, we said eleven," Helen corrected.

"Just testing," Zoe laughed giddily.

"We should go now, too. We were due at the Doyle Gillises' twenty minutes ago," she nudged.

"So we'll be fashionably late."

"I can safely guarantee that our lateness will be the only fashionable thing about this dinner party," she said, stroking the back of Zoe's smooth hair as they left the house together.

After putting Zoe in a cab, Helen and Michael walked the few blocks to the Doyle-Gillis apartment, where the door was opened by their host, who greeted them with a flaccid handshake and a graceless acceptance of the very good bottle of wine they had brought. Dick was an anesthesiologist with the bedside manner of an undertaker, having attended medical school eons before humanity was introduced into the curriculum. While he busied himself hanging their coats in the closet, they wandered into the kitchen, where Denise was leading Lauren Toppler on a guided tour of her pantry.

"The spices are arranged alphabetically, starting with anise, which is tricky because it's sometimes called fenugreek, but I chose to . . . Oh, hi." Denise turned. "Lauren was just asking how it was possible for my kitchen to be so spotless in the middle of preparing for a dinner party, and I was explaining it's all a function of advanced planning and timing."

"Denise, your organizational skills are legendary," Helen said, giving her a light peck on the cheek. *But your taste is indescribable because . . . for all intents and purposes, you have none,* she thought.

But if she were pushed to define Denise's style, the word Helen would have chosen would have been utilitarian. There was nothing left to chance when it came to Denise's appearance: hair kept crew-cut short, clothing generic, and makeup in short supply. Her house was the same: highly functional, zero design, and forget about frivolity.

"You're the only person I know who has one of these in her kitchen," Helen said, pointing to the tall gray steel file cabinet in the corner.

Michael, curious about its contents, read the labels on the drawers: "Birthday parties, vacations, auction, community service. Wow, there's even one just for admissions."

"That's the drawer that I've been in and out of most these days," Denise commented wryly. "Can't wait until that's over."

"Ditto," Helen responded, and then whispered to Michael. "*My* admissions files are on Excel."

"Denise runs a tight ship," Dick added. It was not clear whether he meant it as a compliment.

"Speaking of ships . . . what do you and John think of the auction theme this year, Lauren?"

"Where is John?" Helen asked.

"In the little boys' room on his cell phone, no doubt," Lauren answered with a hint of annoyance.

"Do you mind if we sit down for dinner right now? Dick has to go pick up the kids at ten, so time is a little tight."

Helen looked at her watch. It was only seven thirty. "Sure. Where are the kids tonight?"

"Mark is serving dinner at the homeless shelter, Matthew is sleeping at my parents', and Marissa is over at the Winters', helping April catch up on homework."

"How's April doing?"

"Apparently she had a relapse last week. I gather she pulled herself together to take the SAPS, but then she completely collapsed from exhaustion. And to make matters worse, between you and me, Marissa told me her test scores were dreadful. Poor thing. Anemia is difficult to deal with in adolescence. These kids have such lousy diets to begin with, right, Dick?" Dick grunted.

What is with these people? Helen thought in disgust. *Denise is a smart woman, and Dick is a doctor, for Christ's sake. Haven't they heard of eating disorders?*

Only after they were all seated around the dining room table did

John Toppler make an appearance. With cell phone headset dangling off one ear, BlackBerry in his breast pocket, and pager attached to his belt, he was wired to the hilt.

"Hey, old man, how's it going?" he bellowed, slapping Michael on the back. "What's for dinner? I'm famished," he added with gusto.

"Cornish hens," Dick answered just as Denise entered with an enormous dome-covered platter.

"Under glass," Denise announced as she made a grand gesture of setting the plate on the table and lifting the glass dome.

"Ohhhh . . ." Michael was impressed with the formal presentation. "Huh?" He did a double take when he saw only two small hens huddled in the center of the huge plate.

"Dick, will you do the honors?" Denise asked, handing her husband a long knife.

The guests watched in disbelief as Dick, with the care of a surgeon, proceeded to carve the first miniature bird.

"Who wants a leg?" he asked his guests. Helen didn't dare look at Michael, for fear she would totally lose it.

"I'll take one. I'm a dark-meat man," Toppler answered good-naturedly, not yet having registered that the two Cornish hens represented dinner for six.

"And there's pasta, too!" Denise announced, much to everyone's relief, as she returned from the kitchen carrying two small bowls. After Dick placed a minuscule portion of poultry on each person's plate, he passed to Denise, who added six tortellini, counting as she went, and two branches of broccoli.

Helen wished she had a camera to record the sight of the corpulent John Toppler holding the teeny hen leg between thumb and index finger as he gnawed in search of a morsel of flesh. No one would have believed it otherwise.

On the other side of the table, Michael was taking his time chewing his 1.5 ounces of breast meat while wishing he were drinking the California Zinfandel he had brought instead of the Doyle-Gilleses' sickly sweet Riesling. Helen was methodically cutting each tortellini into four pieces in order to prolong the meal, while Lauren, who had declined the pasta and poultry altogether, made a meal out of two broccoli stalks by nibbling them floret by floret. When Denise apologized for not being able to offer seconds, Helen kicked Michael under the table when she thought she heard him chuckle.

"Let's retire to the living room for coffee and dessert," Denise suggested.

One coffee bean and a thimble of sorbet, Helen thought just as Denise appeared with a plate of six tiny brownies.

Suddenly there was a high-pitched buzz as one of Toppler's telecommunications devices received an incoming signal. He shoved the microphone in front of his mouth and began yakking loudly.

"The fucking surgeon is blaming the pulmonary guy who's threatening a malpractice suit against the idiot anesthesiologist who had the gall to . . ." Lauren grabbed her husband's arm and guided him out of the room as she murmured "sorry" to her hosts.

"Helen, I want to talk to you about the entertainment for the gala. I thought you and I should wear matching gowns, you know, in order to establish our coleadership roles. I have a dress picked out that I think will look great on both of us. That way, we'll be color-coordinated when we perform our song."

"What? What song?"

"The parody lyrics I'm working on. I told you about this weeks ago. It's important for spirit building and getting the sale off to a rollicking start."

"I don't sing. Nor do I do twinsies," Helen replied, certain she wouldn't be caught dead in a dress selected by Denise.

"What's this about singing?" John Toppler returned to the room.

"We were just talking about the musical performance that Helen and I are planning for the night of the auction. The idea is to warm up the crowd before the sale begins. If you beg and plead, I'll give you a sneak preview," she teased. No one did, but that didn't stop her.

"Dick, will you be my accompanist?" she asked, leading her begrudging husband towards the piano.

Dick played a short overture to "When I Was a Lad" from *HMS Pinafore,* and Denise sang:

"WHEN I WAS A MOM
I SERVED A STINT
AS CHAIR OF THE AUCTION

AND WE RAISED A MINT.
I GOT DONATIONS
AND I TOOK SOME BIDS
AND NOW WE HAVE A LIBRARY FOR ALL OUR KIDS.

"And everybody, repeat the last line," she demanded.

"AND NOW WE HAVE A LIBRARY FOR ALL OUR KIDS."

"AS CHAIR OF THE AUCTION
I MADE SUCH A SPLASH
THAT THEY ASKED ME TO ORGANIZE
ANOTHER BASH.
THEY ALL GOT BOMBED
AND MADE OUTRAGEOUS BIDS.
THAT'S HOW WE GOT A JUNGLE GYM FOR ALL
OUR KIDS.

"And everybody, repeat the last line," she commanded again.

"THAT'S HOW WE GOT A JUNGLE GYM FOR ALL
OUR KIDS."

After three more verses the audience applauded.

"Great song, Denise, but please don't make Helen sing. She can't carry a tune with a shovel," Michael said.

"He's right, Denise. But the song is fun. You should do it alone," Helen said kindly.

"No way!" Denise was disappointed. "Dick, will you sing along with me while you play?"

"I'd sooner go into cardiac arrest," he said lugubriously. Denise let it go.

"John, I was hoping I could get you to come up with a few items for the auction. Your divorce package last year was such a big hit, I thought maybe you could offer another kind of legal service this time, like a will or a real estate closing."

"How about leading a class action suit? At least there's some upside potential for me. Last year's divorce ended up costing me about two hundred billable hours. Boy, that couple really went to war." Helen tried to remember who the winning bidder was on the divorce last year.

"Well, maybe it's not a legal service. Think about some of your clients. Who could you ask a favor of?" Denise pressed.

"How about a day at a pharmaceutical factory? I know the people who make Viagra. I could definitely pull that off."

"Ummm . . . not exactly right for our audience," Denise delicately rejected his suggestion.

"How about medical services? I have lots of clients in the health care business," he said, ignoring the fact that his host was an MD.

"We sort of have that base covered. Dick has gotten us laser eye surgery, dermabrasion, and a series of botox treatments."

"And I'm working on our podiatrist to donate a bunion-removal procedure," Dick added stiffly. He wasn't going to lose a game of medical one-upsmanship to some ambulance chaser.

"Think vacations and weekend homes. Those usually generate tons of bidding and make lots of money. Last year I think we got eight thousand for a week at the King's Tennessee mountain retreat, including a day at Graceland with an Elvis impersonator." Denise kept trying. "Think out of the box."

"I've got it! I've got a client in Jersey. He's in waste management. He's got some kind of barocco villa in Palermo. He's shown me the pictures. Looks pretty heavy-duty. He keeps telling me I should take the family and spend a week there. I'm sure I could get him to give it to us for the auction. He's into me for a bundle."

Denise looked to Helen for guidance. She didn't want to keep rejecting John's ideas, but this one sounded a little scary.

"That sounds extraordinary," Helen said with restraint, leaving Denise unsure what she meant. Thankfully, Toppler's pager starting vibrating, and he ran out of the room.

"Lauren, do you know this client of John's?" Helen inquired.

"If it's who I think it is, I would steer clear," she said softly while John was in the kitchen screaming about a car accident.

A few minutes later he returned to the conversation, red in the face, and said, "That call just gave me a great idea. Bodywork. I could get a buddy in the repo business to give us some bodywork. Maybe he would throw in a muffler and a lube job, too."

"That's an original idea," Denise responded politely.

"I love it," said Michael.

"Great," said Helen.

"We're happy to donate our apartment, with staff of course, for the Pamela Rothschild Provençal dinner. That's always a popular item, isn't it, Denise? What did it go for last year?" Lauren offered, trying to compensate for her husband's vulgarity.

"Ummm . . . ," murmured Helen as Denise said, "It sold for about eight thousand last year. That's so generous of you. Thank you, Lauren."

"Uh-oh," Michael whispered to Helen, who responded with a "Shhh."

At nine thirty on the button, Dick stood up and walked towards the hall closet for his coat. The Dragers took this as a cue and departed with him. As soon as they both said, "Good night, Dick," and were out on the sidewalk, Michael suggested that they go for a drink and a bite to eat in the time they had to kill before picking up Zoe.

"Good idea. I'm starving," she said, and took his hand as they walked down the street.

"God, Dick is a snooze," Michael complained.

"What do you expect? He's in the business of putting people to sleep."

"Was that the saddest excuse for a meal you've ever been served?" he asked.

"They're not generous people. That goes for everything they do. Denise is withholding and controlling, and he's just a cold fish. I'm afraid Marissa is turning out to be the same."

"Where are they applying to high school for her? I couldn't bear to bring it up tonight."

"Marissa is a really strong student, so they're counting on her getting into one of the competitive public high schools. I'm sure she will. That's where Mark is, and Matthew will undoubtedly do the same."

"And they're okay with that? I mean, they certainly can afford private school, can't they?"

"I'm sure the decision wasn't made lightly. I would guess Denise conducted an exhaustive analysis and weighed every pro and con, probably factoring in the impact the decision would have on college admissions. And knowing her, I'm sure it will prove to be the right choice."

"Remind me again why we're not applying to those public schools," he asked innocently.

She sighed. "Because we determined—correctly, I might add—that Zoe needs a more supportive environment. She's not an independent worker and requires supervision. She would get lost in one of those huge schools," she explained patiently, even though she thought they had settled this months ago.

But she, too, had paused when she first learned of the Doyle-Gilleses' choice to go the public school route. Denise was such a perfectionist and stickler for detail that her decision at least warranted understanding. The bottom line was that her kids were the highly motivated, outspoken type that thrived in a large, competitive arena. Zoe was not like that at all. She required the security blanket of a smaller community, and Helen had come to realize that she did, too. For the past ten years, The School had provided them with a grounding, a luxury that would be hard for all of them to give up. The cost of that was exorbitant, but once they had accepted the bite of the tuition (not to mention the Capital Campaign, annual auction, scholarship fund, and on and on) and adjusted their lifestyle accordingly, it became just another line item in their carefully monitored family budget.

After walking a few blocks, they ducked into a neighborhood restaurant, found a seat at the bar, and ordered two glasses of wine and something to eat.

"I've been meaning to ask you since this afternoon, how are things progressing with Vince? You seem to be thick as thieves these days," Helen asked.

"What can I say? We've become sports buddies."

"You have plenty of those already. I think getting so close to Gargano could be a mistake. I'm beginning to worry it could work against us."

"Why is that?" Michael was concerned.

"If Vince has strong principles, he may feel like he can't accept

Zoe on the grounds that it might be perceived as favoritism. I think you should cool it with him for a while."

"Then he would be hurt. He would feel like I dumped him."

"It's beginning to sound like a lose-lose. We're damned if you're friends and damned if you're not."

"I don't know, Helen. To be honest, I'm sick and tired of the whole admissions mess," he confessed.

"You're sick of it?" she jeered. "I've been living and breathing admissions for the last three months. I've had it up to here," she said, with her hand leveled to her forehead.

"Well, I have, too," he reminded her.

"*Icchh,* enough. Let's have another glass of wine," she said with resignation.

At a few minutes before eleven they hailed a taxi and Helen gave the driver the Cashins' address. As they pulled up in front of the house, Michael said, "Pretty swanky. Who are these people?"

"Catherine is the girl that Zoe met at Bertha's."

"And the parents?"

"Tell you later," Helen answered as she hopped out of the cab. "Wait here. I'll just run in and get her." A few minutes later she returned with an irate teenager in tow.

"You didn't have to come at eleven o'clock sharp, did you? I was the first person to leave!" Zoe was furious.

"Whoa. Calm down. How was the party?" Michael tried to put his arm around her, but she knocked it away.

"Great."

"Was Max there?" Helen ventured.

"Why do you think I'm pissed about leaving early?"

"It's not early. It's exactly the time we agreed on."

"Why do you always have to be so exact, Mom? You're like a drill sergeant. Other people's parents are always late. I wish you were like that."

"You're making it sound like I'm Denise Doyle-Gillis. I'm not that compulsive, am I?"

"Sometimes."

"Would you prefer if I were a permissive parent and let you slum around with no curfew whatsoever? Michael, help me out on this, will you?"

"Let's drop it; it's late. We're all tired."

They rode the rest of the way home in silence. As soon as they walked into the apartment, Zoe went straight to her room and immediately made a phone call. Helen fell asleep hearing the faint murmur of Zoe's voice intermingled with her memory of Phillip, hand on her waist, whispering, "Call me," as the music and hullabaloo of the party blared in the background.

No sooner had The School opened on Monday morning than pandemonium broke out in the admissions office. Sara arrived to find Brandi already at her desk, working the phones, with the early edition of *The Standard New York Tabloid* spread out in front of her.

"Have you seen this?" Brandi asked excitedly the moment Sara crossed the threshold.

"Seen what?"

"Get settled first. You'll want to be sitting when you read this." As Sara settled in, Brandi ceremoniously placed the journal on her desk, open to page six—the place to turn for the latest installment of high-society gossip. Sara couldn't miss the bold headline on the right side of the spread: DOES THE SCHOOL NOW OFFER EARLY ADMISSIONS?

> As everyone in the New York school world knows, the official notification date for admissions is February 12. So how is it possible that, in the December issue of *Tally Ho* magazine, Tally Easton reported that her son, Montana, has been accepted into The School's coveted Kindergarten class for next year? Has The School instituted a radical new early-admissions policy? Or has Tally Easton been given preferential treatment? If so, why? Is it her celebrity status alone, or did something else pass between the media queen and The School?

"Holy shit," Sara moaned.

"Sara, Katie Couric is on line one," Brandi interrupted with apprehensive excitement.

"Tell her that I have no comment," Sara instructed abruptly. By the time Brandi dispensed with Katie, there were three other reporters on hold, all demanding to speak with the director of admissions. Sara listened to Brandi repeating, "Ms. Nash has no comment," several times before sequestering herself in her office. She needed some time to think but apparently wasn't going to get it. Within minutes Brandi was knocking on the door to tell her Lisa Fontaine insisted on speaking with her immediately.

"Where did *The Tabloid* get this story?" Lisa demanded.

"I believe that their source was *Tally Ho.* In her column in the December issue, Tally blathered about how thankful she is for receiving the greatest Christmas gift of all time—a place at The School for her son. I think everyone here knows Tally had applied, but as far as I know, no admissions decisions have been made. I normally don't even begin to review the applications until January."

"Then can we assume Pamela made this decision independently of your office, and delivered the news to Tally on her own accord?" Lisa continued the cross-examination.

"It seems so," Sara replied. "That is, according to Tally's Kindergarten placement consultant, Lydia Waxman. I called her as soon as I read the article."

"This is the final straw!" Lisa exploded, and then switched to a more officious tone. "Sara, why wasn't I notified about this article sooner?"

"Uh, *I* only learned about it on Friday and didn't think it warranted the board's attention over the weekend. You were first on my list to call this morning," Sara replied, thinking on her feet.

"We need a damage control expert on this right away. I'll call my ex-husband. He's been involved with enough corporate scandals to know who's best for this sort of PR debacle."

"Let me know what you want me to do. Until you tell me otherwise, I'll continue to make myself unavailable to the press, which, by the way, is hounding us," Sara said respectfully.

"When reporters smell a good story, they're like vultures. Thank God the winter break starts on Friday. That will put an end to this madness. We just have to get through this week." Lisa sounded exhausted. "You haven't forgotten that you're meeting with the board tonight, right?"

"Of course. Seven p.m.," Sara replied.

The day continued, with Brandi rebuffing reporters, and Sara behind closed doors. Since the possibility of getting any work done that morning was out of the question, she spread one of the napping mats she had borrowed from the creative movement instructor on the floor and did a series of yoga exercises.

"This came for you," Brandi said, handing Sara a hand-addressed envelope when she emerged from her office an hour later. The envelope contained an engraved card from Mr. and Mrs. Robert Swanson, inviting Sara to join them for a Christmas Eve performance of *The Nutcracker* followed by a midnight buffet supper at their apartment in Carnegie Hill, the sliver of the Upper East Side named for those who occupied mansions there at the turn of the nineteenth century, and which was now populated by those who aspired to do the same. Scrawled in peacock-blue ink at the bottom of the card was a note that read, "Ms. Nash. Did you know Miranda is the *youngest* member of the troupe! She would love for you to come see her dance! Hope you can join us. Gloria."

"*Icchh.* Please write her a brief note thanking her for the invitation but telling her that I couldn't possibly accept. Oh, and wish her a happy holiday."

"Anything about how you're looking forward to seeing her in the New Year?" Brandi asked.

"Oh, you're wicked," Sara laughed.

"And what's this?" Sara asked as she slipped a gold satin ribbon off a shiny red box. Nestled in a bed of gold tissue paper were a large tin of sevruga caviar, an exquisite little mother-of-pearl spoon, and a tiny envelope containing a handwritten note:

> *To Sara Nash:*
> *In Russia, no celebration is complete without caviar.*
> *We look forward to celebrating many good times with you throughout the coming years.*
> *The Romanovs,*
> *Donald, Josh, Anastasia and Alexi*

"Brandi, take a look at this note."

"It sounds like we have another case of presumed early admissions, doesn't it?" Brandi replied.

"I can't possibly imagine why. This family has had no contact with Pamela . . . that I know of. They're friends of Helen Drager's, but that should hardly have led them to conclude that they're a slam dunk. And I've given them no encouragement whatsoever."

"Maybe they're just believers in the power of positive thinking."

"It's really too bad they felt compelled to send a gift. They were actually starting to grow on me. Plus, they're the only gaybee boomers that applied this year. And the Russian angle is kind of intriguing."

"So I should return the gift with a 'thank you for the generous thought, but I don't accept payola' note?" Brandi suggested.

"Exactly," said Sara. "God, you're good."

Helen's morning was shaping up in much the same way, except that instead of the press, she was barraged with phone calls from school parents demanding to know if the *Tabloid* article was correct in asserting that The School had instituted a new early-decision policy.

When the phone rang for the fourteenth time that morning, Helen answered with an uncharacteristically discourteous "Yeah?"

"Mrs. Drager?" a meek voice questioned.

"Yes."

"This is Eva Hopkins from the admissions office at The Very Brainy Girls' School."

"Oh, hel-lo." Helen instantaneously shifted into a deferential mode.

"I'm calling to ask if you are still interested in applying for grade nine for Zoe."

Has Michael Jackson had plastic surgery? Helen thought. "Yes. Most definitely," she said enthusiastically.

"Oh, good. Then I'm pleased to let you know that we're now in a position to offer you an application. Shall I put one in the mail for you?"

"If you could, that would be great."

"And if you could get the head-of-school recommendation, test scores, and school report to us right away that would be helpful. While I have you on the phone, can we set up a tour and interview date for sometime in early January?"

Pleased to have received this news, Helen updated her spreadsheet.

SCHOOL	PHONE #	DIRECTOR OF ADMISSIONS	STATUS
The Fancy Girls' School	674–9876	Justine Frampton	Michael going to France Dec. 22
The Progressive School	563–9827	Soledad Gibson	Sent thank you (no thank you) note
The Bucolic Campus School	475–8392	Vince Gargano	Michael wasting time with V.G. Could be fatal.
The Safety School	498–5937	Shirley Livingston	Sent thank you note
The Very Brainy Girls' School	938–8475	Eva Hopkins	Sending application. Dec. 5 Interview Jan. 8. Hallelujah!
The Downtown School	483–8473	Taisha Anguilla	Gave up

The call from The Very Brainy Girls' School led her to thoughts of Phillip Cashin, and she decided to break down and call him. Since she had asked him to be her spy at the party on Saturday night, the least she could do was respond to his whispered request to call. She reached a member of his domestic staff, who told her that Mr. Cashin was at work, and for some odd reason, that surprised her. She had never pictured him passing the day in the ho-hum context of an office; in her fantasy he floated above and apart from the daily grind of life. The voice on the other end of the line offered to put Helen through, and she accepted.

"Helen! How nice to hear from you. I've thought about you many times since last Saturday. You looked lovely that night," he began warmly. "But you absolutely could not have chosen a better time to call. I'm lounging here with my feet on my desk, staring in amazement at the most gorgeous Gauguin I've seen in years. I wish it were mine, but it belongs to a client who has asked me to evaluate it for him. I wonder if I could ask you to pop over and take a look at it. I would love to get your opinion. Can I lure you over for lunch?"

"I normally charge a lot more for my professional opinion than lunch. And anyway, I'm not free today," she replied defiantly. She was slightly insulted by his presumption that she had nothing better to do than "pop" over to his office in the middle of the day.

"Oh, I'm sorry. That was selfish of me. I meant no offense. I just thought I had come up with a clever ruse to get to see you today. But seriously, this picture is spectacular."

"I'm sure it is. But I was actually calling about the Saturday night shindig. When I ran in to pick Zoe up, you made it sound like you had something to report."

"I wanted to tell you that you were right—Zoe is head over heels for Max. And vice versa."

"I already knew that. What I wanted to know was whether or not they behaved themselves."

"In my opinion?"

"Who else's opinion would I be asking for?"

"It's a very subjective question."

"Put it this way: if it were your daughter who was with Max on Saturday night, would you have approved of their behavior?"

"No."

"So what are you telling me?"

"That I'm a rabidly jealous, overprotective father and a lonely old man."

"You're not being helpful."

"You're right. I was teasing. Zoe and Max were adorable together. They held hands, slow-danced, and fed each other popcorn. Period. I even confirmed this with Catherine just because I knew I owed you a detailed report. Satisfied?"

"Yes. Thank you," she said gratefully, and breathed a sigh of relief.

"What do you have planned for the holidays?" he asked.

"Zoe is going to Cuba with Huts for Humans, that is, if she can tear herself away from Max for two weeks; Michael is going to France on business; and I'm going away for a week, and then I'll be home, writing an essay for an exhibition catalogue. And you?"

"Catherine is going with her grandmother to Sweden. My relationship with my mother-in-law is rather . . . strained at the moment, so I figure I'll be staying here."

"Oh." There was a long, pregnant silence.

"Can I take a rain check on lunch?" She stuck her neck out.

"Nothing would please me more. Call me when you know your schedule," he said, choosing his words carefully.

Meaning, when hubbie is across the Atlantic, Zoe is south of the border, and Catherine is with her loathsome granny, we might actually . . . what? she wondered.

It was after nine by the time Michael returned home from work. Zoe was in her room studying for midterms, and Helen was at the dining room table with a half-eaten piece of lasagna and a pile of papers.

"Dinner's in the oven," she said as he leaned over and gave her a peck on the cheek.

"I'm exhausted," he moaned. "I was on the phone for hours today with Justine plotting out the itinerary for the trip."

"How that woman gets any work done at her real job is beyond me."

"Believe it or not, we actually discussed admissions today," he mentioned.

"Really?" she looked up, expressing more interest in Justine than she had shown in weeks. "In what context?"

"She had recently spoken to Pamela, who apparently told her that The Fancy Girls' School was not our first choice. She wanted to know where we stood on that."

"What did you say?" she asked anxiously.

"I said that we were crazy about The Fancy Girls' School but were told that admissions directors discouraged first-choice letters, and that was why we didn't send one. I thought I cleverly avoided having to tell her that it's not our first choice. Don't you?"

"Uh-huh." Helen's mind was off in another direction, analyzing Pamela's motivation for telling Justine that. She was probably still hoping to secure the spot for April in exchange for Dana's convincing the board to make Felicity the interim head of The School. It would be interesting to see how all this would play out after Pamela's defrocking.

"What are you working on?" Michael asked, looking over her shoulder.

"The application for The Very Brainy Girls' School. Not what I expected to be doing this late in the game."

"But it's good to have one more iron in the fire, don't you think?"

"Absolutely. Especially one that Pamela won't have a chance to meddle with."

The phone rang. It was Sara, sounding so shaky that when she asked if they could possibly meet for a drink, Helen was out the door in less than ten minutes. When she arrived at their neighborhood hangout, she found Sara already there, looking preoccupied and rather distraught.

"Are you all right?" Helen asked with concern as she sat down next to her friend.

"I just came out of meeting with the executive committee of the board. I'm still in shock about it. I'm not sure I should be telling you any of this, but I just can't carry it alone anymore. You're my best friend, above and beyond your role at The School, right? I know I can trust you not to tell a soul about anything I'm going to tell you, can't I?" She was rambling nervously.

"Sara, relax. I can't even believe you would ask if you can trust me. You know you can. And besides, I think I already know most of what you're going to tell me. Lisa has been confiding in me for weeks."

Sara felt betrayed. "I can't believe you knew all along and didn't say a word! I've been desperate to talk to you about everything that's been happening. It's been awful to hold it in all this time."

"I've been dying to talk to you, too, but I'd been sworn to secrecy. And even if I hadn't, I didn't think it was fair to burden you. It would have made working with Pamela even more difficult for you than it already was."

"It couldn't have been more difficult." Sara was still peeved.

"Come on, Sara. The point is, now we can talk, and I, for one, suddenly feel incredibly relieved."

"Me, too," Sara said, and pressed her face against Helen's shoulder to conceal her tears. "I'm sorry. I've just had to hold so much in for so long now."

"Don't apologize," Helen murmured, rubbing her back the way she did with Zoe. "Work must have been a horror show for you. I know she's been driving me to the brink of homicide recently. You must want to wring her neck on a daily basis. I feel like we should break into a verse of 'Ding Dong, the Witch Is Dead,'" Helen joked. Sara sat back, blew her nose, and ran her fingers through her hair.

"Are you aware of *everything* that happened tonight?" Sara asked.

"Not exactly. I assume they told you that Pamela was going to be discharged as of Friday, right?"

"Right. And they offered me the position of interim head of School."

"Really?" Helen took a slow sip of brandy, buying herself a minute. "What about Felicity?"

"She claimed to have no knowledge of receiving unauthorized money from The School, which, given her financial acumen, is believable, but then exhibited uncharacteristically good sense in telling the board that she didn't feel she was qualified to assume the position of interim head. As a result, they decided to let her stay on and teach French for the remainder of the school year."

"That was a good move on her part. I've always thought she was one of those people with a low IQ but a high survival quotient."

"Strong primal instincts," Sara concurred.

"But back to you. That's very big news. How do you feel about it?"

"I'm not sure. You know I've often fantasized about heading a school, but not necessarily The School. And the board has made no guarantees that the interim position will lead to that. I would be on trial for some period of time, which could be a setup for failure. The School's finances are in a shambles, the staff will be demoralized, the children will be discombobulated, many parents will be up in arms, and external relations are already dicey. Which reminds me, are you aware of the Tally Easton fiasco?"

Helen nodded affirmatively. "I spent my morning on the phone with every loony in The School."

Sara continued. "Admissions are still two months from completion, and who knows what the response will be when the news of Pamela's departure hits the streets. We may very well see lots of applicants withdrawing. And then there's eighth-grade admissions, which will certainly be a challenge."

Helen hesitated and then ventured haltingly, "Honestly, Sara, that's the only part of your taking the job that I have any question about. I know you'll make a successful head of The School in the long run. The first year may be difficult, but you'll get through it. But I have to tell you, I'm really worried about getting through the next two months. Do you really think you can get all twenty-two eighth-graders placed into their first- or second-choice schools? You know that's the expectation."

"You mean *your* expectation. Be honest, Helen, all you really care about is getting Zoe into high school," Sara said bluntly.

Helen was mortified. In all the years they had been friends, Sara had never been this overtly critical.

"I mean it, Helen," Sara continued. "Since September you've been incredibly self-centered. You've been acting like high school admissions is the most important thing in the world. I would never have expected you to be so hysterical about it, particularly for Zoe's sake."

"God, have I been that awful?" Helen asked, now on the verge of tears herself.

"Yeah, you have. You've been absolutely impossible."

"I'm so sorry. It's just that I'm really worried about it all the time. You can understand that, can't you?"

"Of course I can," Sara said kindly, handing Helen a tissue. "Believe me, I'm worried, too. I would feel terrible if I failed to get all the eighth-graders into school. But I look at it this way: Pamela hasn't done a thing for anyone this year except maybe April Winter and Julian Toppler, and that's only because she has some outstanding debts to their parents. She actually wrote their recommendations, and I assume she's lobbying heavily for them at a few schools. Everyone else has basically been fending for themselves. Margaret told me she's received calls from almost all of the eighth-grade parents about missing letters of recommendation. So if I'm able to accomplish even a fraction of what Pamela was expected to do, we'll be ahead of the game. Right?"

"I suppose you're right," Helen said halfheartedly. "So you're going to accept the offer?"

"I think I have to, don't you?"

"Yeah. I guess you do."

"Don't sound so enthusiastic," Sara sniffed.

"I'm sorry. Of course you should accept," Helen responded with reserve. "And you know I'll be here for you in any way that I can." Helen awkwardly placed a hand on Sara's arm, making a promise to herself to do something special for Sara during the winter break. It was the least she could do to make up for her selfishness over the past few months.

"Thanks," Sara said perfunctorily. "I'm going to need all the help I can get. And you need to stop worrying so much. You're going to make yourself sick."

"I already feel sick. I'm not sleeping well; I'm getting headaches. *Icccch.*"

"See? But I guarantee you'll feel better when you hear Zoe at the Holiday Festival. She's going to steal the show. She's just glowing these days."

"I hate to burst your balloon, but the glow is amorously induced."

"You don't think I know that? I've been watching them make goo-goo eyes for the last month." Sara laughed. "But hey, they're good kids, and they seem to be behaving themselves. Plus, if it enhances the show, so much the better!"

Since the program always included an exuberant chorus of "Let It Snow" it was fitting that, for the first time in the nine years that the Dragers had been at The School, there was a snowstorm on the morning of the Holiday Festival, and the children would actually get the white Christmas of their dreams.

Helen had arrived early to supervise the setup of the bake sale. The volunteer bakers had all delivered their contributions the afternoon before, and the committee had worked into the early evening tying up little bundles of petit fours, wrapping cakes, and packing loaves and tortes in preparation for the morning rush. At eight a.m. sharp, the doors opened, and the customers pushed and shoved to get first crack at the inventory.

"Mason, grab a dozen of the Newman's rum balls and a bag of those pecan sandies," Mr. Dixon ordered his son.

"Jen-a-fa! I said only two," a nasal mother shrieked.

"Are there nuts in these?"

"Is this wheat-free?"

"Penelope, you may select one treat for each of your friends. Okay, one for your imaginary friend, too. Mommy's your best friend? Well, you're Mommy's best friend, too," Brenda Simpson, as was her habit, articulated loudly so that no one at any time could fail to witness her model parenting.

Helen was always amazed by how many parents felt compelled to wear holiday-inspired garments to this event, or for that matter, how many even owned these absurd articles of clothing. There were the dignified fathers who donned red and green ties, some with patterns of pinecones and holly discreetly embedded in the silk, and others with more blatant motifs like Santas or candy canes. There were always a few Jewish fathers in silvery-blue ties patterned with Stars of David, menorahs, or dreidels. A wackier father might show up in a long, red Santa cap, and every year at least one really out-there guy wore a headband with attached reindeer horns and a red plastic Rudolph nose.

The conservative mothers wore Norwegian sweaters, Tyrolean jackets, or Nordic vests that tastefully depicted wintry scenes of *Tannenbaums* and snowmen. The more risqué revelers wore hand-knit sweaters featuring Nativity tableaux, or factory-stamped sweatshirts imprinted with cartoonish renderings of Santa's workshop. There were always a few with strands of blinking Christmas lights around their necks that, every year, left Helen wondering where the power source was hidden. Her only sartorial concession to the holiday hoopla was to wear two tiny Christmas tree ornaments as earrings.

Balancing pastries atop paper coffee cups, the parents made their way to the auditorium, oohing and aahing over the festive decorations, compliments of their little darlings. They pointed and smiled when they thought they had successfully identified the particular angel or sleigh bell that their child had instructed them to look out for. But who knew for sure?

Parents were busily discussing vacation plans, where to find the newest version of the iPod their children had asked Santa to bring them, and the ever-controversial topic of teachers' gifts. Each year there were always a few parents who broke the rules and gave embarrassingly extravagant gifts to their children's teachers, one of the worst offenders being John Toppler, who, two years ago, gave Julian's math teacher a diamond-studded platinum slide rule that was rumored to have cost five figures. But it was generally agreed that he was outdone the following year by Peter Newman, whose gift to the American history teacher consisted of a two-week chauffeur-driven tour of the Confederate Army Civil War battle sites and a three-day reenactment at Appomattox.

The music teacher tapped her stick, and the elementary string ensemble began playing a just barely recognizable rendition of Pachelbel's Canon in D Minor on their pint-sized violins and celli. The audience was enchanted not only by the music but also by the miracle of the performance itself. Their video-game-and-cartoon-addicted offspring had metamorphosed (for the moment, at least) into credible classical musicians! What a tribute to The School! What a return on their investment!

After two more pieces and a thunderous applause, the musicians were replaced by the elementary chorus, which performed a veritable cornucopia of seasonal melodies, taking multiculturalism to a whole new level: from "Oh, Tannenbaum" to "Oh, Chanukah, Oh, Chanukah," to "Oh, Oh, Oh, the Muezzin Is Calling." Next was a Kwanza song, followed by a pan-Asian medley of winter harvest tunes, followed by the requisite snow song that had those with holiday travel plans watching with dread as the snow piled up on the windowsills. Their final song was a roaring execution of "Mele Kalikimaka," with an audience sing-along made possible by the phonetic Hawaiian lyrics provided in the program.

Once the elementary performance was complete, Sara Nash appeared on the stage and introduced Elizabeth Marcus, the music director from The Public School, and together they welcomed the newly expanded middle school choral group. The program began with The School's half of the group slowly marching onto the stage, softly singing the first verse of "The Little Drummer Boy." Next, The Public School choral members followed, joining in on the second verse, seamlessly blending to create a symphony of young voices. They ended the piece with a multipart harmonization and then faded into "pum, pada pum, pada pum."

"Bravo!" parents of boys shouted.

"Brava!" parents of girls shouted.

"Bravisimi!" opera buffs shouted, all clapping madly.

The program continued, with several equally complex arrangements of holiday favorites, including a round of "Joy to the World" in four different languages.

Next on the program was Max Kupka's solo performance of "Greensleeves," a song that Helen never particularly liked but that today gave her goose bumps. Her response was triggered not so much by the song as by Max, whose pale skin, dark eyes, and bee-stung lips reminded her of photographs she had seen of Michael at that age.

The last piece on the program was Zoe's own arrangement of "White Christmas," a gutsy interpretation that spanned two octaves and several changes of key. Her solo included a series of improvised scats, and Helen and Michael, who normally wiggled nervously in their seats any time their daughter was on stage, were mesmerized, afraid that if they moved a muscle they would miss a note. As Zoe reached the final chorus, she was joined by the entire group, and all, singing their hearts out, performed a virtuoso grand finale.

Helen and Michael were the first on their feet, and within an instant, the entire audience followed. As each of the performers took a bow, there was deafening and continuous applause for what was, by any standards, a notable musical achievement. Lisa Fontaine entered the stage with two huge bouquets for Sara and Elizabeth Marcus and congratulated them both for what she hoped was "the start of a beautiful relationship."

"And now, please, everyone, if you could take your seats, I have an important announcement to make." As she waited for what to Helen seemed an interminable interval, Lisa adjusted the microphone and repeatedly cleared her throat. Once the cacophony had finally subsided, she began.

"The board of trustees has received some very sad news. Today will be Pamela Rothschild's last day as head of The School." She paused as the shock waves zigzagged across the dumbstruck brow of every parent in the room. Even for New Yorkers who thrived on institutional drama, this was an unexpected blow. It would be safe to say that every parent in the room was stunned. It would also be safe to say that all the parents in the room were asking themselves the same question: "What does this mean for my child?"

Lisa continued. "Ms. Rothschild has requested that she be given the opportunity to explain her unexpected departure," she said as she moved aside, making way for the queen of melodrama herself.

In contriving her farewell address, Pamela's objective was simple—there should not be a dry eye in the house. In an effort to elicit sympathy, she had come up with what she thought was an inspired idea: invoke the memory of Elizabeth II in the darkest days of her annus horribilis. To do so she wore a pale-violet silk brocade high-waisted dress with a matching three-quarter-length-sleeved jacket and topped it off with a dainty hat and shoes dyed to match. Her hair was tightly styled in a flipped bob, or bobbed flip, depending on the angle, and her makeup was appropriately subdued. Even though her hands were gloved, she made certain that her infamous charm bracelet was visible around one wrist, the strap of a violet handbag around the other.

"I am standing here today at a crossroads in my career. I have had to make a most difficult choice between doing what I love, with children that I love, with people that I love—and that includes all of you—or following my instinct to devote myself to children who are less fortunate than yours. I have been offered an opportunity—received a calling, if you will—from an internationally recognized, highly funded, prestigious world-class organization, whose name I am not at liberty to divulge at this moment, to be their director of education. The unfortunate news is that their needs are immediate. Therefore, it is with a heavy feeling in my heart that I leave you now. With the wisdom I have gained through the privilege of educating your children, I must now go and use that knowledge to benefit others. Please, find it in your hearts to forgive my abrupt departure. Understand I am doing this for all of us. For the future of our world belongs to *all* the children. Amen and adieu."

Pamela stood glued to the podium, waiting for a contagious flood of sobs to infect the audience. But no one moved. No one made a noise. At last, Pamela broke the deafening silence by snapping open the clasp of her handbag, extracting a lacy hanky, and delicately dabbing the corner of her eye.

Lisa Fontaine returned to the stage and said graciously, "Thank you, Pamela. We all wish you the very best in your new endeavor."

With head bowed, her dowager's hump more pronounced than usual, Pamela skulked off the stage in shame while the room began to vibrate with the murmur of stifled agitation.

"Please, please, bear with me for another moment. I have one more important announcement to make. The board has named Sara Nash interim head of The School, effective immediately. I wish you all a very happy holiday. Thank you."

Michael squeezed Helen's hand, surprised to find it shaking and slightly moist. The audience offered a smattering of weak applause, some as a congratulatory gesture, some as an expression of relief, others because they had no idea what else to do. As the elementary chorus returned to the stage to sing a somber version of "Auld Lang Syne," a few parents stood in place and joined in. But the majority were out the door fast, anxious to find their friends in the lobby and participate in the postmortem. This would surely go down as the most talked-about Holiday Festival in The School's history.

JANUARY

"Funereal" was the word that came to mind whenever Sara looked back on the two weeks she spent alone at The School during the winter break. The fact that it was the dead of winter contributed to the gloom, but it also felt spooky to be in a place that was normally teeming with life and not encounter a soul. The void created by Pamela's departure was filled with the oppressive stench of death, and Sara's impulse was to embark on a psychic housecleaning in order to restore The School to a state of well-being. Unfortunately, even the janitorial staff was away for the holidays.

Even though she really needed to collect and review numerous documents that were presumably filed in Pamela's office, Sara had been avoiding the chore, haunted by a childish fear that the ghost of Rothschild would jump out from behind the door and strangle her. By the second week, when she finally got up enough courage to enter, she was disheartened to discover that the office was more chaotic than a ten-year-old's bedroom after a twelve-kid slumber party. Drawers and shelves were cleared, with every reference book, directory, manual, file, letter, or disk that might in any way be useful to Sara either torn to shreds, dumped on a heap, or stuffed in a ten-gallon garbage can. Pamela had left the office in a "fuck you" state, making good on her promise to do everything in her power to undermine her successor, including, to Sara's vast amusement and relief, prying that ludicrous plaque from the office door.

On the Friday of the Holiday Festival, Sara had made a point of stopping by Pamela's office to say goodbye and wish her the best of luck on her new endeavor (which she knew was fictitious but acknowledged nonetheless). As Sara extended her hand for a collegial shake, Pamela recoiled and hissed, "I hope you're satisfied now. You may think that your clever plot to overthrow me has worked, but you will never be made head of The School. You know nothing about education. The faculty refers to the admissions department as the den of inequality and sees you as the glad-hander that you are. When it comes to finance, bah, I bet the only thing you've ever balanced is your chakras. And just wait, when the auction is a bust, the board will see you're a complete amateur when it comes to fund-raising. And when the rejection letters roll in, every eighth-grade parent will be begging for me to come to their rescue. By the end of February, you'll wish you never set foot in The School, let alone tried to run it."

The blows to Sara's Achilles' heel were dealt with such devastating accuracy that it took her the better part of the winter break to recobble her self-confidence. Plagued with insecurity about the new position to begin with, this articulation of her weaknesses, even by someone for whom she had no respect, was not easy to ignore.

Before departing for their winter holidays, the board had established a new committee, aptly named the transition team, to provide Sara with some guidance in the upcoming months. The committee had decreed that Sara's first priority during the month of January should be admissions, both in and out, followed by an exhaustive review of every department and faculty member, a new budget for the upcoming year, and everything else that they discovered had fallen through the cracks during the last years of the Rothschild regime. The challenges Sara faced as the newly appointed interim head were truly Herculean, and she prepared by spending every waking hour, including Christmas Day, at The School, in a self-taught crash course on school management.

By January 2, Sara finally began to gain a little confidence in her understanding of the big picture and had made considerable headway in laying the groundwork for tackling each assignment. In addition to her board-mandated responsibilities, she had drawn up a list of six projects she hoped to initiate before the end of the school year:

1. Establish an equitable compensation plan for faculty and administration, including the head
2. Establish a bona fide admissions policy, including a statement regarding sibling admissions
3. Schedule a symposium on teenage sexuality for parents and students
4. Schedule a symposium on eating disorders for parents and students
5. Provide a SAPS preparation course for next year's eighth-grade students
6. Discuss dress code with Felicity Cozette

There were moments when her plans and lists seemed overly ambitious and she became discouraged and pessimistic about the prospect of succeeding on any front. But then there were the breakthrough moments, like the day she completed all the letters of recommendation, or the day she received a call informing her that The School was left a substantial bequest from a recently deceased alumna, when her optimism was renewed. On those days she believed that with hard work, support from the board, and a little luck, she might just be able to pull this off.

One morning near the end of the break, she logged on to her computer and was delighted to have received an e-mail from Helen.

Sara-
Happy New Year! I'm back from a fantastic week at the spa. I feel great. Pilates everyday, salt scrubs, body wraps, massages. I shouldn't rub it in. LOL. I even lost the five pounds that Michael will surely gain in France. He and Zoe get back on the 4th.
I'm off today to an "interesting" lunch. How about getting together tonight? I can't wait to hear how your week went. Hope it was productive.

I also want to make a date to take you to lunch before school starts. How about Friday?
Love, Helen.

Helen,
There is nothing I would like better than seeing you tonight. Look forward to hearing all. Eight o'clock at the Bistro? Also, Friday sounds perfect. I need to get out of here for a few days before the deluge.
Sara

Sara,
Great. See you tonight.

Upon her return from the spa, Helen had called Phillip Cashin, who was in the process of evaluating *another* significant painting for *another* one of his high-worth clients. Saying he was delighted to hear from her, he repeated his enticing offer: lunch in exchange for her "invaluable expert opinion." This time she graciously accepted. Still bristling at the idea of Michael cavorting in Provence during the holidays, she had no trouble convincing herself that a thinly disguised professional visit to Phillip's office, and lunch, were perfectly justifiable.

Where else would the offices of the Cashin Group be located than on the forty-eighth floor of one of Manhattan's most notable modern skyscrapers? Helen observed as she rode the elevator up to the tastefully understated suite. An untrained eye would have found the décor dated and institutional, but Helen immediately recognized the significance of his rare vintage modern furniture and art. However, she was less impressed with his client's painting and gave him five good reasons why she was certain it was a fake.

"Really? Are you sure?" he said with concern. "But now that you've pointed it out, I see you're right. The brushstrokes are rather thick. And the signature does look a bit shaky," he agreed, and as he leaned in to examine the surface, he brushed his hand across her back.

As she turned to face him, he took her in his arms and whispered,

"Your mind turns me on as much as your body. I find the combination devastating." She thought that his warm breath in her ear was pretty devastating, too.

She broke the spell by suggesting lunch, and they descended to the ground floor and entered Quattro Stagione, the elegant midtown power restaurant that also functioned as a temple for those who worshipped modernity. The maitre d' greeted Phillip by name and led them to his regular table, adjacent to the serene pond that dominated the center of the room. When the extravagantly expensive lunch arrived, Helen was underwhelmed; it was one of those towering vertical presentations that made her feel like a child knocking over a stack of blocks every time she tried to take a bite. But she didn't care, in part because she had eaten so little while at the spa that she had lost her appetite, but also because being with Phillip turned her insides to mush. Throughout the lunch, difficult as it was, they refrained from touching, both concerned that there were likely to be people they both knew at the restaurant. Their frustration having intensified their desire, they ended the meal abruptly and went to his house, where they spent the rest of the afternoon and early evening on his living room couch.

"I understand your reasons for not wanting to go to bed with me," he said not at all convincingly as he languidly stroked her hair.

"Thank you for understanding. This is very hard for me," she murmured as his hand moved slowly down her neck. She felt like she did when she was seventeen, trying to hold on to her virginity, but at this stage in her life she wasn't altogether sure what she was holding on to.

"These are lovely earrings," he said, fondling her mother's precious garnets.

"I'm the third generation of women in my family to own them. They're very dear to me," she said as she removed the gems from her ears and gently toyed with them.

He took them out of her hands, placed them on the table, and nuzzled her neck some more. As his hands traveled lightly across her shoulders and in the direction of her waist, he whispered, "You're absolutely bewitching." She caught his hand before it slipped beneath her blouse, and glanced at his watch.

"Oh, no! Look at the time. I've got to pull myself together and get across town in twenty minutes," she said, and then quickly tucked in her blouse and searched the floor for her shoes.

As he walked her to the door, Helen noticed a slight hint of defeat in his gait, an attitude she was certain Phillip Cashin rarely exhibited.

"I'm really disappointed to see you leave," he confessed sadly.

"I think it's for the best," she responded philosophically, anxious to depart lest he renew his seduction. She wasn't sure she could resist it again, and was glad she had made the date with Sara, if for no other reason than that it prevented her from doing what, she knew deep down, was out of the question.

Even though it had been less than two weeks since they had seen each other, Helen and Sara embraced enthusiastically. Having spent so much of the intervening time alone, they both craved the relaxed intimacy that only the closest of friends could provide. Their last real contact had been the evening in December when Sara called Helen to task on her neurotic behavior, so they both sought reassurance that any rift that might have existed between them was patched up. No sooner had they sat down and ordered drinks than Sara said, "You first. How were your holidays?"

"Considering I spent them alone at the spa, I would have to say, strange, but very pleasant. Zoe has e-mailed me a few times from Cuba and is having a fantastic experience. But she misses Max and is ready to come home. Michael called last night and also has had a good trip."

"Remind me, why did he go to France?"

"Oh, some business thing," Helen answered vaguely.

"Business! Over the holidays? That seems weird."

"It shouldn't seem weird to someone else who worked her ass off during her vacation," Helen teased.

"That's true. But that can wait. What was the lunch you so provocatively alluded to? I want to hear about that."

"I'm not sure where to begin. I guess I should just come out with it and then work backwards. Are you ready?"

"I'm all ears."

"Okay," Helen said, and paused to take a deep breath. "I'm sort of having an affair."

"You're kidding!" Sara gasped with exaggeratedly wide eyes. "What does 'sort of' mean?"

"It means we haven't slept together but we're acting like we're lovers. And I feel as guilty as if I were cheating on my husband, even though technically I'm not."

"Can I ask who your 'sort of' lover is?" Sara asked, praying it was not another father in The School.

"Of course you may," Helen answered giddily. She had looked forward to finally being able to talk about Phillip and poured out a detailed account of how they met, what he looked like, and almost everything that had happened between them.

"And his wife?"

"She was some sort of Swedish socialite. She died last June. He just told me today, it was suicide," she explained in an appropriately somber tone.

"Oh, how awful. That will leave some deep scars. How has his daughter handled the death?"

"As well as could be expected. She seems like a really solid kid. Slightly lost but highly functional."

"Where does she go to school?"

"That Shaker school. I think it's called The Community School?"

"Quaker," Sara corrected with a chuckle.

"Same thing," Helen answered.

"No, it's not," Sara argued.

"Oh, whatever."

"Helen, this is really dangerous, that is, if you intend to stay married to Michael. He would be devastated if he ever found out."

"And so would Zoe."

"I don't want to sound like Miss Family Values, but why on earth are you doing this?" Sara said.

"I don't know. All I can tell you is that I haven't felt this way since I first started dating Michael twenty years ago. Remember that tingle you get when you're about to see a man you're incredibly attracted to? Or you get just thinking about him?"

"Barely. It's been a while, but, yeah, I vaguely recall feeling something like that with Steve," Sara agreed, referring to the last man she dated, more than four years ago. "In my case it's a distant memory. It's practically ancient history."

"Well, it was for me, too. Until Phillip. He's stirred up emotions I've barely felt for years. The stuff that's lost after years of marriage. It's not about sex or love. That's taken care of with Michael. It's desire, passion, romance. It's the ferocious chemistry that I'm finding so exciting. It's so powerful that I sometimes feel dizzy thinking about him. If I thought I could control myself, I would love to see more of him."

"Can you?"

"I don't think so. Sooner or later he's going to insist we go to bed together, and my resistance will break down. We got pretty close to that point today. I can understand his need. He's not getting laid. I am," Helen explained with a shade of disappointment.

"I have to admit, I'm envious of the romantic part. It sounds . . . so hot," Sara said, searching for the appropriate word and coming up with one she'd heard the kids use. "But the emotional aspect sounds extremely complicated. I don't think I could handle it. It would make me mashikana."

"Meshuggener, with a 'G,'" Helen corrected. "I'm not sure I can, either. I'm glad Michael and Zoe will be back in two days. I need a reality check. Being with them will remind me why I shouldn't sleep with Phillip."

"Will you see him again?" Sara asked with an inflection that conveyed more than just a hint of disapproval.

Helen didn't answer right away. "I know I shouldn't, but . . . we'll see."

Sara certainly understood Helen's temptation but absolutely could not fathom why she would ever put her marriage at risk in pursuit of it. In her mind, Michael was a pretty terrific husband, and she thought Helen was being selfish for even entertaining the possibility of hurting him. But after coming down so heavily on her friend the last time they were together, she was reluctant to speak so candidly again.

"You're not really looking for me to give you a go-ahead, are you?"

"No, not really," Helen confessed. "I knew you wouldn't approve even before I decided to tell you. But I had to tell you anyway."

"It means a lot to me that you told me, knowing how I would respond. And I have to admit, he does sound pretty wonderful. But be careful. I don't want to see my best friends get hurt."

"Neither do I. But enough about me. Tell me about your so-called winter break. Not much of a break, was it?"

"You mean my ten days of solitary confinement? It was an amazing time. Sometimes terrifying, like the day I first set foot in Pamela's office and thought, 'Holy shit, there's no way I can deal with this mess, or the day I reviewed the budget and couldn't remember which was the desirable scenario—being in the red or being in the black."

"I can never remember which is which," Helen laughed.

"But as time went on and I crossed chores off of my list, I started to feel a little better. And then there were definitely some highs, like when Vince Gargano returned my call and invited me to come up to The Bucolic Campus School to tour the campus and discuss our four applicants," Sara said proudly.

"Good for you," Helen commended neutrally.

"And the day I finished the last of the eighth-grade letters of recommendation. That felt like a major accomplishment. And I have to tell you, I got particular pleasure out of writing Zoe's. I went on and on about how she's a spectacular musical talent, has just hit her stride academically, provides a moral compass for her peers, yadayadayada."

"That sounds great. And of course you mentioned how much her fabulous parents have contributed to The School community," Helen joked, and then added, "and I don't mean dollar amount . . . although you might have mentioned that, too."

"Of course." Sara smiled and then declared in flawless Rothschild-speak, "You're referring to the two-million-dollar pledge Michael made at the Capital Campaign cocktail party last month, *chéri*?"

"Make it four million, *mon petit bonbon,*" Helen joked.

"But you know, it's really weird. When I look at myself in the mirror every morning and I see Sara Nash, director of admissions, I have to remind myself that I'm now the head of The School. It doesn't seem real. I still look the same. If I can't see the difference, how can I expect anyone else to relate to me in this new role?"

"You need a makeover," Helen answered.

"You mean like they do on those reality television shows?" Sara was aghast.

"Nothing that extreme. But let's do a little shopping after lunch on Friday and get you a few new outfits. That way, when everyone returns after the break, they'll see a new you. When was the last time you bought some new clothes?"

"When I started working at The School."

"And that was . . . ?"

"A long time ago."

"My point exactly."

A profound sense of relief washed over Helen when both Michael and Zoe had safely returned home from their trips abroad. Zoe was exhausted and wanted to go straight to bed, giving Helen an excuse to lie down with her for a few minutes, stroke her hair, and inhale her familiar odor as she drifted into a deep sleep. The experience brought tears to her eyes, and she felt incredibly lucky to have her back safe and sound. She then joined Michael in their bedroom and had reunion sex with an intensity that took both of them by surprise. It was exactly what she needed, and he made it fairly obvious that he was appreciative, too.

Lured by the smell of melting butter, Helen wandered into the kitchen the following morning and found Michael at the stove, making omelets with dried herbs he had brought back from Justine Frampton's garden. Soon Zoe was also awake, and the Dragers spent the morning sharing anecdotes of their adventures and exchanging the small gifts they had bought for one another. When afternoon arrived, Zoe sheepishly announced that she was going out to meet Max at the corner café, and was relieved when Helen, who had fully anticipated this and wondered why it hadn't happened sooner, told her she was absolutely free to go.

"Let's invite Max for dinner one of these days, okay?" Helen suggested.

"I don't know," Zoe replied shyly. "That might be really awkward. He might feel, you know, like he's on a job interview or something."

"But we really want to get to know him. Why don't we invite him along with a few of your other friends for dinner? Invite Julian," Helen proposed. "You can always count on him to be a good buffer. And maybe . . ."

"Maybe Marissa. She's been much nicer this year, and she helped me a lot on my science project. Plus, she knows Max from the chorus."

"Okay. That sounds good. How about Friday night? I'll make a brisket."

"Yummm," Michael murmured.

"Okay. I'll invite everyone. Bye, Mom. Bye, Dad. Love ya both." Zoe blew kisses as she zipped excitedly out the door.

As the short winter day turned to dusk, Michael proposed opening one of the bottles of wine he had brought back from France.

"Happy New Year." He raised his glass to Helen and smiled. She had forgotten how cute his dimples were.

"It sounds like your trip went well. Justine was bearable?"

"She's a superficial and shallow human being, but in spite of that, managed to be a dynamite hostess. And I must confess, the place is lovely. It will be a spectacular place to shoot," Michael replied.

"Will be? That sounds pretty definitive."

"Perceptive of you to pick up on that subtle distinction," Michael praised playfully. "That brings me to the most fascinating revelation of the trip."

"Do tell."

"Where does Xavier live?" he asked out of the blue.

"Somewhere in Westchester. Chappaqua, I think," Helen guessed, having no idea where this was leading.

"Right. And how many children do the Peñas have, and of which gender?"

"Three girls, I believe."

"Right again. Well, guess what. The Peñas are moving to Manhattan in July and are in the process of applying to private schools for the three girls," Michael revealed slowly.

"And they've applied to The Fancy Girls' School?" Helen gasped.

"It's their first choice for all three," Michael answered, and then grinned broadly.

"Well, la-di-da. So all along Xavier has been playing the same game we have. It explains everything. His enthusiasm for the show. The overexpenditure on the pilot. It even explains this trip!" Helen exclaimed. The knowledge that someone else was as conniving as she had been was exhilarating! It freed her from any sense of responsibility or guilt she might feel when the show was axed in February.

"What a perfect ending to a twisted tale. It's like an O. Henry story," she said gaily. "Only the final chapter remains to be written. Will Justine accept Zoe? Will she accept all three Peña girls?"

"If I were a betting man, I would put one hundred dollars on each girl to place. Justine wants this show really badly. I think she sees it as her ticket out of The Fancy Girls' School."

"Good. Then the story will have a happy ending. There's no reason everyone shouldn't get what they want. You've worked damn hard for both Zoe and Justine. I see you've even put on a few pounds just for the cause," Helen teased, affectionately patting his stomach.

"It was a huge sacrifice, let me tell you."

After a sumptuous lunch at one of the venerable midtown Manhattan French restaurants where quenelle still reigned supreme and waiters would never deign to introduce themselves, Helen and Sara set off on their mission.

"Tell me again why we're going all the way down to Century Twenty-One instead of Bergdorf's?" Sara asked as they hustled into a taxi.

"Because for what you would spend at Bergdorf's on one suit, you can get three that are just as nice there. I just have to warn you, it's going to be a bit more work."

"What kind of work?"

"Just stick with me."

"I've got lots of jackets and skirts. Maybe I just need you to come over to my apartment and give me a lesson on how to put things together. Maybe all I need are a few accessories—a scarf or two," Sara hedged.

"Sara, you know I adore you. But in this blazer with these humongous shoulder pads and this midcalf-length, elastic-waist skirt," she said, plucking critically at Sara's clothing, "you look like one of those Westminster dog handlers. All you're missing is a leash and a shih tzu."

"Eeeww. Is it that bad?"

"Until I saw you in a bathing suit, I never knew what a fabulous figure you have. I say, if you've got it, flaunt it," she instructed. "God knows I do."

"And look where that's gotten you," Sara joked.

"Not funny," Helen retorted.

Arriving at Century Twenty-One, they were propelled by the crowd through the revolving doors and immediately confronted with sensory overload: neon lights, screeching shoppers, scrunching packages, screaming price checkers, jabbing elbows, squabbling spouses.

"I can't take this," Sara said, turning ashen.

"Just remember to breathe. Let's go," Helen instructed, linking her arm through Sara's and leading her up the escalators to the infamous third floor—the preferred hunting ground for the discerning shopper. It was here that the most sought-after designer clothes could be had for bargain prices, but, as when hunting for anything, one had to know how to identify one's prey in order to make a killing.

No sooner had they stepped off the escalator than Helen snatched a cashmere jacket off a rack.

"What are you doing? I look hideous in green," Sara proclaimed loudly.

"Lesson one: don't hesitate. If you see something that has any potential, grab it. You can always put it back."

"Then put it back."

"Be open to new colors. It's celadon; it's not actually green. And look at the price!" Helen coaxed, fishing the ticket out from deep within the sleeves of the jacket. "It's on its third markdown! It's gone from sixteen hundred to two hundred ninety-nine!"

"That's still expensive, isn't it?" Sara was shocked.

"Sara, it's Armani!" Helen said, pulling more tags out of the folds to confirm the importance of the garment. With Sara following obediently, she scrambled over to the next rack, where a fitted teal knit sweater hung with a pair of matching slacks.

"I think this color would look great on you," Helen announced, holding the sweater under Sara's chin.

Overhearing the obviously informed pronouncement, a woman with Sara's coloring sidled over and snagged the slacks.

"Excuse me. We were about to take those," Helen said angrily.

"Got them first," the woman cackled.

"Like they'll fit you," Helen said snidely.

"They weren't my size anyway. I'm hardly a two, either," Sara said softly.

After what seemed like hours of hunting and gathering, they joined the line for the dressing room, each weighed down with a bundle of garments.

"This is my worst nightmare," Sara moaned.

"I promise, you'll be thanking me every morning when you're getting dressed. Oh, I just thought of something! What are you going to wear to the auction?"

"I don't know. Probably that gray cocktail dress I wear every year."

"You absolutely *can't* wear that again. Wait here." Helen threw her pile on top of the one Sara was already struggling to balance. "I think I saw the perfect dress for you over there." She pointed across the room.

"No, wait . . . I can't . . . ," Sara said to no avail.

As the minutes ticked by, Sara became increasingly anxious, unable to spot Helen anywhere. Just as she was about to assume the first position in line, Helen returned, breathless, arms draped with a tangle of sequined gowns.

"I found a few excellent candidates."

"Oh, no . . . I can't possibly try all these on."

"No whining allowed. Come on," Helen ordered cheerfully as they cleared the security person stationed at the entrance.

"You didn't prepare me for this," a modest Sara whispered upon entering the communal dressing room.

"Relax. Nobody is looking at you." She was right. The mirrored room was crowded with every size, shape, age, and ethnicity of woman, forcing, zipping, hooking, tying, or buttoning themselves in and out of clothing. There was a constant rustle (and occasional embarrassing tear) of fabric, and whispering between friends, but otherwise the dressing room was relatively quiet. Other than the occasional

"If you're not taking that may I try it?" there was virtually no inter-shopper communication.

So it was surprising when, just as Sara had redressed after trying on the last of the evening gowns, a fellow shopper approached her and asked, "Aren't you Sara Nash?"

"Yes," Sara answered, racking her brain to attach a name to the face.

"Tamara Riley," the woman said, extending her hand for a shake. "Butterscotch's mother."

"Oh, right. Nice to see you," Sara said dismissively.

"Nice to see *you,*" Tamara replied, and then, leaning towards Sara, whispered conspiratorially, "I wouldn't buy that jacket if I were you. It's looking a little shopworn."

Sara was speechless, so Helen came to her rescue. "Miss Nash has actually owned this jacket for years."

Tamara blanched. "Terribly sorry. I thought I was being helpful. I never meant—"

Sara interrupted. "Don't give it another thought." She and Helen turned and sped out of the dressing room, each with an assortment of clothes over their arms.

The line for the cash register was half the length of that for the dressing rooms, and within half an hour, weighed down with shopping bags, they were out of the store and in a taxi speeding uptown.

"I can't believe I spent two thousand, five hundred ninety dollars and eighty-seven cents! That's probably more than I've spent on clothes in my entire life."

"Look at how much great stuff you got. The evening dress alone would have been close to that if you had paid retail. You looked stunning in everything. I would be thrilled if I were you."

"I am," Sara confessed. "I can't thank you enough for doing this."

"One last thing to complete your new wardrobe," Helen said, pulling a small package out from under the bundles. Sara excitedly unwrapped the paisley, silk, and cashmere shawl they had both admired early on in the hunt.

"When did you get this?"

"While you were in line for the dressing room. I hope you like it."

"It's gorgeous. I adore it. Thank you, thank you, thank you," Sara said effusively, hugging Helen. "For everything."

"Thank you for everything you've done for me this fall. And congratulations on your new job! You're going to be phenomenal. I can tell already."

Sara was never so happy for a school vacation to end. The building was again filled with life, she was reunited with her colleagues, and her temporary stewardship of The School had officially begun. Fortunately, Brandi was now fully trained to handle the hair-raising daily dramas of the admissions department. And the inestimable Margaret, who knew more about the inner workings of The School than Sara would ever have predicted, worked tirelessly by her side.

On the first day of The School's reopening, Brandi buzzed Sara. "Benjamin Whyte is on line one," she announced. "I tried to take a message, but he insisted he had to speak with you."

She had wondered what the Whytes would do when they learned that Pamela was no longer at The School. "Put him through." In true Brandi style, she had the Whyte file on Sara's desk within seconds.

"Happy New Year, Miss Nash!" he said brightly.

"And to you, too. How can I help you?"

"When I asked the receptionist for Mrs. Rothschild, I was informed she was no longer working at The School. That was certainly an unforeseen surprise. In light of that, I thought I should touch base with you on the status of our, ahem, situation."

"Let's see . . . hmmm . . . I see from your file you've submitted an application. But I see it's incomplete. There are no KAT results and no interview report. Maybe you should check with the testing service and make sure they resend the report immediately," she said, knowing that Oscar never took the test, but trying to sound as if she were being accommodating. "And do you have a late interview scheduled with us? I don't see anything in the file that references that. Maybe we slipped," she continued in this vein.

"Uh, Ms. Nash," Benjamin proceeded nervously. "I'm afraid our application is rather . . . unusual," he said haltingly. "You see, I'm an old friend of Mrs. Rothschild, and she said she would take care of everything for us. I thought it seemed rather cheeky, but she said that we shouldn't bother ourselves with the—is it the KAT?—for little Oscar. And she conducted the interview herself in our home."

"I see. Your application is rather unconventional," Sara said, unconsciously mimicking his accent. "But I assume you have applied in a more, uh, conventional manner to other schools, haven't you?"

"Er, no, actually. She led us to believe it wasn't necessary."

"Well, then, you are in quite a jam, aren't you? Look, Mr. Whyte, I really don't understand why Ms. Rothschild stuck her neck out so far for you. It's quite out of character for her and, on top of that, runs counter to The School's admissions policy. If you would be so kind as to explain to me why she would have done that, I might be able to help you to submit a 'conventional' application to The School. But understand, that doesn't mean we'll necessary accept Oscar. It just means we'll consider your application."

He cooed obsequiously, "You would do that for us? That would be super, so kind of you. Otherwise I don't know what we would do." He paused. "Let's see. Where to start? Mrs. Rothschild was very, shall we say, uncomfortable with the fact that I knew her at—how shall I put it?—a time in her life when she had a spot of bother."

Just say it, thought Sara, who had no time for his mincing. "And what time in her life was that?"

"Oh, blast, this is tricky. I'm not usually one to blow the gaff," he paused, and then asked, "Are you sitting in front of a computer?"

"Yes, of course."

"Could I possibly e-mail you an article that will explain everything? That way I won't feel like I was the one who told you."

"If that makes you feel better, okay," she answered. Although impatient, she was sufficiently intrigued to put up with his flabby logic. "Meanwhile, while I'm waiting for the e-mail, let me tell you what you need to do. As soon as you hang up the phone, you must call the KAT center and arrange for Oscar to be tested. If you're very lucky they'll still have a few slots available in the next week or two. You'll have to pay a little extra to have the test processed overnight and then have the results faxed to me immediately. You must also call back and arrange with my assistant, Brandi, to bring Oscar in for an interview next week. I will tell her to give you an appointment."

At that moment her computer told her that she had received an e-mail from BWHYTE@britmail.com. He remained on the phone, breathing audibly into the receiver, as she read an article that had apparently appeared twenty years ago in *The Journal of the National Association of Public School Educators of Great Britain.*

> Headmaster Harold M. Rothschild and second form teacher Pamela Wickham were dismissed last week from The Manchester School. The two were discovered in a situation that can only be described as compromising, according to Elizabeth Rothschild, wife of the headmaster. Miss Wickham's employment was summarily terminated, but Mr. Rothschild was permitted to retain his post. However, on March 30, at the close of the school's fiscal period, it was discovered that Miss Wickham had absconded with school funds of over £80,000, and Mr. Rothschild was implicated as coconspirator.
>
> Claiming it was a misunderstanding, Miss Wickham and Mr. Rothschild confessed to the theft and returned the funds. The school has decided not to press charges.

"That's quite a story," she said, downplaying her astonishment. "But not inconsistent with her behavior here."

"What do you mean?" he asked anxiously.

"Let's just say, the only thing in this article that comes as a complete surprise is her relationship with Rothschild. I assume she married him, yes?"

"That would seem to be the case, although I did hear that Rothschild has since died. He was an old buffer, at least twenty years her senior. But once they left Manchester, I never had any contact with her. That is, until we ran into her in New York last year. I believe you may have been with her at the time."

"Yes, I was."

"Can I assume that you have put two and two together? I'm embarrassed to admit that she bent over backward to assist us because of what I knew about her past. In other words, to keep us quiet. Not that I ever threatened to blow her cover. I didn't even know she was undercover! I would never have done anything like that. Please, Ms. Nash, you must believe me. We've done nothing wrong. As far as we knew, favoritism is standard practice in New York school admissions. We did whatever she told us to do," he whined pathetically.

She felt sorry for poor Benjamin Whyte. He was one of the many victims of the master manipulator and didn't deserve to be punished merely for knowing about her past and keeping quiet about it. She decided that the right thing to do was to view the Whytes as a charity case and give Oscar a fair shake. If, after going through the normal channels, he proved to be a reasonable candidate, she would consider him as such.

The lobby of The Very Brainy Girls' School was lined with campaign posters for an upcoming student council election. However, they were not the garden variety, Magic Marker-on-colored-cardboard kind of posters; they were typeset, multihued photolithographed versions that, anyone could see, cost piles of money to produce. Madeline Gottbetter, the Dragers' twelfth-grade student guide, wore a large round button imprinted with "Caitlin@kins FOR PRES," who was, she went out of her way to let them know, in some way related to the diet doctor.

"But her opponent is outspending her ten to one on campaign paraphernalia. You'd be surprised. A lot of the younger girls are seduced by that crap," she said in a disturbingly blasé voice.

"So much for campaign finance reform," said Helen. Only Michael chuckled.

As they wound their way around the imposing building, Madeline subjected Zoe to the third degree. "Where do you go to school?"

"The School?" Zoe answered in the form of a question.

"Never heard of it," Madeline replied. "Is it private?"

"Yeah?" Zoe again answered with the inflection of one who's asking, not telling.

Don't sound so insecure, thought Helen.

"Do you wear a uniform at The School?" Madeline inquired.

"No."

"As you can see, we do. But we manage to work around it. If you come to school here, that is, if you're one of the lucky few to be accepted, you'll learn that it's important to express yourself through accessories. I can tell a lot about a girl from her shoes, what kind of bag she carries, her jewelry—you know, the *accoutrements,*" she said with an accent that made it clear she had studied at least five years of French.

"Oh, great," Zoe mumbled.

"Like I can see right away, accessories aren't a priority for you," Madeline sneered, her laser-sharp brand scan of Zoe having registered a single-digit number.

"So what's your IQ?" Madeline asked as they walked up the stairs.

"I have no idea," Zoe answered. Helen's glance at Michael asked, "Does this call for a rescue?"

"That's weird. Everyone here knows her IQ. How'd you do on the SAPS? You must know that."

"I do, but I don't think I want to share that with you," Zoe replied with dignity.

Good girl, thought Helen.

"Where do you think you want to go to college?" Madeline wasn't fazed and continued her interrogation.

"Uh, don't know yet," a beleaguered Zoe answered.

"FYI, I got into Yale. Early decision," Madeline volunteered.

Just then a girl came bolting out of a classroom in tears, scrunched a piece of paper into a ball, threw it on to the floor, and fled down the hall. Madeline picked it up, and unfurling it, said with an air of ennui, "B minus. No wonder she's upset. I would be, too."

Helen, noticing that Zoe's lower lip was trembling, put a protective arm around her but was summarily rebuffed.

"Madeline, what kind of social life do the girls have here? Do you have some sort of reciprocal arrangement with any of the boys' schools? Do you have any organized opportunities to socialize with any of them?" Helen thought that if she took control of the conversation, she might be able to neutralize it.

"There is some of that. I don't know much about it. I'm a lesbian," she answered distractedly.

"Oh," Helen answered. "Is there an active gay community here?"—thinking that it was important to let Madeline know she was all right with this.

"Pretty active. But a lot of them are LUGs."

"What's a LUG?" Michael asked.

"Lesbians until graduation," Madeline answered flippantly.

The Dragers all looked at one another and made a collective decision to leave that one alone.

Madeline had led them to an impressive chemistry lab, where a small group of girls was gathered around a teacher, avidly jotting notes as he poured blue liquid from one test tube into another.

"Mr. Bunson. MIT. Undergrad. And grad," Madeline informed them as they moved on to the next classroom. "A.P. Physics. Ms. Pushkin. Undergraduate, somewhere in Moscow. But she did graduate work at Princeton."

"What a relief," said Helen sarcastically.

The last thing she showed them was the gymnasium, where the ninth-grade girls were playing a ferocious game of basketball against a team from The Fancy Girls' School.

"Our biggest rival. It doesn't matter the sport—when we play their team, we play to win," Madeline said. "We even compete with them on college admissions. We always have at least ten percent more students admitted to the Ivy League than they do."

"So would you describe The Very Brainy Girls' School as highly competitive?" Helen asked naïvely.

"Wouldn't you?" Madeline stared accusatorially. "It's commonly understood that we're the best at everything. Academics, sports, debate, college admissions, even fund-raising. We certainly have the most high-powered parent body in New York. A former secretary of state, the head of the World Something-or-other, a future SEC chair, editors of big newspapers—you know the type."

"And what do your parents do?" Helen asked a question she would normally never have posed, but with this girl it was no-holds-barred.

"They're divorced and I rarely see my dad. He's the most important U.S. ambassador in Africa. My mother is the head of plastic surgery at the Hospital for Facial Reconstruction. Ever since she donated a nose job to our school's auction a few years ago, lots of the girls here have gone to her for work. She's done at least six rhinoplasties, two breast reductions, and three augmentations in my class alone. They all say she's the best."

Helen was horrified. "Well, you must be proud of her."

"It certainly seems that The Very Brainy Girls' School prides itself on its excellence," Michael said with an edge.

"It's the best school in New York, and probably the entire country," Madeline added definitively. Period. End of discussion.

She deposited the Dragers in the lobby and instructed them to wait. A few minutes later, Eva Hopkins, the very formal and stuffy director of admissions, appeared and informed them that she would meet with only Zoe. Here the parents were spared the interview; The Very Brainy Girls' School collected the only two pieces of parental data they wanted solely from the application: parents' education and current professional status (use of the word "status" duly noted).

The agonized look on Zoe's face as she followed Ms. Hopkins out the door left them feeling as guilty as if they were committing her to four years of boot camp, or in this case, sentencing her to four years of running laps in Manolo Blahniks.

Twenty minutes later, when Zoe exited the interview, her dour expression said it all: "Get me out of here and don't make me ever come back." They all felt as if they couldn't escape The Very Brainy Girls' School fast enough.

"So, I guess this isn't our first choice," Helen teased as they hailed a cab.

"That's putting it mildly," Zoe added morosely. "I can't believe Catherine wants to go there."

"Does she really?" Michael probed.

"You don't even know Catherine," Zoe snapped at Michael.

"Look, I think if we had had a more amiable, less obnoxious guide, we would have had a very different experience. Madeline embodied the worst of The Very Brainy Girls' School. But there's no question that the education is excellent. I'm sure if Catherine ends up there, she will manage to make it work for her."

"If that's really THE BEST school," Zoe said, imitating Madeline's pronunciation of "the best," "then that's where Catherine belongs. She's one of them—a girl who has grown up with 'the best' of everything. For all I care, she can have it," she said with a degree of anger that caught Helen off guard.

"I have to agree, I found Madeline's qualitative judgments totally offensive. There's no absolute best. What's best for Madeline might not be best for Zoe. Or for Catherine, for that matter," Michael weighed in. As they rode home in the cab, they all asked themselves some version of the same question: *Will Zoe end up in the "best" school for her?*

The next time Helen checked her e-mail, there were several pertaining to school business. The first was from Sara.

TO: All eighth-grade families

RE: Admissions

As we head into the final stretch of the admissions process, I wanted to touch base with all of you on a few points:

1. Please call Margaret in the next few days to set up an appointment for your family to meet with me to discuss the status of all of your applications. It's important that I know where each of you are in the process and at which schools you would like me to make the strongest push.

2. Please call each school and double-check that your applications are complete. Before the winter break there was much confusion surrounding letters of recommendation, and I want to make sure that nothing falls through the cracks.

3. Please feel free to call me or drop in with any questions, suggestions or comments.

4. Bear with me, as I am learning as I go. I assure you, I consider successful eighth-grade admissions to be my number one priority.

The next was from Denise.

Helen,

A few last-minute questions before the auction catalogue goes to press.

First question: The Marxes have offered a day at the races. They own a slew of thoroughbreds and have arranged for a group of four to join them in their box for a champagne breakfast and a special race. One of their horses won the Triple Crown or something like that one year so I think they're pretty big time. I'm not sure it's appropriate since there's gambling involved. What do you think?

Second question: Toppler came through with something really tacky. He's offered to donate his legal services to set up an off-shore corporation, something he claims to have extensive experience with. I'm not comfortable with this. What do you think?

Last: What do you want to do about the Rothschild dinner?

She had no time to answer these now. She had been assigned three reviews, all due the following week, and she hadn't yet seen the shows; she had a Pilates class, a haircut appointment, and had to shop for the dinner with Max they had scheduled for the following night. The School would have to wait.

Sara had arranged for Oscar Whyte to be interviewed by Laura Sue Charleston, the new Kindergarten teacher from Alabama, while she met with his parents. Miss Charleston was chosen because she had never conducted an admissions interview, and Sara thought it was important to give her a trial run. As Brandi led Oscar down the hall, she put her index finger to her mouth to shush a group of children she caught giggling at him. But even she had to admit that with his nubby hand-knit sweater and his Prince Valiant pageboy, he fit in better on the Isle of Wight than the Isle of Manhattan.

"And so do his parents," she thought when she returned to the admissions office and considered Benjamin and Clarissa, both of whom were dressed in burlappy fabrics and homespun tunics, looking like a couple of modern-day Druids on their way to view a solar eclipse at Stonehenge.

"Miss Nash will be with you in just a few minutes," Brandi said politely. "Would you like some coffee while you're waiting?"

"That would be lovely. With milk, please," Clarissa answered.

Sara kept the Whytes waiting for over ten minutes, something she had been loath to do when she was the director of admissions, but was now forced to do with some regularity. She was stuck on the phone with the long-winded Eva Hopkins from The Very Brainy Girls' School, who had called to discuss Zoe Drager and the two other girls from The School whose applications she was considering. Brandi knew not to interrupt Sara after her recently issued edict: "Without exception, admissions directors take precedent over applicants," or, as she pragmatically explained, "We've got to move out the merchandise before restocking the shelves."

When she finally freed herself and apologized for her lateness, Clarissa countered, "No, no, no. We're the ones who should be apologizing. We're so embarrassed about the way this was handled and are ever so grateful to you for your willingness to even consider our application."

These people are so not *New Yorkers,* thought Sara, finding their self-deprecating manner as well as their Cotswold Cottage fashion sense endearing.

"I'm happy to help. I understand the difficulty of moving to a new city, and I certainly know how intimidating the admissions process can be. So tell me a bit about Oscar."

"Kiddywinks?" Clarissa beamed.

"Our little kipper!" Benjamin chimed in affectionately.

"Before you came to New York, had Oscar attended any kind of preschool program?" Sara realized she needed to be more specific.

"Oh, my, yes," Benjamin began. "You see, I am a Montessori-trained teacher."

"And I teach the Rudolf Steiner method," Clarissa added. "Oscar attended a preschool in Manchester—a sort of hybrid, a blend of the two educational philosophies: The Steinessori School. It was a marvelous place. Have you heard of it?"

"That's a new one," said Sara. "Can't say that I have. But, of course, I do know the two methods individually. Didn't Pamela have some affiliation with Montessori?" she asked. Even though she knew it was unprofessional, she couldn't resist the temptation to wheedle more information about Pamela out of the Whytes.

"She claimed to be a certified Montessori teacher and even stated so on her resume. But after she left The Manchester School, which, by the way, was strictly Montessori, it was discovered that she had no certification."

"Wouldn't her lack of training have been evident?" Sara asked.

"Not to four-year-olds," Benjamin replied with an awkward grin. Clarissa giggled.

"But to her colleagues or the school's administration?" Sara couldn't believe The Manchester School would have been so lax.

"Don't forget, she was . . . how shall I put it . . . ?" Benjamin stuttered as he searched for the right euphemism.

"Oh, just say it, Benjamin—she was shagging the headmaster," Clarissa said impatiently. Her husband blushed, and Sara bit her lip.

"It seems old Harold Rothschild was willing to turn the other cheek . . . so to speak," Ben snickered, apparently having decided to let his hair down.

"Ben-ja-min," Clarissa scolded, laughing.

Sara giggled, remembering that the only thing the British enjoyed more than bathroom humor was bedroom humor.

Clarissa suddenly turned to Benjamin and asked, "Did you tell Miss Nash why Pamela was . . . made redundant at The Manchester School?"

Sara sensed Benjamin's fear and hastily interjected, "I learned what happened in Manchester from, ah . . . another source." Benjamin looked at her gratefully.

Meanwhile, Oscar Whyte was cheerfully playing with the Kindergarten class hamster, Fribbles, while Miss Laura Sue observed and scribbled notes.

"So tell me, sweet pea, how do y'all like New York?" she drawled.

"It's okay," he answered. "But I like Manchester better."

"I betcha do. I miss my hometown, too. But ya get used to New York real fast. It only took me 'bout two weeks."

"You mean a fortnight," Oscar corrected.

"A what?" She was befuddled. "Let's take a look at a book, darlin'. You pick one out," she said, plunking herself down on one of the miniature chairs. This was the part of teaching Kindergarten she was finding the hardest. With weak knees and an excess forty pounds, maneuvering up and down all day was an occupational hazard. Some days, to avoid having to repeatedly lower herself onto the floor, she had taken to crawling around the room on all fours, sometimes prompting a child to climb on her back and play horsey, which only made matters worse.

"I'll go fetch one from the Mother Hubbard," Oscar said, skipping over to the cupboard where the books were stored. Choosing a basic primer, he had no trouble reading every word, "See Spot run. Run, Spot, run. Jane called Spot. Come, Spot, come."

"Why, you went through that faster than Grant went through Richmond, sweet potato," she crooned. "You must have read this one before?"

"No. But I've seen some of the words before. Like 'Spot.' 'Out, out damned Spot,' " he explained.

"Why, that's real smart a ya, hon," she said, recognizing the phrase but not sure from where.

"Miss Charleston, I'm hot. May I please take off my jumper?" he asked politely.

She was confused. "You're not wearin' a jumper, sugar."

"What do you call this?" he said with a sigh of frustration as he pulled off his sweater.

Again she was confused. "Oscar, what's your favorite food?" When she was hungry, which was much of the time, she liked to talk to the children about food.

"Mummy wishes it were bubbles and squeak."

"Whatcha mean, sugar?"

"But I'd rather have bangers and mash any day. Or chips."

"I like chips, too," she said with relief.

"Is it time yet to go up the apples and pears and find Mummy and Daddy?" he asked anxiously.

"You make about as much sense as a ripe Georgia peach in the middle of January," she said, furrowing her brow.

"Upstairs to find my mum and dad!" he announced with frustration, and bounded upstairs to the admissions office, Laura Sue huffing and puffing to catch up.

They reached the top of the stairs just as Ben and Clarissa were shaking hands with Sara, and as Oscar leapt into his father's arms, Miss Laura bubbled convivially, "Me and lil' Oscar Meyer wiener had a real swell time, didn't we, sugar?"

Oscar burrowed into his father's shoulder.

"What is it, ducky?" Benjamin asked.

"This lady is all ballsed up," Oscar sobbed.

"There, there," he comforted his son. "Don't get your knickers in a twist about it." And then he shrugged apologetically at Miss Charleston, who looked upset and confused.

Maybe Pamela wasn't completely off base about the language difference, Sara thought.

The last of the interviews completed, Sara spent the rest of the day behind closed doors with Brandi, ensconced in the first phase of the Kindergarten admissions selections. There were dozens of applications that, for a myriad of reasons, were not even in the running, making the first round of cuts quite simple. There were the many children who were patently not ready for school, there were applicants whose KAT reports were drastically below the norm, and there were the applicants whose parents so far exceeded the pain-in-the-ass quotient that Sara refused to consider their application regardless of the child's qualifications. The Belzers fell into this category. Even though Sara felt that Sam would thrive in a supportive classroom environment, away from his parents for a good portion of the day, she rejected him on the grounds that she couldn't bear the thought of discussing his latent genius with his parents for the next ten years.

However, the job became more difficult when they tackled the second tier. This was the group that comprised all the sibling applicants, and there were many. Sara was relieved not to have Pamela breathing down her back, glad of the freedom to make her own decisions about these tricky cases. She and Brandi discussed each application at length, making sure to consider all the variables before deciding yea or nay. For example, Nina Moore was a decent candidate with an annoying father and an absentee mother. Her eighth-grade brother, Nicholas, had been slightly needier than one would ideally want, but wasn't an extreme case. And it didn't seem that he was going to be particularly difficult to place in high school. Ultimately, they both felt compelled to reward the mother for her career choice, since she was one of the few ob-gyns who still accepted patients with high-risk pregnancies; and even though her husband was a shlub, they accepted the Moores' second child.

They spent the next three hours discussing each of the siblings, admitting fourteen, rejecting twenty-three.

After the siblings they had to consider the few applicants who were essentially faits accomplis. Obviously, Montana Easton fell into this category, not necessarily by Sara's choice but by a confluence of unforeseen circumstances and his megastar mom's media savvy. Aurora Dondi-Marghelletti was another one, partially out of Sara's sense of obligation to Simone Savage—she always accepted at least one of her students, and in this case, she liked the family. And although she wouldn't admit it to Brandi, she had a soft spot for Italians and loved the sound of their name. Then there were two children whose parents were, though not exactly related, so tight with a couple of trustees that they might as well have been, whom she had no choice but to accept, as Lisa Fontaine had made abundantly clear in a recent e-mail.

Next they had to focus on diversity. Sara was committed to making sure the class was at least 15 percent nonwhite, and with many appealing applicants from which to choose, she and Brandi reviewed each one and accepted several more than they knew they would enroll. The fact was, all the schools wooed the well-qualified minority children, and each one would most likely have the luxury of receiving multiple acceptances.

In a class of fifty, that didn't leave many open slots to fill, but Sara and Brandi persevered to give every remaining applicant a fair shake.

"I'm sorry the Romanovs knocked themselves out of the running by sending that Christmas gift," Brandi said.

"Me, too," Sara admitted.

"What do you want to do about Oscar Whyte?" Brandi asked, flipping open his application file.

"What are his KAT scores like?" Sara asked.

"Ninety-eight, ninety-four, ninety-seven, ninety-eight," Brandi read.

"Wow. He's very bright. But highly eccentric . . . which I like," Sara began.

"The parents are sort of oddball but seem very knowledgeable about education and really love The School," Brandi added enthusiastically.

"But they haven't looked at any other schools, so they have nothing to compare us to. That bothers me," Sara complained, and then paused to read through his entire file. "At the moment, we don't have any British students. I would like to see at least one in The School. Wouldn't you?"

"Absolutely."

"I just wish he didn't come by way of you know who," Sara said regretfully. "But in a funny way, that's why I'm favorably disposed. She really screwed them, and I feel this irrational compulsion to make it up to them. Let's accept him."

"Miranda Swanson?" Brandi said, going down the list.

"*Icchh,* no," Sara said. "That mother is insufferable, and Miranda is on her way to becoming a narcissist of the highest order. She's one of the few children I have no desire to see in five years."

"The Barton twins, Craig and Greg?"

"Tough call. The boys are nice, but the family situation is a mess, and the father seems dangerous. I vote no. What do you think?"

"They're our only viable twins. And the former nanny, now stepmother is lovely. I say maybe."

"Okay. Maybe."

"Butterscotch Riley?"

"Love the name."

"Yes. No?"

"Isn't she the one who speaks Mandarin?"

"That's her. What do you think?"

Sara recalled her recent dressing-room encounter with the mother and couldn't decide whether to factor that into her decision. She would have to sleep on it.

"Maybe."

"Silvia Clarin?" Brandi continued down the list.

"Is that the girl who's allergic to everything?"

"That's her. I say no."

"Me, too. Just thinking about her gives me hives."

And on and on it went. Four hours later they were interrupted by a visit from Lisa Fontaine.

"Thanks for stopping by," Sara began. She had left Lisa a message that morning saying that something had come up she wanted to discuss. "Just when I thought the Tally Easton problem was resolved, I received a note from her with a donation to The School, intended, as she so eloquently put it, 'as an expression of her deep gratitude for our willingness to overlook her publicity faux pas.'"

"That was kind of her. It's unusual to receive a donation from a new family before the child has actually enrolled, but not unheard of. We received a rather large donation from what's-his-name, that Wall Street honcho, last year before his daughter was even accepted, if I remember correctly, didn't we?" Given the commotion it caused at the time, Lisa's struggle to recall the details rang false to Sara.

"I was slightly put off by Tally's check since we haven't even sent out the letters of acceptance yet," Sara said, maintaining her deferential tone.

"You and I both know their acceptance was a done deal the minute *Tally Ho* hit the stands in December. Tally used the media brilliantly. If we don't accept Cheyenne, or whatever his name is, she'll make our lives miserable. It's just not worth it. So how much did she send?"

Sara gulped. "Half a million."

"That sounds about right, don't you think?" Lisa asked, not really interested in her response.

"Of course," Sara said as if she meant it. When it came to fundraising, she was flying by the seat of her pants. And for one who was accustomed to coach, upgrading to the first-class cabin was going to take some getting used to.

Tacked to the corkboard above his desk were the photographs Michael had taken in France. The numerous shots of Justine in situ, posed in her tiled kitchen stirring large copper pots, or on the garden path carrying baskets of potatoes, were a graphic testament to the surreal quality of Michael's job these days. Generally not a procrastinator, he was having trouble finalizing the production budgets for the fall season. Factoring in the costs related to *La Cuisine de Justine,* which in his mind was still no more than a farce, was stretching the budget beyond tenability. As Xavier talked up the show as though it were the linchpin of the fall schedule, Michael dutifully played along. Some days he thought that Xavier really did believe in the show and that it would actually be produced and aired in the fall. Other days he expected Xavier to crack and confess his real reason for rooting for Justine. But he knew that if he persisted in second-guessing, he could drive himself crazy, so instead he forced himself to stay focused on the tasks at hand: fine-tuning estimates, participating in preproduction meetings, and humoring Justine. Come February 12, who knew what would happen?

He was relieved when his phone rang and on the other end was a chipper Vince Gargano; they hadn't spoken since before the holidays.

"Yo, bro. I'm calling with a proposition. By the way, happy New Year," Vince began.

"To you, too. What's up?"

"Would you believe I'm calling to offer you a once-in-a-lifetime opportunity to play some b-ball with the nineteen seventy-three Knicks?" Vince succeeded in tantalizing Michael.

"Say what?"

"Okay, listen. The Bucolic Campus School auction is coming up next month. You know how these school auctions work, don't you?"

"Oy, do I ever."

"Okay. So one of the items in our auction this year is Fantasy Basketball Camp. The deal is, five guys get to hoop it up with five members of the 1973 Knicks for a whole day, with lunch and dinner thrown in, too. Monroe's gonna be there—Reed, Lucas, Bradley, and Frazier, too. We've got four guys, and we're looking for a fifth to join us. We'll be bidding against some heavy hitters, but there's strength in numbers, and we might just get it. I immediately thought of you, bro. It'll be a total gas and a great chance for you to get to know some of the guys here. We've got one of the cooler phys. ed. teachers, a math teacher, the dean of the upper school, me, and you would make five. Whaddya think?"

Michael wasn't sure what to think. Did Vince mean that he should "get to know" these guys so that when Zoe went to The Bucolic Campus School next year he'd already be chummy with a few members of the faculty? What other reason would there be for him to "get to know" them? But at the same time that he was sweating that question, he was also thinking that it sounded like a gas.

"How much are we talking about?" Michael asked.

"It'll probably go for around twenty-five," Vince replied.

"Thousand?" Michael was not prepared for that.

"Yeah. That's five grand each. Could be a bit more, but we figure we'll set a limit at seven grand each. But hey, it all goes to the school, and it's almost a hundred percent tax-deductible."

"Great, if your kid is in the school," Michael fished, and then waited for a response. But none was forthcoming. "That's a lotta dough. Let me discuss it with the wife and get back to you, okay?"

"Sure, bro. Let me know soon, though; I know a lot of other guys who would kill for it."

"How are things with you otherwise?" Michael fished again.

"Nuts. January is crazy in admissions. I've got to make the final selections this month. You can't imagine what a huge to-do that is."

"I think I have some idea," Michael responded wryly.

In preparation for her meeting with the Winters, Sara was reviewing April's academic records and was disturbed by the fact that, year by year, the level of her performance had markedly declined. When April first enrolled at The School in Kindergarten, she had KAT scores that ranged from the eighty-fifth to the ninety-fifth percentile. When, in the fifth grade, she first began to receive quarterly report cards, she had a 3.5 average. Each subsequent quarter her grade point average dropped until it had reached 2.2 last semester. The teachers' written reports also reflected her troubles. The nadir of her academic descent was her recent SAPS scores, which were substantially below the fiftieth percentile. All this was presumably aggravated by her absenteeism, which had increased at an alarming rate, to the point that in the first semester of eighth grade she had missed eighteen days of school.

Knowing it was bound to be fraught with strife, Sara dreaded this meeting. She could hear the Winters in the reception area in the midst of a hushed but heated argument and waited until they appeared to have reached a momentary standoff before inviting them to enter her office.

"Bring me up to date on your thinking about where you would like to see April next year," Sara began the discussion, with a self-assurance that she hoped to maintain throughout the meeting.

"If you'd been doing your homework, you would know that April is going to The Fancy Girls' School. We've been unwavering in our pursuit of that from day one," Dana stated smugly as Patrick nodded in agreement.

"I'm not sure, given the fragile state of April's health, that would be a wise choice. I would worry that she would find the demands of their program extremely stressful right now," Sara began diplomatically.

"That's absurd," Patrick blasted.

"Ridiculous," Dana echoed.

Sara knew it was her responsibility to exercise her newfound authority and force them to face the facts. As she handed them April's transcript, she said, "I'm sure there's nothing here you haven't already seen, but when looked at all together, the picture is pretty grim."

She waited patiently while they gruffly leafed through the report, hissing barbed remarks to each other as they went.

"What you're looking at is essentially a longhand version of what the admissions directors are working with. In addition, after meeting April, they have all had the same reaction—this is not a healthy adolescent. They have all asked me what kind of treatment April is receiving, and I'm almost embarrassed to tell them none. I have to tell you, I feel that's unconscionable," she said quietly.

They both refused to meet her gaze.

Sara continued, "I'd like to make a suggestion." She paused. "That is, if you're open to hearing one."

"What?" Patrick barked, barely civil.

"I think the best thing you could do for April is to withdraw all of your applications and leave her at The School for another year. This would relieve her of tremendous pressure and give you some time to get her into intensive therapy, possibly a residential program, for the remainder of this school year. She could return to The School in September and repeat eighth grade."

Their reaction was instantaneous: Dana turned red and emitted a choking sound, and a tear or two ran down her cheek, pooling in the ridges of her tightly puckered lips; Patrick quivered as the veins of his neck and forehead swelled and bulged. Sara was frightened by the potential for calamitous cardiovascular episodes on both their parts.

"I told Lisa Fontaine that you're unsuited for this position. You're absolutely unqualified to be talking to us this way. I'm going to tell the board that they should immediately get Pamela back to take over eighth-grade admissions, before we have a total fiasco on our hands!" Dana fumed.

"Why don't you two go home and talk this over? You don't have to make a decision immediately, but I wouldn't let it go much longer. April is in crisis. I just saw her this morning, and she looks dreadful," she counseled calmly. "I realize this is a lot to digest," she added, immediately regretting her choice of word.

"You can be damn sure we're going to talk about it," Patrick exploded.

"I can assure you that this recommendation doesn't merely reflect my own opinion. I've spoken with all of April's teachers, The School's consulting psychologist, and the psychiatric staff at the hospital last month."

"You had no right to do that," Patrick shouted. "That's an invasion of privacy! I knew I should get Toppler involved. Dana, call him the minute we get out of here!" he ordered.

Sara didn't back down. "You should also know that I spoke with Justine Frampton about April, just yesterday. She's extremely concerned about her health and will not even consider her application until April gets help and shows signs of improvement." She hadn't planned to tell them this today, but at this point, felt she had no choice.

"That's absurd and you know it. Just yesterday, Pamela assured me that April was getting into The Fancy Girls' School. All along she's told us that our application is no more than a formality." Hands on hips, Dana bullied like the schoolyard thug Sara imagined her to have been.

"Well, then I suppose it's her word against mine. You can choose which story you want to believe," Sara said, not intending to sound quite so na-na-na-na-na.

"Dana, if we went to that fucking cooking school last summer for no reason, I'm gonna kill you!" Patrick was so menacing that Sara thought he was perfectly capable of making good on his threat.

"Don't worry, Patrick," Dana assured her fuming spouse. "Pamela knows exactly what she's doing. She and Justine are like this," she said, crossing her index and middle fingers and shaking them in his face. She then turned to Sara. "Pamela's known April much longer than you have and is practically a member of our family. She'll take over from here, and it will all work out. You'll see," she said high-handedly, regaining control of her emotions and resuming her haughty stance.

"I'm sure she'll be there for you the same way she was when April was hospitalized." Sara didn't mean to be sarcastic, but the Winters' refusal to face reality infuriated her.

"She didn't come because she knew there was nothing seriously wrong with April. *She* knew her well enough to know it was just anemia," Dana said defensively.

"Open your eyes! Your daughter is dangerously underweight! She has anorexia and bulimia. She could collapse again at any moment," Sara spoke as strongly as she felt she possibly could without causing Patrick to become violent.

"I've had it with your pseudopsychiatric diagnostics! You don't know what the hell your talking about!" Patrick shouted.

"What more do you need? Look at the physical evidence! She's five feet seven inches tall and weighs eighty-three pounds!" Sara exploded.

"She's always been built like a model," Dana argued.

Sara was so frustrated that she pulled out all the stops. "Maybe this image will mean something to you. Last night the janitor called to tell me there was a trail of ants coming out of her locker. We opened it up this morning and found piles of chewed food hidden among her notebooks and gym shoes. How would you explain that?"

"Another invasion of privacy!" Patrick declared assertively.

"Call it what you will, but it's my duty to make sure The School is clean and vermin-free. April's health problems are life-threatening *and* a liability to The School! I'll say it for the last time: GET HELP! For April and yourselves!" she took a deep breath and stood up to signal the end of the meeting.

"You'll be hearing from our lawyer," Patrick warned as he stormed out, his wife hustling to follow. She half expected Dana to turn her head and stick out her tongue.

After they were gone, Sara collapsed; she was emotionally depleted. But the worst was surely behind her, since April's situation was probably the most complicated of all the students in the eighth-grade class. It was just unfortunate that the Winters had been her first meeting—she would have preferred to have had a chance to get her feet wet before diving into the deep, frigid waters of the Winters' emotional abyss. She hadn't quite anticipated their level of resistance and animosity, but as she critiqued her performance, she decided that she had handled it as well as she possibly could have.

Brandi stuck her head in the door. "Are you okay? That sounded really unpleasant."

"I'm okay. Glad to have that meeting behind me." She breathed a sigh of relief. "Oh, no. I just realized that if they follow my advice, they'll be here next year. I don't know if I could survive another go-round with them."

Helen was enjoying the novelty of puttering in the kitchen, especially since the evening represented such a significant familial milestone—the "meet the parents" dinner with Zoe's first boyfriend was not a trivial event for any of the Dragers. Ever since Zoe had gotten involved with Max, she had been much easier to live with, her mood swings occurring with less frequency and much more predictably. Other than her outburst after their visit to The Very Brainy Girls' School, she was more serene than Helen could remember her being in years.

When at last the brisket was in the oven, the noodle pudding assembled, and the carrots and sweet potatoes pureed, Helen sat down to return a few calls and e-mails. First she called Margaret to schedule the admissions meeting Sara had requested. She made the appointment for the following week, early in the morning so that Michael could join them before going to work, and told Margaret she would let her know if Zoe would be attending—Sara had left this choice up to them, and Helen was unsure whether it was better to include Zoe or not. She and Michael would decide closer to the time. Next she returned Denise's e-mail with a phone call.

"I agree with you on the inappropriateness of both the Marx donation and Toppler's," Helen said.

"Good. I think that since we've included his lube job we can say no to the offshore nonsense without offending him. The day at the races I was less sure about. It could go for quite a lot of money," Denise explained with uncharacteristic uncertainty.

"The gambling aspect is dicey. I think we should avoid it. Plus, I'm a little squeamish these days about anything having to do with horses, thanks to our dearly departed," Helen explained.

"Which brings us to the last item on my agenda: the Rothschild dinner. Since I sent you the e-mail, she's called me several times to confirm it."

"Oh?" Helen was surprised. Somehow she thought that after Pamela's humiliating dismissal, she would have kept her distance from everyone connected to The School. "What did she say?"

"She gave me a long harangue about the importance of fulfilling one's obligations and refused to accept my offer to let her off the hook."

"So you agreed to keep the dinner in the auction?" Helen asked.

"I told her I had to clear it with my committee. What do you think?"

"I'm concerned that if we include it, no one will bid on it. Let's be frank: the people who spent a lot of money on the dinner in the past did it to kiss ass with the head of School. Why would anyone want it now?"

"For the food?" Denise responded.

"They could go to Le Bon Take Out and feed themselves for a fraction of the cost."

"Just kidding. So what do I tell her?"

"Oh, let's just leave it in the auction. There're still enough of her fans around. Someone will bid on it. It's been such a good moneymaker for us in the past, I hate to lose it."

"Okeydokey. By the way, what time do you expect Marissa for dinner? She's reading to the blind at four and then has her Junior Junior League meeting until six thirty."

"She can come whenever she's finished," Helen answered. She certainly didn't want to rain on Marissa's do-gooder parade.

Having completed her calls, Helen logged on to the computer to check her e-mail, expecting some information from an editor about a deadline, and another message from a curator about an upcoming symposium she had been invited to attend. She was puzzled when she opened her in-box and saw that there was a message from PHILLIP@CASHIN.ORG. She hadn't recalled giving him her e-mail address.

Helen,
I took the liberty of tracking down your e-mail address through Josh Kirov. I'm not sure why, but he seemed surprised that I didn't already have it.
I wanted to let you know that Catherine found your red garnet earrings in a glass bowl in our living room. She recognized them as a pair Zoe wore to her party last month and assumed they had been here since then. I recognized them as the pair you were wearing when you were here, but didn't say so. I'm afraid she may have told Zoe she found the earrings and I thought I should warn you of that possibility. They are safely in my desk drawer and awaiting instructions. I could messenger them to you, or, as would be my preference, give them to you in person.

The time we spent together last week was splendid. Just seeing you gives me enormous pleasure, touching you gives me even more. So much so that I'm willing to be with you in whatever way works for you.
Just let me know what you want to do.

Phillip

Oh, my God, how could I have been so damn careless. I'm an idiot, she chastised herself. Her recollection of the recklessness that led to the removal of the earrings was mortifying. *Was I actually so transported that I removed my earrings? These are the same earrings that I reluctantly let Zoe wear, only after issuing a stern warning to not remove them under any circumstances. And now I broke the rule that I had insisted my daughter follow only weeks before. How could I have been such a hypocrite?*

She wasn't sure how long she had been sitting there or how many times she read the note, but before she had a chance to respond, she heard a key in the door and, without thought, pressed delete, and the message disappeared.

"Hi, sweetie!" she greeted Zoe brightly.

"Hi, Mom! Ummm. It smells yum. What can I do to help? Should I set the table?"

"That would be great. How was your day?"

"Excellent. We got our math midterm back. I got a ninety-two. Oh, and I got an A minus on my history paper."

"That's great! Have you gotten the science midterm back yet?"

"Yeah. That's not such good news. I got a B minus."

"That's not so bad," Helen said supportively, following Sara's advice to let up on Zoe.

"It would be if I went to The Very Brainy Girls' School. I might have jumped off the George Washington Bridge."

"You've got a point," Helen laughed.

Zoe set the table with more care than Helen had ever seen her use, carefully aligning the silver and artfully folding the linen napkins so that each place setting was a perfect replica of all the others.

"Mom, do I look better in profile or face-to-face?"

"You're beautiful in every way. Especially inside." Helen parodied a folksy singsong style. "Why?"

"I'm trying to decide if I should I sit next to Max or across from him," Zoe debated earnestly.

Helen did an internal eye roll and then, recognizing that from her daughter's perspective this was a serious concern, recommended that she sit across from him. "That way, we can put Max on Daddy's left and you on Daddy's right, which will create a good conversation triangle."

Michael arrived home with a large bouquet of flowers and a Linzer torte he had picked up at one of their favorite bakeries. While Zoe was in her room dressing for the party, Michael helped Helen in the kitchen. As she was standing over the sink washing the salad greens, he wrapped his arms around her waist and kissed her neck.

"Hmmm, that's nice," she said softly. "What's up?" They had been married long enough for her to know that his gesture was loaded with more than affection, and sure enough, she was right; it was a calculated prelude to his presentation of Vince Gargano's proposition.

"You're not seriously considering it. Are you?"

"Not really," he said, and then added, "but it *would* put us in good standing there."

"What are you talking about? Until Zoe's admitted, we have no standing there! I don't think it's right for us to be spending money at The Bucolic Campus School auction. It feels like we're trying to buy our way in. Besides, we have an obligation to support The School's auction this year."

"What good is that going to do us?" he asked.

"Michael! I can't believe you said that," she said sharply.

"At least I'm being honest. Where is *your* sudden burst of moral superiority coming from?"

"Don't talk to me about morality," she snapped defensively. "It's one thing for you and me to be in cahoots against the system. But this is something else altogether. This feels like you're pulling one over on *me,* and I don't like it!"

"That's not fair. All along it's been you who's pushed this relationship with Gargano. Now that he's proposing we cement the bond, you're accusing me of 'pulling one over on you'?" Michael was incensed.

"If you had been honest about your real motive right off the bat, I wouldn't have reacted this way. Admit it, Michael. This is about fulfilling one of your deepest childhood fantasies. You've dreamed of going to basketball camp your whole life." The opportunity for moral grandstanding was irresistible.

"What's up with you two?" Zoe interrupted, bursting into the room. "My friends are going to be here any minute."

"We'll talk about it later," Helen snarled through clenched teeth.

Knowing the importance the success of the evening had for Zoe, the Dragers demonstrated their social dexterity by temporarily burying the hatchet and putting on their best we're-one-big-happy-family faces. When the doorman buzzed to announce the arrival of the first guest, Zoe instructed, "Pleeeeaaase, guys. Don't do or say anything to embarrass me."

"Do we ever embarrass you?" Michael asked with genuine concern.

But Helen teased, "So we shouldn't pull out the photo albums and show Max your naked baby pictures?"

"Mo-o-m," Zoe laughed.

Max arrived with an exquisite little box of chocolates for Helen and a kiss on the cheek for Zoe. As Michael warmly shook his hand and led him into the living room, Zoe followed Helen to the kitchen and whispered, "Isn't he adorable?"

"Very," whispered Helen as she opened a bottle of sparkling cider for the kids and wine for the adults.

Julian's arrival was, as usual, marked with a burst of fanfare as he shed multiple layers of outerwear, revealing an elaborately embroidered kimono beneath. While wildly gesticulating and delivering kisses and hugs all around, he complimented Helen on her haircut, which both Michael and Zoe had failed to notice.

"Maximilian, how goes it?" Julian sat down and began to tell an animated story about his cab ride, amusing Zoe and Michael with his exaggerated tale of narrowly averted dangers.

Meanwhile, Helen was conversing with Max. "Is Maximilian your real name?"

"Fortunately not. I'm just Max," he said shyly.

"It's a wonderful name. Max Liebermann is one of my favorite painters," Helen said warmly, working hard to help him relax.

"Really? That's such a coincidence. My grandmother studied painting with him in the forties. She used to tell stories about him when my mother was a little girl. That's how she decided to name me Max," he told her, relaxing as they conversed. "Zoe told me you're an art historian. You have some beautiful photographs," he said, looking around the room. "Is that one by Frantisek Styrsky?"

Helen was impressed by a fourteen-year-old that could identify the work of an obscure Czech photographer.

"It is. Have you studied photographic history?"

"Not at all. But we lived in the Czech Republic until I was seven, and my parents are both Czech. I think we once had a book about Styrsky, and I remember seeing pictures that looked like that."

Michael had now turned an ear to their conversation. "I didn't know you were Czech. That's really interesting. We went to Prague a few years ago. We loved it, didn't we, Helen?"

"It's a beautiful city," she answered.

"Do you follow the Eastern European basketball players?" Michael asked, eagerly engaging Max.

"Totally! I root for the Sacramento Kings 'cause they've got Divac, Stojakovic, and Turgalu. They're awesome players." Max lit up as he and Michael talked about this ethnic pocket of basketball that Helen had no idea even existed.

She excused herself to greet Marissa, who had arrived lugging a canvas tote filled with spiral-bound books. She pulled one out and handed it to Helen.

"A gift for the hostess. It's hot off the press. Your own copy of the Centenary Edition of the *Junior League Cookbook.*"

"Thank you so much." Helen accepted it graciously and, thumbing through, came upon a recipe donated by Justine Frampton, member, New York Chapter, for, of all things, pissaladiere!

"I know several people who would love to have this recipe," she told Marissa, and then announced, "Dinner is on. Please, everyone, come to the table. Zoe will show you where to sit."

"Did anyone watch the Golden Globes last night? Tally Easton was wearing the tackiest off-the-shoulder number." Julian launched into an imitation of Joan Rivers on the red carpet and had everyone in stitches.

"My mom said Tally Easton's son is going to go to The School next year," Marissa said in her Miss-Know-it-all manner.

"Is that true, Mom?" Zoe asked.

"That's what I'm hearing," Helen replied.

"Too bad none of us will be there next year to dally with Tally," Julian quipped. "Tally ho," he added with a giggle.

"I got her autograph at the mayor's Christmas party," Marissa bragged. "She was there the night we performed."

"Really? Zoe, you didn't tell us she was there," Michael said.

"I forgot about it. She's not high on my list of hot celebrities," Zoe said, looking to Max for his opinion.

"Me, neither," Max concurred.

"She's a god-awful dresser. That night she was wearing some sort of double-breasted fur jacket. Very bad idea for anyone under five five. Fur adds at least ten pounds," Julian continued his riff.

The guests all complimented the meal and ate heartily, accepting Helen's offer of seconds and, in some cases, thirds. Marissa unabashedly ate more than anyone, which, given the compulsive portion control she was subjected to when she ate at home, was not a surprise. Even though she loved her mother's brisket, Zoe ate like a bird, self-conscious about seeming a glutton in Max's presence. Despite the fact that it offended every feminist bone in Helen's body, she related to Zoe's girlish impulse and guessed she would find her picking at leftovers after the guests departed.

Julian was back to nattering about who wore what, when Max interrupted.

"Julian, you should be a designer. Have you thought about going to the Fashion Center High School?"

"And become a garmento? Over my dad's dead body. He'd rather see me become a nurse than go into the rag trade. I would love to, but it's not gonna happen," he lamented dramatically.

"That's too bad. Some kids from The Public School are going there next year. You'd love them. You'd really fit into their group," Max said encouragingly.

"My father specifically wants to send me to a school where I don't fit in. That seems to be his goal," Julian complained.

"So where do you think you're gonna end up?" Max asked.

"A boarding school for manly men," Julian answered, raising a fist and flexing his biceps.

"And how 'bout you, Marissa?" Max asked.

"I'm hoping to go to one of the public science high schools. I think I did really well on the entrance exam, and I've always gotten nearly perfect scores on every standardized test I've ever taken, so I think I'll have my pick," Marissa answered with the precision her mother had trained her to use. "What about you?"

"The High School for the Musically Gifted. Lots of The Public School kids will be going there, too. They have an excellent orchestral program, great voice training, and are also strong on musical composition, which is what I'm really interested in. Plus you do all the usual mandatory academic stuff. It seems pretty good. For a public school, that is," he added in deference to the Dragers, who, he knew from Zoe, were partial to private school.

"You have no idea how lucky you are that your parents support the idea of your following your passion," Julian said with a downcast look.

"They're both musicians, so they're thrilled that I'm interested in studying music," Max responded, and then turned to Michael and said, "Zoe has a wonderful voice."

"Thank you. We think so, too. All of you were fantastic at the Holiday Festival. It would be so great if the group could perform together again. Are there any plans for that?"

"Not that I know of," Zoe said with regret. "Have you guys heard anything?"

"Now that Ms. Nash is the acting head, she probably won't have time to do the choral program. We'll be back to singing 'My Favorite Things' with old Mrs. Barker," Marissa complained.

"Old Mrs. Barker has whiskers like kittens. She'll never have me, but I know she's smitten . . . ," Julian began singing a parody, and the other kids cracked up as Helen and Michael cleared the table.

"What do you think of Max?" Helen asked quietly when they were alone in the kitchen.

"Nice kid," he answered distractedly.

"That's all? Nice kid?" She was disappointed in his lack of imagination.

"What? Don't you think he seems like a nice kid?" he asked with a hint of hostility.

"Yes, Michael, he's a nice kid," she said condescendingly. "Are you being so terse because you're still angry with me for not jumping on the Fantasy Basketball Camp bandwagon?" she asked angrily.

"It's you who's picking the fight," he retorted under his breath.

Julian's singing in the other room became louder. "When the bitch bites, when the kids sing, then I'm feeling bad . . ." They returned to the table and served the dessert.

After the guests departed and the kitchen was cleaned up, Helen went into Zoe's room to chat while she was getting ready for bed.

"Tell me everything you and Max talked about," Zoe pleaded. The reality was, Helen's mind had been elsewhere for most of the evening, and other than her astonishment at Max's ability to identify Frantisek Styrsky, she had only a sketchy memory of their conversation.

"He seems very bright. We talked a little bit about his parents, who sound very interesting, and then he and Daddy got into basketball. Otherwise, I mostly listened to you kids talk, and I thought he seemed very composed and articulate."

"So do you like him?" Zoe asked anxiously.

"Very much," she said. She could tell Zoe wanted her approval, and she had every intention of giving it. But she was so preoccupied with the dilemma presented by Phillip's e-mail that she had no capacity for anything else. She knew she would never be able to sleep unless she had ascertained whether Catherine had told Zoe that she had found the earrings.

"Have you spoken to Catherine lately?" she asked with a casualness that downplayed her sense of urgency.

"Yeah, yesterday. Why?" Zoe was annoyed that her mother didn't seem to want to talk about Max.

"How was her trip to Sweden?"

"She said it was fun. She did a lot of skiing with her grandmother."

"That's nice."

Zoe busied herself brushing her hair as Helen watched quietly, lost in thought. After a few minutes, Zoe began hesitantly, "Mom, something weird happened. I think I need to tell you."

"What's that?" Helen said, masking her nervousness.

"Remember Catherine's party before Christmas? Remember how you generously let me wear your garnet earrings? Well, Catherine called yesterday to tell me that she found them at her house. At first I thought they couldn't be yours, because I was positive I never took them off at the party. So I looked in your jewelry box and they weren't there. So then I thought I must have left them at her house. But I'm totally freaked out because, I swear, I can't remember ever taking them off," Zoe said, almost crying. "I feel like I must be going crazy or something. Then I started wondering if maybe someone had slipped some drugs into my soda, and now I'm worried that I might have done other stuff that night that I don't remember."

Helen was overcome with confusion, guilt, and self-hatred. Clearly, her first obligation was to relieve Zoe of her anxiety, so she finessed and concocted an explanation that straddled the line between fact and fiction, closer to the latter than the former.

"That's a funny mix-up," she began, feeling duplicitous as soon as she started. "I had to drop in at the Cashins' last week, while you were still in Cuba," she continued, keeping it light but provoking a prickly response from Zoe nevertheless.

"Really? Why?"

"A little business," she said, wondering where she was going with this. "You know Catherine's dad is an important art collector, right? Well, he asked me if I would come over to look at a painting he was considering buying."

"Really?" Zoe was skeptical.

Helen nodded. "The day I went there, I was wearing the garnet earrings, and there happened to be another woman there who asked to see them. I took them off for her and forgot to put them back on," she explained feebly. She was deeply ashamed at the ease with which she told the lie, but the alternative was unthinkable; she would never in a million years consider telling Zoe what she was really doing at the Cashins', especially since she was hard-pressed to explain it herself.

"Well, I'm glad to know I'm not losing my mind," Zoe said sleepily.

"Of course you're not, sweetie," Helen said, kissing her daughter on the forehead and quietly leaving her room.

But I think I *am,* thought Helen, and then made a vain attempt to sublimate her unbearable feelings of shame. *An analyst would have a field day with this story. It's got it all: mother-daughter dynamics, the family jewels (everyone knows what they symbolize . . . and they're red, no less!), adultery, deception, triangulation. . . .*

After the Dragers had scheduled their meeting with Sara, Helen had sent her an e-mail telling her that Zoe would not attend. Sara found the decision curious, given the lip service Helen had been paying to the importance of keeping Zoe involved. But a few comments that Helen had recently let slip led Sara to suspect that the Dragers had a few issues that they were anxious to discuss and had apparently determined that this was best done without their daughter.

"Let's start by reviewing where you stand with each of the schools you have applied to," Sara began.

"Okay. First there's the noncontender—The Progressive School. None of us liked it at all, and we agreed that even if it were the only school that accepted Zoe, we wouldn't send her there," Helen explained.

"Fair enough. I agree it's not the right place for her, although it does have its virtues," Sara said. She had several other students for whom it was a good fit, and had determined it was good practice not to speak negatively about any school.

"Next on our list is The Safety School. I think we all agree it's our last choice, don't we, Michael?"

"Definitely," he said.

"So you consider The Safety School your fallback? That is, would she go there if that were the only place she gets in?" Sara asked.

They both nodded affirmatively but halfheartedly.

"I spoke with Shirley Livingston last week. We have eight students who have applied to The Safety School, all of whom she thought were good candidates. She asked me to tell her which of the eight I think will attend if accepted. I think it's unlikely to be Zoe's only choice, so shall I tell her that she will most likely not attend if accepted?"

"If you think that we're covered," Helen replied, wishing that Sara were telling them what to do, not asking. But she also remembered how belittling it was when Pamela barked directives, and given a choice between the two, she had to admit, she preferred Sara's more inclusive and honest approach.

"Next are the two single-sex schools, The Fancy Girls' School and The Very Brainy Girls' School. In my mind they're tied," Helen stated, clearly not having consulted Michael.

"We hated The Very Brainy Girls' School!" he exploded, surprising them both with his vehemence.

"We had the tour guide from hell," Helen explained to Sara, "so we didn't get a good feel for the place. But their reputation is so strong, I think we have to consider it if she were accepted."

Michael pouted but remained silent.

"I spoke to Eva Hopkins yesterday about Zoe. She was noncommittal about her and said she sensed some ambivalence from you two," Sara explained.

"She never spoke to us!" Michael said angrily.

"Really? She led me to believe she had gotten a strong sense of both of you."

"We introduced ourselves. That was all. Maybe she didn't approve of Helen's shoes," Michael said sarcastically. Helen scoffed but also wondered how they could have managed to make a negative impression when they had virtually no contact with the woman.

"I would recommend, if Zoe is accepted, that we ask her to arrange for you to make another visit. That would be perfectly reasonable under the circumstances," Sara advised, and then, turning to Michael, asked, "You're leaning more towards The Fancy Girls' School?"

"Between the two, I would have to say yes," said Michael. "But we would much rather see Zoe at a coed school."

Helen cleared her throat audibly. "Excuse me? When did we make that decision?"

"I thought we had agreed on that a while ago," Michael responded.

"Maybe *you* made that decision. But I would love to see Zoe in an all-girls school. I think she's leaning in that direction, too."

"Really? As of when?"

"The last time she and I discussed it. A few weeks ago."

"Maybe she said that just to please you. She knows you've had your heart set on a girls' school from the very beginning," Michael said with a distinct tone of irritation.

"Okay. So I have. But I also think it would be good for her," Helen continued defensively.

"Well, I don't think that's what she wants. And I don't think it's right for her, either. Even though I'm ninety-nine percent sure she'll get in to The Fancy Girls' School."

Helen shot him a querulous look. It was not lost on Sara, who was growing increasingly uncomfortable with the tension between them. In the years that she had known the Dragers, she had rarely witnessed this level of antagonism, and wondered if there was an underlying cause above and beyond the stress of admissions.

"The last time I spoke to Justine Frampton she was positive about Zoe but by no means definitive. Do you know something about The Fancy Girls' School that I don't know?" Sara asked.

Before coming here today, Michael and Helen had agreed not to tell Sara anything about *La Cuisine de Justine.* But now that Michael had dropped a hint, Helen unilaterally decided to tell her the whole story.

Sara was astonished and thoroughly amused. "That is so great! I love it! It bears out what I've always believed about Justine—she's a status-seeking social climber who's purely out for herself. I always suspected that she and Pamela had some kind of quid pro quo deal going with the cooking school. It was no coincidence that the families who vacationed there ended up with children at The Fancy Girls' School. The Bakers, the Cookes—there have been at least three or four others."

"The Winters," Helen added.

"We'll see about them," Sara replied evasively. "The way you figured out how to play her is hilarious. Whose idea was it?"

"Hers," Michael said, pointing his thumb in Helen's direction.

"I have to take the rap for this one," Helen confessed with a smirk. Sara was relieved to see her reach out and take Michael's hand.

"If it means Zoe's acceptance, I applaud it. It will definitely go down in the annals of bizarre admissions stories. Last is The Bucolic Campus School, right?"

"We all love The Bucolic Campus School, don't we, Michael? If we decide to go the coed route, that's our first choice," Helen said in a conciliatory tone.

"Vince Gargano and I had lunch last week. There are four students from The School who have applied, and he and I met to discuss each one. But he seemed to be completely enamored with the Drager family, and I had trouble getting him to focus on anyone else. You seem to have made quite a good impression on him," Sara reported enthusiastically.

"Um . . ." Helen shrugged and cocked an eyebrow. Michael nodded and said, "Why not?"

"Your turn," Helen said, and Michael told Sara about his cultivation of "Vinnie."

"And the funny thing is, I really like him. He's a good guy. He's someone I could actually imagine hanging out with," Michael explained.

Again Sara was astounded. "Boy, did I underestimate you two!"

"This was also Helen's idea," Michael volunteered.

"Nice going. I never knew you had it in you," Sara said.

"You and I have never been on opposing teams," Helen laughed. "I can be cutthroat."

"I'll have to remember that. Well, it looks like you're in good shape. I don't think you have anything to worry about. I'm fairly certain Zoe will have a few good options and will be in the enviable position of being able to make her own decision instead of having it made for her. My advice would be to let her take the lead. She's the one who has to attend the school every day, and you want her to feel that wherever she ends up is her choice. Do you agree?" Sara asked, making certain to look at both Helen and Michael.

"Absolutely," they said in unison.

They left The School together but were heading in opposite directions: Helen to the library to do some research, and Michael to his office. Even though they were both under pressure to get to work, they lingered on the corner for a few minutes, discussing the prudence of sharing Sara's optimism. Michael was more inclined to do so than Helen, who was concerned about Sara's lack of experience. She thought that accepting the words of the various admissions directors at face value was naïve and therefore risky. She refused to breathe a sigh of relief until she had an acceptance letter in hand.

"So your pessimism negates my optimism and we remain neutral. That's probably a healthy attitude for us to convey to Zoe during the final waiting period," Michael said sensibly.

"Well put," Helen agreed. "What time do you think you'll be finished with work tonight?"

"Not late. What time does Zoe get home?"

"Tonight's the night she's going to The Public School to see the performance of *Guys and Dolls.* Max told us he's playing Nathan Detroit. Remember? He's invited her to the cast party after the show, so she'll be home on the late side. We could meet somewhere for dinner, if that works for you, and get home before she does," Helen suggested.

"Let's do that. The Bistro at seven?"

"Great. See you there."

The only eighth-grade parents that Sara dreaded meeting with almost as much as the Winters were the Topplers. In the past few days, she had spoken to the admissions directors at the five boarding schools to which Julian had applied, and while all of them were impressed with his scores and school records, they questioned, as one put it, "his emotional maturity," or, in the words of another, "his personal style." She took this to mean that they were uncomfortable with his sexual ambivalence but, lest they be accused of discrimination, couched their concerns in the most euphemistic terms possible. She had several conversations with Julian in which he talked extensively about his desire to stay in New York, convincing her that it was her duty to go to bat for him in what she knew could potentially be an explosive battle with his father. She had even gone so far as to call Soledad Gibson at The Progressive School, to float the idea of the Topplers submitting a late application for Julian. She felt a little like

Pamela when she dropped a hint about Toppler's wealth, but was willing to pull out all the stops to help Julian secure a spot in an open-minded, supportive environment. The Progressive School certainly fit that bill, but convincing John Toppler of this wasn't going to be pleasant.

Lauren Toppler had arrived on time for their appointment; John was twenty minutes late and, when he finally arrived, was belligerent towards both Margaret and his wife and barked, "This better be important; it's costing me five hundred an hour in lost billings."

He barged into Sara's office and demanded she drop whatever she was doing (speaking on the phone to Lisa Fontaine, who, hearing the unmistakable growl of John Toppler, understood when Sara abruptly signed off).

Sara wasted no time presenting her case and, as she talked about the importance of taking Julian's uniqueness into consideration when making a decision about school, heard Toppler grunt and harrumph. Lauren looked at the floor as Sara finished explaining to them why she thought a school like The Progressive School was the best place for Julian.

"Look, Miss Nash. I don't know what your credentials are or why you presume to know what's best for my son. Miss Rothschild never talked about any of this crap. Open, supportive, nurturing—that's the kind of mushy stuff you look for in a Kindergarten, not a high school." He glowered.

"John, dear, I think we should listen to what Sara has to say. Julian has told me that she has spent quite a bit of time with him lately. He thinks the world of her and respects her opinions tremendously. I think we owe it to him to consider her proposal."

"Thank you, Lauren," said Sara as John gave them both a look of resentful resignation.

"Okay, so assuming we decide to keep him at home for high school—which I'm not saying we would, but, for argument's sake, let's say we did—why The Progressive School? Who the hell has ever heard of The Progressive School? I mean, I've heard of The Preppy Boys' School or The Very Brainy Boys' School. Why haven't you suggested one of those?" Toppler questioned in the staccato style of a prosecutor.

"To be frank, those schools are not going to be any better for Julian than Extrover or Mannington. They both demand a certain degree of conformity that I think Julian would find oppressive. He needs a place where he will be valued for who he is. A place that fosters individuality. An accepting, nurturing environment. The other possible option, which I haven't mentioned, is . . ." She hesitated. ". . . a public school."

"WHAT! Did I hear you correctly?" he blasted.

"Not *any* public school. One of the specialized public high schools that foster creativity. Like The School for Fashion, or The School for Theater Arts. He would thrive in one of those places. There would be dozens of kids like him, and . . ."

Toppler emitted a loud Bronx cheer, spraying Sara's desk with saliva. "Don't waste our time, Miss Nash. That's the most ridiculous thing you've said so far." Toppler shook his head in disbelief.

Having had enough experience with Toppler to know he had a short attention span, Sara worked quickly. "So let's go back to The Progressive School. Would you consider submitting an application there? I think I could talk them into considering Julian, if you move quickly. There are no guarantees he would be admitted, nor are you committed to sending him if he is, but at least it gives you a New York City option, which is what Julian really wants," she added, looking directly at Lauren, who, she knew, cared deeply about doing what was best for her son.

"I think we should do that, John. It doesn't lock us into anything. We have nothing to lose," Lauren suggested softly.

"Damn it, Lauren! Whose side are you on?" he demanded. "I'm tired of all this simpering. You treat my son like a hothouse flower. No wonder he's such a pansy! He needs to get out on his own and become a man!"

Sara watched curiously as Lauren patiently waited for her husband to finish his diatribe before beginning to speak and then chose her words carefully. "John, dear, our son is probably a homosexual."

"What the hell are you talking about?" he roared. "Did you get that from her?" he demanded, pointing a finger at Sara.

"No, dear. I've suspected this since he was nine. Julian's just recently discovering this about himself. It has nothing to do with Miss

Nash," Lauren said as Sara marveled at her serenity. She had no patience for Toppler, but out of respect for Lauren and a true fondness for Julian, she jumped in.

"Julian needs both of your support as he comes to grips with his sexual orientation. It's a difficult challenge for an adolescent, and he needs all the help he can get," Sara explained.

"It's all your fault!" Toppler glared at his wife. "He got it from your side of the family. You're the one with the queer brother. This can't have come from me, that's for sure. I've tried to make a man out of him, but he prefers the company of the *laaa-dies,*" he pronounced with disdain. "Or the decorator. I take him golfing, but when we get to the club, all he wants to do is hang around with your bridge group."

Miraculously, Lauren remained composed and maintained her stoicism while her husband continued his crass assault, proving himself to be even more bigoted and Neanderthal than Sara had previously known.

He continued with his litany. "I remember the time, ten years ago, when he fought with Zoe Drager over who got to color with the pink crayon, and you broke the crayon in half so they could both have pink. You should have made him color with the blue crayon! That would have straightened him out. You allowed this to happen! It's your fault!"

"Enough!" Sara shouted, startling all of them. "I think it would be more productive to talk about Julian's future than to dwell on the past. Could I ask you, one last time, to please consider applying to The Progressive School?" she said directly to Toppler.

"I've had enough of this bullshit," Toppler said, looking at his watch. "I've gotta get back to the office . . . where I'm paid to listen to this kind of crap," he said, and stood up. As he was halfway out the door, he turned around and grudgingly muttered, "Throw in an application to that pussy school, if that will make you both feel better," then added, "But just remember, an application doesn't mean jack shit."

Lauren smiled at Sara and said, "He's really not so bad."

Sara returned the smile, thinking that Lauren was hovering somewhere between sainthood and catatonia.

When Helen and Michael returned home after a pleasant dinner at the Bistro, they were tired but, as was generally the case with parents of adolescents, had no intention of going to sleep until Zoe was safely home and tucked into bed. In order to stay awake, they turned on the television and immersed themselves in an episode of *Law & Order* in which a private school admissions director was murdered. Just as the head of school, the primary suspect, was about to be arrested, Zoe returned home and plunked herself down on their bed, announcing that she had something important to discuss. Seeing that she was flushed and agitated, they reluctantly turned off the television, fully expecting a momentous announcement concerning her love life.

"Are you both awake enough to discuss something really, really important?" she asked.

Do we have a choice? Helen wondered. "I suppose I am. Are you, Michael?"

"For you, baby? Of course," he replied sleepily.

"Okay. You're sure? It's pretty heavy." They yawned and nodded.

"It's important that you know this isn't coming out of left field. It's something I've been thinking about for a long time. And I spent a lot of time thinking about it when I was in Cuba."

She's joining the Venceremos Brigade? Converting to Catholicism? Getting her nose pierced? The possibilities flashed through Helen's mind.

"I've decided that I want to go to a public high school. The High School for the Musically Gifted."

First there was silence and then a series of dull thuds, as Helen and Michael pounded their pillows into upright positions, their heart rates shooting from an amble to a sprint in ten seconds flat. It was a rude awakening.

"I must say, this isn't what I expected," Helen confessed, making a valiant effort to remain calm.

"It does come as a bit of a shock," Michael added.

"You're not serious, are you, sweetie?" Helen asked.

"Of course I am. Do you think I would ever dare say this if I weren't one hundred percent positive? It's all I've thought about for weeks," Zoe said with surety.

"You can't be," Helen said again.

"Helen, this is a difficult subject for Zoe. Let's listen to what she has to say," Michael said sternly.

"Zoe, I need to understand your thinking. Take a minute to explain how you reached this decision," Helen requested formally, as a way to mitigate her exasperation.

"All right, I will." Zoe stood her ground. "Number one: there is not one school that we have looked at that I feel superenthusiastic about. Number two: the kids at the private schools seem elitist, consumerist, and class conscious. I have a hard time relating to that kind of stuff these days, and it makes me feel like I don't fit in. Number three: none of the private schools are really diverse. They all talk a lot about it, but they really only have a few token minority students. I have problems with that. I want my friends to come from all sorts of backgrounds, not just the upper class. That's gross. Number four: private school costs a fortune."

"The fourth reason, the financial part, shouldn't be a concern. We've factored tuition into our budget and aren't worried about it, so neither should you be," Helen said, not looking for Michael's agreement on this point since she was not sure she would get it. "So you've told us why you don't want to go to private school. Now tell us why you want to go to public school," she challenged.

"Ever since the chorus began to work with The Public School, I've felt differently about myself. I used to take everything I had in my life for granted. I acted really smug and superior a lot of the time. When I met the kids at The Public School and learned how much harder they have to work for everything they have, I started to feel more and more disgusted with my life. Getting to know these kids, and then being in Cuba, has really forced me to examine who I am and what kind of person I want to be. I'd rather be in a school that's maybe not 'the best' academically but where the kids have better values. And since I really want to pursue music, it makes sense to me to go to a high school that focuses on that. Plus, from what I'm hearing, the good colleges give more serious consideration to kids who do well at public schools than private."

"I really respect your thinking on this, Zoe. It sounds like you've given it a tremendous amount of thought," Michael said gently.

"Well, I think that you're being unfair to yourself. You've never been a snob in any way I'm aware of. You've never taken what you have for granted. I think you have excellent values. Just because we haven't had to struggle to make ends meet doesn't mean we don't work hard. Everything we have, we have because we work for it. Including your education." Helen became increasingly self-righteous as she spoke. She couldn't believe that this was happening after all they had been through over the past five months.

"I appreciate how hard you and Daddy work so that I can have a good education. But I'm saying that money doesn't necessarily buy the kind of education that I want," Zoe said calmly. "Or is necessarily the best for me."

"I'm going to ask you a question that may anger you, but I want you to give serious consideration before answering. Does this have anything to do with your wanting to be at the same school as Max?" Helen asked, knowing full well that this would unleash a fury.

Right on cue, Zoe instantly became enraged. "I knew you would say that! I just knew it! You've objected to Max from the very beginning. You think he's not good enough for me because he goes to public school!"

"That's ridiculous, Zoe. I have nothing but good feelings about Max. If I object to anything, it's the intensity of the relationship. You've gotten deeply involved very quickly," Helen explained calmly.

"Like you and Phillip Cashin?" Zoe countered.

"Who?" Michael asked. "I'm lost."

Helen was speechless. She never expected her daughter to hit her with such a low blow.

"Phillip Cashin is the father of Zoe's friend Catherine. He and I have become friendly. He invests in art and has asked me to evaluate a few paintings for him. We've developed a bit of a professional relationship. Period. So no, Zoe, it's not like Phillip Cashin and me," she said, struggling to remain composed.

"Zoe, that was really mean. I don't understand why you said that. You owe your mother an apology," Michael instructed in his best rendition of chivalrous knight defending fair maiden.

"I'm sorry," Zoe said contritely, refusing to look at her anguished mother. "That was totally inappropriate."

"I think you should give your mother and me some time to discuss this alone. We can talk about it again tomorrow. Okay, love?" Michael proposed gently.

"Yeah, I guess. 'Night," Zoe said, and stalked out of their room.

Helen and Michael were awake until four in the morning.

"Don't you think that your bias towards private school might have something to do with the fact that *you* went to an exclusive private school?" Michael accused.

"It wasn't exclusive," Helen replied angrily. "It was in Philadelphia, for Christ's sake."

Then she went on the offensive. "You always talk about what a lousy education you got. As long as I've known you, you've been angry with your parents for not sending you to private school. Talk about baggage! When it comes to education, you've got more baggage than a luggage carousel at JFK."

"That's because it was a lousy school. Not all public high schools are that bad," he retorted.

"I saw the expression on your face when she made the remark about the money. You looked just like your father. You've always resented spending twenty-plus grand a year on tuition," Helen attacked again.

"I have not. But it would make paying for college a hell of a lot easier, that's for sure," he argued.

"That's true. But it's not a good enough reason to let her do it."

"Do you really think she made this choice just to be with Max?" Michael asked.

"I wish I could say no . . . but in part, yes. Maybe not just Max per se, but his whole lefty gestalt. I think a lot of the kids at The Public School come from working-class families, and that appeals to her. I can definitely understand how she feels. The public-school kids feel more . . . authentic to her. But I think it's our duty to make sure she gets the best education that we can give her. She'll be grateful to us for the rest of her life. She just doesn't know that now. She's not mature enough to make this decision on her own, and it would be irresponsible of us to let her."

"Remember what Sara said about letting her choose," Michael said.

"She was talking about making the choice between two or three private schools. You know that," Helen said impatiently.

"But I still think we have to factor public school into the equation. Zoe is. So we have to, also."

"I'll call Sara tomorrow. I'll be interested to hear what she has to say," Helen said sleepily, her eyes closing against her will.

"Helen? Why do you think Zoe said what she did about this Cashin person?" he asked, for the first time revealing an iota of jealousy.

"My guess would be that in the course of her sexual awakening, she's experiencing feelings of guilt. So she's sublimating that guilt through a fantasy about my having an illicit relationship with Phillip Cashin. That way, she can be free of the guilt she's feeling about Max by transferring it to me," she explained lamely. If Michael hadn't been half asleep, her wobbly psychoanalytical construct might never have held up. As it was, it was as shaky as a vertiginous five-year-old on the top rung of an eight-foot-tall jungle gym.

"You're sure I shouldn't be worried?" he asked again.

"At the moment, we've got bigger things to worry about than Phillip Cashin," she answered. He took that as a no.

Early the following morning, Helen called Sara at The School, having correctly assumed that, even though it was Saturday, that was where she would find her. Trying hard to control her extreme agitation, she told Sara about the two-ton bomb that Zoe had dropped the night before.

"Oy," was the first thing out of Sara's mouth.

"I love that you've become such an oyster," said Helen wryly.

"I'm glad you're finally able to see some humor in all this. So what would you like me to do? I'd be happy to talk with her if you think that would be helpful," Sara volunteered.

"I was hoping you would say that. She really looks up to you and would probably be more receptive to what you have to say than she is to us right now," Helen answered gratefully.

"I'm very interested in hearing what she has to say. I'll also make an appointment to visit The High School for the Musically Gifted. I've heard good things about it from Elizabeth Marcus."

"Are you saying that we should actually consider it?" Helen asked with surprise.

"Out of respect for Zoe, I think you have to. Be open to the possibility. Look at it as another option. It's not as if you're going to withdraw the applications you've submitted to all the other schools. And who knows? Zoe could change her mind again before February twelfth. I think it's entirely possible that if and when she gets an acceptance letter from The Bucolic Campus School, the whole thing will blow over."

"I hope you're right," Helen said.

"The important thing is that Zoe doesn't feel like she's being backed into a corner or ganged up on."

"I agree," Helen said, and sighed resignedly. "So how are you doing?"

"Overwhelmed. Crazed. But I've got to tell you, I've never felt so excited about work in my whole life. This job is so incredibly complex. I'm faced with new challenges almost every day. It's like being the CEO of a company with the most demanding clients in the world. I don't have to tell you how intense New York parents are when it comes to their children's education."

"Present company included?" Helen joked.

"At least you're self-aware enough to know you are. Most of the parents I'm dealing with these days are positively myopic. But Zoe aside, how are things with *you*?" Sara asked.

"*Icchh,* complicated," Helen answered.

"That must mean you slept with him."

"NO! Michael just stepped out of the shower. He says hi," Helen said, deftly sidestepping further questioning.

"Hi, Michael. How's the auction shaping up? It's in less than three weeks," Sara said.

"We're in good shape. I've got to find a dress today. Denise was a little insulted when I told her I refused to wear matching gowns, so I compromised and agreed that we'll wear the same color. But I look horrible in red."

"Just be glad she's not making you wear a scarlet 'A,'" Sara teased.

"Not funny."

"I've got to go. The board has asked for a first draft of next year's budget by the end of the month. Crunching numbers was never my forte."

"Really? You've always been the crunchy type," Helen teased her back.

"I'll call you on Monday after I've had a chance to speak with Zoe."

It could have been a case of the Monday morning blahs, but more likely, Michael was suffering from an overdose of the bad vibes that had permeated the Drager household all weekend. To make matters worse, on his desk was a phone message from Vince Gargano; he dreaded having to tell him he wouldn't be able to participate in the Fantasy Basketball Camp. When he finally made the call, Vince was disappointed to hear that his bidding consortium would have to continue its search for a Middle-Aged Male Willing To Spend Five Thousand Dollars To Fulfill a Sports-Related Fantasy.

"What can you do, bro? Your old lady has gotcha by the cahones," Vince said snidely.

"I gotta tell you, I kind of see her point," Michael said defensively. "If Zoe ends up at The Bucolic Campus School next year, we'll be more than happy to participate in the school auction. But right now . . . it doesn't really seem . . . kosher," he said, hoping he might succeed in tricking Vince into giving him a prenotification date thumbs-up. Sara's optimism about The Bucolic Campus School was encouraging, but like Helen, he would feel much better hearing it from Vince.

"Well, if my guys don't win the bid this year, maybe we'll have another shot at it next year. Okay, bro?" Vince offered generously.

I could construe that to mean that an acceptance letter is forthcoming . . . or not, Michael thought morosely.

"By the way, I'm playing in a three-on-three game up here in the school gym tonight. Want to join us? I think we need another guy," Vinnie extended a conciliatory invitation.

"Don't think I can make it, but thanks anyway," he answered. Last week he would have jumped at the invitation, but today he felt as though he needed to get home as early as possible.

"No problema," Vince replied, and hung up.

Michael's thoughts were jolted back to the Cooking Network when Charlotte poked her head in to tell him Justine Frampton had arrived for the production meeting.

"Take her to the conference room. Let the team know she's here, and I'll be there in a minute," Michael instructed, and gathered his *La Cuisine de Justine* files. He couldn't believe he had to participate in yet another game of charades with this ridiculous woman. And in the presence of his staff again, no less.

Everyone was assembled around a large table and was passing around eight-by-ten prints of the photographs Michael had taken in France, admiring Justine's country kitchen as she looked on eagerly.

"I adore those tiles, too. Do you know, I bought them from an old monk right before his monastery was demolished? He was so happy to know they would be put to good use. Thank you. The view is lovely, isn't it? And in the spring it's divine. You can all look forward to seeing it then!" she gushed. "Oh, hello, Michael."

"Hello, Justine. Okay everyone, let's get going here. We have a lot to cover. First of all we need to go over how we plan to block the basic shots in Justine's kitchen. Notice, the width of the door is slightly too narrow to accommodate the cameras. We may have to widen the doorway slightly. Justine, how would you feel about that?"

"Well . . . it is an historic building, sixteenth century, mind you, so it would have to be done *very* carefully. Hmmm . . . but if you're going to the trouble of bringing in a crew . . . I was just thinking . . . you might want to consider raising the roof ever so slightly. It's awfully low. I've always thought a cathedral ceiling—with skylights, naturally—would be so much more attractive. For the show, that is. Don't you think?"

"I'm not sure about that. Let me talk to the set designers and get back to you," Michael said evasively. "Cynthia, what do you think about Justine's stove?" he asked the head of the cooking department.

"Gorgeous. I love the ancient look of the burners. And that old brick oven is so authentic."

"Ahhhemmm," Justine cleared her throat loudly. "I agree, the antiques have their charm. But let's be honest—not for the kind of serious cooking we're talking about here. I really think we need to upgrade all the appliances to top of the line. Don't you, Michael?"

"I agree with Cynthia about the authenticity. Let's continue to look at it. We don't have to make a decision now," he answered diplomatically.

"Look at this shot of Justine's cookware," Michael said, passing another photograph around the table. "Aren't these old pots wonderful?"

"Gorgeous."

"Lovely patina."

"So real."

"Worn thin. Broken handles. Downright dangerous. They all need replacing. For the show, that is," Justine insisted.

Cynthia looked sideways at Michael. "We'll decide about these details, Justine. Cynthia has a great eye for what works on film. Trust us."

"When you see how shabby they are, I'm sure you'll agree with me," Justine said stingily.

"Now, what about a second pair of hands in the kitchen? I was thinking it might be nice to have a young French chef. Someone Justine is sort of training on the set with her. Get some nice little back-and-forth going. Mentor-protégé kind of feel. What do you people think about that?" He directed his question to the marketing experts.

"Marvelous idea!" Justine responded enthusiastically. "I was actually going to make the same suggestion. And I have the perfect person."

"Lovely young local female talent, perhaps?" Rubin, the dirty old head of international syndication, inquired.

"Er, not exactly local. Or young. But she does speak French. Michael knows her. An extraordinarily competent student of mine named Pamela Rothschild."

Michael gagged and splattered his coffee. "WHAT?"

"Rothschild, eh? Lots of panache and great name recognition. Didn't know you knew a Rothschild, Michael." Rubin seemed impressed.

"Ah, yes. I do. Um . . . could you all excuse us for a minute. I need to speak with Justine alone. Let's take a ten-minute break."

Perplexed, the staff straggled out of the room and Michael closed the door. "Why the hell would we EVER want Pamela Rothschild on this show?"

"Oh, my, oh, dear," she clucked like the Little Red Hen. "Because . . . she's a marvelous cook? And a dear friend?"

"Bullshit."

"Because without her this show never would have happened and she has a little free time before she starts her new post and asked me to get her a part on the show," she explained nervously, moisture beginning to accumulate on her forehead and upper lip.

"It's not going to happen. Got it?"

"Michael, you must be more considerate. I mean, after all she's done for you. For Zoe, I mean," Justine said righteously, and flung her braid over her shoulder.

"She hasn't done SHIT for me OR my daughter!" he yelled.

"Are you forgetting your candidacy at The Fancy Girls' School? Without Pamela in your corner, Zoe would never have been considered. There are dozens of applicants who are more qualified than she is. But Pamela never let up. She's pushed and pushed . . . ," she pressed.

Michael stood up and, towering over the still-seated Justine, declared with a certitude that, in retrospect, even he found astounding, "From this moment forward, consider our application to your Fancy-shmancy Girls' School officially withdrawn!"

"You're not serious. You can't be serious. And my show. What will happen to my show?"

"That's between you and Xavier now. I hereby resign as producer of this travesty," he said, throwing his folder onto the table. Photographs scattered, Justine trembled, and Michael stormed out of the room.

After suffering through a tension-filled weekend, Helen was glad when Monday arrived and she was finally alone in the apartment. She had really hoped that she and Zoe could have spent some time together, knowing that if they had had a chance to get out and do something they both enjoyed, they would have reached a more peaceful accord. But Zoe had put up a wall and made sure she had scheduled plans with her friends for every hour of both days. It wasn't until Sunday evening, when Zoe finally settled down and Michael was at the gym, that Helen had an opportunity to broach the subject of Phillip. But as soon as she uttered his name, Zoe recoiled.

"And I would prefer if you never, ever said his name in my presence again!" she shouted melodramatically. "And on that subject, I never want to see or talk to Catherine Cashin, either. She's a spoiled brat!"

Helen had not expected that but was hardly in a position to argue with her. She then said, as calmly as possible, "If that's what you want, that's your decision. But it's important for me to know that you understand that Phillip and I are no more than colleagues, as you implied the other night."

"Mom," she shrieked, "I said I don't want to talk about him!" And she ran into her room and slammed the door. Later, when Helen gingerly went in to say good night, Zoe impassively accepted a kiss.

After a sleepless Sunday night spent thinking about all that had happened (and not happened) with Phillip, she woke up on Monday morning knowing that she had to end whatever it was that was going on. Unsure what Miss Manners had to say about an electronic Dear John letter but having concluded that the phone was awkward, a rendezvous was unwise, and snail mail was too slow, she settled on sending an e-mail.

Dear Phillip,

I couldn't bear the idea that Zoe blamed herself for leaving the earrings at your house, so I invented a flimsy explanation as to why I had been there and how they came to be left behind. It was truly pathetic and I'm embarrassed even thinking about it.

We once joked about me being your wake-up call. In a way you provided the same for me. You woke me up to the fact that I have a loving husband and a trusting daughter. To risk the loss of either of these relationships for an amorous adventure would be self-indulgent and ludicrous.

You're a gracious, kind and outrageously sexy man who deserves a compassionate, devoted companion. Alas, that cannot be me. I wish you only the best.

Fondly,
Helen

PS. Please send the earrings via mail or messenger at your convenience. Thank you.

She read it several times before pushing "Send" and then, as she had been on the verge of doing all weekend, had a good, long cathartic cry. Within minutes her computer announced that an e-mail message had arrived.

Dearest Helen,

Although terribly disappointed, I respect your decision to put an end to the adventure we seem to have begun. It is more painful than you can imagine, as being with you has been the only bright spot in my life these days. Understandably, your commitment to your family must come first.
Would you possibly agree to let me see you one more time? Since Margot died so suddenly I have learned the importance of saying goodbye. It would mean so much to me if you would allow me this one indulgence. And I promise to bring your earrings.
Just tell me when and where.
Yours always,
Phillip

Phillip,

How can I refuse? I'll be near your office for a meeting tomorrow. How about tea at Quattro Stagione at 4:00?
Helen

Michael came home from work in the late afternoon looking bedraggled. With scraggly hair, blotchy face, and stuffy nose, Helen was not at her best, either.

"Are you okay?" he asked. "You sound like you're getting a cold."

"I'm fine," she sniffled. "Maybe it's allergies. You're home early. What's up?"

As he poured out the story of the production meeting, raising his voice at least three decibels as he reported on Justine's proposal that Pamela have a part on the show, Helen listened intently, emitting sympathetic murmurs along the way. Visibly nervous, Michael dramatically paused before revealing the denouement and then, having reached the end, warily awaited her reaction.

"You're not angry?" He gaped in disbelief.

"Michael, I'm really proud of you. What you did took a lot of guts," she said sincerely. "You should feel really good about it."

"You know what? I do. But I was scared to tell you. I thought you'd hit the roof."

"Zoe has no interest in going to The Fancy Girls' School, and you at least had the balls to support her choice. I respect that. For some stupid reason I let Pamela talk me into thinking it was THE school for her. Now that I've finally accepted the fact that everything Pamela told us is utterly bogus, I'm finally ready to let go of my preconceived notions of where Zoe *should* go to school," Helen explained with a lump in her throat.

"Fuck Pamela and the horse she rode in on!" Michael announced.

"I second that," Helen added, taking Michael's hand and holding it against her cheek to catch the tears that were streaming down her face.

"What's the matter?" he asked gently.

"Nothing in particular. I haven't cried in such a long time. I just need a release. I've been holding in a lot of stuff."

They sat that way for several minutes.

"I guess one reason I'm feeling so sad is because I'm coming to grips with the fact that Zoe isn't my baby anymore. I'm no longer in control of her and have to learn to stop trying. I once read that good mothering means giving your child roots and wings. There's no doubt that we've given her good, solid roots. Now she's beginning to spread her wings and is ready to fly. I have to let her," Helen sniffled as she spoke.

"Allowing her to choose where she goes to school next year is a good way to start," Michael said firmly. Helen closed her eyes and nodded.

"Good morning, Michael. Sorry to call so early," Sara apologized, "but I just heard some very troubling news.

"I don't think I can take any more bad news," he moaned.

"What? What's wrong?" Sara was concerned.

"Nothing, nothing. Just some stuff at work," he finessed.

"Oh, it sounded serious," she replied dismissively. She knew from Helen that Michael often exaggerated the gravity of his professional travails.

"So what's up?" he asked.

"I got a call this morning from Lisa Fontaine, whose ex-husband's step son goes to The Bucolic Campus School. She had just heard that Vince Gargano is taking a three month leave of absence. Apparently, his eighty-four-year-old mother broke her hip and he's gone to take care of her."

"Oh shit," Michael responded. "This IS bad news. Should I give him a call? Figure out some way to make myself useful?"

"I don't think there's much you can do. He caught a flight to Rome late last night. She lives in some place called Finale Ligure."

"He just dropped everything and blew out of town?"

"From what I hear, his father died a year or so ago and he's been worried about his mother ever since. He's an only child so the whole burden has fallen on him. He really didn't have any other options," Sara explained.

"Three months? That's a long time to be away. Especially smack in the middle of you-know-what."

"Admissions? I know," she responded flatly.

"How do you think The Bucolic Campus School will handle it?" he asked.

"I gather that his assistant will be jumping in. Did you meet her when you were there?"

"No. All of our contact was with him," he said sadly, and then, with a perceptible increase in panic level, added "She won't know us from a hole in the wall. We'll be just another name on the list. It's a disaster!"

"Whoa. Slow down. I have to believe he made extensive notes after all of his interviews. He was certainly enthusiastic about Zoe when I spoke with him, so let's just hope that was recorded somewhere. If we're lucky, he may have already made his first round of selections and she was one of them. There's a good chance of that."

"Yeah, I guess." He sounded crestfallen.

"One more thing. I spoke to Zoe yesterday and she's still very stuck on the public school idea, so I went ahead and set up a meeting at The High School for the Musically Gifted later this week. I'll let you know what I learn."

"Thanks, Sara. I'm glad we've at least got you on our side."

"Talk to you soon. And, Michael? I'm really sorry," she added.

As soon as Helen returned, Michael broke the news.

"This is totally insane! Poof! In the last twenty-four hours our two best shots have disappeared into thin air. Just like that. I can't believe it!" She was in tears again.

"The Fancy Girls' School is out of the running. But The Bucolic Campus School isn't. Sara's still very optimistic about our chances there. She thinks it's highly likely that Vince had already made his selects before he left. When I talked to him yesterday, I got the sense that he was in the middle of doing that. I have to believe that Zoe is at the top of his list and that whoever takes over will honor that," Michael said stalwartly.

"I don't know. I don't know what to think," Helen said, shaking her head. "It's just too bizarre."

As he was leaving for work, he remembered to tell her about Sara's appointment at The High School for the Musically Gifted. "I'll be anxious to hear what she thinks," he added.

"You and me both," Helen replied.

It was a cold, gray day with a forecast of sleet, one of those dreary days when the sky hung like a blanket of wet cement. Helen spent a good part of the afternoon in a meeting with Ruth Noble, a program officer at the arts foundation that she had been counting on to fund her exhibition. As the meeting progressed, Helen became increasingly frustrated as Ruth repeatedly asked such uninformed questions that it was obvious she hadn't read the proposal. Normally Helen would have persevered in guiding Ruth through the particulars, but given her overall state of mind, she instead sank into despondency. She was beginning to feel as though everything she had done over the past three months was futile, like she'd been madly spinning her wheels and was getting nowhere. It was in this mood that she arrived at Quattro Stagione to meet Phillip.

"Are you all right?" he asked with concern once they had been seated at his regular table.

She stared into the luxurious, placid pool and whispered, "Yes . . . no," as tears welled up in her eyes. He instinctively reached across the table and touched her cheek. She had promised herself she wasn't going to cry in front of him, and he had sworn to himself that he wouldn't initiate physical contact with her. So much for good intentions.

"This isn't about us, is it?" he asked. "Because if so, I'm sure I'm to blame. I should never have insisted that we see each other. I'm so sorry. Shall I just give you the earrings and you can leave?" he suggested, gallant as always.

"No, no. It's not about you. I mean, I'm very sad about what happened between us, but that's not why I'm crying," she said, struggling to contain her emotions. "It's the rest of my life that's got me down. I just had a frustrating meeting over at the foundation about my exhibition. Ruth Noble seemed totally disinterested."

"There are plenty of other sources for funding. I might be able to give you a few suggestions, if that would be helpful," he offered.

"Thank you, that's very generous," she replied appreciatively. "But I'll get the museum staff working on it. I had just thought Ruth would come through since she's funded other projects of mine in the past."

"I'm sure it will work out. From what you've told me, it's a great show. A real crowd-pleaser."

"I'm sure it will, too. But that's not my biggest worry right now. I'm much more concerned about the school situation for Zoe," she confessed.

He looked surprised. "Why? You've applied to plenty of schools. She'll get into at least one," he said guilelessly.

"Phillip, you have no idea, do you? *You* may have nothing to worry about. You're virtually New York royalty. You're connected up the wazoo. But the rest of us plebes are up against a wall," she said harshly.

He was embarrassed. "Really? I'm so sorry. That hadn't occurred to me. I'm so self-immersed and insensitive. But you're absolutely right. Margot was on the board of The Very Brainy Girls' School, and we made a substantial five-year pledge to their capital campaign. I guess they have to accept Catherine, don't they?"

Duh, as Zoe would say, she thought, but said, "They'd be idiots not to."

"Did you ever submit an application there?"

"You mean, did they finally permit us to?" she said with rancor. "Yes. Right before Christmas. We were just there a week or so ago for Zoe's interview."

"Hmmm," he murmured as he looked past her, preoccupied.

"Let me get the earrings from you and be on my way," she said, suddenly uncomfortable with the thought of prolonging their goodbye. She had also just noticed Sir Basil sauntering in and had no patience for the "didn't we meet at the so-and-sos'?" that was sure to take place between the two men.

He reached into his pocket and pulled out a small silk pouch and placed it on the table. As she reached for it, he took her hand in his and held it for a few moments before saying wistfully, "I wish I had met you at an earlier time in our lives."

"But then there would be no Zoe or Catherine," she answered sharply. "I'm sure neither of us would ever wish for that."

"I didn't mean to suggest that," he apologized.

"I'm sorry. It was mean of me to suggest that you did."

"Oh, Helen . . . I can't bear for us to end with bad feelings," he choked, sounding as though he, too, was fighting back tears.

Oh, shit. This is about Margot, not me. It's classic transference. He's traumatized about saying goodbye to me, but this is really about him working through his guilt about never having had a chance to properly say goodbye to his wife. Icchh, *I can't handle this,* she thought, and then quickly stood up, squeezed his shoulder, and said, "Phillip, I have only good feelings for you. I always will. There is nothing to be sorry for. Goodbye—take good care of yourself and Catherine."

Once outside, she wrapped her large black shawl around her head to shield her against the sleet, conceal her bleary eyes, and prevent herself from succumbing to the persistent ardor of Phillip Cashin.

She was gratified to discover that there was *some* practical use for a chador.

With clipboard in hand, furiously scribbling notes, Denise presided over the final meeting of the Auction Committee before the big event. As she fired questions at each of her crew members, her attitude was that of a ship captain preparing for an assault on an unsuspecting enemy. But this enemy's only defense was a checkbook.

"How much do you think we'll get for the canoe?" she asked Neal Moore, chairman of the classroom creations committee.

"I'm not sure . . . There are a limited number of people who are going to be interested in a six-foot-long, hollowed-out hunk of wood. I know *we* don't intend to bid on it . . . I'm not sure how stable it is, either . . ." He whined until Helen interrupted.

"We'll have to hope that someone is tipsy enough to buy a tippy canoe."

"Not to mention the other fifty items in the sale," Denise added, flipping the pages on her clipboard. "Let's see. The schedule. Has everything been cleared with the crew? Sail at seven, return at eleven?"

"Aye, aye, Captain," Barbara, the bosomy bosun, saluted.

Denise spent the next two and a half hours drilling everyone in the room about every detail of the auction: decorations, menu, music, catalogues, even an emergency escape plan in the event of a maritime mishap.

"Do we have an exact head count? Three fifty? Has someone confirmed the number of life vests on board?"

About halfway through the meeting, Sara stuck her head in the room and asked Helen to come see her when she was finished. Finally, at one o'clock, Denise dismissed her crew, and Helen went up to Sara's office.

"I'm perplexed by a phone call I got this morning from Eva Hopkins," Sara reported.

"Really? You told me she was pretty negative about us the last time you spoke with her."

"She was. Absolutely noncommittal and pretty low-key. But this morning she had a totally different attitude."

"That's odd. What did she say?"

"She began by asking if you and Michael liked The Very Brainy Girls' School. I told her that you had been disappointed in your tour guide but that you were impressed with the school itself. Was that fair?" Sara asked.

"That was very politic of you."

"Then she apologized profusely for anything you may have found offensive and asked what she could possibly do to put your mind at ease because, as she said, 'we very much want Zoe to be here.' I swear, those were her exact words. And then she positively gushed about all of you and said that you're exactly the kind of family they're looking for and you fit their parent profile so well. I listened and said 'uh-huh' about six times, wondering what could possibly have caused her about-face. I can't, for the life of me, figure it out."

Helen could. But she decided not to breathe a word of it to anyone, even Sara. Dear Phillip. He couldn't bear the thought of her being upset. And for the hundreds of thousands, if not millions, of dollars he had pledged to The Very Brainy Girls' School, he was entitled to throw his weight around with them. She never thought she would be one to condone such behavior, but if he was willing to be the miracle worker, she was more than willing to play Helen Keller.

"It would be nice to get an acceptance letter from The Very Brainy Girls' School, but I don't think there's even a remote chance Zoe would attend. It would mean dragging her there kicking and screaming, and I'm not about to do that, and I know Michael feels the same."

"That's what I thought. But of course I didn't tell her that. At the end of our conversation she asked if I thought Zoe would attend. I was intentionally vague and said that I didn't know where you were leaning at this point."

"Well put. Oh, everything just feels so up in the air right now," Helen groaned.

"I also wanted to tell you what I've learned about The High School for the Musically Gifted. I was there yesterday and met with the new principal. She's a very bright and dynamic African-American woman who has some very innovative ideas about public education. I was really impressed with what she had to say. We talked for about an hour, and then she gave me a tour and let me sit in on a few classes."

"What did you think?" Helen asked anxiously.

Sara chose her words carefully. "The music program is, without question, excellent. The facilities and equipment might not be as glitzy as what you've seen at the private schools, but the quality of the music curriculum is as good, if not better. They have an incredibly diverse and, I have to say, appealing student body. I think that the fact that they're all there for the music program breeds a certain sense of camaraderie. Overall I thought the teachers seemed fresh, enthusiastic, and committed to good education. The classes are bigger than I would ideally like, but not impossibly large."

"It sounds like you came away with a pretty good feeling about it," Helen responded flatly.

"I did. And the best part is, she's been accepted. Elizabeth Marcus had spoken to the principal about Zoe's musical abilities and got her preapproved. She doesn't even have to audition."

"Well, that's a nice change," Helen said.

"Helen, I hear the disappointment in your voice. I hope you don't sound like that when you talk to Zoe about it."

"It's never going to be my first choice, but if you're telling me that it's a decent and safe place, then I will make sure to let her know I'll support whatever decision she makes."

"Look, is it as good a school as The Bucolic Campus School? No, it doesn't come close. Is it as good as The Safety School? Probably."

"Would Zoe be happy there?" Helen asked.

"I think the chances of that are as good as anywhere."

"Will she get a decent education?"

"If she works hard to connect with the right teachers, asserts herself in the classrooms, and falls in with a good group of kids, I think she probably can," Sara said realistically.

Helen was both relieved and disappointed. Part of her had hoped that Sara's report would be so negative that they would agree to drop the idea. On the other hand, she was relieved to have another viable option and, most important, one that Zoe had chosen herself.

"Will you do me a favor and share your observations with Zoe?"

"I've already asked her to come talk to me after school today."

"Thanks. You're the best."

"Unfortunately, I don't think all of the eighth-grade parents would agree with your assessment right now, but thanks."

FEBRUARY

In the wake of the past few months, Sara expected February to be relatively smooth sailing. She had a good feeling about the direction things were heading, particularly tonight's annual auction. If A Night to Remember was the success she predicted, thanks to the competency of Helen and Denise and their tireless committees, The School's financial woes would be alleviated and school spirit would be renewed.

Knowing that she would be busy with last-minute preparations until the final hour, she brought her new evening dress to the office that day. At five o'clock, when she was certain that everything on her to-do list was done, she changed her clothes, applied a trace of makeup, and ran a comb through her hair while scanning the catalogue and a printout of the guest list that Brandi had left on her desk. She was surprised to see that the Winters had bought three tickets for tonight's event, and while wondering who they could possibly have invited, she heard a cab pull up in front of The School and dashed out.

Also dressed in the prescribed "nautical festive attire," which meant navy blue and white for Michael, and Denisian red for Helen, they escorted Sara into the taxi and each snatched a copy of the catalogue. Ardelle Flax, a third-grade class parent and associate editor at

Nouveau Biche (a magazine for bichon frise owners), had designed this year's catalogue in partnership with the witty advertising copywriter and mother of second-grade twins, Michelle Ferrone.

"Here's a perfect one for you, Michael," Helen read, " 'Hey, Good Lookin'! What's Cookin'? Unleash a new you with a haircut at the Cut Above Salon on Madison Avenue. Then show off your new do at a power lunch for four, complete with wine pairings at Chanterelle.' "

Michael groaned. "That's one I WON'T be bidding on! I made myself a sacred promise never to mix business and school ever again!"

Fifteen minutes down the West Side Highway later, the threesome arrived at the World Yacht Marina. What appeared to be a fairly well oiled crowd was sipping into something comfortable at the dockside bar near the foot of Pier 81. Helen spotted the Moores, the Newmans, the Reynoldses, and a bevy of lower-school parents she recognized but didn't know by name. She felt a momentary pang of sadness as she recalled auctions past and realized this would likely be the last time they would be socializing with this circle.

Helen and Michael maneuvered their way up the gangplank of the *Spirit of New York* and embarked on the mid deck, where two enormous striped papier-mâché smokestacks, made by the Arts and Crafts Club (and available for purchase in the silent auction) sat squarely. A tricolored flag, hand embroidered by Mrs. Frailey's fourth-graders, with "A Night to Remember" in cross-stitch (and also available to the highest bidder) fluttered at full mast. The musclebound captain, an uncanny dead ringer for Popeye (available for birthday party entertainment), welcomed the passengers aboard and then directed them towards the white-jacketed waiters, who, under the supervision of Dana Winter, were pouring generous flutes of champagne.

"Ahoy, there, maties." Already two sheets to the wind in a custom-made-for-the-occasion white pleather sailor suit, Dana greeted the Dragers.

"Shiver me timbers," Helen said under her breath to Michael. "Requesting permission to come aboard, Captain Winter," she saluted.

In a corner of the deck, and likewise feeling no pain, Peter Newman was boring Patrick Winter with his favorite joke: the one he told at every school function about Jefferson Davis, the cocktail weenie, and the Confederate soldier's widow.

Gia Hancock, a sexually frustrated single mother of two, sauntered up to Newman and encouraged him to repeat the joke, and while she was whinnying with loud peals of laughter, Patrick snuck off in search of another drink.

An exuberant group of Kindergarten parents, school auction virgins, sailed their auction paddles like Frisbees and threw confetti streamers from the poop deck.

"It's better than throwing poop from the confetti deck," one of the tipsier fathers slobbered to anyone who would listen.

Finding Brandi manning the registration desk, Helen exchanged her credit card information for a paddle number, turned down a "Hello, My Name Is . . ." name tag, and, with a glass of champagne and Michael in tow, circumnavigated the ship.

"I'll hold the paddle tonight, Michael," she said, reminding him of the year he got stuck for thirty-six hundred dollars trying to bid up a Cooking Network–sponsored wine-tasting trip to Napa Valley.

"Hey, it beat the rainy weekend at the Moores' moldy beach house we went in on with the Fontaines. Twelve hundred dollars for head lice."

Braving gusty winds from the deck, Sara sized up the crowd at the registration desk and hypothesized that there was a direct correlation between people's outerwear and the way they generally bid. The goose-down-encased Michelin men were well insulated from the inclement weather but generally didn't spend much. The wool wearers would spend but always came with an established limit they would exceed only if sufficiently inebriated. The Cashmere-clad could go either way, while fur, though decidedly un-PC, meant "Clear the decks 'n' raise those paddles high!"

For most parents, flaunting their good fortune at the benefit auction was significantly more gratifying than writing a large check to the Capital Campaign. It was here that one could receive a hearty applause for spending an obscene sum on something as mundane as a mosaic-framed bathroom mirror or a decoupage Clorox bottle turned piggy bank. All it took were two alpha dads with my-wallet's-bigger-than-yours complexes to send the price soaring. And the winner got to go home and tell little Daphne that Daddy loved her *sooooo* much he was willing to spend five grand on the wooden bat house she assembled and painted in art class.

While Michael was chuckling with a group of fathers, Helen wandered into the grand ballroom, where the Grateful Dads, a four-piece pop combo fronted by seventh-grade parent Nicholas Argento, was wrapping up an instrumental version of Three Dog Night's big hit "Mama Told Me Not to Come." The band featured a fourth-grade father on bass, a Kindergarten dad on drums, the geometry teacher jamming on rhythm guitar, and Nick on lead. Over the years, the Grateful Dads had become a staple at all The School's events: Guacamole Night, Parent-Teacher Trivial Pursuit Night, Head of School for the Day Night.

For this Night to Remember, the band featured a special guest artist, Adrienne Badeaux, second-grade mom and mezzo-soprano with the Opera Company. A spotlight followed her to center stage, where she launched into an operatic rendition of "My Heart Will Go On," the love theme from *Titanic.*

Having had enough of Adrienne's heart-wrenching performance, Helen went to look for Michael. She followed a small convoy of waiters bearing silver platters of pâté, smoked salmon, and miniature quiches into a stateroom on the lower deck, knowing that where there were hors d'oeuvres, there would be her husband. Michael had always loved finger food.

The custom-fit stateroom was home to the silent auction, where parents competed, in semi-anonymity, by writing their paddle number on bid sheets in incremental dollar values for goodies like Sunday (brunch) in the Park with George (Stephanopoulos), an ice-skating birthday party with the New York Islanders, or a personalized voice mail message recorded by Howard Stern.

Helen was perusing the various bids, trying to figure out whose paddle number belonged to whom, when she saw Dana Winter, looking even more dyspeptic than usual. Pen clutched tightly in hand, she stood guard over several items while draining another glass of bubbly. She was poised, ready to pounce the moment anyone wrote in a higher bid for the TaylorMade golf bag signed by Tiger Woods.

"Dana, are you feeling all right?" Helen asked.

"The nerve of some people," Dana sputtered. "On three separate occasions Cally Reynolds has tried to steal the cosmetic tooth whitening right out from under my nose." She scratched out the underbid and upped it by $500.

"I don't know. You're looking a little green to me. Have you had anything to eat? The bok choy egg rolls are really good." Helen reached to snatch one off a passing tray and handed it to Dana.

"Oh, God, no," said Dana reflexively, pushing away Helen's hand. "I can't possibly eat a thing."

"Maybe you should go outside and get some air."

"And have somebody outbid me on the golf bag? If I lose it, Patrick will be furious," Dana slurred.

"Why don't you go out on deck, take two Dramamine, and I'll keep an eye on the Tiger?"

"Well . . . Maybe just for a minute," Dana gagged, trying to hold back the spew. "But when Pamela comes by, tell her I'll be right b-b-b-baaaccccckkkk." She ran out of the room, hand over mouth.

Pamela? Helen couldn't believe her ears. She couldn't have meant Pamela.

But it was true. Surrounded by an adoring throng of parents who had no idea of the true story behind her ouster, the former head of The School held court atop the ersatz Versailles staircase that led to the grand ballroom. Always eager for approbation, Pamela basked in the attention.

"Please come back," her minions begged. "For the good of the children, you must change your mind. What are we ever going to do without you?" Champagne glasses clinked. Toasts were tendered to her selflessness as St. Pamela regaled her faithful with tales of teaching malnourished Haitian youngsters how to read, bringing comfort to babies in Yemen, and founding the first all-girls school on the Isle of Man.

If any of these sycophants had a blood alcohol level remotely south of 96th Street, they'd realize that Pamela had made her bed and was still lying about it, Helen thought wryly.

"What the fuck is she doing here?" Sara demanded.

In all the years he had known her, Michael had never heard such enmity in Sara's voice.

"I don't know." He tried to diffuse her rage. "I always thought rats were supposed to *abandon* the ship."

"Do you think Helen knows about this?" Sara snapped.

"Absolutely not," he replied, sure that she couldn't have known and not told him. "I've been looking for her for the last twenty minutes. I thought she was with you."

"What the fuck is she doing here?" Lisa Fontaine confronted Sara. "The board made it expressly clear that Rothschild was no longer welcome at school functions. Whose responsibility was it to check invitations anyway?" she demanded at the very moment Dana Winter, the heaving heavy, tore through the banquet hall, hands cupped over her mouth. Sara nodded in her direction.

"Two-faced cow!" Fontaine spat.

"What the fuck is she doing here?" Helen demanded as she charged over to Sara and Lisa.

And the band played on.

Despite Pamela's unique ability to turn the end of the rainbow into a pot of poo, the evening had all the earmarks of an unqualified success. As was his custom, Christie's Alasdair MacIntyre got the bidding off to a roaring start.

"Anyone who has never bid at an auction before, raise your paddle." About half the room lifted their numbers. "Excellent," Alasdair complimented them. "Now you know how to bid." And he began with item number one.

Nearly halfway through the live auction, Helen calculated that they'd already netted close to two hundred thousand dollars. She had to hand it to Denise Doyle-Gillis: she couldn't have done it without her. Any school that took Marissa as an incoming freshman should consider itself lucky; they'd be getting a dynamo of a mother as well.

"I'll never forget the first time the girls had a play date—they were probably around five years old," Helen reminisced across the table from Denise, who was seated next to John Toppler. "Marissa asked me if it was all right to watch the *Power Rangers*. God, what was the name of that pink one?"

"Kimberly," Lauren Toppler said. "Julian always wanted to be her, too." Her husband harrumphed.

"Denise had already told me that Marissa wasn't allowed to watch action shows," Helen continued, "so I said to her, 'I don't know about the *Power Rangers*—isn't it a little violent?' And without missing a beat, Marissa said, 'Oh, no, all they do is save the day.' "

Denise beamed at the early manifestation of her daughter's altruism.

"My favorite was the time you and I chaperoned the first-grade class trip to the museum," Lauren Toppler said to Helen. "Remember the Rubens nudes?" The memory caused tears to well up in Helen's eyes.

"Remember when Julian said at the top of his little voice, 'Why don't they put clothes on these people? They're all naked!' " Lauren paused to let Helen pick up the story.

"Then Zoe walked over to a magnificent nude, stared at it very intently, and yelled at the top of her lungs, 'Hey, Julian, her butt is even bigger than April's mom's!' " Everyone found this to be amusing except for John Toppler, who excused himself to get his Chivas refreshed at the bar.

Normally Helen found incessant reminiscing about one's children to be deadly dull, but tonight she actually enjoyed sharing fond memories with old friends. Only the unsettling pall of Pamela's presence at a nearby table broke the spell. Like someone unable to stop picking at an annoying scab, Helen kept stealing furtive glances over her shoulder to where the former head of The School sat between her two most faithful acolytes, Dana and Patrick Winter.

"Item number forty-two," Alasdair MacIntyre announced from the rostrum. " 'Zelebrate with Zigglebaum.' Armand Zigglebaum, Johan and Wolfgang's talented papa, has graced us with a number of his fully orchestrated CD sets including the Second Horn Concerto, 'Metamorphosen,' and the Duet-Concertino. These recordings are private-edition collector's items and are not available in stores. Get ziggy with the artist that the *Philharmonic Monthly* describes as 'the man who brings the oh, boy to oboe.' Do I have a bid for four hundred? Four fifty? Five hundred? I have five fifty in the back of the room . . ."

Helen craned her neck to see who actually wanted this snoozer, when she caught a glimpse of Pamela, buttonholing John Toppler near the bar. The receptive manner in which he greeted her made Helen wonder if Pamela was still on his speed-dial.

"Item number forty-three: Houston, We Have a Drinking Problem. Join fifth-grade parent Lenny Camacho, lead singer of Space Case, America's hardest-partying band, for two weeks on the road during their comeback tour starting this Memorial Day weekend. Doctor Larry Bridges, the School physician, assures me that penicillin will be provided . . . heh, heh. Must be twenty-one or older please. Do I have a bid for two thousand? . . . do I see three thousand? . . . four thousand . . . six thousand . . . eight thousand . . ."

"Twelve thousand!" shouted Grateful Dad front man Nick Argento, jumping up and nearly knocking over the high hat and cymbals. As he stood up to take a bow, the whole place went nuts. People were stomping. High-fiving. Whooping it up Texas-style. If Sara hadn't stopped her, Gia Hancock looked as if she might rip off her bra and throw it into the fray.

"I wonder how high they'll go for a piece of pissaladiere?" Helen whispered sardonically to Denise Doyle-Gillis as they eyed the next offering in the catalogue.

"Item number forty-four: The Last Supper. The School's famous six-course dinner for twelve, a farewell fete cooked by Pamela Rothschild . . . ," Alasdair read from the catalogue.

There was a hush of suspense as everyone awaited the first bid.

"I have an opening bid of one thousand," Alasdair announced buoyantly. "Do I hear fifteen hundred? Two thousand. Twenty-five hundred to the lady," he acknowledged a first-grade mom sitting to the left.

"Would you like to bid three thousand, sir?"

"I have four thousand. Five thousand." Alasdair injected urgency by rattling off the bids at a breathless pace. "Seven thousand, to the lady on the left."

"Seventy-five hundred." Alasdair pointed to Dana's raised paddle.

"Eight thousand," shouted a well-heeled father who still operated under the misconception that his slacker son was a freshman at The

Very Brainy Boys' School due to Pamela's efforts last year, when, in fact, the boy swam the fastest 440 butterfly in the state.

"Ten thousand!" Dana Winter shouted as Pamela nodded approval.

"I have ten thousand; do I hear eleven thousand?" Alasdair said, looking at the previous bidder, who shook his head and bowed out.

"I have a bid for ten thousand. Am I selling at ten thousand? Ten thousand once . . . ten thousand twice," he announced, looking directly at a quaking Dana.

"Fifteen thousand!" a voice boomed. Every head in the room turned to see John Toppler with his paddle held straight in the air.

Pamela nudged Dana with a sharp elbow. "Twenty thousand!" Dana yelled, to get the auctioneer's attention.

Toppler's paddle didn't budge. "Twenty-five thousand."

"John, what are you doing?" Lauren whispered, laying her hand firmly on her husband's arm.

"I know what I'm doing," he mumbled gruffly, pushing away her arm.

"I have a bid for TWENTY-FIVE THOUSAND DOLLARS," Alasdair enunciated every syllable.

Everyone applauded.

"Thirty thousand," Dana bleated, as much from the sharp kick she had just received under the table as from the murderous look she had just gotten from Patrick.

Toppler's arm never wavered as he yelled, "THIRTY-FIVE THOUSAND."

"John, what's going on?" Lauren asked through clenched teeth.

He hushed her harshly and whispered, "She said she would get Julian into boarding school."

"Who did?"

"Rothschild. She promised if I bid up her damn dinner she would get him into Extrover."

"I thought we agreed that boarding school isn't right for Julian. And besides, Sara spoke with them and they told her that he's not the right fit."

In the rear, Pamela yanked on Dana's arm and pushed it into the air. "Forty thousand. . . . We have forty thousand over here!" Pamela yelled as Patrick Winter tried to wrestle the paddle out of Dana's hand.

"Forty thousand dollars for frogs' legs? What are you, crazy? It's either this or the side-by-side Sub-Zeros. You can't have both!" Patrick snarled forcefully.

"We have FORTY THOUSAND DOLLARS from the lady in the back of the room," cried Alasdair as the crowd went berserk.

"Patrick, you have nothing to worry about," said Pamela, joining the paddle tug-of-war. "John Toppler promised me he's going to pay a record price for the Last Supper. My dinner will go down in private school history," she explained excitedly.

Alasdair looked at John Toppler. "Sir, the bid is to you. Will you bid forty-five thousand?"

"John, let it go," Lauren pleaded. "Julian doesn't want to go to boarding school, and they've made it clear, they don't want him, either," she urged.

Toppler lowered the paddle a few inches. "He's a cream puff."

"He's our baby." Lauren choked back a tear.

"He needs to be tougher."

"So you want his childhood to be miserable just because yours was?"

"Rothschild gave me her word." He remained intransigent.

"Pamela's word is worthless and you know it," Helen cut him short, and said rapidly, "John, Julian is a joy. Any man who doesn't recognize how lucky he is to have a son like Julian doesn't deserve to be a father. You should be happy that he wants to stay at home and be near you."

Alasdair looked at John Toppler again. "Sir, the bid is still with you. Will you bid forty-five thousand?"

Slowly John Toppler lowered his paddle to his lap.

"Going once, going twice, SOLD TO THE LADY FOR FORTY THOUSAND DOLLARS!" Alasdair shouted, and slammed down the gavel over thunderous applause.

For the third time that evening, Dana Winter made a mad dash for the deck.

And the band played on.

* * *

Pamela ran to follow Dana out the starboard door, leading to the third deck, where a thick fog made visibility almost impossible. She stumbled over to the rail and found her doubled over, violently vomiting overboard.

"It will be the grandest fete ever. We'll do the *boeuf en croute,* the *pommes de terre* Anna. I'll even make my famous chocolate torte with butter ganache." Pamela rested her hand on Dana's back and patted her assuredly.

"Don't talk about food. You're making me . . . ," Dana barely managed to say before heaving once again.

"Oh, Dana, here you are." Denise Doyle-Gillis approached. "How do you want to pay for the Last Supper? Check or credit card? You hadn't left your card imprint before the sale, so we weren't sure," she said officiously, as though oblivious to Dana's retching.

"I don't know . . . I'm not even sure I really meant to bid that high," Dana groaned softly.

"Don't you dare betray me. Of course you did," Pamela insisted indignantly. "It will be the most celebrated soiree in the history of The School. For years people will talk about how you stood up to the pressure and stepped up to the plate. The dinner will be a celebration of April's acceptance to The Fancy Girls' School. She will be the guest of honor."

At that moment, Sara appeared on the deck. Concerned about Dana, she, too, had followed her out, only to be greeted by a wet slap of wind and a glacial stare from Pamela's ghostly, enshrouded silhouette. Above the hum of the engine and the churning waves, Sara faintly heard Dana murmur, "Yes. We'll all toast April when she starts The Fancy Girls' School. I can't wait to see her in the little skirt and blouse. I always loved their uniform."

"Dana, please," Sara interjected emphatically, "I don't know why you've chosen to believe Pamela, but I promise you, The Fancy Girls' School is not going to accept April. Dana, think about April's health. She's very fragile. She can't handle that kind of pressure now. Maybe next year, if she's better by then."

Dana looked from Sara to Pamela, to Sara, to Pamela.

"She's LYING!" Pamela shrieked, and then, jutting out her chin and baring her teeth, growled, "You've been after me and my job for the last year, you slag! You lied to the board and to the parents. You poisoned them against me. Well, no more! You see what she's doing, don't you, Dana?"

Suddenly another figure emerged from the fog and felt her way towards the muffled voices.

"Everything I've ever done, I did for the good of The School. I've devoted my life to these people and their children," Pamela declared as she made a sweeping gesture towards the new arrival, Helen.

"Zoe Drager was a timorous little mouse when she came to The School. I built her confidence. Gave her courage. I made her join the chorus. I helped her find her voice. And she thanks me for it every time I pass her in the hall. And you, Helen. You were a simpering sheep when you first arrived. I made you a room parent. I made you a tour guide. How do you think you became president of the Parents' Association? That was my doing. And how do you show your appreciation? By taking sides with this, this Brutus, that's how! *Et tu,* Helen?"

"Pamela, get a grip. Maybe we should go inside," Denise took her elbow and tried to steer her away from the others.

"Leave me alone, you übermother! I hate your type. So self-righteous!" she shouted, shoving Denise aside. "All you people who think Sara knows what she's doing are in for a shocker. The only way any of your children are getting into high school is because I've called in favors for all of you. And this is the thanks I get. Dana, April is signed, sealed, and delivered to The Fancy Girls' School because of me. Denise, I had the power to get Marissa into any school in the country, but you cheaped out and chose public. But that's your prerogative. And you, Helen!" she shouted, and jabbed her finger in the darkness. "You should know I've used every bit of my influence to get Zoe into The Bucolic Campus School—even though they had their doubts, I may add. Thanks to me, you can rest assured I've taken care of everything. I've had several meetings with my dear friend Vince Gargano over the course of the last month. In fact, just this morning we had breakfast and he said to let you know she's in."

Sara squeezed Helen's hand and whispered, "Are you going to tell her, or should I?"

"Tell me what?" Pamela snarled.

Helen cleared her throat. "Vince Gargano has been in Italy for the last three weeks. He's taken a leave of absence from his job."

At least ten very awkward seconds passed, and then a fury was unleashed. "You INGRATES! Every one of you! After all I've done for you, your pathetic children, and your little school." As she ranted, she grappled with the clasp on her infamous charm bracelet. "You've ruined this for me forever. You've turned it into a meaningless trinket." Dramatically she tore the bracelet off her wrist and tossed it overboard, into the icy waters below. "Farewell, all my children!"

As they all leaned over the rail, futilely scanning the inky blackness for a glint of the discarded treasure, they were suddenly knocked off their feet as the ship, with an enormous thud, lurched backwards. The stateroom doors burst open, and hundreds of terrified people came stampeding onto the deck, tripping over deck chairs, pushing and shoving and screaming, "Life vests! Everyone grab a life vest!"

"Man the lifeboats! Man the lifeboats!"

Two heroic lower-school fathers tore the tarpaulin off the first lifeboat, uncovering a disheveled Gia Hancock in a rapturous embrace with Peter Newman.

"I guess we're not going down tonight," he quipped as she scrambled into her skivvies.

A siren blared over the loudspeaker. The captain's voice came shouting out of the mounted speakers: "Do not panic. I repeat, do not panic. Move in an orderly fashion to the aft. Move slowly to the aft of the ship!"

"Michael! Michael!" Helen called out. As she was swept along by the panic-stricken hordes, she clung tightly to Sara's hand. They finally reached the rear of the ship, where they were handed life vests, and as they stood shivering, awaiting instructions for boarding the lifeboats, Helen could see faint lights in the distance. Suddenly, through a transitory opening in the dense blanket of fog, she just barely made out what looked to be the Staten Island ferry terminal. The *Spirit of New York* had run aground no more than thirty feet from the southern tip of the Island of Manhattan.

It was truly a night to remember.

* * *

By the time the *Spirit of New York* was towed to a vacant pier, and all the passengers were safely on solid ground, it was three a.m. By the time the exhausted and shivering Dragers reached home, it was nearly dawn. Having piled their damp clothes on the bathroom floor, they drew the drapes, crawled under the covers, and slept until noon. Zoe was startled to find them still in bed when she returned in the early afternoon from the Doyle-Gillises', where she had spent the previous night.

"How was the auction?" Zoe asked brightly, plunking herself down on their plump duvet.

"Coffee. I can't possibly function until I've had coffee," Helen blearily answered.

"You deserve breakfast in bed," Michael said, hauling himself up and heading towards the kitchen.

"Tell me, tell me," Zoe asked playfully.

"It was a crazy night," Helen began, and told Zoe an abbreviated version of the *Spirit of New York* running aground.

"That's so scary! You must have been terrified!"

"Only for a moment. As soon as I saw the lights of Manhattan, I knew we were safe. From a fund-raising point of view, the evening was a great success. I don't know the final figures yet, but we definitely exceeded our goal. People were bidding wildly, and a few lots sold way above the estimate," Helen explained.

"Really? What was the highest item?" Zoe asked.

"Are you ready for this? Forty thousand dollars for the Rothschild dinner."

"No way!" Zoe was stunned. "Who in their right mind would have paid that?"

"Who said the buyer was in their right mind?" Helen teased.

"Who was it, Mom?"

"Guess."

"John Toppler? It had to be him. Nobody else is that crazy with money."

"Close. He was the underbidder. He lost out to a nasty redhead—scowler, squinter, daughter April . . ."

"Dana Winter! Why would she have done that?"

"It's too long and complicated to explain right now, but I promise, I'll tell you the whole story soon," Helen hedged.

"What story?" Michael asked, returning with a tray.

"The story of the auction. Zoe, listen to this! You won't believe what Daddy bought as a present for my fortieth birthday. The week at the villa in Tuscany!"

"That's so cool!" Zoe exulted, and then spent the next few days preoccupied with planning the month she thought they should spend in Europe the following summer, including a week in Prague.

The Dragers all knew that Tuesday was February 12, but in order to conceal their apprehension, they went out of their way to adhere to their normal morning routine as closely as possible. As usual, Zoe and Michael left the house together, and Helen followed a few hours later, having a meeting and lunch date with one of Sir Basil's associates at the museum.

As Helen was pulling on her coat, Sara called.

"Hi. Are you okay?"

"I'm fine. How are you?"

"I'm good. What are your plans today?"

"I'll be out for most of the day. Why?"

"What time does your mail usually get delivered?"

"Two-ish, but I probably won't be home until three or so."

"You'll call me the minute you have any news, won't you?"

"No. I'll call Pamela first. What do you think?"

"Just checking. I'll be in my office all afternoon."

Helen finished up at the museum at around three and, anxious to be the first one home, made the short trip quickly by taking a taxi.

"Is the mail in, Carlos?" she asked the doorman as he helped her out of the cab.

"Yes, Mrs. Drager. I believe Mr. Drager took it upstairs with him," Carlos answered matter-of-factly. He didn't think it was appropriate to let on, but he'd been working in the building for twenty-odd years and had figured out what February 12 signified.

"Honey, I'm home," Helen called out as she let herself into the apartment, her eyes immediately lighting on the four envelopes lined up across the Mackintosh table. Without bothering to remove her coat and gloves, she called out again, "Michael, I'm home!"

He waltzed out of the kitchen. "If these mean what I think they mean, we have something to celebrate!" he said, glancing at the envelopes—two thick eleven-by-fourteens and two thin four-by-nines. Since the envelopes were all addressed to Zoe Drager, there was never any question of their opening them. But it didn't take X-ray vision to know what they contained.

"Not until Zoe gets home," Helen said, smiling.

"I know, I know. But I'm getting ready to celebrate. I'm chilling a bottle of champagne, and I've opened the can of caviar I bought at the duty-free shop in Paris. I think we should let Zoe have her first glass of champagne today, don't you?"

"She's only fourteen. I don't know if it's such a good idea."

"C'mon, Helen. Loosen up."

"What are we going to do if, after she considers these acceptances, she still wants to go to public school?"

"We celebrate her decision. We're obligated to do that whether we agree or not. Right?"

Helen hesitated. "I would have a hard time with that. I think we would want to revisit the options with her and . . ." she stopped when she heard Zoe's key in the lock of the front door. "Hi, sweetie!"

"Hi, Mom. Dad, what are you doing home?" she asked suspiciously.

"Slow day at the office. You got some mail. It's over there."

Zoe threw down her backpack and ran over to the table. She waited a few moments before making a move.

"Don't they say size doesn't matter?" she asked, biting her lip to stifle her nervous laughter.

"Come on! The suspense is killing us," Michael said, and Zoe ceremoniously ripped open the first and most important of the four envelopes.

"Yeeess," she said quietly, consciously working to temper her enthusiasm. But from the quiver and turn of her upper lip, Helen could tell that she was elated. She handed the letter of acceptance to Helen, who read it aloud.

"Congratulations, sweetie. You did it! You got into The Bucolic Campus School!" Helen said, hugging her daughter.

"Great job, Zoe," Michael said, hugging her so exuberantly that he lifted her off her feet.

Zoe opened the second of the thick envelopes. "Wow, how weird is this? An acceptance letter from The Very Brainy Girls' School. I didn't like this school at all and for sure didn't think they liked me, either. Boy, did I read them wrong."

"I think we all learned that there's no way to predict how this process works," Michael philosophized.

"That's for sure," Helen agreed. *But rubbing shoulders with the right people certainly didn't hurt,* she thought.

"Are the other two envelopes what I assume they are?"

"Wait-listed at The Safety School," Zoe answered, opening the first of the thin envelopes. "And rejected by The Progressive School," she announced ambivalently, having opened the second. "And the great thing is, I don't feel bad about that at all."

"You shouldn't. As everyone says, it's all about finding the right fit, and we all knew that was *not* the right fit. And wait-listed at The Safety School is nice because that says that they didn't want to reject you, because they knew you were well qualified, but didn't want to accept you, because they knew you weren't that interested in them."

"That makes me feel really good," Zoe replied.

"It should."

"By the way, did you notice you didn't get a letter from The Fancy Girls' School?" Michael asked gently, remembering that he and Helen had irresponsibly neglected to tell her about the withdrawn application.

"I'm not going to an all-girl's school, so it doesn't matter if I get in or not. Right?" she replied.

"Right," he answered, and welcomed Helen's affirmative nod. "Let's pop the cork and have a toast," he suggested.

"Wait, wait. I promised Sara we would call her as soon as we had news," Helen remembered.

"I'll call her," Zoe said, grabbing for the phone. When she reached Sara, her parents listened attentively to her side of the conversation.

"Thank you. Yes, I'm really, really happy. Getting into The Bucolic Campus School *is* wonderful. I never expected *that* to happen. Yes. Uh-huh. Yes. Uh-huh. I will. Thank you so much for everything. Okay. Here she is." She handed the receiver to her mother and followed Michael into the kitchen.

"Congratulations! You must be thrilled!" Sara gushed.

"Thrilled and relieved. Now she just has to make a decision between that and public school," Helen said.

"She already has," Sara replied.

"Has she?" Helen answered.

"She made it weeks ago. From the time you all visited The Bucolic Campus School, she's wanted to go there. But she smartly explored the public school option, partially as a way of asserting herself but also as a defensive measure. We have Pamela to thank for undermining her confidence and convincing her that her chances of getting in anywhere were slim to nil. So really, Helen, in the face of that, you have to give Zoe tremendous credit for formulating her own backup plan. I think it was incredibly pragmatic of her and shows great maturity, don't you?" Sara urged.

"You're absolutely right. I just wish she could have shared those thoughts with us," Helen said, slightly miffed that Sara presumed to know more about what had gone on in her daughter's head than she did.

"I was under the impression that she tried but that you weren't particularly receptive," Sara offered gently.

"I suppose you're right," Helen conceded. "Oh, Sara, I'm so glad it's over!"

"You should be so proud of her, Helen. She handled the whole thing beautifully."

"I am. Sara, thank you again for everything," she said tearfully. "By the way, you looked amazing last night."

"I have *you* to thank for that."

"I'm more than happy to do anything I can to help you with your new job. Here comes Michael with a glass of champagne. I wish you were here with us."

"Me, too. Here's a hug," Sara said warmly, and rang off.

The Dragers stood closely together and raised their glasses. "To Zoe," Michael toasted.

"To Zoe," Helen added, taking a sip.

"Icchhh." Zoe crinkled her nose at her first taste of champagne and put the glass down on the Noguchi table. "Max should be home from school by now. I've got to call him," she announced sheepishly, and kissing her smiling parents, excused herself, and softly closed the door to her room.

Helen and Michael raised their glasses again.

"To you. My brilliant, ballsy, slightly wacky wife," Michael said warmly.

"To you. My honorable, faithful and . . . highly obedient husband," she laughed. "But seriously, don't you think there must be a lesson to be learned from this ordeal? I'd like to think we benefited from this experience in *some* way."

"How about this? We make a promise that in three years, when it's time for Zoe to apply to college, we remain sane."

"That depends. What's your definition of sane?" Helen asked.

"The opposite of the last six months," Michael replied.

Admissions resolved, the Dragers raised their glasses.